Praise for Kerrigan Byrne

"The romance is raw, edgy, and explosive . . . deeply satisfying."

—*Publishers Weekly*

"This is a dramatic, romantic, and utterly lovely read."

—*BookPage*

"Byrne is a force in the genre."

—*RT Book Reviews* (Top Pick!)

"Captured me from page one and never let go. Romantic, lush, and suspenseful."

—Suzanne Enoch, *New York Times* bestselling author on *The Highwayman*

"A passionate, lyrical romance that takes your breath away. From the first page, you'll fall in love."

—Elizabeth Boyle, *New York Times* bestseller

"Byrne makes a stunning debut with a beautifully written, intensely suspenseful, and deliciously sensual love story."

—Amelia Grey, *New York Times* bestseller

ALSO BY
KERRIGAN BYRNE

The Highwayman

The Hunter

KERRIGAN BYRNE

St. Martin's Paperbacks

THE HUNTER

For information address St. Martin's Press, 175 Fifth Avenue, New York, NY 10010.

ISBN: 978-1-250-07606-9

Printed in the United States of America

St. Martin's Paperbacks edition / February 2016

St. Martin's Paperbacks are published by St. Martin's Press, 175 Fifth Avenue, New York, NY 10010.

10 9 8 7 6 5 4 3 2 1

To Janet Snell

I couldn't do it without you.

ACKNOWLEDGMENTS

A writer's life, anyone's life really, is full of unexpected pitfalls and terrifying unknowns. I wouldn't be able to survive it without the tireless support and love of my incredible friends, fellow writers, and critique partners, Cynthia St. Aubin and Tiffinie Helmer. You both are a constant source of encouragement and inspiration.

I'll always have an incredible amount of gratitude to Christine Witthohn for her inexhaustible hard work. She is not just an exceptional agent, but a cherished friend.

I want to express my eternal and fathomless appreciation to the brilliant and extraordinary team at St. Martin's Press, specifically Monique Patterson, Alexandra Sehulster, Erin Cox, Angela Craft, Heather Waters, Danielle Christopher, Amy Goppert, and the myriad of people who I haven't had the pleasure to meet, who have expended their time and effort to allow me the chance to build a life doing what I absolutely love. I can't thank you all enough.

Of course, a special thank you to my husband and family for their patience and pride. It means the world.

And always to *you*, the reader, who gives me a reason to bring the characters in my head to life.

I kiss'd thee ere I kill'd thee. No way but this,
Killing myself, to die upon a kiss.

—William Shakespeare, *Othello*

Prologue

Newgate Prison, London 1855

This was nothing short of torture.

Christopher Argent's muscles shook with uncontrollable strain. Sweat mingled with the freezing rain and made infuriating trails of moisture, mirroring the sensation of small vermin crawling down his twitching flesh. He'd have given his soul to scratch them away. Teeth clenched until his jaw ached, Christopher dared not show anything but relaxed features, for fear of the consequences.

Sliding his gaze to the man next to him, he mimicked his Sifu's actions accurately, in a desperate attempt to keep up. Or, rather, to match the impossibly slow pace of the flowing movements Master Wu Ping guided him through with unnatural precision.

"You understand why we drilling the *siu lim tao* in the rain, boy?" Master Ping inquired in his thickly accented English, never once breaking form or pace. They were the first words he'd spoken to Christopher since they'd begun their lessons for the day.

It was more difficult for Christopher to speak and move correctly at the same time, such utter focus did the forms require, but he made a valiant effort.

"I am being punished," he ventured. "For beating John and Harry . . ."

"And?"

Christopher heaved a breath, hoping to unburden himself from the yoke of shame, but it interrupted his actions so that he had to recover and concentrate to get back in rhythm with his *sifu*.

"And Hugh," he mumbled.

Master Ping was silent for the breaths it took to move his bladed hand from an extension in front of his chest back into the protection of his body. "I am your Sifu, boy. What does that word mean in your language?"

Christopher knew this. "It means *teacher*."

Wu Ping gave a short jerk of his chin in acknowledgment. "Then, it not my place to punish. It my responsibility to teach."

Silence stretched on for what seemed like an eternity as they performed the physical drills of precision and line work Christopher had been learning for the better part of two years. Now, at eleven, he was almost as tall as the teacher who had taken him under his wing.

"Today, I teach you, boy, to be like the water." Master Ping had always called him "boy."

Staring ahead at the gray, wet stone of the courtyard of Newgate Prison, he listened intently. The old man had lectured on water before, but Christopher had to admit, he hadn't listened. He would certainly listen now. Drenched as he was in the aforementioned substance, shivering, suffering, and exhaustion made a more distinctive impression.

"Water is adaptable and fluid," Ping began. "It soft; conforming to the shape of whatever contains it, finding the lowest places and the path of least resistance. It sustains life. It easily redirected for the benefit of others. You understand?"

"Yes, Sifu." He didn't really, but knew he would once Master Ping made his point.

"But water also most deadly," Master Ping continued. "It crashes with a force that not even stone can withstand. It floods. It drowns. It destroys everything in chosen path without thought. Without mercy. Without *remorse*."

The old man ceased his movement, turning to face Christopher, who also dropped his trembling arms in relief. He stood looking at the small Chinaman, remembering that he once thought Master Ping looked like a sausage, round and bent and encased in tough skin. The small, gentle foreigner was simply the most dangerous, lethal man housed at Newgate Prison.

"What are the five responses to conflict?" Ping asked.

Christopher listed them from memory. "Avoidance, accommodation, collaboration, compromise, and aggression."

Ping gave another of his short nods. "Notice that fists and force are needed only once in five times. Do you know why that is?"

Christopher looked down at the filthy stones of the yard, following a dark ribbon of grime with his eyes as it oozed toward the sewage drain. "Because I shouldn't fight," he mumbled.

"*Wrong,*" Ping snapped, but his hand was gentle as it lifted Christopher's chin so they were eye to eye. "Because the kung fu I practice not for fighting. It for killing. And you shouldn't use it, except to take a life, defend yourself, or protect another."

Christopher's teeth clenched for a reason other than cold and exertion, a familiar heat compressing his organs against his rib cage. He couldn't keep the defiance from his eyes. "You didn't hear the disgusting things those others said about my mother."

"Was it true what they say?" Ping asked.

"*No.*"

"Then why it matter?" The Sifu shrugged.

It mattered for so many reasons, but Christopher couldn't identify them by name, and so he kept silent and fumed.

Ping's black eyes softened and crinkled a bit at the corners, the closest he ever came to smiling. "You already much like water, but your emotion run too deep. Too strong. Like ocean. You must learn to quiet feelings like anger, hatred, fear . . ." Ping put his hand on Christopher's shoulder, an unprecedented gesture of affection. *"Love."*

"How?" Christopher breathed.

"You redirect them, like a farmer would redirect a river to feed crops. Turn them into patience, logic, ruthlessness, and power. Only then can death flow from your hands with all the destructive force of raging flood." Master Ping turned from him, set his hips, grounding his feet to the stones, and slapped the walls of Newgate Prison with an open palm. The stone crumbled beneath the blow and cracks branched from his hand in the mortar.

Christopher gaped, rain pouring into his open mouth. "How—how did you do that?"

Ping winked. "I show you tomorrow. If you don't hit the mark, but punch through it, then power is transferred, and it must fall before you."

"Can you show me now?" Christopher asked hopefully.

Ping shook his head. "Your mother will want you back in your cell. It is almost time for meal."

"How do you—"

A clock chimed the lateness of the hour, and Christopher's head whipped around toward the guard tower, flinging droplets of water into the shadowy storm. It seemed that even on days such as these, when the sun couldn't be seen, the mysterious old man was always aware of the time.

When Christopher turned back to Master Ping, he found himself alone in the yard.

Vibrating more from excitement than from the cold, Christopher scrambled through the rain to the hallway beneath a rusted grate the prisoners at Newgate had come to know as Dead Man's Walk. Veering through the various catacombs of the prison, he hailed a few familiar faces before knocking on the iron door that separated the male prisoners from the female.

"Who's that, then?" A thick Scottish brogue reached through the bars above his head before the youthful round face of Ewan McTavish peeked down at him. "Well, little lad, ye're certainly lucky ye're back before the changing of the guard here. If Treadwell were to find ye on the wrong side of the door, he'd likely leave ye there to the nighttime mercies of the damned, ye ken?"

Christopher had been born inside these walls. He understood better even than McTavish the hellmouth Newgate Prison became at nightfall. His lullabies had been the echoes of chains, the screams and whimpers of the weak, and the dragging footfalls of the condemned who walked the long, grated hallway and never returned. His mother cried sometimes for those who marched to the gallows, but Christopher never did. A dead prisoner often meant new shoes or a belt.

The rusted iron door scraped along the stone floor with an earsplitting sound as McTavish pulled it open wide enough for his thin hide to shimmy through before pushing it shut and throwing the bolt.

"Mum always sends me to wander on easement day." Christopher hopped from one bare foot to the next, trying to keep warm. He liked McTavish, and followed the stout, dark-haired guard around some days when he'd nothing else to do.

McTavish's liquid eyes matched the smart dark blue of his uniform. They were touched with pity as he nodded. "Aye, lad. I know."

"The guards don't like me around when they bring wood for the fire or fresh tins of food. Mum says I'm in the way."

The guard's attention slid down the dank hall lined with iron bars. "They're finished now," he mumbled, not quite returning his gaze back to Christopher. "Why don't ye find yer ma in time for supper?"

Looking forward to a fire with distinct relish, Christopher skipped up one hall and down another, flattening himself against the wall as two guards sauntered past, one adjusting his belt. Here in Newgate, it was just as important to know which guards to avoid as which prisoners.

McTavish had been right about Treadwell. The big, golden-haired oaf had cuffed him, shoved him, and caned him more times than he could count over the years.

"Bitch needs to learn a bit of gratitude," Treadwell muttered to his companion as they passed. "I should let the real brutes loose on 'er, give the quim some perspective. Then she'll be begging me for a toss."

"We could throw that freckled bastard of 'ers into hangman's row, make 'er watch them tear 'im apart," suggested the other.

In the shadows, Christopher covered his cheeks with his hands and wiped, as though the action could rid him of the offending freckles.

"We keep records of the shackleborn now," Treadwell spat, using the nickname given to the forgotten waifs born into custody of the prison system. "We'd 'ave to explain why 'e'd gone missing . . . Besides, it's not the bastard I'm sore at, it's the mouthy whore 'e calls a mother."

Struck with concern, Christopher's hands dropped from his face to his thudding chest. He stood in the puddle made by his sodden, ill-fitting clothes until the pair turned the corner of the cell hall, before scampering to the end of the women's block he'd called home for his entire life.

A coal bed glowed beneath the grate that barely passed as a window, and Christine Argent was adding a large log to the fire with trembling hands.

Though it let in the cold in the winter and the unbearable heat in the summer, Christopher and his mother counted themselves lucky to have the opening, no bigger than a porthole, to let air filter through their tiny space. In a place that smelled foul on a mild day, a crosswind was more precious than gold.

"Mum?" Tiptoeing around the open bars, he knelt next to her, the heat from the flames instantly bringing the sting of warmth to his numb limbs.

Her long, curly auburn hair had been brushed and braided this morning; now it hung in tangled ringlets, hiding her bent face from his view.

"Oh, Pigeon, it's you." The smile in her voice sounded watery as her hands disappeared behind the curtain of her hair and dashed below her eyes. Pushing herself to stand, she turned before he could see her and faced the homemade calendar etched by a stone on the wall. "I thought you were out with Mister Ping." Lifting her tattered apron, she used it to wipe at her face while her back was to him.

"It's . . . *Master* Ping," Christopher said softly, staring into the pitiful flames. There wasn't as much wood this time. It would barely last the week, and easement day only came once a month.

"Oh yes," she said brightly, covering a sniff. "I knew that, of course." With her worn piece of shale, she made the mark that ended another month within Newgate Prison. Her movements were stiff, almost pained. The mark she made on the wall with an oddly unsteady hand was deeper than the others, and wider. "Did you—" She cleared her throat. "Did you enjoy your time with Master Ping?"

"I did," he answered after a careful pause. "Mum. Look at me."

Her hand dropped to her side, palming the shale, but she made no move to turn around, pulling her threadbare gray shawl tighter across her shoulders. "Forty-eight more months, Pigeon, can you believe that?" The false bravado in her normally soft-spoken voice alarmed him. "Four more years and you and I will be free. Free to do whatever we like. I'll get a job as a seamstress, and I'll make beautiful lace for fine ladies. I used to be famous for the quality of my lace, you know."

"I know, Mum," Christopher whispered, very worried now. He'd heard these words before, but they meant little to him, as he'd never seen a piece of lace in his life and her descriptions of them made no sense. "Let me see your face."

"And you can apprentice with a tradesman. Maybe Mr. Dockery still works at the shipyards. We'll have rooms of our own with a woodstove *and* a fireplace with a stone hearth. We'll never be cold."

Gaining his feet, Christopher left the heat of the fire and padded over to his mother. He wanted to fling his arms around her long waist, but didn't because he was still rain-soaked and it would chill her. Instead, he slid in between her and the wall, lifting his hand to brush the hair back from her face.

It wasn't as bad as he'd expected. Her lower lip was split, but wasn't bleeding.

Christopher squeezed his eyes shut for a second. He was eleven now, old enough to know that it was the wounds he couldn't see that caused her pain. It was what the guards did to her whilst he wasn't there. What she let them do. All so he could be afforded whatever scraps they were willing to throw him.

She was pale, and her eyes were red from crying, but she was still his mother. His tall, beautiful, sturdy mother. The woman who gave him everything, from strong bones, good teeth, and hair the color of rust on the ancient iron hinges, to the last morsel of her meal and a smile that was the only beautiful thing in their gray world.

A familiar hatred surged within him and he bared his teeth. "You shouldn't let them in here anymore, Mum," he growled. "I don't need a fire."

Watery eyes, the same light blue as his own, blinked rapidly as she slicked his sopping hair away from his eyes. "Of course you do, Pigeon," she crooned. "Just look at you. As wet as a drowned Irish rat." Her strong, capable hands seized him and began to peel the dripping shirt from his chest. "Come over here and warm up before you catch your death. I'll go after our tins of supper."

She limped a little, he noticed, and his teeth banged together from sheer helpless frustration. But she was a stubborn woman, and there was no talking to her when she was like this.

They ate their meat in silence, both of them staring into the flames. Christine a little dazed and distracted, Christopher seething and fuming.

Wu Ping didn't know what he was talking about. He didn't understand. How was one supposed to quiet his love for someone like this? How did he not hate the men who used his mother? Or fear what they might do next?

It was impossible to calm emotion.

He would tell the old fool that next time he saw him.

"Christopher," his mother whispered, pulling his gaze from the glowing coal bed. She rarely called him anything but "Pigeon," her pet name for him. "Christopher, I want you to know that I'm all right. And that everything I do, I do because I deserve it, and because you deserve better."

"That's bloody bollocks, Mum, you don't deserve to be . . . they shouldn't . . . not for me." He couldn't say the words, but his cheeks burned with shame.

"You watch your tongue," she said firmly, but then immediately softened. "My son, you don't know what the world is like out there beyond those walls. How strange and wonderful. Beautiful and terrible. You don't know what a real life is like. You've never seen a true sunset, or had a fresh meal." Fresh tears welled in her eyes. "That's all because of me. Because I'm a criminal."

"That doesn't matter," he argued, but she cut him off.

"You'll see someday, Pigeon. You'll see what you've been denied, and maybe you'll hate me for it."

"I could *never* hate you," he vowed, scooting over to settle into her side as she wrapped her shawl around his bare shoulders.

"I hope for that, son." She perched her cheek on top of his head. "But you never know what you're capable of until . . ."

"Until what?"

Letting out a beleaguered breath, she stood and tested his shirt hanging from a rusty nail. It was impossible to dry anything in this dank place, even with the heat of their meager fire. But it was good enough for her to hand to him, though the cold almost burned his skin as he slipped the shirt on.

"Time for bed, Pigeon." The sounds of iron bars clanking together and heavy doors swinging shut as the prison locked down for the night echoed above the calls of the guards and sounds of other prisoners. A stocky, sour-faced woman came by for head count and closed their cell, and then Christopher and his mother separated to their pallets.

They used to huddle together for warmth, Christopher remembered with longing. She'd curl her body around his and sing him songs in hopes of drowning out the horrible noises of the night.

Not anymore. Not since he'd started dreaming and woke racked with a strange and burning pleasure tightening in his loins and spilling into his trousers.

She'd separated them then, laughing almost wistfully

as she tried to explain growing into a man to him through a crimson blush.

Christopher didn't want to be a man, he thought glumly. Not if they turned into rutting brutes like Treadwell, or old leathery fools like Master Ping.

He just wanted to be held.

What had begun as a gentle rainstorm turned into a tempest. Thunder shook the old stones of Newgate, and lightning slashed arcane shadows through their tiny window.

"Should we sing tonight?" his mother asked, and Christopher smiled in the darkness. He'd been secretly hoping she'd ask. The storm had unsettled him, and the noises of Newgate were particularly grotesque.

"What should we sing?" he asked.

"How about my favorite Irish tune."

They sang.

Hush Hush in the evening,
Good dreams will come stealing.
Of freedom and laughter
and peace ever after.
Ye'll smile while you're sleeping.
And watch I'll be keeping.
Hush hush now my darling
No tears til the mornin . . .

A terrible scraping sound reverberated through the stones against Christopher's ear, ripping him out of a warm dream and dumping him onto the cold floor. He sat up, blinking against the darkness. The storm still raged outside, and a flare of lightning illuminated his sleeping mother. Thunder immediately boomed overhead. For a moment, he'd thought it could have been the thunder that woke him, but the sound in the stone was so singular, he only knew of one source.

The heavy iron door that separated the male prisoners from the female cells.

Deep voices filtered down the hall. Male voices. Not guards, either. He knew the sound of the guards. Their footsteps were more clipped against the stone made by cobbled boots with sturdy soles.

Christopher put his ear to the floor. These steps were shuffled. The feet were bare.

Terror ripped through him as lightning once again threw menacing shadows against the wall. But these shadows were no illusion.

They belonged to the men invading his cell.

These were no guards, that much he could tell from the brief second he'd seen them. They were filthy, even by prisoner's standards. Frightening. Leering. Growling.

Seized by painful hands, Christopher fought like a savage. Panic hid all the teachings of Master Ping from his memory. He couldn't find his center line from the floor. Couldn't form a fist. He couldn't get the weight of the man three times his size off him, no matter how violently he tried.

"Christopher!" His mother cried his name in the darkness. "Christopher, run!" Pure, paralyzing horror held him just as captive as the giant with the knee in his back, grinding his cheek into the ground.

Treadwell had made good on his earlier threat.

"Please don't hurt my son," his mother pleaded.

"We're not here for the boy," one of them snickered. "But make a noise and we'll gut him. Now which one of us will have you first?"

Christopher fought until his captor held his cheek down by the coal beds. The orange glow turned everything past it into writhing shadows. The raging storm didn't drown out the grunts, the moans . . .

His mother's whimpers.

He came to fear the lightning. To dread the illumination of the violent depravity they forced upon the person who was his entire universe. Tears streamed onto the filthy stone beneath him. His meager supper crawled its way back up his throat, threatening to choke him. He wanted to look away. To disappear. He wanted to die. To kill.

"Look away, Pigeon," his mother gasped.

But he forced himself to watch. To watch them as they held her down. To memorize and catalog every sneering, rutting, grunting bastard's face with each electric slash of light. Four of them in all.

Rage ripped through him, fueled by heat and fear and youth and helplessness. His soul became as enraged as the storm.

When the man restraining him was replaced by another readying to take his turn, Christopher lunged, catching the brute in the throat, and he didn't stop punching until he felled the man.

He dimly heard his mother's weak and hoarse scream before pain exploded behind his eyes, and he crashed to the floor, stunned.

The world spun around him, dipped and tossed in such a way that made him want to hold on to something, to reach out and make it stop. Shadows rose and fell, doubled and then transposed. Thunder crashed, or was it the door?

Then the storm hurling itself against the roof was the only sound ripping through his pounding head.

Mother. Where was his mother? Was she—

"Christopher?"

With herculean effort, he turned his neck to see her shadow draped on the opposite side of the quickly dimming coals. She crawled toward him on her elbows, but couldn't seem to make it around the fire pit.

Fear chased the vertigo away and he summoned the strength to lift himself from the floor.

"Mum," he croaked, staggering to where she'd collapsed.

"Christopher." Her voice, barely above a whisper, mirrored his terror. "Are you hurt, my son?"

"No. I'm okay. Mum, don't move. I'll call the guards." He knelt over her, afraid to touch her. Afraid to put his hands anywhere.

"There was a knife, Pigeon, did they—" She panted a bit, as though trying to catch her breath. "Did they cut you?" Her hands, usually so strong, so sure, feathered over his face, his shoulders, and down his torso.

"A knife?" He shook his head, still trying to clear it. "They didn't cut me . . ."

A warm, sticky sensation pooled against his knee and he suddenly wondered if he hadn't been somehow stabbed. But there was no pain. No cut.

A new dawning horror licked at his soul.

"Throw another log on the fire, Pigeon, it's so cold."

The warm liquid slid down his leg as he hastily fetched two small logs and steepled them over the coals. Lightning flashed before the logs caught flame, illuminating the most grim sight of the entire horror-filled night.

Blood. Spreading from the prone form of his mother, threatening each wall of their tiny cell. He cried for help, clinging to the bars and pressing his face as far against the opening as he could. He called out for someone, *anyone*. Female voices answered from the darkness. Some concerned, some angry.

But no one came.

Breath exploding from his thin chest, he turned back to his beloved mother, now wreathed in the golden glow of their pathetic fire.

"Mum." He knelt next to her on the side the blood had

not yet reached; distressed to see how fast it crawled toward him, the edge of the red pool beveled in the light of the flame. "What do I do?" He groaned, hot tears blurring his vision. "Tell me what to do."

"Oh, Pigeon, there's nothing . . . to be done." Tears streaked from her own eyes, but she could no longer reach for him. She sounded afraid, which intensified his own despair. He gathered her head against his chest, clutching her to him as though if he held on tightly enough, he could keep her with him.

"Don't leave me," he begged, not caring how small he sounded. "I'm sorry I didn't stay still. I'm sorry. I was angry. I didn't know about the knife. Don't leave. I'm sorry!"

"Sing me the lullaby, Pigeon," she whispered. "I can't see you anymore."

He forced the words through a throat blocked with terror and pain.

Hush Hush in the evening,
Good dreams will come stealing.
Of freedom and laughter
and peace ever after . . .

His mother smiled, though blood leaked from the corner of her mouth and trickled into her hair. Her skin was so cold. Waxy. But the pool in which he sat was warm. Enveloping them both.

Ye'll smile while you're sleeping . . .
And watch I'll be keeping—

His voice caught on a sob. Then another. He couldn't go on singing. But he didn't have to.

She coughed. Her chest heaving. Then it deflated, hot

breath hitting his skin like the words she could no longer say. Out and out and out until she was perfectly still.

Christopher couldn't hear. Someone was screaming. Loud, long, ear-shattering peals of desperation. Screaming like their soul might escape through their throat. Screaming loud enough to wake the gods. Loud enough to be heard over the cacophony of the nightmarish place he'd called home. To be heard over the storm, and the thunder, and the silence of his dead mother.

Christopher wished the screaming would stop. But it didn't. Not for a long, long time.

Eventually the fire died. The stones cooled the blood beneath him and turned it to ice. The shell of his mother cooled also. As the warmth seeped out of her corpse and she stiffened to a heavy weight in his young, trembling arms, all that was warm leaked away from him, as well. He felt it leaving with a mild sense of curiosity.

It felt . . . like water. Sitting in pool of water. It was only water. Surrounding him. Covering him. Caked to his skin. Filling the cracks of the stone. The space of his container.

Water. He understood now. He'd learned the lesson Master Ping had been trying to impart to him. There in the stormy darkness he was learning to be like water. Patient. Ruthless.

Laying his heavy mother on the slick ground, he stood, feeling as though he had no bones. As though he didn't reside in his body. But out of it. Around it. Like the water.

All the water on the stones.

He stood facing the door, still as the stone, and began the forms he'd been drilling earlier in the rain. When the door opened he would go to Master Ping. He would tell him that he understood now. That he was like water.

Ready for death to flow from his hands.

Chapter One

London, 1877
Twenty-two Years Later

"I don't kill children," Christopher Argent informed the solicitor who seemed to be attempting to hire him to do so. "Or deliver them to their deaths."

Sir Gerald Dashforth, Esquire, perched uneasily behind the desk, and persisted in eyeing the closed door as though he anticipated the need to scream for help at any moment. The man matched the furniture in his Westminster office, expensive, waspish, delicate in an almost feminine manner, and the most offensive shade of puce. He peered at Argent from behind wire-rimmed spectacles perched on ears that had long since outgrown his head.

Argent pondered the few observations he'd made about Dashforth in the minutes since he'd met the lawyer. The man was paid above his station, and yet still spent more than he made. He conducted business with the unscrupulous desperation of someone living well above their means. He was fastidious, vain, intelligent, and greedy to the point of immorality. He'd made a career of being the unassuming absolver of his clients' malevolent misdeeds by whatever means necessary.

For example, hiring the empire's most expensive assassin.

"I have three unequivocal policies that my clients *must* be aware of." Argent ticked them off on his fingers, beginning with his trigger finger. "The first, I don't intimidate, maim, rape, or torture, I *execute*. Secondary, I leave no messages, clues, or taunts behind for the police or anyone else, handwritten or otherwise. And tertiary, I don't kill children."

Dashforth forgot to be afraid for a moment, and his thin, dry lip curled up in an imperious sneer. "An assassin with a code? How very droll."

"Not so droll as a confirmed bachelor who pays to bugger young, foreign boys." Argent didn't only rely on observation.

"How dare you accuse me—"

Argent stood, and the lawyer gasped in a breath so abruptly, he choked on his own spittle. It wasn't just his uncommon height that reminded the man of his fear, Argent knew. It was the contrast of his appearance. The flawless press of his expensive suit against the unfashionable breadth of his body. The crook of his repeatedly broken nose against his aristocratic features. The gold and diamond cuff links above hands so scarred and callused from years of forced labor, they could never have belonged to a man of blue blood.

"The daylight is fading, Sir Dashforth," Argent stated calmly over the man's indelicate fit of coughs. "And I mostly work in the dark." Turning from the sputtering man, he counted out five measured paces.

"Wait!" The lawyer wheezed, hacking up a last bit and pressing a trembling hand to his heart as though willing it to slow. "*Wait,*" he repeated. "My employer doesn't wish the child harm, I promise . . . It is his dreadful mother that is to be—disposed of and the document recovered from her."

Argent faced Dashforth, who cleared his throat once more behind a fist and loosened his tie. "Go on."

"So long as the boy cannot be traced back to his father, whether the child lives or not is inconsequential."

Argent blinked. It was not uncommon for nobility to try and get rid of their bastards; he only had to ask his employer, Dorian Blackwell. "And this woman," he inquired. "What did she do to incur the wrath of your client?"

"Does it matter?"

"Not especially." Argent ambled toward his vacated seat and lowered himself back into it, unsure of the structural dependability of the chair beneath a man of his size. "What matters is how much you pay me to do the job."

Bending to his desk, Dashforth made quite a show of dipping his pen and scrawling an astounding sum on a scrap of paper. "My employer is prepared to offer *this* recompense."

Had Christopher Argent been prone to sentiment or emotion of any kind, he imagined astonishment would have been where his features would have landed. As it was, he wondered if he might need to show some just so he could perform the human expressions and responses he'd been practicing.

"That's quite a sum," he affirmed tonelessly. "Who does your employer want me to murder, the queen?"

Behind his spectacles, Dashforth's eyes widened at the word *murder,* and again at the treasonous implications at the mention of the death of the British monarch. "Have you heard of Millicent LeCour?" he rushed on.

"Who hasn't?"

"She may be London's darling, but she's nothing but a treacherous viper."

Still looking at all of the zeros on his scrap of paper and doing some quick calculations in his head, Argent gave the man a distracted, "Is that so?"

"Millie LeCour is not just an actress on stage," Dashforth continued. "She's a thief, a prostitute, and a blackmailer, who has forced my employer's hand in this matter."

Argent stood again, crumpling the paper in his hand and tossing it into the fire. "I'll take half the payment up front, and when the job is finished, I'll return for the rest."

Dashforth also stood, though he steadied himself on his desk before shuffling to the Diebold safe in the corner of the room. Though the gold dial gleamed and the safe was obviously new and expensive, the bulky item seemed as out of place in the frilly room as Argent, himself.

Once Dashforth extracted a leather satchel from the safe, he turned and pushed it across the desk at Argent. "This is more than half. Millie LeCour premieres as Desdemona in a special presentation of *Othello* at Covent Garden in two days' time."

"I know." Looking inside the case, Argent picked up a pile of banknotes and counted them.

"She's constantly surrounded by people," the man continued. "But we know she has apartments above Bow Street not far from the theater. That's where she keeps the child."

Argent snapped the satchel closed, causing Dashforth to start. "I do my own reconnaissance. I'll contact you within three days when the job is done."

"Very good." Dashforth put out his hand for a shake, but Argent only looked at it before striding for the door and retrieving his jacket from the stand.

"Don't let her fool you," the solicitor called after him. "She's the best actress in London for a reason. That gutter whore has left a trail of corpses in her rise to the top. The woman deserves less than the swift death you'll give her, make no mistake. She may be incomprehensibly beautiful, but she's unfeeling and unspeakably ruthless."

"If that's the case, then she and I have much in common," Christopher remarked. "Except my trail of corpses is indisputably longer and bloodier than hers."

Millie LeCour strained her vision through the stage gaslighting to once again find *him*. He wasn't hard to find. Though he was cloaked in shadow, his magnetic pull was indefinable and unmistakable.

Two thousand two hundred and twenty-six seats at the Covent Garden Theater, and each one was occupied. But the moment Millie's eyes had alighted on the rough-hewn gentleman in the impeccable suit, he may as well have been the only audience member she'd ever played to. She'd thought that he seemed more like a character in one of the Bard's more violent plays than a connoisseur. Something about his presence excited and enticed her, and also made her utterly nervous.

The spotlights were dimmed by the light boy to illuminate only Iago and Rodrigo whilst they pontificated onstage upon *her* fictional demise. If she hugged the crimson velvet curtains just so, she could peer out at least three boxes on each tier of stage left without garnering any attention.

"Are you nervous?" Jane Grenn, who played Emilia, settled a friendly chin on Millie's shoulder and peeked into the crowd. Her golden ringlets tickled Millie's bare skin as they mingled with her ebony curls.

"No." Linking her arm with her friend's, Millie didn't look away from the arresting shadow that hadn't so much as shifted in the entire time she'd been watching him.

"Really? Not even for your debut at Covent Garden?"

"All right, I'm petrified," she admitted with a whisper. "This is the biggest night of my life thus far, and the crowd seems so subdued tonight, don't you think? What if it's a disaster?"

Jane wrapped her arms around Millie's corseted middle in an encouraging hug. "They're all just waiting breathlessly for the great Millie LeCour to make her appearance."

"Oh go on." Millie waved her compliment away with an embarrassed huff of breath. "They're here to see a Shakespeare play."

Jane's unladylike snort tickled her ear. "*Othello never* sells out Covent Garden like this, trust me. They're here for Desdemona."

"Or perhaps to see Rynd play Othello." Millie gestured to the strong, coffee-skinned actor whose deep voice sent thrills through every lady in the audience, whether she deigned to admit it or not. The golden lights shone from his sharp cheekbones and illuminated the brilliant white of his smile. He was exotic, sexual, and powerful as the Moor of Venice, and when she was on stage with him, even *her* body responded to the sparkle of mischief in his dark eyes.

"We're *all* dying to know if he's as horse-cocked as reputation suggests. Is he?"

Millie hid her gasp behind a hand and backed away from the curtain lest she be caught by the audience making such a gesture. "I'm sure I wouldn't know!" she stage-whispered at Jane, shooing her away with playful, indignant slaps.

"Don't be coy." Jane giggled. "Everyone knows you're swiving him. It's the reason you won't take Lord Phillip Easton's offer to keep you."

"Bite your tongue," Millie admonished. "There are innumerable reasons why I won't take Lord Easton's offer, all of which are my own. Besides, Rynd is married to that adorable woman, Ming."

Jane wrinkled her nose. "Being married never stops anyone from swiving whomever they please. And while

Ming is a dear, I heard they're—you know—not right *down there*." She made a discreet gesture between her legs. "Sideways or some such."

"That is a malicious rumor," Millie insisted. "*Really*, Jane."

"How would you know? Have you seen one?"

"No, but they're *people*. And we're all pretty much made the same. I'm not discussing this further with you." Millie sidled back as close as she dared to the edge of the curtain, sure to stay out of the way of the entrances and exits of the various actors from the stage that made up the populace of a fictional Venice.

"Who are you playing to tonight?" Jane asked, assuming her place by Millie's shoulder and peeking into the shadows of the Covent Garden audience. She referred to Millie's habit of picking one figure in the crowd and delivering her lines through a connection she created just for that individual. Of course she performed to the entire audience, but through her awareness of that link with her chosen theatergoer, she was somehow able to convey more emotion, sentiment, and passion. If she ever lost herself, she would find her mark and it would ground her back in the moment. She attributed much of her success to the practice, and never failed to pick her ritualistic audience-of-one before each performance began.

"See that man there, sitting alone in the second box back on the second tier?" She pointed to the lone figure.

"My, but he's a giant shadow," Jane marveled. "Not hard to pick him out of a crowd."

"No, indeed, and his eyes are so shockingly blue, I could see them from the stage when the houselights were up."

"Giving Rynd a run for his money, is he?" Jane poked her in the ribs with a sharp elbow.

Millie poked back. "Of course not, since we've already established that Rynd and I aren't involved."

Jane smoothed her coiffure and sent Millie a sideways wink. "Sure you inn't. *Anyone* just has to watch you on stage to know you're setting each other's bed linens on fire, you lucky wench." She swept onstage for her cue, cutting off Millie's chance at a retort.

"It's *called* acting," Millie muttered under her breath. Rynd was a startlingly handsome and unerringly friendly man, to be sure, but he was also self-involved and bombastic. No one would guess this, but Millie preferred quiet gentlemen. Someone with unimposing intelligence and unfailing kindness. Forgiving. Patient. Indulgent.

Safe.

Her notice returned to her shadow man. He'd taken off his hat, yet sat taller than most. And still. So impossibly motionless. But a sensation creeping over the fine hairs at her nape caused her to wonder if those eyes, pale and cold as a winter sky, were watching her right now. Something about the idea caused a wicked stirring inside of her laced with a delicious sort of anxiety.

She knew nothing about him, but had a feeling that he was neither unimposing *nor* safe. Something about his watchful stillness unsettled her. She took an involuntary step back into the safety of the velvet curtains and her own shadows, thinking that her bedsheets were a midnight-blue satin, and those eyes would glimmer from amongst them like crystalline stars against the darkest night.

Catching a sudden breath, she shuddered and brushed away the secret thrill from low in her belly. Best not even to fantasize. Everyone in her life was held at arm's length but one. Marriage, or even a lover, was strictly out of the question.

Her secrets were simply too dangerous.

Chapter Two

Reconnaissance. Argent answered his own internal question. That's what he was doing at the gin-soaked club at midnight. The Sapphire Room was little more than a veritable mélange of shadowed nooks and private rooms sprouting from the main dance hall with no shortage of cushioned furniture from which to drape oneself.

The cacophony of the revelers packed beneath the crystal chandeliers all but drowned out the chamber musicians. Everything sparkled. From the gowns of the waltzing *demimondaines*, fashionable in their jewel tones, to the ladies' intricate coiffures, to the champagne, all glimmered and winked like fallen stars beneath the new electric lights of the Sapphire Room.

Christopher had to suppress a wince as a woman's high, fake cackle breached his eardrum. He never understood why people pretended amusement or hilarity. It was as though they believed that if they laughed loudly enough, they would create happiness where there was none. Their worthless lives wouldn't seem so meaningless if they could drown out the sound of their own empty existence with enough champagne and laughter.

What fools.

At times like this Christopher appreciated his uncommon height, as he could stand a head above the crowd, and scan the herd for his prey. It wouldn't be difficult to find *her* here. Millie LeCour's hair was an uncommon shade of ebony. Her eyes, though nearly black themselves, shone with such life, they reminded him of multifaceted volcanic glass.

Those eyes. He'd watched the abundant life drain out of them as Othello had strangled her with his large, dark hands. Above them, alone in his box, Argent had held his own breath as the light that captured all of London dimmed and extinguished to rousing, thunderous applause.

He'd leaned toward her then, gripping the railing of the box. Willing her to wake, truly wondering if he hadn't just watched someone carry out his own charge to murder her in front of an audience of hundreds.

Argent had seen the real thing so many times he'd lost count, and she captured the dull lifelessness with such precision, *he* didn't breathe again until the curtain lifted for a final bow. And there she was, her smile brighter and more prismatic than Covent Garden's crystal chandelier.

He'd actually slumped back into his chair.

She'd turned to him, pressed her hands together, and curtsied with such grace, her eyes sparkling with unshed tears. Alive. Not only alive. *Full* of life. Brimming with it. Pressing her rouged lips to her hand, she'd tossed a kiss to the crowd. And again, he could have sworn, she turned and tossed one to him.

She'd been happy. He'd observed enough of humanity very closely to recognize the emotion. The true glow of transcendence. And as she'd waved at the boxes, *his* box, beaming that elated smile at him, he'd felt the most peculiar impulse to return it.

He'd become unsettled by that. Restless, chilled, and uncharacteristically prone to movement. His fingers curled and uncurled. His jaw clenched. His heart quickened its pace along with his breath. A pressure exerted itself against his heavy ribs and squeezed.

At first he'd considered apoplexy. Now he was altogether convinced it was something else, entirely.

He'd . . . felt. Not only that, the phenomenon hadn't abated.

For the first time in more than twenty years, he'd been a victim of affect. Something he'd thought himself rid of indefinitely.

Even still, at this moment, he was searching the crowd for her with a stunning sense of . . . what he could only identify as anticipation. Not for the violence, but just for another glimpse of her dark and mesmerizing eyes.

Grimacing and shaking his head, he took up a silent guard against the far wall, hoping the odd sensation would dissipate. That she could affect him so was an impossibility. What sort of creature was she? According to Dashforth, Millie LeCour was a liar and blackmailer. A charismatic narcissist dancing with a death sentence. A mark with private rooms above Bow Street. It was all Argent needed to know.

Wasn't it?

So . . . why was he here prowling amongst the crowds of common people like a serpent in a container of mice?

Oh yes. *Reconnaissance.* He'd do well to remember that.

A murmur of pleasure and surprise swept through the crowd, followed by a swell of applause directed toward the entrance.

The first thought that occurred to Argent was that Millie LeCour couldn't be more porcelain white if she were, in fact, a corpse. His second, that the crimson and white striped dress accented her pallor so absolutely, she brought to mind the Countess Bathory, a woman famous for bathing in the blood of virgin peasants to maintain her skin's youthful perfection.

Her smile was brilliant in every sense of the word, and

Argent found himself with his hand pressed to the chest of his jacket. It happened again. That curious little jolt in the cavern of his ribs. It was the same when she'd smiled at him from the stage. A startle of sensation. A current of awareness that singed along the nerves beneath his skin with warmth and maybe a touch of pleasure.

It seemed, if she was the Countess Bathory, tonight he was Vlad Tepes, dead but for strange, lethal animation and his insatiable hunger for blood. Not for physical sustenance, like the vampire, but just as necessary for his survival.

For in the spilling of blood, he made his living.

Beaming, Millie LeCour let go of her foppish escort to execute a curtsy at the top of the stairs before descending down to her adoring public, rouged lips pursed to receive and return a plethora of air kisses.

Of all the jewels on display at the Sapphire Room, she gleamed the brightest. Christopher had marked the tired cliché that men would often tell their female companions. They would say that a woman lit up a room. In the past, it confounded him that such a sentiment would occur to either party as a compliment.

But now . . .

What was once a tepid room filled with the press and stench of people flirting with debauchery, now seemed to glow with whatever luminescence was contained beneath her nearly translucent skin.

Objectively, it was a shame to rid the world of such beauty. Such talent. Though her smile might just be an illusion, and her graciousness may amount to artifice, her loss would further tip the scales toward the desolation of humanity by means of mediocrity.

It wouldn't stop him, though. If he fulfilled his vocation, she wouldn't live to see the dawn. He could do it here, he supposed. Draw her into a corner and snap her pretty neck, drape her limp body across a chaise and disappear before the alarm was raised.

He'd have to charm her. To lure her into the darkness with him, into his realm. As a creature of the spotlight, she'd be vulnerable there. She'd be defenseless.

The idea shouldn't excite him, but he'd be a liar if he didn't admit having Millie LeCour to himself in the darkness didn't arouse urges other than the one to kill.

Dangerous urges. Dangerous to him.

Though surrounded by people, Millie found him at once. Her head snapped up as though she'd heard his thoughts articulated above the drone of the crowd.

But Argent was certain she knew nothing of his intentions, because her eyes became warm midnight pools of delight the moment she noted him.

Excusing herself from her adoring public, she pressed through the throng as the orchestra began to play once more. She didn't stop until she stood in front of him, unaware, or uncaring, that all eyes were on them both.

"I have found you," she announced with a coy smile.

Argent had no idea what she meant. Maybe she knew why he was here. Maybe someone had warned her of the contract drawn against her life. Perhaps she was as unafraid and unfeeling as himself. A human free from the chains of pathos.

It still didn't change anything.

"It is I, Miss LeCour, who have found you."

And it is I who will end you.

Millie couldn't believe her luck. Here *he* was, the night's audience of one. She'd never had the pleasure of actually *meeting* one of them before. And to be in the presence of this particular man was an unexpected pleasure. Could it be that somehow he'd felt that strange, electric connection that she had experienced from the stage?

That would be terribly romantic, wouldn't it?

"I thought this was a private gathering, Mr. . . ." She looked at him expectantly, offering her hand for an introduction.

"Mr. Drummle," he answered, leaning over her hand, but not kissing it. "Bentley Drummle."

Millie was unable to hold in a sound of mirth.

"My name amuses you?"

Everything about him amused her.

"Not at all." She rushed to cover any offense. "It's only that you don't look like a Bentley."

"Oh? And what name would you deem appropriate for me?"

Millie regarded him with gathering interest, somehow unable to answer his question. He didn't look like he'd have a proper English name at all. He was nothing like the slim, elegant, fashionable men-about-town she was usually introduced to at these parties. Indeed, with his thick locks of hair the most uncommon shade of auburn, startling blue eyes, and raw, broad bones, he seemed as though he belonged on a Celtic battlefield wielding a claymore against Saxon intruders. Though his handsome features were relaxed into a mild expression, something dangerous shimmered in the air about him. Something . . . she couldn't quite put her finger on. It wasn't violence or anger. Nor was it anything unbalanced or wrong. Could it be that when he smiled, it didn't reach those fiercely blue eyes?

She searched those eyes now, her smile fading just a little. They were like ice, and not only because of the color. A glacial chill emanated from behind them. Charm and geniality warmed the slight curve of his hard mouth, but looking into those eyes was like staring across an endless arctic tundra. Bleak and empty.

Suddenly she was anxious, and, truth be told, more than a little intrigued. "I fear I'm drawing a blank at the moment," she admitted, surprised how breathless she sounded as she pulled her hand away from his.

He seemed to loom over her, a menace affecting a purposefully nonthreatening air. A wolf in sheep's clothing, perhaps? Though he was fair-skinned and light-eyed, he evoked a current of darkness. As though he carried the shadows with him in case he needed their protection.

However, Millie was fair certain that there was precious little that didn't need protection *from* him. A chill raised her skin, even though warmth suffused other parts of her. Parts she studiously tried to ignore.

"How did you say you came to be here?" she asked.

His expression changed from mild to sheepish, which sat uncomfortably on a face as brutal as his. "I was invited by a friend of a friend, actually. I forget her name. Quite tall, fair hair. Younger than she looks, but then older than she claims." He winked at her, his eyes crinkling with endearing groves. Not yet a smile, but the promise of one.

"Oh, do you mean Gertrude?" she asked.

"That's the one." He nodded, then scanned the crowd as though halfheartedly looking for the lady in question. "We have a mutual acquaintance by the name of Richard Swiveller, do you know him?"

Millie shook her head. "I'm afraid I don't."

He shrugged a gigantic shoulder and the movement rippled over his expensive evening jacket. "No matter. These private parties are hardly intimate, are they?"

Millie took a moment to scan her surroundings, taking in the hundred or so dancers and revelers in various stages of drunkenness and excess. "I suppose that depends on your interpretation of the word," she remarked wryly.

There was that sound of amusement again. It hailed from deep, deep in his cavernous chest. A sound more suited to the shadows of the jungle than an English ballroom.

"Would you care for a waltz, Miss LeCour?" He stepped closer, invading her space, towering over her like a wall of heat and muscle.

Millie hesitated. Not because she was afraid, but because she very much doubted that a man of such height and width and—she looked down—large feet, could waltz worth a damn.

One tread of his heavy soles upon her feet and she feared he'd break them.

"I'll step lightly," he murmured, reading her mind.

She looked up, and up, into those unsettling eyes. There. Not a feeling, not an emotion, per se, but a glimmer. One of enjoyment . . . or regret, she couldn't be sure.

Lord, but he was fascinating.

"See that you do," she teased. "One cannot act if one cannot walk, and so, Mr. Drummle, I am at your mercy."

"So you are." He took her gloved hand in his—enveloped it, to be accurate—and led her to the floor. She paused to wait for an opening amongst the swirling couples, and gasped as he pulled her forward, seizing a place and twirling her into it with powerful arms.

It became instantly obvious that her fears regarding his dancing skills were completely unfounded. Indeed, he was the most graceful, skilled man on the floor . . . or perhaps on any dance floor in London. He held her close, scandalously close, his hand on her back securing her to him like an iron clamp. The warmth of that hand seeped through the layers of her clothing and corset, an undeniable brand. Yet, the hand that held hers was gentle, but just as warm.

The arms beneath his suit coat were even harder than she'd guessed. The swells of muscles where her hands rested flexed and rolled with his movements, and Millie found herself entranced by them. So much so, that she stumbled and lost her footing around a turn.

He pulled her even closer, allowing her to seamlessly recover while supported by the strength of his astonishingly solid body. Regaining the rhythm of the waltz, she threw him an appreciative glance.

"It seems, Miss LeCour, that it is *I* who should have been worried about injury to my feet."

She laughed, dipping her forehead against his shoulder. Her heart sped along with the tempo of the waltz, sending warm flurries of nerves flooding through her. Perhaps her scruples about him had been as mistaken as her worries over his dancing capabilities.

"Tell me, Mr. Drummle, what is it you do?"

"I'm a longtime partner in a business enterprise," he answered.

"Anyone I've heard of?" she pressed.

"Undoubtedly. My partners handle the day-to-day running of the business, meetings, mergers, acquisitions, and so forth. I'm over contracts, damages, and . . . personnel."

"My," she flirted. "You sound like an important man to know. Tell me more." She used this ploy often. Men loved to talk about themselves. But this time, she found that she truly was curious about him. About how he spent his days. His nights.

And with whom.

"It's all rather dull and workaday compared to what you do." Millie felt, rather than saw his head tilt down, inching closer toward her. The din and atmosphere of the Sapphire Room suddenly melted away. Everything seemed darker, somehow. Closer. Their feet waltzed over shadows and their bodies synced in a flawless rhythm that felt, to her, sensuous. Sinful, even.

His scent enveloped her, a warm, masculine musk of

cedar trunks, shaving soap, and something darker. Wilder. Something that smelled like danger and sex. The kind of sex that marked you afterward. The kind she'd heard in the wailing of ecstatic obscenities and pounding of headboards against thin walls in the days before she could afford her own apartments.

Tilting her head back, she'd meant to smile an invitation into his eyes, but her gaze never got that far. They snagged his lips. Soft against the hard, almost cruel brackets of a perpetually masculine visage.

Those lips *would* indeed mark her. The russet stubble would redden her skin and tickle any flesh she exposed to him.

"I believe," she whispered, breathless again for the second time in his presence. "I believe that you want to kiss me, Mr. Drummle."

His answer wasn't the witty flirtation she'd expected. Just as suddenly as she'd found herself whisked onto the dance floor, he twirled her away from it. The crowd melted before them, artists and actors mixing with lower nobility or wealthy merchants. Those with money, power, influence, but not burdened by the more strident social morals of the upper class.

Eyes followed them as they left. Millie was used to it. Because of her celebrity, people watched her wherever she went, but this time, she had a cloying suspicion *she* wasn't the center of attention for once.

The farther into the Sapphire Room they ventured, the darker and seedier it became. In a gloomy nook of the hallway, two bedazzled women were locked in a passionate embrace, one lovely head buried in the other's neck. There was desperation in their passion. One born of unfulfilled desires denied too long.

Millie found an echo of that desire surging within her own body, as she followed Mr. Drummle's wide back into a narrow nook beneath the grand stairway. Here, the entry chandelier was dimmed to create a wicked atmosphere, but it provided enough light to cast their corner in complete shadow.

That shadow became theirs as they claimed the darkness.

Gasping, Millie found herself pressed against the wall, imprisoned between it and Bentley Drummle's unyielding torso.

A willing prisoner, but a prisoner nonetheless.

Lord, she never did this. Certainly, she'd stolen a few kisses, or gifted them as favors. She'd shamelessly flirted, openly admired, and even allowed the pursuit of men on occasion. But never like this. Publicly, with a man she barely knew whom she didn't need to charm for money or gain.

Just pleasure.

He stood like that for a moment, or it could have been an eternity. Their breath mingling in the darkness. Wine and port and desire.

She couldn't see his face clearly, backlit as it was by the chandelier that cast a halo around his vibrant hair. Millie knew for a certainty that neither of them were angels, and with a man as mysterious and sensual as this one, she could pave her way to hell in only an evening.

Best get started, then.

She strained toward him, lifting her mouth in invitation, but he didn't allow her to move. He just stood against her, his chest pressing her breasts higher as those big hands rested on her waist. She read hesitation in the movement, a hesitation she didn't understand.

Millie knew he could see her a little. She didn't have to fake the come-hither look this time, and finally, those hands began to move.

This man never seemed to do what she expected him

to. Even now, his hands weren't exploratory, but purposeful. They spanned the indent of her waist. Then her ribs, increasingly confined by her ever-quickening breath. His own inhale hitched when he reached her breasts, but he didn't stop there. Didn't cup or test them, didn't reach beneath her low bodice to find the straining, aching nipples. His hands merely kept moving upward, across her bare chest and shoulders, the calluses on his palms abrading her tender flesh and unleashing chill bumps everywhere.

And *still* he didn't kiss her. Merely stood with a whisper between their lips, his hands inching toward her throat.

Millie released a whimper of need, unashamed of the frenzy beginning to build within her. Who could have known? That desire would be this delicious? That anticipation could lock you in its hands—its large, callused hands—and strip away your pride until you wanted to beg.

"It won't hurt, I promise," he whispered as his fingers gently reached the nape of her neck, and then her jaw, and paused there.

It already hurt. She *ached,* ached in places generally best left ignored. Millie's breath had now been reduced to little more than needy pants. "If you don't kiss me, I'll die," she confessed.

He froze.

Vibrating with frustrated arousal she surged against him, lifting to her toes and grinding her lips against his.

The kiss was as hungry as it was sudden. While his eyes may have been cold, his mouth was hot and tasted of wine and male. She kissed him with abandon, enjoying the way his entire body jolted and went instantly rigid.

From the rough fingers at her throat to the hard sex in his trousers.

At the press of his arousal against her, Millie's sensitive breasts likewise swelled beneath her corset, becoming full and heavy. Her clothes felt confining, her skin itched to be bared to him. Demanded it.

At last, his tongue invaded her mouth and she moaned her approval. His thumbs, at first resting against her clavicles, caressed the dip of her throat, the curve of her chin, the line of her jaw, all while tasting her with the insatiable gluttony of a hedonist.

Millie had a sense that he was as lost to her as she to him. More so even, and the sensual, feminine power that surged within her fed her desire. She wanted him nigh gone for her. Drunk on her. Atop her, beneath her, and within her.

Perhaps they were *meant* to meet tonight. Maybe he was the man she'd been waiting for, the mythical hero that would sweep her off her feet and capture her heart.

His fingers tightened again against her throat, just a little, and she gasped. Then moaned as a thrill of fear titillated down her nerves and settled as a pool of moisture between her thighs.

"Again," she demanded, her arms winding around his neck, her body rubbing against his like a cat demanding to be stroked.

His curse was lost in the cavern of her mouth, and she knew in that moment that they both needed to see whatever this was between them to fruition.

A commotion warned them before the door from the hall burst open. Two female bodies spilled into the entryway floor in a heap of skirts and spitting, swearing, scratching violence. One of them they'd seen kissing another in the hall.

The aggressor was a stranger.

Millie and Mr. Drummle leaped apart, suddenly surrounded by a riotous group of men crowding behind them, shouting pleased and lusty approval and encouragement to the fighting women. Millie watched them for a moment. Stunned that ladies could be so vicious to one another.

But, she supposed, jealousy was a powerful emotion.

"Well," she called over the din, looking back over her shoulder to her would-be lover. "Would you like to—"

Her words died away, as there was no one to offer them to.

He'd disappeared.

Chapter Three

Millie knew she'd had a touch too much to drink when she had to wonder to herself if the carriage she'd hired to take her the scant distance from Covent Garden to Drury Lane had, indeed, stopped. Because the world still rocked ever so slightly.

She wasn't one to imbibe overmuch, but tonight was a special occasion.

Tonight she'd been abandoned.

Well, of course she'd had a splendid opening night at Covent Garden. There was that. But also, she'd had the most sensual, romantic moment of her entire life and then . . . nothing.

Bentley Drummle. What a *stupid* name. She was certain now that she'd heard it before, and not under the best of circumstances.

"Here you are, Miss LeCour." The driver opened the door and cold November air blasted her with sobering force. "Watch your step, now."

Millie took his offered hand and gathered her skirts before stepping down onto the street with a shiver. She overpaid the driver, Higgins was his name, a kind rather jowly man with a lovely top hat and bow tie. She thought at least he might be able to take the rest of the morning off and catch what few hours of sleep he could before the sun came up over the London rooftops.

She hiccupped and shuffled to her door.

Bentley Drummle. What a sod. She'd not give the man another thought. She was supposed to be celebrating her unbridled success and good fortune. Perhaps the man was sent by the powers that be to humble her on the night where her fame climbed to its greatest pinnacle yet. To remind her that in this world, she could still be treated like a common gutter slut.

God knew she'd acted like one with him.

Not only that, she'd been brought even lower by his rejection. Lord, but she was too romantic. Too willing. Too . . .

Lonely.

"Do you need help inside, Miss LeCour?" the driver asked with the careful voice reserved for drunks, invalids, and little children.

"No, thank you, Higgins." With a turn of her key, she lurched inside and slammed the door on the evening.

Her apartments were not spacious, but for a suite in the middle of the city, they were downright palatial. As Millie stepped into the entry that served as a parlor, she let the warm glow of the welcoming fire melt her until she felt as though her bones were made of dough.

She loved this place. Draped in imported silks from the Orient, furnished with everything from Indian cushions to Louis the XIV antiques and bedecked with Turkish tassels, it paid homage to every example on the color wheel, and still maintained a balance between cozy and opulent.

"Millie, me love, you're 'ome!" Millie found herself clutched to the plump bosom of Mrs. Beatrice Brimtree, her housekeeper. "An' you're as frozen as a snowman! Get in 'ere and take off your cloak. I drew ye a bath when they sent word that the celebration was beginning to thin."

If either of them resembled a snowman, it was Mrs. Brimtree. Her round, pillowy breasts rested neatly on a figure that would never require a bustle to be fashionable. Every bit of the woman from her cheeks to her backside bounced as she walked, much to the delight of her ever-randy husband, George, who still called her "young lady" after twenty years of marriage.

"It's after two in the morning, Bea, you shouldn't have stayed up to wait for me." Millie fought the woman over her cloak until she somehow became stuck in the folds and had to stand patiently like a child while Mrs. Brimtree uncoiled her.

"Nonsense, I couldn't sleep until I 'eard all about your debut as the star of the London stage." With a wrinkled nose, her housekeeper drew her toward her rooms at the back of the apartment, the carpet muffling their steps. "Lord, but you smell of gin and cigars and men who are up to no good."

"As it so happens, I spent the after party much in the company of all three." Millie giggled a bit, wishing the edge of bitterness hadn't crept into the sound. Still, the night had been an incredible success, and through it all she'd been feeling as though her feet would never actually touch the ground.

The gin had helped reclaim her good mood, she suspected.

"I take it opening night was a success."

"Oh, Bea, they called me back for three separate bows. Three!" Millie twirled in place while Mrs. Brimtree checked the temperature of the water in the deep copper tub and poured a bit of lavender oil into it. "You should see how many flowers are in my dressing room. It smells like a hothouse. It was so exhilarating that my heart still hasn't slowed."

And it had nothing to do with Bentley *sodding* Drummle and his unforgettable mouth.

"Is Jakub sleeping?" Millie asked, hoping to free her mind from the velvet chains of the memory.

"Sweet lad only made it to 'alf past one afore nodding off in your bed. 'E wanted to congratulate you 'imself and 'e drew you in your costume and everything."

That familiar sense of warmth and pride lifted Millie's lips into an irrepressible smile as she floated from her washroom to her adjoining bedchamber. Lifting the curtains back from the poster bed, she crawled in and nuzzled the downy cheek of the creature she loved most in this world. Her greatest joy and her most terrible secret.

"Mój Syn?" My son?

Jakub's hair, the color of wet sand, tickled her nose when he lifted his head.

Millie pulled her ridiculously fluffy blankets over him, almost causing his thin body to disappear in the mountain of down-stuffed comfort. "I'm home, *kochanie.*" She used the nickname she'd called him since he was a child. The word for *darling* in their native Poland.

"I waited up for you," he mumbled.

"I can see that." Smiling, Millie pushed a lock of hair from his forehead in hopes of seeing his soft doe eyes, but they remained closed. Her sweet boy was locked in that magical place at the surface of sleep where he'd sink back into the depths as soon as she released him to do so.

"You smell." He wrinkled his nose.

Her smile became a tender laugh as she kissed the forehead she'd just uncovered and rolled off the cavernous bed. "I'm going to bathe and then I'll come carry you to bed."

"I'll be awake," he insisted.

By the time Millie had gathered a silk wrapper from her wardrobe he'd already fallen into a slack-jawed slumber.

As she watched him, exhaustion began to chase alcohol and excitement from her veins and replace it with weariness. Better finish that bath while she was still able.

Mrs. Brimtree laid out a towel, her imported Parisian

soaps, and the scented almond oil that she liked to use to detangle her hair and rub on her skin to keep it soft.

"Go up to George, Beatrice, you know he doesn't like to sleep without you. I'm too spent to be much company tonight. I'll tell you all about it over breakfast and I promise I'll be much more interesting then."

"All right, dearie." Beatrice bustled around a moment longer, lighting another lantern and smoothing her wrapper and nightgown where they draped over a screen. "You're right about my George, of course. 'E's such a love. Drinks too much and curses too often, but I adore him for all of that."

"Well, give him this for me." Millie kissed the lady on her flushed cheek and began to untie her stays, which laced up the front, thus negating the need for help during costume changes.

Mrs. Brimtree hovered, her brow furrowing as Millie peeled her garments from her body. "Miss Millie, can I speak freely?"

"Of course." Millie pulled pins from her heavy hair, her scalp switching from aching to itchy. Sweat caused by the stage lights and the close quarters of the after party had chilled and dried on her skin, and she looked forward to being clean with a lustful relish.

"It's just that, you never bring a man 'ome."

Millie froze with both hands locked in her hair, the statement astonishing her into stillness. If Mrs. Brimtree knew how close she'd come to bringing one home tonight. If she knew the manner in which she'd conducted herself. The woman would bundle her back up and ship her off to church.

"I have Jakub," she said gently. "It wouldn't be seemly." Mr. and Mrs. George and Beatrice Brimtree had been her butler and housekeeper for almost two years now, as she'd been able to afford them, but in such a short time, they'd become like family. Though they were a couple deeply in love, they'd never before dared to remark on Millie's solitude. What was it about tonight that she must be constantly reminded of her loneliness?

"It's just that, women like you, wot have a mind of their own, and money besides, they tend to wait for the perfect gent to come along."

Millie blinked, lowering her hands. "Do they?" she asked, feigning nonchalance as a familiar pang of loneliness stabbed her in the gut, where excitement and arousal had been only hours before.

"I worry all the time, that you spend yer nights acting out stories about 'eroes spouting sonnets, killing themselves in the name of love, or fighting off tyrants and monsters and saving the damsel. That man. That perfect 'ero, 'e's not out there, but there are plenty of good'uns worth your time."

Like who? Bentley Drummle? Lord, she was really terrible at keeping him out of her thoughts. The brigand. The ne'er-do-well. She should have gone with her first impression of him.

Beatrice didn't look her in the eyes as she spoke, and Millie thought her hesitance and concern was endearing. "You sometimes have to make allowances for them. For example, maybe 'e's 'ansom, but smokes like a chimney. Or maybe 'e's kind, but milk gives 'im the brimstone winds. Or say 'e's rich, but 'as a few bad teeth."

"Are you saying you think I'm a snob?"

The fact that Mrs. Brimtree didn't deny it hurt worse than Millie thought it would have.

"Sometimes, accepting a man just as 'e is, flaws and everything, chases the loneliness away, and over time those edges dull. If 'e feels like you love 'im for all that, 'e's more likely to be loving you still when your youth, fame, and beauty 'ave gone the way of things."

"I'm not lonely," Millie lied. "I have Jakub."

"Inn't right that the boy 'as no father. And in no time, 'e'll grow up and 'ave a family of 'is own. And then where will you be?"

Millie turned away from Mrs. Brimtree, the conversation making her feel more exposed than taking off her clothing. "Trust me, it's better this way." Jakub needed more protection than most boys, all because of his mother's terrible secret.

"But—"

"*Good night,* Beatrice," Millie said firmly. "Please don't forget to give my love to George."

A quiet moment ticked by, then Millie moved to the tub.

"Yes, mum."

Millie waited for the door to click before she stepped over the rim of the copper tub and sank into its depths with a breathy sigh. Bowing to her public on that stage, she'd thought nothing could cast a pall on this brilliant night. The most wonderful and affirming of her life thus far.

She'd been wrong.

Beatrice only called her "mum" when she was displeased about something. The woman thought she was giving kind advice, but she didn't know how dangerous the world was out there for her and Jakub. That allowing just any man into her life would shatter the safety and comfort that she'd created for them.

Jakub deserved to be safe and grow up without fear. He deserved the best she could give him. Better than her parents and brothers had done for her. Better than the rakes and noblemen who chased her skirts, but not her heart.

And better than Bentley Drummle.

Damn it. How was it that he wormed his way into her thoughts every ten seconds? It was the paradox of his face. Had to be. Warm skin, fair and yet darker than his red hair and eyes warranted. Like he'd lived in sunnier climes.

There were other contradictions she'd experienced first-hand A hot tongue. Cold eyes. Rough hands. Gentle fingers. Hard mouth. Soft lips.

Millie cursed, splashed the water, and cursed again, this time in Polish.

Forget about men. She had a career to build. A son to raise. And for now, for *him,* she'd just have to content herself with her onstage heroes, because she knew that Mrs. Brimtree was right about one thing.

They did not exist out here in the real world.

Christopher Argent's hands ached with cold. He'd scaled a wrought-iron gate and climbed the stone stanchion to the lower ledge of Millie LeCour's apartments. His fitted waistcoat had hindered his reach, so he'd abandoned it, leaving it hanging from one of the many tall iron points of the gate. The wind snaked through the narrow corridor of Drury Lane and stung his flesh through his shirtsleeves like the lash of a whip. In fact, the similarities of the pain were uncanny. Except, he supposed, a whip was a more localized pain, and the chill of the wind could be felt over his entire flesh. Regardless, the residual burn was remarkably comparable in both cases.

The empty street had an apocalyptic quietude that appealed to him. A cold like this, one that left crystalline swirls of frost over the whole of the city, drove even the stoutest of night stalkers and criminals indoors.

Argent was used to the cold. Was born to it and honed from it. He only had to worry about it when it affected his physical performance.

Like now, when he could sense the joints in his hands stiffening with each passing moment. Galvanized, he judged the length of distance to the second story with a few hurried calculations, and crouched to leap.

The coarse brick of the ledge bit into his fingertips, but he ground his teeth together and used all the honed strength in his arms and back to pull his chin above the ledge. Once his upper body was secure, he checked to see that no one was looking out of the window toward the street.

The soft glow of a lantern pierced the night, but from his precarious vantage, he could tell he wasn't in danger of being detected as a Japanese screen protected the window from view even though the drapes were open.

With a grunt, he swung his leg up and found purchase enough to lift the rest of his bulk and stood, turning so his back was against the narrow red brick wall between two arched windows.

He'd conquered walls with thinner ledges, but not many.

Tucking his hands beneath his arms to warm them, he strained his neck to peer into the window. The Japanese screen about four paces inside consisted of three panels skewed into diagonal sides so they could stand upright. A panel depicting an Asian landscape blocked his view.

Argent could only see the gleam of a copper tub through a slivered crack in the bent screen. Steam rose above its rim, so he waited a few minutes to make sure no one was submerged.

The time he spent waiting unsettled him. If nothing else, he was a patient man. His profession was about timing. The time it took to enter someone's home. The time it took for a mark to strike out, pass out, or bleed out. How long it would take him to make his escape. Or, most importantly, how long it took his clients to make their payments. So taking the time to decipher whether Millicent LeCour's head would appear above the bathwater took on a distinctly anticipatory edge.

Argent blinked. And just what did he anticipate? He

couldn't say. In fact, he couldn't remember anticipating much of anything before. And so his brain wouldn't dare answer the question.

But his body did.

His lips throbbed with the exquisite memory of her mouth pressed against them. His skin felt warm, the heat radiating out from his quickening blood. His cravat became tight, his clothing binding. Especially his trousers. His lungs seemed to need more room than his ribs were willing to give, and suddenly it was impossible not to fog the window with his overheated breath.

There it was again. Desire. A thing as foreign to him as were warmth and kindness.

He wanted Millie LeCour with an intensity he'd never before felt.

But . . . why? He'd fucked plenty of women in his lifetime. Willing, trained, and uncomplicated.

Disposable.

Why her? Why now?

What was it about the actress that entranced and aroused him? What about her was different from everyone else?

His unerring eye for detail was a greatly relied upon attribute. Once his notice touched something, it was calculated, analyzed, prioritized, and then shelved in its correct location. Things, people, places, events, they were all part of the landscape and each held an equal measure of curiosity and emotional ambiguity. He thought the same of a lovely clock as he did about a lovely woman. They were both curious and complicated with cogs and bits that took a man's intense scrutiny and precision to understand. Both of them served a useful function in the world.

And both were easily broken.

But for some perplexing reason, Millie LeCour refused to be shelved or classified. Her details were so . . . they were too . . . bemusing? Uncommon? Curious?

After his first attempt at her life had been thwarted, primarily by that thoroughly unexpected kiss, Argent had stalked her all night, suffused with fascination. How had she manipulated him with something as simple as a kiss? Why had he paused when a quick snap of her lovely neck would have uncomplicated things immensely? How had she recovered so quickly from their encounter when *he,* the man hired to snuff out her life, still itched with the memory of her downy skin beneath his hands?

A slew of noble rakes and roguish upstarts had vied for a word with her all night, for a touch, a dance, or a smile. And she'd given of them freely. Flitting from one admirer to the next like a coy butterfly, ever avoiding the net.

She was an expert at this subterfuge, he realized. At making every person in her scope feel as though they were singular to her, all the while treating them with abject equality. She never lingered for too long. Never said too much. Never touched more than was appropriate.

Except for him. Among her entire bevy of admirers, some handsome, others titled, and rich, she'd allowed *him* to lure her into the darkness. Allowed his hands to sample her soft flesh and softer lips. Why him? What draw had he over her that those others didn't?

While she radiated warmth, each move was as calculated as his own. She was as unattainable as a beloved goddess. Remote as a tropical island.

And he was as dark and cold as the denizens of hell. Had to be. So whatever this mothlike fascination he had with her light and warmth, it was past time he snuff it out and return to the darkness that was his domain.

Millie LeCour had to die.

Tonight.

His cold musings had taken too long. Argent surmised that if anyone was in the tub, and they stayed below water that long, they'd be dead. So either way he could make his move.

Unsheathing a long, thin dagger from his boot, he shimmied it between the crack in the windows and ran it up the middle softly until he felt it brush against the latch. Angling it forward, he felt it give and pulled the window out. Turning his body sideways, he slid into the room and stepped down onto the flat of his foot, lowering his bulk onto the washroom carpet. Simultaneously, he pulled the window mostly closed and resheathed his knife. One of the many secrets to a successful assassination was economy of movement.

Now that he was inside, humid, aromatic warmth suffused his lungs and spread a bewildering heat along his frigid limbs. His shirt, made of the finest, softest linen, abraded his tingling nerves.

It would have been disturbing, if he was capable of being disturbed.

Everything about this contract had been a little skewed from the very beginning, and the need to have it done with was becoming more and more imperative.

Two doors mirrored each other in the southwest corner of the room. One on the west wall stood open, while its companion on the south wall was latched shut. Through dim lamps flickering on the other side of the open door, Argent could see a hallway stretching toward a parlor. Three doors stood closed in the hallway, two on the south wall, and one on the north. Argent guessed that the southern doors belonged to bedrooms, and the northern door to the stairs leading to the top floor.

Her staff lived up there. A married couple. Middle-aged, overweight, and slow moving. They wouldn't be a problem.

A floorboard creaked in a distant room, having as much

effect on the silence as a cannon blast. Argent ducked behind the silk screen, his ears straining for more noise.

A soft hum. A whisper. But nothing close.

Argent stood, again using the flats of his feet to walk lightly across the room and ensconce himself behind the hallway door.

This room was a small annex to a master suite. Many women would use it for a salon, or for entertaining visitors. Millie LeCour had decorated hers with dress mannequins, costumes, gowns, wigs, memorabilia, the large copper tub, obviously, and a vanity with a confounding amount of bottles and baubles strewn across every possible surface.

Argent was glad that only the lone oil lamp flickered in the room—which he'd dimmed further on his way to his current hiding spot—or the glitter and brilliance of it all would surely have blinded him.

After a few eternal minutes, a hall door opened and closed and the shuffle of feminine footsteps angled in his direction.

His timing must be flawless. One strike. One quick, decisive turn of the neck upon a gentle exhale.

And she'd be gone.

His chest constricted, but he ruthlessly ignored it, taking a few centering breaths.

He was like water, ready for death to flow from his hands.

Her scent drifted into the room before she did. Vanilla and lavender, like the heady, fragrant oils from the bath. A flash of an ebony braid against a pale nightgown crossed the thin thread of light coming from the crack created by the door hinges. Five more steps and she'd turn the corner of the door and be within his reach. Three more heartbeats. Two. One.

He lunged for her, reaching for her throat. One twist. One snap. He'd done it dozens of times. Hundreds.

But . . . his hands. They weren't obeying. Instead of twisting they were grasping. Instead of dropping they were pulling. Instead of killing, they were—holding?

What?

She struggled against him, a shocked cry tearing from her as he gripped her tightly to him from behind. Perplexed as he was, he subdued her easily, locking her arms to her sides with one arm and banding his other beneath her throat. He tried not to notice how lush and soft she felt. How clean and sweet-smelling she was, or how her round backside pressed intimately against his thigh.

He could feel her ribs inflate with a deep breath, readying for a scream.

"Make a noise and I slaughter whoever else comes through that door," he threatened in a low voice. "I don't leave witnesses."

Her lungs deflated in a quiet whimper.

Argent did his best to analyze the situation, but something in his mind was refusing to work. He struggled to search his subconscious for a solution to the problem he'd just created for himself. This lovely, soft creature was trembling in his arms, toying with his senses and muddling his thoughts.

What in the bloody hell did he do now?

She still hadn't seen him, he could tighten the arm about her neck and she'd be out in a matter of seconds. The job would be finished with only this minor hiccup.

You could take her first, right here on the plush carpets. The soulless evil that had been with him for fifteen years whispered the vile thought in his ear. *Be the last to taste her.*

Argent squeezed his eyes shut against the idea. *Never.* He'd taken lives, but he'd never in his entire existence considered taking what a woman hadn't offered him freely.

Or charged him for.

He clenched his teeth in helpless frustration as his cock swelled against her back.

What was happening to him? What was *she* doing to him?

The woman whimpered again, a powerful tremor of fear coursing down her body as her breath sped to short bursts of terror.

Argent didn't want her to be afraid. Didn't want to be doing this to her. He wanted those whimpers to stop. His arm tightened on her throat slightly. No matter what she'd done, a woman didn't deserve to be terrorized. Not by an unfeeling killer like him. So why couldn't he just squeeze? Why wasn't she dead yet?

Because earlier her dark eyes had shimmered with life. Her smile had held the kind of joy that life tended to smother out of most adults. Because . . . though he was a godless man, something whispered to him from the ether that he didn't have the right to take such light from the world.

Because she'd kissed him, and in this moment he had to admit that he'd never again be the same. She'd awakened something he'd thought he'd live without.

A hallway door opened. *"Mama?"* a small voice called into the darkness.

They both froze.

The hallway floor creaked twice with little steps. One more time and the boy would be moments from discovering them.

Fuck.

"Please," she breathed, softer even than a desperate whisper. "Do what you want with me, but—*please—don't hurt my son.*"

Chapter Four

Millie couldn't breathe. She'd never prayed so hard in her life. If only her son had stayed in bed. If only . . .

"Follow my lead, and I'll leave you both unharmed," he growled into her ear.

She didn't know how she was suddenly facing him, or why, until he grabbed a fistful of her braid, wrenched her neck back, and slanted his lips over hers. *Oh God.* She *knew* who he was. Would recognize the feel of those lips anywhere.

She'd kissed them only hours ago.

Suddenly his hands were cupping both sides of her jaw, his thumbs pressing her lips apart so his tongue could make its wet sweep into her mouth.

She should bite him. Claw his eyes out. Knee him between the legs, grab Jakub, and run screaming from the house.

But this man was someone you never escaped from. She could tell by the way he kissed, by the unmitigated power in his arms when he'd seized her.

This was no gentle, questing probe she'd received from gentlemen. Or soft, seductive kisses that she'd allowed from exciting men who had no idea what the word "gentleman" meant. It wasn't the hungry, thrilling kiss they'd shared before.

There was something wild in his lips. Something dark

and desperate that, it seemed, astounded even him. Even if she'd allowed this kiss in regular circumstances, Millie didn't think she'd be ready for the overwhelming intensity of it. It felt like something had shattered inside her attacker. Almost as certainly as if she'd heard it.

He made a sound in his throat. A sound of pleasure. A sound of agony.

"*Matka?* Mama?" The door moved. "Ew!"

When Millie pulled away, it surprised her that her assailant allowed it.

Jakub stood gripping the door handle, his honey-fair hair sticking up in wild disarray, and an openmouthed expression of childlike disgust frozen on his beautiful little face.

"Kochanie," she gasped, her heart pounding loud enough for everyone in the room to hear. Though whether it was from fear or from the kiss, she couldn't honestly say.

"I heard a noise," her son said by way of embarrassed explanation.

Her attacker stood absolutely still as Millie lunged for Jakub, and she sent a silent prayer of gratitude that he'd let her go. "I know. I'm sorry. L-let's get you back to bed." Desperate to get him away from the intruder, she scooped little Jakub up and ran for his room. Once inside, she set him down and locked the door, leaning back against it and trying to slow her panicked breaths.

"Who was that?" Jakub's eyes remained as large and round as an owl's.

How did she answer that question? He was a dangerous man. One she'd allowed to kiss her earlier that night, one who'd followed her home for Lord-knew-what nefarious purpose. Her behavior had brought this on them, she'd acted like a wanton and put her child in danger.

"Why was he kissing you?" Her son didn't wait for an answer to his first question before pressing forward.

Millie opened her mouth to answer, distressed that she could still taste the masculine flavor of his lips on her own. Had he broken in to molest her? To finish what they'd started in that nook beneath the stairs? Had he intended to rape her?

"Is that my father?"

Millie's hand flew to her chest. "What in God's name would make you think that?" she puffed, reaching for the bell-pull in Jakub's room and tugging on it twice, with a pause and then once more.

The signal to George Brimtree of danger. He would bring his gun, and this would all be over.

Jakub followed her around as she checked the lock on the door, paced away, checked it again.

"At school Rodney Beaton said that mothers had to kiss fathers whenever they were told."

"Rodney Beaton is a half-wit," Millie muttered without thinking, before taking Jakub into her arms and holding him tight. "That man . . . he's not your father," she said more gently. "He's . . ."

She heard the attic door burst open and George Brimtree's heavy footfalls pounded toward the locked door.

"An intruder, George, in my rooms," she called through the heavy wood.

"I'll get 'im with old Francesca, 'ere," George bellowed back. Francesca, of course, being the name of his rifle.

Millie could hear him charging her rooms. "Be careful!" she called belatedly. George was a big man. He'd been a foot soldier for years, and worked his way up into a rifle brigade. But somehow she knew that, even with the weapon, he wasn't going to stand a chance against the profligate who'd followed her home.

Praying for his survival, Millie didn't breathe again until she heard her butler limping back down the hallway.

"All clear, Miss Millie. Inn't no one there. I checked every crack and cranny."

Hesitantly, Millie unlocked the door and peeked into the dimly lit hallway, shaking more now than when she'd actually been in the clutches of the brute. She would have laughed at the sight of portly George in his nightshirt and hat, clutching the ancient rifle to his chest, if she wasn't so shaken.

"Are you 'urt, Miss Millie?" he asked. "Is wee Jakub all right?"

"We're fine, George," she said, hating the tremor in her voice.

"Must've lit out the window. Though I can't see 'ow he'd do it without breaking 'is legs." The old man looked stymied.

"Best send for Scotland Yard, George," Millie said, shutting the door and turning back to poor wide-eyed Jakub, gathering him into her arms again.

That's it, tomorrow she was installing bars on all the windows, or she'd never sleep again.

CHAPTER FIVE

Please—don't hurt my son. The words echoed through the cold, biting February rain as it whipped through the narrow streets of the East End. Argent couldn't tell whose voice roared against the storm rolling down from the north. Millie LeCour's? Or his mother's?

Numbness stole the dexterity from his limbs, though whether the culprit was the freezing temperature or the pounding in his head, he couldn't be certain. Suddenly he felt as though he'd run several leagues. His ribs tightened around his lungs, inhibiting his breath. His heart tossed itself against its cage, throbbing in his ears, through his muscles, and in the very marrow of his bones.

Was it truly so cold outside? Or could it be the startling contrast between the chill of the evening and the warmth of the flesh he'd had pressed against him only moments ago?

Trying to remember how long he'd been running, he plunged into darker streets, down the most dangerous alleys, with names like Cutthroat Corner or Hang Tree Row. He couldn't seem to stop. If he stood still his skin might peel away from his body. And with nothing to shield his awareness, he might blow away in the storm.

Objectively, he'd always wondered if the black, cold void in his chest would expand to swallow him whole. Maybe that's what he was running from. Evisceration. Oblivion.

For as long as he could remember. Since . . . since the night he'd been left alone in this world, he'd often felt as though he existed *outside* of his body. That he walked alongside himself, behind his own head, detached, apart, an emotionless observer to the blood he spilled. His body existed as an animated corpse, bone and vein, but bereft of a soul. Of whatever passion that made a being fundamentally *human.* What caused them to sigh at a poem, or see themselves within a painting. Take offense at their neighbor or start a war out of greed.

He'd thought he lacked this intrinsic element.

He didn't fear death. Didn't appreciate life. He was fond of nothing and therefore didn't fear pain or loss.

So why was he chasing his own body through the streets of predawn London? Why couldn't he feel his skin? Or the breath in his lungs? Was this trembling a sign that his body was shutting down, or becoming more powerful?

Images transposed themselves over the stormy darkness. A lake of blood the size of a prison cell, growing larger with each lifeless body he tossed into it. Large, lovely marble-black eyes flickering with the last vestiges of life to roaring applause. A small boy, watching his mother die. What had he done? What had he left undone? What was the strategy for his next move?

Please—don't hurt my son.

His chest tightened so abruptly, he gasped as his hand flew to cover it.

He needed to *think.* He was too scattered, too caged. How a man could be both detached from his body and imprisoned by it was infuriating. He needed to center himself, needed release, and knew exactly where to find it.

Veering to the left, he crossed Limehouse Street and turned down what they called "Poplar Alley." Not for the foliage, but for the small lodgings made of the poplar tree.

The smell of foreign spices, street vendors roasting

strange delicacies on spits, penned animals, and raw sewage mixed with things better left to the shadows and fog.

Exotic food was not the only delicacy on display. Petite women with blue-black hair and robes of glimmering silk beckoned from white tents filled with sweet-smelling smoke and bodies limp from one excess or another. Opium, drink, food, sex, any of it was for sale here in the Asian markets, and Argent had tasted it all without developing a taste for any of it.

The markets and back alleys were clogged with too much humanity, even at this time of night, to maintain his jog. Though wherever he walked, people made room. Argent was a tall man in any place he found himself, but here in the Asian quarter, he stood out like a flame-haired beacon in a sea of darkness. Eyes followed him, but he didn't meet them. Nor did he look down.

He'd always avoided looking directly into anyone's eyes. He stared through them, or focused on the space between them. He imagined it was because life, itself, resided in the eyes. He'd learned that early on. And if he watched life drain away once, he'd watch it again. Every time he slept. Or sometimes tattooed on the back of his eyelids when he blinked.

The next gaze he met could belong to a potential victim. At first that thought had sickened him, and then it didn't. It—drew him. Made him feel powerful. Like a god. As he grew older, he realized that the only time he felt alive was when he took a life.

And that came with its own dangers.

There was no shame in taking pleasure in a kill, but for some, it became an obsession, an addiction, and Argent didn't want to give anything that power over him.

So he used other means with which to fill the void.

"I know you," a sweet voice crooned from one of the silk tents. "You only want girl on her knees."

Argent turned, looking down at a small woman with long, long black hair and startlingly red lips painted on a face so white, he could barely distinguish it from the color of the tent.

She was right. He only took women from behind. He didn't want to look them in the eyes, either.

Reaching for him, she placed a demure hand on his jacket. "I get on my knees for you," she offered in a husky voice. "I not afraid like the other girls."

She said that now . . .

"Some other time, perhaps." He brushed her off.

It was a different vice he searched for tonight. A different woman he wanted on her knees . . .

God, what that image did to him. Millie LeCour bent over for him, her creamy skin bared and her body accepting his.

Christ, he needed some kind of release or he'd immolate there in the frigid London night.

When a door opened and two men dragged a half-naked body to bleed into the gutter, Argent knew he'd found the right place. Nodding to one of the house employees he'd known for years, he caught the gleam of greed in the man's eyes. "You going to give me time to place my bets?" the man asked, dumping his charge and wiping filthy hands on his trousers.

"Only if you place mine, I'll give you six percent of the winnings." Retrieving his clip of notes from his pocket, Argent tossed the entire thing to the man, Wei Ping was his name, and mounted the rickety stairs into the unmarked building.

Three flights down into the bowels of the earth the sound became so deafening, it drowned out the storm. Men. Hundreds of them. Some in white-tie finery and others in tatters and rags, all screaming, sweating, and swearing at the fighter upon whom they'd risked their money.

Ducking below the door frame, Argent nodded to the corpulent Chinese, Pan Lee, who leased the building from Dorian Blackwell who took a commission from the business. The man held up two fingers, raising a questioning eyebrow.

Argent held up three.

Receiving a nod from Pan Lee, Argent strode toward the pit. His jacket hit the filth that covered the floor. Then his tie, his waistcoat, and finally his shirt.

People always gasped when he removed his shirt. He'd stopped noticing years ago.

Rainwater and sweat dropped from his hair and ran down his spine. His muscles were warm from his run. He was ready.

He was like water.

Pandemonium spread through the crowd when they saw him. Christopher Argent. Last student of the Wing Chun Kung Fu master Wu Ping. The weapon of the Blackheart Brothers of Newgate Prison. The youngest, highest-earning pit fighter of the previous decade. The Blackheart of Ben More's master assassin.

The coldest, deadliest man in all London.

He knew what they saw when he removed his fine shoes at the side of the pit, certain that even in this den of thieves, no one would dare to swipe them.

Please—don't hurt my son.

Those words had followed him around for two decades.

They'd hurt him plenty in the years after his mother died. The guards. The prisoners. Even his allies. In a world like Newgate Prison, pain was how one communicated, it was the only language they all understood. And once they'd hanged Wu Ping a couple years later, pain had become Argent's *new* teacher.

His torso was a large, pale record of lessons learned, of lashes he'd returned and pain he'd answered in kind.

Of brutish strength gained through forced labor, disciplined training, and pits like these in the early days, when he'd followed Dorian Blackwell into the hells of the East End. They'd each done what they had to do to earn money. Unspeakable things.

Like the cavern carved through time by a single trickle of water, Argent had honed himself into a sharp-hewn weapon, an instrument of death. And he'd *never* failed to deal the fatal blow.

Until tonight.

The question remained . . . Why?

Three men filtered into the round pit, a hole in the ground, really, the depth of a grave and the width of a small bedroom. Once you entered Pan Lee's pit, you left broken or victorious. There was no in-between.

And no one had *ever* broken him.

Argent studied his opponents. Size never counted in his calculations, though only the large African outweighed him. It was skill he looked for, and only two of them had it. The dark man with Anglo features dressed in nothing but a dingy wrap about his waist. East Indian, Argent guessed. And more skilled with a weapon than his bare hands.

Though weapons weren't allowed in the pit, that didn't stop some, as the consequences weren't enough to deter a dirty trick every now and again, as long as it pleased the crowds. Though where the Indian man would hide any weapon was beyond imagining.

The African was heavy-fisted and strong-jawed. Argent knew he'd better outmaneuver this one and avoid going to the ground.

And finally, the sharp-boned Spaniard was the least of his worries. More swagger than skill, and obviously overcompensating with bravado, loud threats, and crowd pandering.

He'd asked for three opponents, not two and a half. He had a great deal of thinking to do.

The gong had barely sounded before the first punch was thrown.

His opponents thought because he didn't dance or weave, because he rooted himself to the earth and found his center line, that he would be an easy target.

Apparently, they were not locals.

He allowed the Indian to land the first blow to his jaw. Argent's cheek ground against his teeth, his mouth filled with the metallic tang of blood. The pain pulled him back inside his body. Centered his awareness where it belonged, behind his eyes. It opened the cold void within his chest, and also filled its yawning mouth.

Argent had known it would.

Now he could think. *Now* he could consider the consequences of his actions and formulate a plan.

Spitting the blood into the Indian's eyes, he used the element of surprise to buckle the man's leg with a swift kick. Gripping the man's hair, Argent felt the Indian's cheekbone break against his knee.

The crowd erupted.

One down.

He never took a contract he didn't intend to finish. So why could he not finish off Millie LeCour?

He'd killed women before. Mothers, even. One had been contracted by her own son, a desperate ploy by an aristocrat to stop her from signing away his inheritance to her beloved dog. Another had been a midwife, stealing bastard newborns from young, unmarried mothers and selling them to whoever paid the highest price.

He'd allowed Dorian Blackwell to offer a discount for her demise.

Once he'd strangled the madam of a whore he'd bought, who was trying to sell the whore's twelve-year-old sister.

She'd paid him in trade. A good bargain, that.

Argent squared off with the African, aware that the Spaniard was moving behind to flank him. But really only one danger remained in this pit. He bared his bloodied teeth at his opponent. One of few men in this world he had to look up to see clearly. *That's right,* he thought. *You think I'm wounded. Cornered. You'll come at me with all your strength.*

It was that strength Argent would use against him.

And why couldn't he use it against his lovely mark?

He'd like to blame it on the idea that forcing the boy to watch his mother die at Argent's own hand affected him in a way he'd not expected. And, indeed, it had, quite intensely. However, he'd hesitated to snap Millie LeCour's lovely neck *before* the child had been an issue.

And while her words, the exact replica of his own mother's plea on his behalf all those years ago, pushed him over the edge of his cold, hard sanity, he'd been walking toward that edge since the moment he'd watched her die onstage.

The African lunged, his long arms swinging with wide hooks that would land like a steam engine. Instead of ducking the fists, Argent leaped toward the man, stepping inside his reach and stealing the power of his punch. Blocking one meaty arm with his own, he simultaneously struck his opponent's throat. Or, rather, punched *through* his throat, as he'd been instructed all those years ago.

He caught a kidney punch from the Spaniard for his troubles, but it didn't break his focus, and he leaped atop the falling African and landed two more devastating blows on his way to the ground.

Two down.

What was it about Millie, *specifically,* that differed from all the rest?

Was it a question of simple chemistry? An unfulfilled lust as primal and animalistic as what happened in this pit?

God knew his body became instantly hard the moment their skin made contact. Hell, he was thickening now just at the thought of it. Touching her was electric. Potent.

And dangerous.

Kissing her . . . well, that defied description. It was more excruciating than any torture. More exquisite than any memory.

Millie LeCour overflowed with life, with enthusiasm, with emotion and warmth, and while their skin was connected, all that somehow transferred into him.

And for a precious instant he could . . . *feel* it.

How was that possible? How did a woman, reportedly a thief, a blackmailer, a greedy social climber with a heart as cold as his, have such a profound effect? The woman he'd seen so selflessly and desperately protecting her child didn't match the accounts of the woman he'd been hired to murder.

Was her love for the boy in earnest? Was she such a consummate actress that she fooled even him? His mother had been a criminal, a thief, and a whore, and still she'd loved Christopher to distraction. In fact, many cold-blooded killers, criminals, and warmongers were family oriented.

It was their weakness. One he'd often exploited during the Underworld War he and Dorian Blackwell had started against the criminal element of London more than a decade ago.

Argent didn't like unanswered questions. Didn't want unknown variables. And at the very least, he couldn't have Miss LeCour going to the police with his description. He'd never left a witness before, and he and Blackwell had already become too familiar with Chief Inspector Morley in recent years to risk it.

The gasp of the crowd and the gleam of metal warned him to roll away, dodging a knife in the spine. Gaining his feet just in time for the Spaniard to charge at him, knife first, Argent used one arm to lever the inside of the man's elbow and the other to push the Spaniard's knife hand toward his own chest.

And so it was decided, Argent thought with satisfaction as the blade, which could have been sharper in his opinion, pierced the chest of the struggling, screaming Spaniard and drove in to the hilt. Dropping the bleeding man, Argent walked to the door of the steps leading out of the pit, which opened upon his approach. The crowd parted for him, and he left the cacophony behind, struck with a singular purpose.

He'd retrieve his winnings later.

What he needed were answers to the many questions tumbling around the flawless form Millie LeCour.

He had to see her again, and this time there must be absolution. He had to logically and objectively analyze this power she had over him. And this *time,* once he understood the stakes, he'd make the final decision. He'd either kill her . . .

Or claim her.

Chapter Six

"An assassin?" Jane asked, reclining into the salt bath with a blissful sigh. "Are you certain that the chief inspector isn't making more of this than is necessary? We've all had our share of overzealous pursuers. And you said, yourself, he'd done nothing but break into your apartments and kiss you."

The steaming water caused Millie to take a few shallow breaths before she could finally settle herself into the bathing pool with a great exhale. "I also found that particularly strange about the attack," she agreed. "He had his arm around my neck as though he planned to strangle me, but he just . . . stood there . . . holding me against him." Millie tried not to think of the warm, hard body belonging to those cold, cold eyes. It upset her. It upset her because she should have been more upset about the entire ordeal. But sometimes the memory conjured heat, and that distressed the most.

Jane cast her a sympathetic look through the gathering steam. "You must have been terrified, you poor dear."

"I was," she admitted, pulling the pins from her hair and letting it tumble into the bath. "When I thought he might hurt Jakub, I nearly came out of my own skin. I wanted to die. I wanted to kill him. I believe I would have if he'd laid a hand on my son."

But he hadn't. He'd disappeared again.

"And then he just . . . kissed you?" Jane wrinkled her pert nose. "Doesn't make a lot of sense, does it?"

"None at all."

"Well, you know you've really made it to the top when those touched-in-the-head admirers break into your house to steal a kiss." Jane had a way of making light of everything, even the horrible. It was how she kept such a sunny smile in a dark world. "Do you still have those two monsters following you and Jakub around?"

She referred, of course, to the guards Millie had hired for Jakub and herself the morning after the attack. Large Irish brothers with a preponderance of shoulders and little neck to speak of. McGivney, their last name was, and they smelled as frightful as they looked. Which added to their effectiveness, Millie decided. They came highly recommended, and Jakub liked that they stood still enough to let him draw them.

"Mr. McGivney is stationed at the entrance to the bathhouse," Millie admitted. "And his brother is with Jakub at school. I had to charm the headmaster in order for him to allow it."

It'd been three days now, three performances gone by, three sleepless yet uneventful nights had passed, and Millie had finally begun to feel safe again.

That was, until she'd been summoned to Scotland Yard this afternoon to talk to Chief Inspector Carlton Morley.

Millie's troubled groan echoed off the cream-tiled walls of the bathhouse as she tried to reconcile the event and her strange emotions toward it.

She loved this place with its gold embellishments and Turkish ambiance. It very much could have been plucked out of a Jean-Auguste-Dominique Ingres painting. Greek pillars. Roman tiles. Turkish draperies. Moroccan lanterns. A taste of the exotic Mediterranean in downtown London. A place where anyone respectable could never be seen and anyone infamous simply must show their face. At night, it became an exclusive playground for wealthy men and expensive courtesans. But as their nights were spent at the theater, Jane and Millie frequented the establishment in the early afternoon when the water was clean and the baths all but empty. Jakub was at school, and they could meet, practice lines, gossip, and lunch at Pierre de Gaulle's café on the corner and listen to him brag about having been the Countess Northwalk's landlord once upon a time before heading to the theater for the performance.

Their Wednesday afternoon ritual just wasn't the same when one had a rather offensive-looking Irishman the size of a small railcar following one around.

Better, though, than risking another encounter with Bentley Drummle.

But then, that wasn't his name, was it? As Chief Inspector Morley had pointed out, Bentley Drummle was a lesser known Dickensian character, as was the contact name he'd given her at the after party, Richard Swiveller.

She'd felt like such a fool sitting there in Morley's orderly office, unable to meet his pitying gaze across the giant mahogany desk. She'd been an utter ninny. Really, for a woman who considered herself so worldly, so capable of reading a man's intentions and twisting him around her little finger, she'd certainly been played by the best.

By a professional.

An assassin, Inspector Morley had suggested.

Millie had a personal acquaintance with Sir Carlton Morley since the tragic death of her dear friend Agnes Miller not five years ago. Though the killer had never been found, he'd kindly kept her updated on any new leads regarding the investigation, and she had wanted to make certain that he never caught on to the most important clue.

Jakub.

"Jane," Millie said carefully. "I want you to be . . . more careful, as well. Promise me."

"Why?" Jane popped a plump grape she'd pilfered from the fruit bowl at the edge of the pool past her lips and dipped her head back to wet her scalp. "This man's after *you,* not me."

"But if what Chief Inspector Morley said is true, then he's after more than one woman. He's killed many, it sounds like. In fact . . ." She trailed off, not really wanting to share the revolting news. Not wanting to make it real by giving it voice. If she said it here, the walls would echo it back to her, and that was almost like tainting one of her favorite places with the horror of it all. "He's targeting women with children, it seems. Boys. They've found the bodies of the women, but they've not found the children. Those poor boys have all gone missing."

The whites of Jane's eyes glowed at her even through the steam. "That's beyond dreadful!" she exclaimed. "How many?"

"Half a dozen, they think."

"They . . . *think*?" Jane crossed the pool to sit next to her, and Millie was secretly glad. She'd suddenly begun to feel vulnerable. Chill bumps raised the fine hairs on her body, even in the steamy water, and sweat tickled down the back of her neck. The corners took on more sinister shadows, the walls pressing closer.

"Do they *think* it was this man in your apartments?" Jane seized Millie's hand, taking the situation much more seriously now. "But he kissed you. He let you go. What do they *think* about that? Do they *think* he's still after you? What are they doing to protect you?"

Her friend's concern touched her, and Millie gave her hand a grateful squeeze. "They don't know what to make of my assault. According to Chief Inspector Morley, he's only just begun to make the connections. You see, these women didn't all reside in the same boroughs. They didn't frequent the same places. Their ages varied. And . . . they weren't . . . murdered in the same manner. Some of the deaths were brutal, others . . . less so, if there is such a thing. Some were raped, others were spared that. They were strangled, stabbed, or . . . beaten. One was shot."

"Good Lord." Jane crossed herself.

"The only common link between the murdered women was their missing sons."

Jane was shaking her head, a hand against her mouth. "Do you think those poor boys are . . . dead? Or worse?"

Millie saw moisture glimmering in the eyes of her soft-hearted friend similar to what gathered in her own lashes.

"No one knows. They've simply vanished."

"How long have these—has this been happening?"

"Inspector Morley said there have been five in the space of two months."

"Why haven't we heard of this?" Jane demanded, her hand splashing the water in anger. "Why isn't this story in all the papers, warning the mothers of London?"

"Because the deaths haven't technically been connected until now. Some of them made the papers in their local boroughs. And one, I think, was the daughter of a local wealthy miner, Mr. Randall Augustine. I remember reading something in the *Daily Telegraph* about his grandson being missing, don't you?"

Jane nodded, pale and teary. "I think so. I don't usually pay attention to that sort of news. It's so very dreary."

"I didn't mean to distress you, Jane." Millie had forgotten how dramatic her friend could be, prone to hysterics and fainting couches. No one had had such a thing where Millie had grown up. She'd never fainted in her life. "I just wanted to warn you to be extra vigilant. Take extra care with your security."

"Why?" Jane sniffed, though she wasn't truly crying. "I don't have a child."

"I know, but . . . even so."

Jane looked into Millie's eyes, her mind working over a ponderous thought. "Millie, if this man who broke into your apartments was this assassin, why didn't he take Jakub? Why kiss you and then . . . let you go?"

Millie put her head back against the edge of the bath and closed her eyes. "I don't know, Jane." She'd been asking herself that very thing since he'd vanished from her rooms. "I really don't know."

It was too late, Argent realized. Too late to go back now.

He'd taken too long to prepare. Too long to cleanse her fire from his blood and become like water again. Three days of nothing but training, fasting, meditating, and sleeping had cleared his mind and cleansed his body. He was cold again. Ruthless. Focused.

Ready for death to flow from his hands.

Or not, depending.

How apropos, then, that he should meet her at a bathhouse. That they should finish this in the water.

He climbed the stairs to the House of the Julii and nodded to Ellis McGivney.

"Weel, sweet baby Christ, if it isn't Christopher Argent," the Irishman sang in a voice surprisingly lyrical for such a grim-looking man. "Is it the stage dove ya're after?"

"She's mine." Argent paused, wondering if the Irishman was daft enough to try and stop him.

"Ta kiss or ta kill?" Ellis asked, biting down on a well-worn cigar.

"That remains to be seen."

A worry crossed the man's craggy face. "I'll only try and stop ya if ya've already been after Ely." Though the look in the bodyguard's bloodshot eyes said that he knew doing so would be the death of him, as well. But a man like Ellis McGivney didn't leave the death of his twin unavenged.

"I have no quarrel with you or your brother," Argent said. "I imagine he's still at his post."

Ellis's shoulders relaxed a notch. "Then I'll abandon my own post to ya. Though if ya don't mind me sayin', this isn't good for business. How can one make a living as a *garda* if your clients end up dead?"

"Then best not to guard anyone I'm after."

The Irishman's jaw tightened with temper, his meaty hand curling into a hammer-sized fist.

Argent stared at him. Waiting.

"We backed Blackwell in the Underground War," Ellis said quietly. "We're still loyal ta him. Ta ya both. Remember that if ya have any jobs ta throw our way."

"Blackwell never forgets." Argent nodded. *And I couldn't care less.*

Ellis glanced toward the colorful stained glass of the exotic bathhouse door wedged between two Roman columns. "She was kind ta us both. Fair. Good ta her boy. Paid us in advance. Don't much like the thought of her screaming, with fear or with pain."

"She won't," Argent promised.

"Very well then, I'll be on me merry way."

With that, Ellis McGivney jogged down the bathhouse stairs, light-footed for such a square-shaped man. He tipped his hat and flashed blackened teeth to a passing lady, chuckling at her gasp as he made his way into the afternoon.

The humid steam filled Argent's lungs as he crept down the long hallway from the ladies' dressing room to their baths.

Feminine voices echoed off the thick, unencumbered walls and bounced down the hall toward him. One high and sweet, the other soft and low.

Millie.

He cursed the increasing speed of his heart, the intensity of his breath.

There it was again, anticipation. There *had* to be something he could do to get rid of it.

Listening to the ladies' conversation, Argent kept to the mist, unable to see them, his back against the far wall until he positioned himself in a dark corner, using the shadows and steam as a cloak.

The fact that she'd gone to Morley would frustrate Blackwell, but it didn't surprise Argent in the least. He'd wondered how long it would take for the chief inspector to bring this serial killer business and lay it at the Blackheart of Ben More's doorstep. As the reigning king of the underworld, Dorian Blackwell had taken his fair share of blame for crimes he'd not committed.

And had gotten away with plenty. They all had.

As far as Argent knew, Blackwell didn't employ many assassins. Neither did he deal in the risky business of kidnapping. So who was murdering these women? And what had happened to the missing boys? In Argent's experience, killers generally had a similar modus operandi for how they did their jobs. A pattern or habit they stuck to, whether on purpose or not. They raped, or they didn't. They killed slowly, or quickly. Some favored guns. Others, such as himself, used closer, more personal means. Something the budding science of ballistics and forensics could not trace back to him. His garrote, his hands, sometimes a knife. All three his most deadly weapons.

So the fact that Chief Inspector Morley had informed Millie that these unrelated deaths were likely perpetrated by the same killer seemed extraordinary.

Fascinating, even.

Were the chief inspector correct, who could the killer be? Crowley? Maybe. The old bastard had been in the profession so long, why not take on five contracts in two months? His liver probably wouldn't hold long enough for them to send him to the gallows. Dorshaw? Argent had assumed he'd retired. At least, the police had lately stopped picking organs and such off the cobblestones. Perhaps the Algerian. Or the Prussian.

Maybe someone new stalked the streets. *His* streets.

Something he'd have to discuss with Blackwell. And if other mothers of young sons were being murdered around the city, did they have something to do with the lawyer, Gerald Dashforth? Was Argent's own contract against Millie connected? It could be a coincidence. But coincidences were rare in the underworld. *His* world. He had a few minions watching Dashforth, and the few clients of his who could afford to hire Argent. So he intended to find out.

"Millie?"

Argent's ears pricked at hearing her name, and it wasn't the only part of his anatomy that paid attention.

"I'm getting overheated, are you ready for lunch?"

"I'm afraid I can't lunch today. I'm going to fetch Jakub from school after this and take him with me to the theater."

It was her voice, Argent decided. It . . . did something to him. Physically. Unlike most women, her voice took on a low resonance that carried—no—enthralled. To listen to her speak was like being chained, but sweetly. One couldn't escape the rich vibrations, but why would one desire to do so? It conjured wicked curiosity. What would her moans of pleasure sound like? Her cries of release?

"It makes me anxious being away from my son even long enough to send him to school," she was saying. "I know I'm being overprotective."

She wasn't. Someone wanted her dead, and maybe the boy, too.

"I don't blame you." A long, lean form stood and stretched in the sunlight. The moisture blurred her lines and angles, but Argent wasn't interested in seeing a naked woman at the moment.

At least, not the golden-haired one.

"I'll pick up something for you and Jakub to eat at Pierre's," the woman named Jane offered. "I'll put it in your dressing room."

"Thank you, dear." The blonde bent to receive a kiss on each cheek from Millie, who was only a dark head above the pool of water from his vantage.

At the sight of Millie and her nude friend kissing, he had to brace a hand on the wall as his body surged to life and lust flared with an entirely new level of intensity.

Jane climbed out of the bath and retrieved a wrap and towel before padding toward the hall leading to the ladies' dressing rooms.

She passed not three spans from him and didn't even bat an eye.

Argent waited until she was gone to creep closer to his prey. He felt like a true predator. Hungry, impatient, but aware that waiting for the precise moment to strike made all the difference in capturing his quarry.

Millie's delicate hands gathered long and heavy ebony hair over a shoulder slick with water and oils, uncovering the flesh of her bare back to him. When she shifted to scrub suds into the slick length, Argent caught sight of the two columns of sleek, small muscle that bracketed her spine.

Blood rushed right beneath his skin in an almost tangible race to his core. Once congregated there, it made a distinct journey south.

And then she stood.

For a moment he couldn't draw breath. He opened his mouth and took a gulp of air, and drowned in humidity and desire instead.

Never in his life had Argent known that one could be

paralyzed by lust. Up until the moment he saw her nude form, he'd always regarded sex as a biological imperative. Something he did because his cock wanted him to. Because it afforded release, pleasure.

One by one, his fingers curled into tight fists of need.

The droplets of water sluicing down the curves of her body and into the water took on a musical lament, melancholy as the rain. What moisture clung to her seemed to do so with desperation, reflecting the thin shafts of afternoon sunlight in such a way that the illumination transformed from gleam to a sparkle.

She was a creature of the sunlight. Where the bright illumination painted so many women with a sickly pallor, she wore it like a golden cloak, a sun-kissed warmth that embossed the rich warm tones in her dark hair.

When she bent to reach for the soap on the ledge, he almost tripped.

Three days. Argent gritted his teeth. Three days he'd prepared for this. He was a man of ultimate patience and discipline. He wasn't brave, he was fearless. His will wasn't strong, it was iron. He'd been burned, whipped, stabbed, and beaten without so much as a moan of pain.

So why did the sight of Millie LeCour's glorious ass have him swallowing a whimper?

She sank back down just before his knees gave out.

Her ebony head disappeared beneath the water to rinse her hair, and Argent seized the moment. If he'd made any sound, the fact that her head was submerged would smother it.

But he didn't.

This couldn't go on. He had to end it. Now. Sweet or no, chains were chains, and Argent had long since promised he would *never* be imprisoned again. Not even by the velvet ropes of Millie LeCour.

The water barely made a ripple as he lowered himself

into the bath, reached down, and pulled her naked, glistening body up from beneath the surface.

She came up fighting.

Gasping for breath, she made a wild swipe at his face. The force of it, combined with the water, actually stung.

Argent barely stopped himself from bending her over and taking her against the edge of the pool. He was hard as a diamond.

Turning her, he subdued her easily, shackling one arm around her middle, chaining her arms to her sides. This time, instead of wrapping his arm around her neck, he clamped his hand over her mouth.

He could drown her. It would only be fair. For, though he had her in his clutches, he was the one being pulled under. Her skin, made slippery by water and soap, created a delicious friction even through the layers of his wet clothing.

Her bare bottom rubbed against the hard sex straining behind his wet trousers, letting it rest in the cleft between the two supple curves.

They froze. Both unsure of what he would do next.

Chapter Seven

Through her panic, Millie recognized the solid body pressed against her naked back. She'd been in quite this same position before.

Except then she hadn't been aware of the true danger. This was no obsessed admirer. His hold was firm but painless. The hand cupped over her mouth bowed as though to spare her lips the pain of being ground against her teeth.

Though the sex pressed against her posterior caused tremors of terror violent enough to ripple the water.

"I made a promise to Mr. McGivney that I wouldn't make you scream," he rumbled against her ear. His breath was hot against the wet, sensitive skin of her neck, but his tone was flat and cold as the Thames. "If you make a liar out of me, you'll regret it. Do we have an understanding?"

Millie swallowed a sob of terror, seeking composure. Panic served no purpose. She had to keep her wits about her.

She nodded and he released her mouth. When she licked her lips, she instantly regretted it. They tasted of salt and flesh that was not her own. A flavor she did not find repugnant.

And damned if it didn't make her nipples tighten.

"What do you want with me? What have you done to Mr. McGivney?" she whispered, disgusted with her body's reaction to his nearness.

Then another thought lanced through her, followed by a flash of hot rage. "If you've hurt Jakub, I'm going to—"

"I have not gone near your son, but he *is* in danger."

Millie's gasp brought her breasts closer to the arm encircling her waist like a steel vise. "Is that a threat?" she hissed.

"It's a fact."

Her throat clogged with alarm. "Don't do this," she rasped. Her fear evaporated, changing into equal parts determination and desperation. Her survival meant nothing in the face of Jakub's safety. "I'll do anything you want."

He was quiet a long time, and still as the dead, but for the steady pulse of his manhood against the cleft of her ass.

"Anything?" he finally breathed against her ear.

The full weight of her offer hit her between the eyes with enough force to make her knees weak. "Who are you?" she demanded with a bravado she didn't come close to feeling. "I know the name Bentley Drummle was a cover."

"We all have our characters we play," he said cryptically, his hand falling to her shoulder and pressing her closer against him. "But be assured, your son was never in danger from me. I don't kill children. My name is Christopher Argent. I have been employed by the solicitor Gerald Dashforth to assassinate you."

Millie could scarcely believe it. He sounded like a gentleman making introductions in the parlor. He may as well have said, "Hello, I'm Lord So-and-So, it's a pleasure to make your acquaintance."

"Are you a murderer or a mercenary?" she asked, calling upon all her skills to keep her voice modulated, so as not to excite him to violence.

"Both. Either."

All right. That revealed nothing. "You say this man, this Gerald Dashforth, he's paying you to kill me?"

"Yes."

Cold. His voice was so cold she shivered.

"I'm a woman of means, Mr. Argent. I can pay you double the price of the contract for my life." There, that didn't sound so desperate. She could be like him. Businesslike, terse, logical.

"That would be . . . unprecedented." He paused. "It couldn't be known that I would turn coat for a rate increase. Then every one of my marks would barter for their lives thusly. They'd have seen my face. They'd know who I work for. It's an excellent way to get caught."

As hope died, fury took its place. For a reason beyond her, his tone, more than the words, sent her temper rushing to her head with such force her ears burned and her mouth opened. If he was going to kill her, he'd get a piece of her mind first. "You. Are. *Insane*," she gritted through her clenched jaw.

He paused again, and she had the distinct feeling she'd bemused him. "What?"

"You heard me." Heedless of her nudity, she began to squirm in that limp, boneless way Jakub had done as a toddler when he'd wanted to escape her clutches. "Lying your way into my after party, using that ridiculous Dickensian name. Risking your life to sneak into my apartments in the middle of the freezing night. To what purpose? To toy with me, terrorize me? To *kiss* me? And then here you are *again,* in the middle of the blasted city, broad daylight even, in my *bath* with your bloody *shirt and trousers* still on, telling me you don't *kill* children. That you don't break a contract for the sake of your—industry reputation. I tell you, you're mad. A *lunatic*."

"You would rather I were naked?"

"*No!* God! That's not—I just—" Her struggles were getting her nowhere except closer to that intimidating arousal behind his wet trousers. "Turn me around, blast you! I at least deserve to look my murderer in the eyes."

To her complete shock, he complied.

But he didn't meet her eyes. As he held her at arm's length, his gaze touched her everywhere else but. The column of her neck, her breasts, the planes and hollows of her stomach, the nest of curls between her thighs.

Millie remembered what he looked like, but hadn't been thoroughly prepared to see him again. Not like this. Standing as they were, in shafts of brilliant sunlight, his appearance was more evocative of an archangel than a murderer-for-hire, and the paradox again took her breath away.

There was no denying that he was beautiful. Beautiful in that way that a lightning storm was beautiful, or a tidal wave. Awe-inspiring and utterly dangerous. Standing in front of him like this was akin to unexpectedly coming face-to-face with a wolf or a bear in the wild. Terrifying, and yet one had the indefinable understanding that this predator was a rare and exquisite creature. Every muscle, every sinew carefully crafted for hunting.

For killing.

The sun ignited embers of gold in his auburn hair. The water turned his white shirt iridescent, molded as it was to a body better suited to a barbarian than—well—a suit. The swells of his chest and the thickness of his arms killed any thoughts of escape, but awakened something else, altogether. Something primal and distressing. This was a man who would defeat all other men. One who, in some other time, would have fought legions and laid siege to tyrants.

Or might have been one.

There is no fighting him, she thought with a terrible acceptance. No escape. No denying the absolute power in those muscular arms. She could sense it in the rough hands gripping her shoulders.

He continued to watch her. Inspect her was more like it, with those pale, remote eyes. If Millie had felt naked before, now she was positively *exposed.*

And just like a lightning storm, just like that heart-stopping moment before a wild animal tore out one's throat, the dreadful anticipation tightened her nerves until they snapped.

"Do it," she dared. "What are you waiting for?"

He struck without warning, but not with a lethal blow.

Instead, his mouth surged against hers.

Too shocked to resist, Millie gasped involuntarily, which parted her lips for the invasion of his tongue.

The kiss was brutal. Or, at least, Millie was certain he'd meant it to be. But for a man with such a stern mouth, his lips were surprisingly full against hers. Stunned and defenseless, Millie was unable to move, to deny her body's unwanted reaction to the intimate flavor of him.

He locked her against his body, consuming her with unrepentant hunger. The bristle of his jaw abraded her skin as he explored her mouth with strong sweeps of his tongue. Millie became suddenly aware of how wet and slick everything was. Her skin, his tongue, her sex, the hand he moved to the nape of her neck to press her closer. To plunge deeper.

She could feel his arousal building, feel it pulsing against her like a heartbeat. Like a promise, or an inevitability. His other hand drifted down her back, finding the curve of her ass.

The intimate contact pulled her out of her astonished haze. With a strangled sound, she ripped her mouth from his, wrenching out of his grasp, as well.

He let her go, his lips slightly parted. He stood still but

for the heaving of his powerful chest and regarded her as if *she* had astounded *him*.

For some reason, that confused and infuriated her all the more.

"You're so cruel," she accused, lifting her arms to cover her breasts and clenching her thighs together, desperately ignoring the brands of sensation his fingers had left on the back of her neck. His mouth looked fuller, and gleamed with the aftermath of their kiss.

"Why do you torture me like this? Why is it that every time you attempt to kill me, you kiss me instead? Is this some perverted game you play with your victims? Well, I refuse to be afraid of you! I *refuse* to be a plaything for your sick amusement." Her voice rose and thickened like the steam in the air, and she cursed the shrill note of hysteria creeping into it. "If you're going to kill me, do it and be damned!"

"I'm not going to kill you," he informed her flatly, though his nostrils flared with each of his breaths.

"What?" She blinked. "Why not?" The questions felt absurd, but she'd been pushed beyond her abilities in regard to improvisational vocabulary.

"Because." He met her eyes then. Almost. There was no cruelty in them. Instead, something completely unexpected lurked in their sapphire depths. That was, besides the smoldering lust. She couldn't identify it, not exactly. Bemusement? Uncertainty?

"I've decided to take you up on your offer," he informed her. "Tonight."

Her heart thudded, hope and elation causing it to run like a stallion at full gallop. "I have a performance tonight," she rushed, quite out of breath. "I can have the money by then, and give it to you afterward at the theater. Just tell me how much."

"No." His fingers slid up one shoulder, capturing the droplets of water that had yet to run down to the bath and creating a wet trail to her neck, where he caressed the pulse jumping beneath the thin flesh there. "Your *other* offer."

"But I haven't made another—" Her breath caught. But she had.

She'd said she'd do *anything*.

Dear God.

When he saw the dawning of understanding on her face, and the resulting fear, he dropped his hand. "I will protect you and your son from those who want you dead, in exchange for a night with you."

Millie's mouth went bone-dry, and she dare not look down at the arousal pulsing against his thin trousers beneath the surface of the water. She took an involuntary step back, her quivering legs encountering the ledge beneath the water.

"D-don't be ridiculous."

"I'm never ridiculous."

Somehow she didn't doubt that. His mouth was set in such a grim line Millie would stake her livelihood on the certainty that it had never truly formed a smile.

"I don't want protection from a man like *you*."

"You won't survive without a man like me."

"I'll go to the police," she warned.

He closed the gap between them. "You've been to the police already. You hired a personal guard." He glanced pointedly around the vacant room. "And yet, here I am."

Here he is. Large and strong and utterly lethal. The truth of this was more disturbing than she'd like to admit.

He folded his arms across his chest, looking very much like a statue of Poseidon rising from a fountain she'd once seen in Florence. All but for the beard.

"If I got to you, others will, too. But they *won't* get past me. I'm the best at what I do." He said this without bravado or pretension, and didn't wait for her to argue or validate.

A new fear stabbed her in the gut. "How—how many others are after me? And you say they're after Jakub, as well? Who wishes us harm? This Mr. Dashforth who hired you, I don't know of him. Who does he work for?" Her head swam and began to pound, and she knew it wasn't just the heat that made her dizzy.

The assassin in front of her was silent for a beat. "I didn't think to ask." He narrowed his eyes down at her. "You have *no* idea who would wish you dead?"

She could think of only one threat. One she'd thought had died with her dearest friend five years ago.

"Jakub's father," she whispered.

"And who is that?"

Millie closed her eyes, gathering her courage. "I . . . don't know."

Another of his now familiar pauses. "You don't know?"

"There was a party I was paid to go to," Millie lied. "One for the rich and the powerful. Everyone wore masks. Jakub's father could have been . . . anyone there." All right. So it made her sound like a prostitute, but of the two of them in this room, in this bath, hers would still be the lesser crime. Wouldn't it?

The two oldest professions for hire. The two greatest sins.

Fornication and murder.

Gathering her courage, she glanced up at him and didn't find the disgust or judgment she'd expected. Only a strong brow furrowed in thought. "I'll have to find out from Dashforth just who his employer is."

"Wait," she cried. "But I haven't acquiesced to your proposition—we haven't come to an agreement."

"But we will. *You* will." His eyes traversed the length of her body again, and she abruptly sat on the ledge, seeking refuge in the water, crossing both arms over her breasts, just to be contrary if nothing else.

"You're so certain of that, are you? So certain I'll lie with you. So certain you're the best. I can't believe your arrogance."

"It's not arrogance if it's accurate. You are the best actress on the London stage, and I'm the best—"

"Killer?" she interrupted.

"Yes. Among other things."

She shuddered to think of just what those things were. *Wait,* had he just paid her a compliment? Millie put a hand to her head, as the room had yet to stop spinning.

He didn't move. Not once. But somehow his voice seemed closer. "One night," he repeated. "One night in your bed and I'll keep you and your son alive until the threat has passed. Is that such a high price to pay?"

She couldn't answer that. It was a higher price than he realized.

So why was she tempted? Why did the cold danger emanating from the hard man in front of her speak to that primal part of her soul? Who knew that desire and fear could feed each other in equal measure?

"Why?" she whispered. "When you could have stacks of money, why trade it for a night with me? It makes no sense."

"I already have stacks of money," he answered. "You said it yourself. I haven't been able to keep my hands off you. Or my mouth. I can't be in the same room as you without getting hard. Without wanting to take you."

Millie's head snapped back in shock, and she instantly knew it had been a mistake. His hips were at eye level, his erection just above the water in which he stood, pressing against his trousers as though to prove a point.

How could he deliver news like that so laconically? Had he no shame?

Of course he didn't. He stood like a god, his arms still crossed over his deep chest, looking at her in his matter-of-fact way.

"I want you," he said, with no inflection at all. "And before you found out what I am, you wanted me, too."

Millie gasped. She hated him in that moment. Hated that he was right. She *had* wanted him. Had begged him to kiss her when he was Bentley Drummle. Had entertained all kinds of salacious fantasies about him.

She'd even pictured him in her bed.

Before she'd known that someone was after her. Before her world had spun out of her control.

The worst part was, her body wanted him still. A disquieting heat throbbed in her loins, pulsed against her lips where the pressure of his mouth had just been. Where she wanted it to be again, damn it all.

"You could have just . . . taken me. At any time. Why make this devil's bargain?"

Lord, had she just put that thought into the head of a man who had no conscience? Was she daft?

"I've *never* raped a woman," he said rather firmly. "And I never will."

"But coercion is acceptable?" she spat.

"Yes." His honesty was almost . . . horrific in its bluntness. It was disconcerting. And yet strangely comforting.

"Answer me this," she said wearily. "Did you have anything to do with the five women recently killed in London, all mothers to missing sons?"

"No." She wanted to look into his eyes, to ascertain his veracity. But it seemed to her that he avoided eye contact.

"How do I know you're telling the truth?"

"You don't. But I assure you that I would tell you if I had. I have nothing to hide. Though I'm not convinced those deaths aren't related to your own predicament. That is something we'll have to find out. If . . ." He let the thought trail into the steam. A hot, scandalous, unspoken ultimatum.

If she yielded. If she said yes. *If* she allowed him into her bed tonight.

There never really had been an *if,* had there? Not when Jakub's safety was at stake.

"A-all right," she forced around a heavy tongue and suddenly dry lips. "I'll do it."

His chin lowered in a nod, and she thought, for a moment, that she saw something flare in his eyes. Not heat, but . . . something deeper. Something that had no name because it was an amalgamation of so many different emotions.

Perhaps only present because she wished it there. Because she feared emotion wasn't something Christopher Argent was afflicted with.

"I'm going to send for someone while you dress," he informed her. "He'll go with you to retrieve your son and accompany you and Ely McGivney to the theater while I interrogate Dashforth." He placed his fingers under her chin, lifting her head. "Then I will return for you."

Millie nodded, feeling alarmed, dizzy, relieved, and frightened all at the same time.

"Promise me something," she said. "Promise me you won't hurt me, or Jakub. That you'll never come for us in the future. *Ever.* After this is done with, and we part ways, I never want to see you again."

"I give you my word," he said, releasing her.

Millie searched his face, so aware of her vulnerability. Aware of the sheer lethal power of the man towering over her. Entranced by it. Repelled by it.

Aroused by it.

Whatever she'd been looking for, she couldn't find. His features were frustratingly blank.

"Does your word truly mean anything, Christopher Argent?"

He paused, then turned from her. "I suppose we're both about to find out."

Chapter Eight

London was known for a great many things, not the least of which, in Argent's opinion, was the legion of grubby, wiry errand boys ready to scamper through the city for a coin. He sent one to Hassan Ahmadi, to whom he'd entrust Millie's safety for the afternoon. The Arab was a longtime employee of Blackwell's, and would be a large, very visible deterrent to any possible threats.

The fact that the Mussulman was zealously celibate had no bearing on his decision to send for Mr. Ahmadi.

Whatsoever.

Another boy scampered away to bring his butler, Welton, with a carriage and change of attire. Welton had arrived first, as Argent had known he would. While he dressed in dry clothing in the men's private rooms at the House of the Julii, he instructed his butler that they were to entertain a woman and her son that night.

Welton blinked several times, which was akin to an all-out fit of vapors for him, and promptly took the hired hackney that Mr. Ahmadi arrived in to make the necessary preparations.

"I will keep your black-eyed woman and her son alive and untouched by the filthy, godless hands of any who would wish harm upon them," the Mussulman promised.

Leaving his carriage to convey Millie to retrieve her son from his school and then to deposit her at Covent Garden for her performance, Argent strode away, confident that the only filthy, godless hands to touch her would be his own.

By the time he reached the white stone building where he would again find Gerald Dashforth's offices, Argent's fists clenched to keep from shaking. He conquered the three flights of stairs wishing there had been more, that buildings were taller and he could keep climbing. It would explain the thudding in his chest.

The hallway where Sir Dashforth's office was located appeared longer than he remembered. For a man who filled any hall nearly to capacity, this passage still seemed remarkably small, and somehow shrinking as his steps echoed against the expensively papered walls. The floors pitched against his feet, like the planks of a ship tossed by the stormy English Channel, and Argent worked at not giving in to the impulse to run and kick open Dashforth's door, shattering the expensive gold lettering on the tempered glass.

As it was, the door dashed off the wall as he opened it, and the glass rattled loudly, as though trying to decide whether or not to stay intact.

Dashforth made a ladylike sound of shock and lost what little color he had in his face to begin with.

"I have business to discuss with you," Argent informed him, trying to squelch the strength of a strange emotion surging through him. Something murderous. Something dark. Something to do with the fact that this man was a threat to Millie.

"How interesting that you should come by today," Dashforth remarked, scurrying to regain his composure. "I assume your charge is finally carried out and you're here for your payment?"

Argent ignored the question, stalking closer to the wiry man. "Which of your clients wanted Millie LeCour dead?"

The corners of Dashforth's mouth appeared beneath his

mustache in a consternated frown. "I fail to see how that is relevant—" He made a choking sound as Argent's hand almost encircled the entirety of his scrawny neck.

"It is not wise to make me repeat myself."

Dashforth squeaked, scratching at Argent's hand with frantic fingers. "You don't—understand," he wheezed.

The worm was right, Argent didn't understand. Couldn't comprehend why anyone would want a brave, vivacious, desirable woman like Millicent LeCour dead. He didn't understand the power she had over him. And he couldn't begin to describe the physical phenomenon awakening in his body.

A storm surge of strength, power, viciousness, and violence. A beast of some kind stirred in his cold, dormant heart, and this beast was hungry for blood. For sex.

And for something else he had no name for. Something he knew only Millie could provide. Something he desired above all else, and couldn't for the life of him identify.

"Tell your employer that Millie LeCour belongs to me now." Reaching in his pocket with his free hand, Argent retrieved a banknote for the obscene amount Dashforth had offered, and tucked it into the breast pocket of the solicitor's suit. "She's not planning to reveal the boy's parentage. She has no need for blackmail, notoriety, or legitimacy. Millie is not a threat to anyone, but *I* certainly am." He released the gaping solicitor to grapple with something he'd thought long dead.

His temper.

"Y-you're canceling a contract?" Dashforth sputtered, his fingers pressed against his tender throat. "A-are you certain that's wise? Your reputation . . . let alone your livelihood—"

"I know you're not threatening me, Dashforth." Argent stepped toward him again, and the small man paled impossibly further. "My threats are infinitely more fatal."

"I'll tell you nothing but this." Dashforth dropped onto

the dainty couch, his beady eyes gleaming with smug secrets. "They'll keep coming after her. Though you think you are the only monster that stalks the night, I assure you there are more dangerous men out there, and they'll do the job you weren't man enough to do. They'll kill you, and then slaughter your precious actress."

An audible crack reverberated through Argent's bones, as dangerous as a rift in a dam. Except it wasn't cold water being released from a reservoir. But fire. It ripped through him, crawling through the sinew of his body with startling strength. He was drunk with anger. Swollen with it, awash in the delicious, violent heat of it.

He snatched up the solicitor by the lapels and gave him a shake like a mongrel's chew toy. "Listen here, you weakling boy-fucker, if you don't tell me what I want to know, *I* will kill you. Slowly."

"Not as slowly as some," the solicitor said, an odd sort of acceptance creeping into his eyes. "If you want the actress, take her before *he* comes for her. Because nothing will stop him."

Awash in a rage the likes of which he hadn't been subject to for decades, Argent growled as he slammed Dashforth into the wall, relishing the sound of the man's head cracking against the solid wood. "Give me a name!"

The solicitor slumped, his eyes rolling up behind fluttering lids, his neck no longer holding his head aloft. It lolled to the side, and Argent could see blood painting the wallpaper where the skull had collided. In his anger, he'd forgotten the true force of his strength.

He didn't have much time.

"Talk, damn you." Argent commanded, shaking the limp body.

"Thurston . . . Thinks . . . he's the father . . . of the boy," Dashforth roused himself to say. "You're too late . . . took . . . too long. There's another."

"What do you mean?" Argent demanded.

The man slumped, completely unconscious and heavy in his arms.

Argent let him drop in a heap to the floor, and then ran trembling hands through his hair. He'd been too hard, too out of control. He could have used different means to extract information, manipulation, intimidation, or compulsion. Now, though Dashforth was still alive, he might not survive his head wound. If he did survive, he might warn Fenwick that Argent was coming for him.

Because come for him, he would.

Extracting his garrote from his pocket, Argent stood over the prone man who'd landed on his face. Blood trickled from his slick hair down his thin neck.

This wouldn't take long.

Dashforth wouldn't be visiting the bordellos tonight. The young boys would be safe from him. The wealthy would have to find another unscrupulous solicitor to do their bidding.

In a fluid motion, Argent made certain the man would never again wake.

"Sir Dashforth?" A shadow appeared behind the tempered glass a moment before the rap of a knock slammed Argent back into cold reality. "I heard a commotion, Dashforth. Are you all right?"

Argent dove for Dashforth's office as the handle rattled, and he barely made it behind the wall in time for the door to open. He used the astonished exclamations and calls for the police and doctor to cover the noise of the window latch as he stepped out onto the ledge and pressed the window closed.

Damn. The streets were full of people. The bobbies were being sent for, and if he didn't work fast, the ruckus would draw attention to the building and he'd be spotted for certain.

The building next to Dashforth's offices, a red-brick mercantile of haberdashery supplies, was only separated from this structure by perhaps the width of a coffin. *Excellent.* Balancing with his back to the wall, he inched along a ledge that barely deserved the name until he came to the tight alley. The trouble with buildings in this up-and-coming part of town was a preponderance of embellishments, such as ledges, for example, that only adorned the front of the building facing the street. The alley, barely half again the width of his shoulders, was hardly more than a glorified gutter and, apparently, a place to store rubbish.

Argent glanced out to the street. For a late-winter day, the sky was surprisingly clear. The chill kept people bundled, their necks bunched down into their scarves and cloaks, scurrying on their way, hoping to find a warm hearth at their destination. No one seemed to be looking up.

Three tall stories separated him from the ground. From freedom. His only option was to use an ability that he'd acquired by climbing the flat stone walls of Newgate, and perfected during bloody ambushes in the Underworld War.

He'd have to act quickly.

His legs were long enough to bridge the gap. Keeping one foot firmly on the ledge, he kicked his other leg and arm out to catch his weight on the adjacent building. Once secure, he pulled his foot off the ledge and caught his downward trajectory with one hand and one foot braced against each wall. He ignored the sharp brick that abraded his palms as he spider-crawled down the building sides, allowing his legs to slide, and then his arms in succession, until he could safely drop to the cobblestones below.

He caught his fall with a crouch, and only one bundled-up woman passerby started at his landing. A true city dweller, she decided it was safer not to question odd happenings, nor tarry in their wake, and she sank deeper into the hood of her cloak, quickening her steps along the way.

Straightening, Argent curled his throbbing palms into fists, knowing the pain would subside the colder he let himself get.

Though how the cold could penetrate the flood of molten heat still pouring through him would confound even the most scientific minds.

What the devil had just happened up there? What he'd meant to be a patient and informative interrogation had quickly become an unmitigated disaster. And here he stood, in the shadow of an alley, blood throbbing, hands smarting, and none the wiser.

His sound of frustration echoed off the stones before his fist collided with them. Though his knuckles didn't splinter, the skin broke and bled. He needed the pain. Pain always grounded him. Focused him. Sharpened his edge to lethal.

This time, it was little help.

He hurried away from Dashforth's office until he found another dark, narrow alley, where the windowless stone walls could see nothing, and therefore tell nothing. To mitigate the feverish throbbing, he turned and pressed his head to the cold, cold stone, trying to absorb some of it back into his soul.

The alley became his purgatory, a place to endure, to reflect. Alone in the center of a city nearly as heartless as he'd always been.

If you don't kiss me, I'll die.

The chill in the wind became a memory of Millie's warm breath against his mouth. If he hadn't kissed her that night, she *would* have died—by his own hands. He wondered if she knew that now. Now that she knew who he was. *What* he was.

There, even in the darkness of the stairwell where he'd first kissed her, her features had glowed with a light he'd never seen before. He'd been about to do it. About to snap the pretty bones in her neck, and break the spell she'd cast upon him while dancing. It would have been so easy to extinguish the light glowing from beneath her golden skin, from inside those obsidian eyes, on the night they'd shone the brightest for all of London.

If you don't kiss me, I'll die.

She'd said it as though she'd known her life was in his hands, and with a kiss, he could save her.

He'd never *saved* anyone before. Never given in to impassioned pleas for a victim's life. He showed no mercy, gave no quarter, and hadn't even been aware that he was capable of hesitation. The ghosts of his sins didn't haunt his dreams. For he never had any. Easier not to dream than to rip oneself from nightmares that never seemed to end. Fear had been equally as absent from his life as regret. What had he left to fear? Whatever nightmares the future held were dreams compared to what lay buried in his past.

But in that moment, standing with their bodies pressed together, everything had changed. She'd not been afraid of him, nor had she been aware that she'd begged death, himself, to kiss her. She'd been nothing more than a woman stripped of artifice and pretense, a woman trusting the touch of a man, letting instinct and sensation suffuse that vibrant light inside of her until Argent had been certain with every fiber of his black soul that if he didn't kiss her she would, indeed, have died.

And . . . He'd desired her to live. So he could have her. So she would be *his.*

For a man like him, desire was dangerous. To want something, to *have* something, gave him something to lose. Something for his enemies to use against him.

He never should have given in to desire. Because now the softness of her lips haunted his every moment. The warmth of her mouth suffused him until need and lust twisted and ached within his very core.

She'd *wanted* him. He couldn't let that go.

She'd been panting and open, soft and willing. No woman had done anything to or for him unless money had changed hands. No one had cared to. In his world, one didn't get swept away by passion. No one crept into dark nooks to share sighs and pleasure and flesh. Someone like *him* might be lurking in the shadows. And money mitigated the risk.

But that night, on the eve of her greatest stage triumph, Millie LeCour, London's darling, considered the most beautiful woman in the empire and beyond. She'd desired *him*.

Well, she'd desired Bentley Drummle.

But it had been sweet, *unbearably* sweet to think that for that moment in the dark it was Christopher Argent, not Bentley Drummle, that she'd begged to kiss her. A shackleborn bastard. A man who'd once been a weak boy. A boy who'd been beaten, raped, whipped, stabbed, starved, and terrorized. A boy who'd lost his humanity in a dank cell surrounded by blood. By the blood of the last human being who'd cared whether he'd lived or died.

He'd lived. To spite them all, he'd lived. And in order to do so he'd given his life to the spilling of blood. At first for vengeance, then for survival, and finally for profit. Under the careful tutelage of Wu Ping, he'd learned to kill a man before he'd learned to lace a boot.

It was all he knew. All he was good at. And never in his life had he questioned his place, never looked back into the abyss of the past. Never thought of that pathetic, powerless boy he'd once been.

Or of that night he'd lost his soul.

Until *her*. Until Millie had begged for her son's life. Until she'd submitted to his demands in order to survive, because life meant enough to her that she would not only suffer the indignity of lying with him, she'd overcome it.

She'd not only endure, as he did now. As he'd always done. She'd thrive. He knew this about her intrinsically. He had a feeling that, as strong and pitiless as he could be, even the ruthless Christopher Argent couldn't snuff out her light. Certainly, he could kill her. But her light would remain in the glow of the lamps on every stage she'd ever graced. In the smile of her son, secure in the knowledge of her love. It would live on in the many portraits and photos of her.

Millie LeCour was immortal.

And for one night in his wretched life, she was going to belong to him.

He couldn't fucking believe it.

Curling his wounded fist, he stepped into London's heavy afternoon foot traffic and angled west, toward Mayfair. He had one more place to go. One more loose end to tie up before he returned to claim what was his.

Chapter Nine

Of all the employees of the New London Metropolitan Police currently housed at Scotland Yard, Chief Inspector Carlton Morley was Dorian Blackwell's least favorite. No, that was putting it lightly.

He despised the man.

It could have been, he supposed, because Morley had made it his personal mission to bring Dorian down and throw him back into the hellish prison in which he'd already spent so many, many years. It could have been because of all the coppers on the force, Morley was the hardest to outwit.

But mostly, Dorian Blackwell, the Blackheart of Ben More's intense repugnance for the man stemmed from the fact that, to his knowledge, Morley was the only other man on the planet who'd kissed his wife. Of course, they hadn't been married at the time. In fact, Farah had been a long-time clerk at Scotland Yard, and had yet to meet Dorian. But the very moment after she'd said good night on that fateful evening three years ago, Dorian had swept her away to Ben More Castle, his Highland keep, and promptly forced her to marry him.

Farah was his. Of that he had no doubt. From her white-blond ringlets to her ridiculously tiny feet. Her body, her heart, and her soul belonged to him. And his heart, black as it was, always had been and always would be at her mercy. His body was hers to command and only hers to touch. And his life was dedicated to filling her every need, serving her every whim, and being the source of her every smile.

So when Farah's angelic gray eyes lit with a warm fondness as she handed a cup of tea to Morley in *his* parlor, Blackwell had to clutch at one of the silk pillows on the couch to refrain from picking up the china teapot, throwing the scalding water into Morley's handsome face, and shattering the blasted thing over his head.

But this room, with its French paper and velvet-upholstered furniture, wasn't the dank stone walls of Newgate. And in such a room, a man like the Blackheart of Ben More resorted to other means by which to show possession and disdain.

Besides, Farah would be cross if he ruined the soft blue carpets with the blood of her former employer.

"It's been too long, Inspector Morley." Farah settled in the ornate pale silver chair stationed between the two men like a referee in a fighting match. Except here, each man was dressed impeccably and faced each other from identical long couches.

Dorian sat back, arms splayed, his leg over one knee, eye patch covering his weak eye against the dimness of the fading light filtering in through the large windows. "I say not long enough," he murmured, and took a sip of his own tea to avoid the sharp look from his wife.

"To what do we owe the *pleasure* of your visit?" she asked sweetly.

Morley perched on the edge of the opposite couch and leaned forward to put his teacup on the table in front of them. "This visit is more business than pleasure, I'm afraid. I've come to talk to your husband about a few of his . . . associates."

"Oh?" Her fair eyebrows lifted and she slid her soft silver gaze across to Dorian.

"Farah—" Morley began, but was cut off by a warning sound from deep in Dorian's throat. "Lady Northwalk," he corrected. "This business is of a delicate nature, perhaps you'd like to leave your husband and me to discuss it without distressing you."

Farah's sweet smile never faltered as she downed her own tea and folded elegant hands across her lap. "Not a chance, Carlton. You should know me better than that. I worked at Scotland Yard for a decade. I don't believe there's anything you can say that I haven't heard before. What are you here to discuss? And how do you think we can help?"

Morley looked away from her when she said *we,* and Dorian couldn't help but feel sorry for the lout. Losing a woman like her would break a man. Even a stuffed shirt like Morley.

"There's a killer stalking the streets," Morley said severely.

"This is London," Dorian scoffed. "There's always scores of killers stalking the streets."

"And some of them are in your employ." Morley shook his head, grappling with frustration. "Women, *young* women, are dying. All of them mothers. And their children are vanishing. Not one of them have turned up, not one. No body. No trace. It's like they've vanished."

Farah tapped the tiny divot in her chin. "And that's how you know these particular murders are connected?"

"More importantly, you think I have something to do with these murdered women and vanishing children?" Dorian demanded.

Morley looked him square in the eye, not something that many men had the constitution to do, and answered, "I think that if something like this is happening on such a large scale in London, there is an even larger chance that you're either profiting from it, allowing it, or at very least have an idea who's responsible."

Dorian was not a superstitious man, despite his Highland heritage, but how the unmistakable auburn head of Argent appeared on his terrace in that very moment, as though conjured by conversations of assassins, Blackwell would never know.

Their eyes met through the glass of the giant parlor window—as much as Argent's eyes ever met anyone's—and when Morley turned in his seat, Dorian made a gesture toward his study.

"What you're insinuating is ridiculous," Farah said gently. "My husband is involved in no such thing. He may not be a saint." She looked at him askance. "But I would not have married a man who was capable of such evil."

Dorian warmed to the faith in his wife's soothing voice. She'd made him a good man by believing it was so. Well, not so much a *good* man . . . but a markedly better one. A work in progress, some might say.

"Perhaps not, Lady Northwalk," Morley said, obviously trying to maintain his air of carefully practiced civility. "But like it or not, your husband built associations with some rather ruthless criminals, in his tenure at Newgate. I have it on good authority that many of those associations still exist."

Dorian lifted a brow. He was no mere associate to the men he'd met in Newgate. He was their king. "In business like mine, one does not openly discuss their associates with any agent of Her Majesty's and hope to keep his head attached to his neck."

Especially when one of those associates was currently climbing up the back trellis, letting himself in the French doors of the second-floor balcony, and dropping through a secret passage into the study below. Dorian kept an ear open for the *thunk* of Argent's arrival.

"Care to admit what business that is, Blackwell?" Morley asked sharply.

Dorian's lip twitched. "I believe that's Lord Northwalk to you, *Sir* Morley." Dorian had been interrogated by this man in many less well appointed rooms, and under much less pleasant circumstances. Those times, it had been Dorian's blood on the floor. Luckily for him, Farah's marriage came with a title, and for the bastard son of a marquess like Dorian, it gave him great pleasure to remind Morley of that fact.

"Pick a business to discuss, Inspector. I am a vintner, landlord, business proprietor, investor, entrepreneur, and recently I've become a restaurateur."

Thunk. Argent was in place, and for such a big man, the assassin could always land quietly. Dorian didn't flinch, having complete faith in the man to know how not to make himself known.

"Don't *toy* with me, Blackwell." Morley stood. "We all bloody well know you're king of the London underworld. You fought the war. You won."

"What we both know, Inspector, is that the London underworld, by definition, can have no king."

Turning to the very window that had only just framed Argent, Morley heaved a great sigh, rubbing at the bags beneath his eyes. "*Lord* and Lady Northwalk . . ." He faced them again, an earnest pain in his blue eyes. "You know I wouldn't be here if I wasn't at my wit's end. These women, if you saw them, the looks frozen into their dead eyes, the ones who have eyes left in their skulls. The terror, the confusion, the . . . pain. Five have been murdered so far, in such brutal ways, all with missing children. Particularly sons under the age of ten. These women are being *assassinated.* I know this. Maybe you don't care, Lord Northwalk, but I thought your wife still might." He turned to Farah. "Because she, I think, is still a decent lady. A mother."

Farah, cheeks and hips still delectably plump from the birth and nursing of their own beloved daughter, Faye, turned to Dorian with concern. "Have you heard *anything* about this, darling?"

"All I need is a name." Morley's face became more hopeful with each passing moment. "An inmate number, a *fucking* direction. I fear that these boys are being taken somewhere and killed, or worse."

Dorian assessed the chief inspector with his one good eye. The man reeked of desperation. Should he tell him the truth? Should he admit his own incompetence?

"Dorian?" Farah pressed.

Goddammit.

"Seven months ago an . . . associate of mine, Madame Regina, contacted me to say that one of her employees had been brutally murdered on the premises and no one had seen a thing. Her young son, Winston, had disappeared from under their noses." Dorian sniffed, galled to admit that he had had just as much, if not less, success tracking the serial murderer down.

"You let them keep children at the whorehouse?" Morley hissed.

"We've set up rooms for child care, where they can be safe and protected, not just from the streets, but from what is going on at Madame Regina's," Farah cut in, picking up her tea. "Many of these women have chosen this profession, many have not, but at the very least we can care for their children."

"That's very magnanimous of you, Farah," Morley stated, and Dorian sensed the man was in earnest.

"I've been looking into the death at Madame Regina's ever since, and so far have not found the culprit, though I've drawn the same conclusion. Whether in Soho, the East End, Hyde Park, or the Strand, these other deaths and disappearances must be related."

Morley almost seemed relieved. "I'm having a devil of a time convincing the commissioners or anyone above me of that."

"That is because they're fucking idiots," Blackwell said.

"On that, at least, we agree."

Dorian pondered a moment, preparing to make one more galling move before the inspector left. "Should I learn anything, it will be dealt with, in my own way, but I will make certain that you are informed, Inspector." It was an olive branch. Or, more aptly, an olive leaf, but it was the most Morley could expect from him.

"Actually . . . I appreciate that." Morley nodded "And, I'll extend the same offer. Though if it's dealt with my way, you'll likely learn from the papers."

"My way might just as well end up in the papers." Dorian smirked. "But the pictures won't."

They'd be too gory.

"We have an understanding, then," Morley stated. "All I want is this killer stopped . . . by any means possible."

"Indeed." Dorian stood, enjoying his superior height to the man, and bent to kiss his wife. "Now get out of my house." With that, he strode to his study and shut the door.

He and Argent stared at each other in silence as they waited for the sounds of Farah kindly bustling Morley down the hallway to fade to another part of the house.

Dorian Blackwell had known Christopher Argent longer than almost anyone else. And yet, he knew him not at all. They'd grown up in hell together, except Argent had been an expert at survival there, because he'd been born to it rather than sentenced. They both had blood on their hands, though Dorian's was generally more figurative, and Argent's literal.

What he knew about Argent: the man was a killer. He was loyal, but had no emotional ties to Dorian. To anyone.

He was cold, unfeeling, and broken. What caused Dorian occasional pause was the utter lack of hesitation or humanity in the face of brutality. The dead, empty eyes that never quite met his, but always seemed to be looking somewhere in between.

Waiting. Ready to be lashed at, to be struck down. Waiting for an excuse. Any reason to retaliate. To kill.

Dorian had cultivated a ruthlessness, his own wall of ice behind which to keep his heart. He did what he had to. He manipulated, intimidated, maimed, and killed men when the situation called for such brutality. He'd struck down everyone who'd dared oppose him until he controlled the parts he wanted and left the rest for the dregs. His whole life he'd had a mission, a reason, a vengeance, and a search for salvation that had ended better than he could ever have dreamed.

But Argent. Dorian still didn't know what drove him. The man was built like a Viking, and seemed to have a similar code. Which wasn't much of one by anybody's standards.

Once the door closed behind Morley, Dorian narrowed his eyes and asked the question haunting him for a few months now. "Is it you?" he asked. "Are you the killer Morley is looking for?"

Argent's pale eyes swung between the brass globe paperweight on the desk and the fireplace poker hooked on the very expensive wrought-iron stand for other such implements on the hearth.

No doubt, he was identifying anything in the room that could be used as a weapon. Newgate habits died hard deaths, and counting the means by which one could protect oneself to the death was a habit not exclusive to the assassin.

"I don't kill children," Argent stated matter-of-factly. "You know that."

"I didn't think so . . . but people change." God knew Dorian, himself, had changed since he'd been married.

"Do they?" The question took Dorian completely by surprise. Before Argent turned to face the window, Dorian thought he caught something on his face he'd never before encountered.

An emotion. Specifically, vulnerability.

What the devil?

If Dorian knew anything about weakness, it was that once one caught sight of it, it had to be exploited. Such was the only way to find out what he wanted. "As much as I hate to admit it, Morley has a point. This kind of brutality against women and children hasn't been seen since—"

"Since Dorshaw," Argent supplied.

"Precisely. Uncontrolled violence such as this creates chaos and fear out there on the streets, both of which are bad for business." Dorian studied the broad back of his associate. Of a man he'd call a friend, if men like them had friends. Which they didn't . . . He knew what riddled the flesh beneath Argent's clothing, and for Dorian, a man with his own scars, who only had the use of one good eye because the other had been made milky by a knife fight at nineteen, Argent's wounds still evoked a wince. For a man to endure what the assassin had was unthinkable, and Dorian had often found himself wondering if the cold, unfeeling man, who'd been his most ferocious ally, might someday turn into his greatest liability.

"If this serial murderer is you . . ."

"I told you it isn't."

"You're the only man alive with whom I cannot decipher truth from lie."

Argent was silent. Still as a reflective pool on a windless day.

Dorian had tried to make ripples in this particular pool

before, without success. But something told him that he was close. That the pool wasn't as serene as usual.

"Argent, if I find out otherwise, I'll have to put you down . . ." Like a dog who'd turned on his master.

Auburn hair glinted in the late-afternoon sunset as Argent turned his chin to his shoulder, but didn't look back at Dorian. "You could try, Blackwell," he challenged.

The moment darkened, suffused with masculine challenge. This had always been an unanswered question between them. Something they'd danced around since puberty. Who would survive a clash of the two? Once violence erupted, would it be Blackwell's fire, or Argent's ice that won the day?

Though they were surrounded by plush carpets and expensive furnishings, draped in tailored suits of the most expensive wool and cotton and silk, they both knew what lay beneath.

Animals, both of them. Predators. With the capability to rend flesh and rip at the throat with the precision born of experience and the lack of conscience that was required for survival in the wild. It was what kept them at the top of the food chain. What protected them from becoming prey. But if lines were drawn, and both of them bared their teeth at each other, striking for the jugular, the collateral damage would be astronomical. And the outcome uncertain. The difference between their lethality could starve a mouse.

The moment that had always shimmered in the air between them turned into a vibration. Dorian again sensed that weakness in Argent, a tension or a battle. A deliberation that split his focus. If he was ever vulnerable to attack, it would be now.

The question remained, was such an action warranted? Was Argent telling the truth?

"Dorian, my love." Farah's soft rap against the study door dispelled the moment with flawless timing. "I'm taking Faye in the pram about the park to watch the sunset. I thought I saw Lady Harrington, and would like to say hello. Are you interested in joining us?"

That was exactly what Dorian wanted to do. He'd like nothing more than to see the sun glint off his wife's lovely pale hair as it dipped below London's singular skyline. Tossing a perturbed look at Argent, he called through the door.

"I have some business to attend to here for a moment. Please take Murdoch with you and I'll join you when I can, darling." As honest as Dorian was with his wife, he didn't necessarily want her to know Argent was here until he'd gotten to the bottom of this strange visit.

She paused. "Very well. Would you like me to send Gemma in with some tea?"

"Don't bother yourself, dear. I won't be long enough for tea."

"But Dorian, did you offer your guest any tea?" Farah asked sweetly, a smile coloring her voice. "If I recall correctly, Mr. Argent is fond of oolong."

Dorian grunted and pinched his forehead. It was damned difficult loving an intelligent, observant woman sometimes.

Argent shook his head.

"No, thank you. No one is in need of any tea at the moment. Enjoy your outing." He turned from the door, then paused and called out. "Make sure you're both warm enough. I'll be along."

"Good evening, Mr. Argent," Farah called before her steps retreated down the hall, as she knew generally not to expect a response.

Dorian joined Argent at the window and they both looked out onto the corner on which Blackwell resided whilst in town. From one side of the house, white rows of opulent Mayfair homes lined the clean, cobbled street, buttressed by columns and lorded over by stalwart, titled society matrons. From the study, only Park Lane separated the Blackwell home from the perfectly manicured Hyde Park.

These days, more and more merchants and wealthy, self-made men like Blackwell acquired property here in the West End of London. Though a title certainly made the generations-long occupants more comfortable.

For an extended, silent moment, the men observed Farah and her middle-aged escort, Murdoch, another former guest of Her Majesty's at Newgate, stroll through the neighborhood of well-dressed people in their furs and capes. It was a particular point of pride to Dorian that his wife was not only the loveliest, but also the most elegantly attired. His tiny daughter was wrapped in the softest furs to match her mother's extravagant golden pelisse.

A strange anxiety rose within him. His entire life was taking in another beautiful evening, and he wanted to be with them. Now.

"What are you doing here, Argent?" he asked shortly, surreptitiously checking Argent's transparent reflection in the glass. "Is this about the delay in fulfilling your contract?" A rather expensive one had crossed his desk today, this one calling for the blood of a rather famous actress. Dorian had only noted it because he'd heard days ago that Argent had taken that very job. A delay in Argent's work was not only out of the realm of normalcy, it was unheard of.

"I killed a man today," Argent murmured.

"Only one? I take it business is slow?" Dorian smirked.

Argent's reflection frowned and undid the top button of his coat. Then the next. "I killed a man because I wanted to. Because he deserved it. Because . . . he made me angry." Apparently changing his mind, he redid the second button.

Dorian watched Argent fidget with a growing sense of alarm. "If you've suddenly developed a conscience and are inclined to make a confession, you've come to the wrong man."

Argent made an irate sound so completely out of character that Dorian's eyebrows climbed toward his hairline, as the assassin swung away from the window. Stalking to the sideboard, he poured a liberal splash of Ravencroft's finest Scotch and downed it in one gigantic swallow. "I know who is killing those mothers."

Dorian blinked, bemused by the abrupt change of subject. "And who is that?"

"Lord Thurston. At least, he is the one drawing these contracts against the lives of these women and giving them to men like me. Do you know him?"

Dorian searched through the images in his flawless memory, sifting through data like a clerk in a file room. "Lord Thurston, yes. I've never made his personal acquaintance, which is to his credit, I suppose. He married a St. Vincent, I believe. The St. Vincent family owns several ancient titles, including an earldom, but lives on overtaxed tenants, parceling family land, and the credit of unscrupulous men such as I." Dorian pulled his seat out from behind his desk and claimed it. "What would Lord Thurston, by all accounts a respectable and wealthy peer of the realm, have to gain by ordering the murders of women, and likely children, from the West End to Cheapside?"

"I don't know." Argent tossed back another drink and set his glass down, stepping away from the Scotch with that legendary discipline of his. "I—killed his solicitor before I was able to extract that particular information from him."

"Oh?" This was not the lethal man's modus operandi. In fact, for Argent, this was incredibly erratic behavior. Argent might be deadly, but he was paradoxically imperturbable. He didn't strike without reason. That reason usually being money.

"He hired me to get rid of Millicent LeCour."

"The actress, yes, I heard." Dorian's sense of impending doom inflated. Something about the way Argent had said her name . . .

"I broke the contract, murdered the solicitor, and—" Slowly, Argent lowered himself into the chair opposite Blackwell's desk, his impressive width dwarfing the leather monstrosity. He seemed about to speak, but the words wouldn't pass through his tight lips.

"And?" Dorian pressed. If a man this notoriously fearless was nervous, then Dorian worried that an international incident loomed on the horizon.

"I claimed the woman."

"The . . . you . . . what?" Dorian gaped. He couldn't remember a time he'd been struck dumb in the last two decades. And he remembered *everything.*

"I think I want her to be mine . . . I'm taking her."

The somber veracity on Argent's face caused Dorian to wonder if he were perhaps hallucinating. "But . . . you gave her a choice, yes?"

"Did you give Farah a choice?"

"Of course—eventually—after a fashion. See here, we're not discussing Farah and me, the situation was completely different from this. She's mine. She's always *been* mine. And you—well . . ."

"I kill people for a living." Argent stared at the globe on the desk with unblinking eyes.

"And that is merely the first reason that this is a very bad idea for you both."

"I want her," Argent stated again. His voice colored, not

with passion, per se, but with something that could be painted with the same brush as need, or even desire.

"Do you . . . love her?"

Argent's glacial gaze flicked about the wall behind where Dorian sat, as though he could find the answer in the expensive volumes lined on the shelves there. "I can't kill her."

Dorian let out a mirthless bark of laughter. "I suppose that's more than some can say."

"I've tried, Blackwell." Argent looked at the space between them. "My hands were around her neck and then . . . I kissed her."

Blackwell gaped, struck dumb.

Argent wasn't known for his exploits as a lover. In fact, Dorian had it on good authority that Argent's sexual tastes ran to the more . . . detached variety. According to Madame Regina's whores, the assassin refused to face them, demanded they keep quiet, and never kissed, caressed, or even looked them in the eye. He finished on them, not in them, paid promptly, and left without a word. Dorian knew the secrets and proclivities of many powerful, important, and dangerous men; after a drink, a fuck, and a cuddle, these secrets would drip from their mouths.

But Argent never spoke, though he had secrets to tell. He never used the same whore twice. He had no type of female he gravitated toward. An anomalous man, this assassin, and one of his many anomalies was his penchant for telling the truth when other men would protect their pride.

"That poor woman, she must be absolutely traumatized." Dorian had to work hard to keep his alarm for the accosted lady out of his expression.

"She kissed me back."

"Are you certain?"

"I'm fair certain. At least . . . one of the times." Argent's expression turned pensive.

"Good God."

"She's agreed to my terms."

"Which are . . . ?" Dorian had a feeling he shouldn't have asked.

"To fuck me."

"Christ," he whispered, swiping a hand on his forehead.

"Just the once."

"You have to be joking."

"She has a son."

"I don't want to hear any more." Dorian put up a hand. "Argent, I do appreciate the information you've supplied me about Lord Thurston, and I will, of course, look into it. The contract on Miss LeCour has been reissued, you know."

Argent's nostrils flared and his eyes flashed with a blue flame as he leaned over the desk. "I want you to let it be known that *no one* takes that contract."

Dorian stood as well, placing both fists on the desk. For the first time their eyes clashed. "Do you presume to issue commands to *me*?"

"Only if you want your men to retain their heads."

"Be careful, Argent, this is dangerous ground. Making a move like this is bad for business; not only yours, but mine, as well."

Argent pushed off the desk with a guttural sound and hefted the bronze globe above his head. Smashing it down onto the smooth surface, he cleaved the wood in two.

It should have been physically impossible.

Dorian's hand moved to the long knife sheathed beneath his suit coat.

"You may rule the underworld, Blackwell, but you were never *my* king," Argent seethed. Red began to crawl from beneath his white collar and climb into his face, blood rushing beneath the skin with long-suppressed emotion. Dorian watched it with bemused fascination. And more than a bit of understanding.

"I've worked, suffered, fought, and killed beside you for many years," Argent ranted on. "I kept your secrets and I came when you called me to your side. But you *never* owned me." He knocked the large chair over with a fist, as though to punctuate his point. "So when I say to pull the fucking contract, you do it, because Millie LeCour is *mine*. She's under *my* protection and may God have mercy on the man who gets in my way, because I don't know the meaning of the word. So help me, I'll flay the meat from his bones before I—"

"Christopher, I *know*." Dorian interrupted his tirade, and the enraged man paused at the use of his given name. "I know," he repeated, more gently this time. He recognized exactly what drove Argent in this moment. The primal, tight ache of it. The hot, needful possession. "I'll pull the contract. No one will go near it without answering to one of us. And Thurston—"

"Thurston is also mine, to deal with as I will," Argent gritted out.

Dorian nodded. "Fair enough."

As he glanced at the ruptured desk, the overturned chair, and the discarded globe, Argent's shoulders visibly slumped. "This isn't—I don't usually—"

Dorian waved it away with a knowing smile ghosting at his lips. "This is what a woman brings into the lives of men like us."

"I'll pay to replace it," he muttered.

"Don't bother." Dorian stepped around the carnage. "I'm sure I owe you for one dead body or another." Striding to the study door, he opened it and waited for Argent to step through, then followed the assassin to the entry and out into the chilly evening. He was looking forward to catching up with Farah. He loved to see the chill turn her cheeks red beneath the freckles she insisted she didn't have anymore. He wanted to discuss this most intriguing turn of events.

Their breaths churned the air, all semblance of tension dissipated like the puffs of their exhales.

And they were allies again.

"What's it like, Blackwell?" Argent squinted across the distance to the nearly empty Hyde Park, where a distant Farah glimmered like a silver fae creature in the rapidly fading sunlight.

Dorian stared in the same direction. Though she was too far to make out the angelic features of her face, he could tell that Farah was smiling. It reached out to him, as always. He puzzled over Argent's question. It had been many years, and he'd read many books, and still the words to aptly describe his feelings for his wife didn't appear to exist.

"It's madness, at first, or maybe always. It's . . . possession and fear, passion and joy. It's indescribably sweet, and utterly terrifying. It's different for everyone, I imagine."

Argent made a noise, whether agreement or despondence, Dorian couldn't be sure. "Watch yourself, Argent," Blackwell advised. "This is a path you may not be ready to tread."

Ever, he said silently to himself.

The sky licked the cobblestones with copper as Argent turned to slink back into the shadows. He muttered something that was carried away by the early evening breeze. Dorian thought it was something like, "Just for one night," but he couldn't be certain.

Argent might not be one to lie to others to spare their

feelings, but if he believed he could let that actress go after only one night, Dorian truly wondered if the assassin lied to himself.

In any case, he thought as he pointed his boots in the direction of his wife. Did Millicent LeCour know just what she was involved with and if she had the wherewithal to deal with a man like Christopher Argent?

If not, God help her, because no man alive, himself included, had ever been able to.

CHAPTER TEN

If she had to identify the most surreal moments of her life, Millie was certain *this* would be near the top of the list. It had taken her some time to charm the stoic Hassan into saying more than two words. But she'd done it, by Jove, and now he was expertly applying charcoal color to outline her eyes at her behest. Millie had done her own stage makeup for years, but the precision with which the Arab accented his chocolate eyes sent her into fits of envy.

It was certainly to her benefit that she had her own dressing room, as Hassan had garnered so much attention backstage at Covent Garden, she was certain they'd never make the curtain call.

Though his features were sharp enough to etch glass, his wide-set gentle eyes reminded her of the good-natured carriage horses of the West End. When he leaned this close to her, she inhaled the scents of sand and musk and a spice that reminded her of flowing white tents, veiled women, and strong, dark vagabond tribes.

She'd found him fascinating and instantly determined they must be friends.

The dark blue of his head wrap and multitude of robes blurred with each swipe of the brush he used to apply the kohl as the gentle pressure pushed her lid against her eye.

Another face, with large, breathtakingly blue eyes and hair the color of dark sand, leaned on her knee and watched the process with fascination. Jakub, her son. Her small, sweet, beautiful boy. The boy for which she'd give her life, because he gave her life meaning. The boy for whom she'd made a deal with the very devil, himself.

She couldn't think about that now. About *him*. Christopher Argent. A mercenary, assassin, and her soon-to-be lover. He'd return for her. Soon she would be in his bed.

Or wherever he decided to have her.

Suddenly her skin budded with chills so exquisite they ached, and she let out a trembling exhale.

"Remain still," Hassan commanded gently.

"Mister Hassan, why do you line your eyes with black?" Jakub queried, his wire-rimmed spectacles magnifying his eyes from innocent to owlish.

"Because, little *rassam walad,* in my homeland the sun is so close and so unrelenting that the kohl protects the eyes from its fire and allows a man to see far across the desert."

Jakub nodded, plucking at the collar of his crisp shirt. "Mister Hassan, why do you call me *rassam walad*?"

The Arab never faltered in his task as he used a small piece of linen to expertly smudge the liner around her lid and draw it out to accentuate the almond shape of Millie's eye. "In my language it means painter boy." Hassam gestured his bearded chin toward Jakub's pile of art supplies arranged compulsively in a little corner. "In my homeland, painting is a sacred profession, a gift bestowed by Allah."

"Oh." Dimples appeared on each side of the boy's chin as his round cheeks pinkened with a bit of embarrassment and shy pleasure. Then his brows drew together as a thought struck him. "But Mister Hassan, the sun is not so close in London. It barely visits at all."

"This is so, *rassam walad*, but when far from home, it does one good to maintain the traditions of one's people, so that the heart can remain close to those he loves but must live without."

Sadness swam up from the depths of the Arab's liquid dark eyes as he paused to gaze down at Jakub with nostalgic affection. Millie caught herself wondering if Hassan had a little *rassam walad* of his own. Not for the first time, she wondered what the Arab was doing so far from his beloved homeland and who he'd left behind. Was he a refugee? A criminal? Could he be a hired killer like Argent? It didn't seem likely, though she'd caught the gleam of the hilt of a long jeweled dagger hidden in his voluminous robes.

"Mister Hassan, do you—"

"Jakub, *kochanie*." Millie cupped his little chin in her gentle hand. "Why don't you give poor Mister Hassan a rest and set up your easel?"

Her son's little mouth puckered and he looked down and to the side. "Yes, Mama," he mumbled.

Jakub scrambled to his makeshift art corner and flung open his box of paints, gingerly selecting a few umbers, golds, reds, and blues for careful inspection. Next, he would mix them with the precision of an alchemist and the focus of a savant, all the world disappearing for him until he created the perfect pigment.

Millie offered an apologetic smile to their interim guardian, but his expression conveyed that it was not necessary. It was true that Jakub was an exceptionally intelligent child, and that came with a profusion of inquisitiveness, but in general his extreme shyness kept him from speaking more than a few words to strangers. She supposed the boy's fascination with all things odd and new overcame his timidity with the imposing Arab.

Indeed, Millie had to bite back a barrage of her own questions. Such as, how did the foreigner come to know

Christopher Argent? What did he know about the assassin's proclivities, sexual and otherwise? What had he gleaned about who was after her and why?

"I have finished, madam." Hassan stepped back and squinted at his handiwork before dipping his chin in a satisfied nod.

Millie turned to the mirror and caught her breath. He'd done a splendid job. She'd never felt more like Desdemona. An innocent, virtuous woman, slandered by the whims of wicked men and killed for a sin she'd never committed.

Lord, who could better relate than she?

"Bless you, Hassan, you've performed a wonder."

He gave another bow. "And I am certain Madam will perform a wonder upon the stage tonight, secure in the knowledge that I will give my life unto the safety of her son."

Millie had to suppress the urge to throw her arms around the fatherly man with the gentle eyes and the dangerous knife. She had a feeling such contact would offend him, so she bowed her head to him, mimicking his previous gesture. "Thank you," she whispered, before clearing emotion out of her voice.

"What do you think, *kochanie*?" She faked a relaxed smile she didn't at all feel.

"You look splendid, Mama," Jakub encouraged, never once glancing up at her from where he knelt surrounded by his paints and studying his canvas.

Sighing, she shook her head and stood, tugging on the front of her silk robe to make sure she maintained her modesty around the Mussulman. Her costume, a wine-red velvet dress with fake pearls beaded across little gold braids on the bodice, hung from a mannequin perched in front of a dressing screen. "Pardon me whilst I dress," she murmured.

"Madam." Hassan hesitated, his dark eyes cast at the

floor. "I mean you no offense, but I am already skirting a sin, being almost alone in a room with an unmarried woman. Since your son is here, it is my hope that Allah, God, forgives me. But if you were to disrobe . . . even behind a screen . . ." He trailed off politely, keeping his judgment of her lifestyle to himself.

Embarrassed by her ignorance, Millie bit her lip. "Would you like to step outside the door? I'll call you back when I'm finished."

"That isn't something either of you need to worry about now." The dark voice sliced through her room like a sudden arctic chill.

Millie's head snapped toward the doorway, where Christopher Argent filled its width shoulder to shoulder. Dressed in a fine gray suit, he again resembled Bentley Drummle, the man she'd met before. Charming, charismatic, affected with the same ennui bemoaned by so many wealthy Londoners.

But she knew better now, didn't she? Beneath his unnatural stillness and enigmatic expression lurked someone much more sinister and, alternately, more intriguing.

"You may go, Hassan." Argent pulled an envelope from his suit coat, and handed the graceful Arab what Millie assumed was payment for her protection.

With no small amount of curiosity, Millie wondered what her life was worth.

"Thank you, Argent." Hassan dipped his head with respect as he took the envelope. "Convey my regards to Blackwell." Turning to Millie, he bowed to her. "It has been an honor to know you and your son. *Fi Amanullah.* May God protect you."

"Fare you well, sir." Millie curtsied to him, and in a soft swish of blue robes, he glided past Argent and was gone.

Millie was alone with an assassin.

Again.

They stared at one another in silence, and only when Millie's lungs began burning did she realize that she'd been holding her breath.

She released it in a tumble of words. "Mr. Argent, this is my son, Jakub. Jakub, come and meet Mr. Christopher Argent, our—guardian." She'd explained their need for temporary bodyguards to him the morning she'd hired the McGivney brothers in as vague and careful terms as possible. It angered her that her son didn't always feel safe. That he had to fear the shadows.

Even when he stood, Jakub's little neck had to tilt back so far his head rested on his shoulders to look the towering man in the face. Though his spectacles always seemed to magnify his eyes, they were wide with obvious wonder.

"Are you a giant, Mr. Argent?" he asked.

"No." Argent blinked, but showed no offense.

"Jakub," Millie reprimanded, worried that a man who killed people for a living might not take care with the feelings of a small, inquisitive child.

Jakub straightened at the censure in her voice and wandered over to Argent, remembering his manners. "I mean, it's a pleasure to make your acquaintance," he amended.

Looking much like a barbarian in a gentleman's suit, the assassin regarded the little boy's upstretched hand with undue assessment before reaching down to take it with two careful fingers.

"Likewise," Argent muttered, letting the boy shake twice before snatching his hand back.

"Was your father a Viking?" Jakub resumed his interview.

"I couldn't say," the assassin answered blandly. "I never knew my father."

At that, the little boy brightened. "Neither did I."

Millie's heart squeezed, but she couldn't instantly identify the cause. Because her son was without a father, a fact he now stated with little to no sorrow? Perhaps because he had common ground with such a villain? Or because she'd never seen the boy so animated around anyone except for the two mysterious and dangerous men she'd been forced to allow into his life. Could the cause be that the stoic assassin had just been so gentle with her boy?

Lord, it would do her well to not notice such things.

"Maybe you're half a giant," Jakub assessed. "Like your father could have been one."

Argent peered down at the child as though examining a queer sort of oddity. "I very much doubt it."

"But you don't *know* that he wasn't, if you never met him."

The assassin paused. "I suppose there's a certain logic to that."

"It's only that you're so *big*." Jakub held out both of his hands to demonstrate the largest size he possibly could.

"Jakub." Millie shooed him back toward his paints. "You're being impolite."

"Sorry, Mama," Jakub mumbled, chastised. "Sorry, Mr. Argent."

"Why don't you finish your portrait, *kochanie,* while I get dressed?" Millie kissed him and turned to Argent, noting that she'd subconsciously placed her body in between her son and the so-called giant.

The assassin hadn't missed it either, though if it bothered him, Millie couldn't tell. His features were smooth and cool as pressed satin.

"Would you . . . like to step out while I dress, sir?" She gestured to the door, and again to her robe, beneath which she only wore her corset and underthings. As an actress, she wasn't used to adhering to the rules of modesty as her life was full of backstage costume changes. But she suddenly felt quite shy.

"No." His gaze sharpened and his features tightened.

Millie found herself breathless yet again. Something told her that to insist would be folly, and she certainly wouldn't want to create a scene in front of her child. If they were truly going to be lovers this night, then why make an issue of diffidence?

Because he unnerved her. Because she'd been unprepared for him to invade her space and claim it as his own. Perhaps . . . because she'd forgotten how intensely compelling and frightening and awe-inspiring his presence truly was in the scant hours they'd spent apart.

"Then—may I induce you to sit, Mr. Argent?" Millie gestured to a chaise, one of the only available surfaces in the disarray of her dressing room. She silently wished he'd take it. He *was* an unusually large man, and somehow her dressing room had become too small with him inside it. As though he'd claimed all the air, the space, the notice of every little sensory nerve on her body. And while his eyes were arctic, his effect on her was anything but.

Her skin bloomed with warmth when he was nearby, even though he sometimes caused chills to spread through her. She found the paradox rather alarming.

He made no move to sit, just stared at her silently with those blue, blue eyes, and for a moment, Millie wondered if he'd heard her.

"Please," she entreated. "Sit down? Rest yourself."

His chin dipped in a nod, sending a gleam of lantern light through his thick auburn hair. Bending his long legs, he claimed the seat, looking almost ridiculous on such a dainty piece of furniture.

"Right. Yes." Millie remembered herself, snatching her costume from the mannequin and dragging it behind the screen with her.

The cream silk of the screen did little to truly cover her, and Millie moved one of the lanterns from behind it so she would only cast a nominal shadow while she dressed. Not only because she didn't particularly want to entice him further, but because his presence in her rooms caused little jolts of anxiety and awareness to sing along her veins. Everything she did took on a distinctly erotic undertone. The whisper of her silk robe over her skin when she slipped it off. The heavy warmth of the velvet dress. When she tucked, and tied, and shimmied into it, she could feel an extra tingle in her breasts, was aware of the feminine curve of her waist beneath her corset. She thought of all the places that might be bared to him later. All the places where he would put his hands.

Or his mouth.

Millie suddenly felt dizzy, and succumbed to her own need to sit down as her head swam. Though she didn't look at him, she could sense the assassin's eyes on her as she made her way to her dressing table. Somehow, she knew that despite her efforts, he'd watched her shadow behind the screen.

"Did you get enough to eat, Jakub?" she asked, glancing toward her son in the corner as she lowered herself in front of the large mirror. "Jakub? *Kochanie?*"

Lost to his paints, he didn't even acknowledge her.

Which left her only one companion for conversation, the terse giant with the startling eyes.

Drat.

Fumbling for her rouge, she refused to look at him as she added more color to her cheeks. Her hand paused just as the brush reached her face. Even beneath the makeup, it was obvious her color was unnaturally high. She reached for her lip rouge instead. Try as she might, she simply couldn't ignore her assassin-turned-protector. It was utterly impossible. He sat so immense and motionless and silent.

She hazarded a glance at him, if only to make certain he still breathed.

Which, indeed, he did, his big chest lifting and flexing

beneath his suit coat. He gazed at her with unparalleled intensity, watching the movements of her fingers with undue interest.

Clearing nerves from her throat, she met his eyes in the mirror and was startled to see that he was the first one to look away.

"Do you enjoy the theater, Mr. Argent?" She ventured a moment of civility.

"I've only attended the once," he replied, seeming to study a wig of long crimson ringlets, going so far as to reach out and test its texture between his thumb and forefinger.

Millie had to look away. "And . . . did you like it?" she prompted. When she gathered the courage to glimpse at him again, she was surprised to see him seriously considering the question.

"Your performance was without a single flaw," he said with no trace of flattery or farce in his voice. "But I find myself unable to suspend disbelief in the manner that is required to truly enjoy a production. I don't understand why people dress in their finest to watch others pretend to be in love. To feign jealousy and cruelty and even death. Why *play* at fighting and killing? There's plenty to be done out in the real world."

And he'd done plenty of his own.

Millie swallowed audibly, trying to decide whether to be pleased at his honest compliment, or to be offended by his dismissal of her entire profession. "Not all of us live a life as exciting and treacherous as yours, Mr. Argent," she said as she added a few more jeweled pins to her intricate coiffure, if only to give her restless hands something to do. "Most of us merely like to be kissed by danger or violence or death. Maybe even let it kiss us, upon occasion. We like to make it a spectacle at which to gasp and laugh, or cry. Though it is only the thrill we want to take home with us, not the reality. We still desire to return to our warm beds, all safe and sound, when the night is over." She considered her words only after she'd said them. She was taking the danger home with her tonight, wasn't she? There was a very good chance her bed would be anything but safe.

And, Lord forgive her, it was more thrilling than she'd like to admit.

"But not everyone makes it home safe and sound," he rumbled.

Not with men like him about.

Millie's heart stalled and her hand froze halfway to her hair. "True . . ." She drew the word out, searching for what to say next. "But we expect to. We hope to, don't we?"

"I know nothing of hope." He leaned forward and placed his elbows on his long, powerful legs. "So people attend the theater to feel afraid and safe at the same time?"

Millie chewed her lip, considering her words carefully. "Sometimes, surely, but mostly they go to play voyeur to the human experience. Drama, I think, does one of two things for a person, it allows us to be a little more grateful for the humdrum of the everyday, or makes us yearn for something above whom and what we are. It can remind us to not let every moment slip into the next without reaching for more. Whether we reach within ourselves or for something we want out in the world. A dream, a home, money, adventure . . . or love."

Feeling impassioned, she turned in her seat to gesture at him. "Drama can make you experience the very extremes of emotion. A good playwright, Shakespeare, for example, can use language to allow an actor to convey an emotion that resonates with the audience. That allows them—sometimes even forces them—to *feel*. Coupled with the performance and the right music and lighting . . . I think that emotion is contagious and complex, and often a person doesn't know which until they experience it under the Bard's very own tutelage. It's quite extraordinary, really, almost magical and—" Millie let her voice die away, noticing that Christopher Argent hadn't blinked for an astonishingly long time.

In the middle of her dressing room, done in all shades of chaos and color, he was a monochromatic study in dove and granite. All but for his eyes and hair, both of which were uncommon in their variegation. His jaw was too wide to be called handsome, his mouth too caustic for its fullness, surrounded by brackets that made him look alternately cruel and somehow inanimate. His eyes made him appear ancient. Not so much in years, but in experience.

What horrors he must have seen in his life, some of them perpetrated by his own hands.

"Forgive me," she breathed, entranced by the moment, as though he were a serpent and she his prey, mesmerized by his menace. "I do tend to get carried away."

He once more brushed aside her words. "You have . . . experienced all these emotions?"

What an odd question. "Most of them, yes."

"Are you—in love—with someone?"

She hadn't realized that someone so still could become even more motionless. It was as though he'd stopped breathing in anticipation of her answer.

"No," she answered honestly, and had the impression that his chest compressed.

"Have you ever been?"

"I can't say that I have truly loved anyone, except Jakub." She glanced at her son, still oblivious to the world around him, and then back to the assassin.

An expression flickered across his features, but was gone before she could identify it. This time when he looked at her, his eyes were gentler, somehow. Still frightfully opaque, but they had lost some of their frost.

"Do you wish to be in love?"

Had any other man asked, she'd have told him that it was no business of his. She'd have lied or misdirected him somehow, to avoid the question. But behind the callousness of Christopher Argent's expression was an earnest curiosity. A lack of judgment or malice.

It was a sincere question that deserved a sincere answer.

"I—I'm never really certain. If there's one thing I've learned from Shakespeare, from most any playwright, it is that love is just as dangerous an emotion as hatred or anger or the lust for power. I think love can make you a stranger, even to yourself. Maybe even a monster. It can be a wild creature just waiting to be unbound. A beast. A feral and selfish thing that will turn you against the world, against nature or reason, against God, Himself. And every time I'm tempted to allow myself to fall, I wonder . . . is it worth the risk?"

His brows drew together. "What if there is no risk? What if God, if He even exists, has turned away from you, and so to turn from Him would be no great sin? There would be nothing in the way of reaching for what you wanted."

Millie blinked, startled by his bleak assessment. "Is that what is going on here? Do you believe God has forsaken you, and so you no longer fear Him? Is that how you're able to . . ." She paused, checking on Jakub to make certain he wasn't listening in. "To *do* what it is that you *do*?"

He lifted his massive shoulders in a dismissive gesture. "Perhaps. I have no fear of God."

"So you do not believe in heaven?"

"This world is all I know."

"What about hell, the devil? Are you not afraid you'll have to answer for your sins, for the blood you've spilled?"

He shook his head, a more adamant gesture than she could remember him making—apart from the times he'd kissed her.

"I do not know what happens when this life is over; therefore it does little good to speculate. All I know for certain is that God and the devil are symbols. Beings greater than ourselves to be loved or feared, blessed or blamed. And to me it doesn't matter which. It is an easy thing to commit a sin and say that 'the devil made me do it,' and then cast that sin on him. But this life has taught me that we make ourselves into the monsters that we are. That the blood we spill is on our own hands.

"I've been able to cast my burdens on no one's shoulders but my own. Carrying them makes me strong, and I've needed that strength to survive. For God has never saved me from the evil I've seen in the eyes of men. And it's hard for me to imagine that hell is worse than some of the places I've already been. So instead of fearing that which I do not know, I've made of myself a symbol, of sorts. A man to be feared, whose vengeance is immediate rather than ultimate, and for many so-called godly men, my form of justice is effective." This time it was Argent who seemed to remember himself, and clamped his hard jaw shut.

Millie wondered if that might be the longest he'd ever spoken at one time. Even though his tone had been dispassionate, his words carried with them a cavernous sort of pain. Only hell could spit out such a cold and lethal man, surely.

"Do you mean for me to fear you, Mr. Argent?" she whispered solemnly, not for the first time dreading the devil's bargain she'd made.

"I do not blame you if you fear me," he answered, his eyes nearly meeting hers. "But for all that is unknown, you can be unequivocally certain that I do not wish you harmed."

Mutely, Millie nodded and turned back to her mirror, unable to bear the intensity between them as he watched her smooth crimson color on her lips. A small vine of sadness appeared beneath her ribs and blossomed into compassion. What he must have endured to fashion him into the heartless killer he'd become, she thought.

Millie knew she understood him better now, but that didn't mean she feared him any less.

Chapter Eleven

"I have to use the necessary." The boy standing next to Argent bent his knees and blinked up at him with a grimace.

Argent frowned as he glanced from a luminous Millie on stage, to her light-haired boy, and back. "Can't it wait until she's finished?" he asked.

"I've already been trying, but Mama said not to leave your side. It's critical. I'm afraid I won't make it until she's done with the scene."

It was *the* scene, as well. The one where she died and had to remain on stage for a long while.

Swearing under his breath, Argent glanced around the backstage area. People bustled about in Elizabethan costumes, ducking around ropes, pulleys, curtains, props, and each other. It was difficult to be vigilant with this much chaos. Argent knew he couldn't relax until he'd taken her somewhere safe.

And alone.

He didn't want to take his eyes off Millie. He'd known her to be exquisitely beautiful, but before tonight, she'd been just that. A rare and dark gem, sparkling despite the danger and blood surrounding her. Something to be possessed. To bring him pleasure.

Something he coveted.

But now, after he'd seen the passion in her eyes, watched

her gesture with fervency and emotion and animated affectation . . .

"Mr. Argent." Jakub tugged on his arm with urgency.

He knew she'd be relatively safe on stage in front of a thousand people. Millie had told him that her son was to be his first priority. If there was a good time to take the boy, this would be it. "Where is the closest one?"

"In the dressing room."

"Why didn't you go before we left the dressing room?"

"I didn't have to go then."

He glanced sharply down at the boy once more, wondering if all children lacked any kind of foresight. "You must hurry, understand?"

"I promise."

Millie's dressing room was visible from backstage, and Argent followed the boy to it, amused at how the child walked with his knees together.

The dressing room seemed less brilliant and filled with more useless clutter without Millie there. Argent swept through the room and checked every corner and hiding place before he returned to the door to allow Jakub some privacy.

The boy hurried, as he'd promised, but dawdled at his painting corner.

"Come on then." Argent gestured to the door.

"I just have to take something with me." Jakub bent to retrieve two boxes and a long brush. "These are too valuable to be left—" A sound of terror escaped the child, just as a slow creak of the door closing behind Argent ripped a chill through his already taut muscles. He whirled to see the gleam of muddy eyes he'd thought never to encounter again.

"It's the fifth act, Argent," said Charles Dorshaw as he oozed from the shadows of the doorway. "Desdemona is in the middle of being murdered."

"I should have known you were back," Argent muttered as he sized up the pale assassin with the mischievous eyes and the sharp throwing knife brandished at the ready. "The blood in the streets, the tortured, degraded women."

The man across from him maintained an expert grip on his knife as he gave a relaxed chuckle. "Some of us *enjoy* our work. We can't all be cold fish like you." He licked thin, refined lips. "Though we can savor the bodies . . . when they've gone cold."

Ladies fanned themselves over Charles Dorshaw's lean, handsome elegance. They posed seductively and dropped their handkerchiefs for him. They angled for introductions and indelicacies. What they didn't know was that catching his attentions was worse than drawing the notice of hell.

Demons had a shorter attention span and weaker stomachs, and there was a chance even the denizens of hell liked their women to be warm and alive when they bedded them.

Dorshaw didn't.

"America and I failed to suit, I'm afraid. It posed no challenge for me." Much like a cobra, he used his hypnotic eyes, melodic voice, and impeccable manners to disarm his prey. "So much of it is still as good as lawless, and the women are all loud, opinionated, uncultured swine, or worse, religious fanatics. The men all wear pistols on their hips, and business is slow as those industrious upstarts all seem to do their own killing." Dark hair and soft, thin eyebrows lent an almost androgynous symmetry to Dorshaw's wicked good looks as he made a dismissive gesture in his starched evening attire. "Indeed, London is my home, Argent, and her streets have always been big enough for the both of us, wouldn't you agree?"

"As you say." Argent nodded once. "But this room isn't, so get the fuck out."

Dorshaw tsked and motioned with his chin to the child blocked by Argent's body. "Can't do that, old boy. The contract on these two has been . . . renegotiated. You failed to deliver, and it's back on the open market."

"Not as of this evening," Argent informed him. "Blackwell's pulled it. The LeCours belong to me."

Dorshaw shook his head. "There must be some dreadful misunderstanding. I didn't get this contract from Blackwell. In fact, he and I have never particularly got on. You see, this client has employed me before, and I should be very loath to disappoint." He thumbed the razor edge of the dagger for which Dorshaw had become infamous. "I'll leave the child alive, if that's any comfort to you. I merely have to *deliver* him."

A gasp and a whimper sounded from behind them and Argent did his best to shut it out. If he could reach for his garrote, or his own knife, he could bloody Dorshaw's throat before he took his next breath. But something about the tiny rattle of whimpers behind him stayed his hand.

"Listen carefully, Dorshaw," Argent said, nonplussed by the difficulty he had in maintaining his monotone. "I have claimed the woman and the boy. They are under my indefinite protection. You leave now, and you leave them *alone* . . . and I'll let you escape with your life."

Dorshaw threw him a look of regret that had little to no sincerity in it. "I *could* have done, Argent. The money is good, but not the best. I could have let you have her; I could have let her go, if I hadn't seen her first." His face turned rapturous, and Argent knew in that moment Dorshaw was going to die.

By his hand.

But that throwing knife in Dorshaw's hand was poised to fly, and Argent had to take care of it before he made his move. He inched to his right slightly, to be sure his body blocked that of the child.

"It isn't often men like us get a mark filled with such an overabundance of life as Millie LeCour . . ." Dorshaw showed even, white teeth in a wolfish grin. "It will take extra time for me to drain her of it."

"Don't you fucking say her name." The red returned, and Dorshaw must have recognized it in his eyes, because his smile died, and with a masterful flick of his wrist, his knife flew right at Argent's throat and was followed by a deft lunge, charging to take him down if the knife failed to do so.

With reflexes honed to that of a viper's, Argent reached his right arm across his body and slapped the knife out of the air with his open palm, changing its trajectory to embed into the wall to his left. That put his elbow in the perfect place to solve the problem of Dorshaw's advancement.

A sharp lunge forward connected his elbow with the man's eye socket. But his colleague was no stranger to a strike in the face.

Dorshaw absorbed much of the force of the strike by spinning away from it, and coming full circle to face Argent with a larger, sharper knife in the same hand. The flash gave little warning before a burning pain ripped through the meat beneath Argent's forearm.

Gritting his teeth, Argent cut Dorshaw's victorious smile short by stomping out at his chest, the force of the blow lifting the smaller man off his feet and throwing him against the door. It was a testament to Edward Middleton Barry's architectural brilliance that the door remained intact.

In the time it took for Argent to retrieve the knife from the wall, Dorshaw had nearly recovered, and they brandished their blades at each other with absolute absorption.

"We should have done this in the ring, Argent." Dorshaw sneered. "Imagine the money we would have made, the best slashers in the empire, hand to hand, as it were."

Argent's only response was an attack.

With his free hand, Dorshaw seized Argent's knife arm, his fingers digging into the smarting wound while simultaneously stabbing at Argent's torso.

Gritting his teeth against the pain, Argent plucked the man's wrist mid-slice, keeping his skin unmarred and his organs right where they preferred to be. *Inside* his body.

Trembling muscles on both sides locked each man in a momentary impasse, but Argent had a few advantages the other assassin did not. The first being an almost inhuman tolerance to pain. Second, superior size and strength. And tertiary, a knowledge of the body's reflexive tendencies and how to manipulate them.

A slight press on the right point of his wrist, and Dorshaw yelped as his fingers sprang open and the knife clattered to the floor. A shift in weight alerted Argent to the incoming kick aimed between his legs.

None of that; he was planning on using that particular part of his anatomy in a short while.

His foot shot out to block it successfully before kicking at the man's other knee, buckling it from under him.

Argent followed him to the floor and impeded Dorshaw's attempt at gaining the upper hand by rolling them both once before pinning the man beneath him, the knife levered toward his adversary's wide eyes.

"The world is well rid of you," he murmured as he pressed down with his weight, some of the blood from the wound on his arm dripping onto Dorshaw's already wounded cheek. The man used both arms in a fruitless struggle to push Argent's knife arm away.

A muffled sob startled him, and Argent looked into the magnified, tear-reddened rims of wide, blueberry eyes.

"Look away, boy," he snarled, cringing at a softening—no—a pause in his cold, lethal ferocity.

"No, do watch." Dorshaw laughed maniacally. "You and me, Argent, we'll create the next generation."

Argent punched him in the throat.

"Look. Away. *Now,*" he ordered softly over Dorshaw's wheezes.

The child nodded, hugging his art supplies closer and squeezing more droplets out of his eyes as he clenched them shut with all his might, using his round cheeks to help.

Satisfied, Argent went in for the kill.

"Stop right there!" The door bounced off the wall.

Argent squeezed his own eyes shut and let a hiss of breath out of his throat, swallowing a surge of intense irritation. If there was one thing worse than a useless, provoking, bothersome, inept, ill-timed policeman, it was a gaggle of them stuffing themselves into the dressing room door, preventing him from carving Dorshaw's defective brain out of his skull.

CHAPTER TWELVE

Argent stood with Inspector Ewan McTavish of Scotland Yard in silence, both their eyes following Dorshaw's shackled progress out the door. The smile on the psychopath's face could only be identified as serene.

"Watch that one," Argent warned. "He's escaped us before."

"We'll take extra care," the Scotsman promised. "Not often ye find a murderer at the scene of the crime."

"A few more minutes and you never would have found him at all," Argent muttered, then McTavish's words struck him. "The scene of *what* crime, exactly?"

McTavish turned to him, waiting for the other coppers to clear the room before he spoke in a whisper so as not to let Jakub overhear. "It's Hassan . . . we just found him in the alley."

Something surged through Argent that surprised and alarmed him.

Anger?

"Is Dorshaw one of your contracts, Argent?" McTavish asked.

Argent shook his head. "He's after the boy and his mother, who's under my protection." Surreptitiously, he motioned with his eyes to Jakub, still standing in the corner next to a knocked-over easel, clutching the same art supplies. He looked very small and very lost.

Aware that he was no longer being ignored in the chaos, the boy took a tentative step forward on unsteady legs. "W-where's Mama? I want her here." His chin wobbled and his eyes began to leak again, but his voice was clear and sure, if hesitant.

McTavish crouched down to the boy's eye level, and the child regarded him with anxious uncertainty. He kept glancing over at Argent as if with an expectation gleaming in his eyes, but buggar if he could tell what the child wanted.

"Are ye hurt anywhere?" the Scotsman asked gently.

He shook his head and wiped a runny nose on his sleeve.

Argent made a face.

"What's yer name, son?"

There was that questioning glance at Argent from beneath long, sandy lashes again. What did the boy want him to say? He knew his own name, didn't he?

Lifting an eyebrow, Argent looked at the child askance before his gaze needed to dart away.

Somehow, the boy took it as an encouragement. "Jakub."

"Yer ma's still on stage, Jakub," McTavish consoled. "Do ye want me to go wait in the wings, and I'll bring her to ye as soon as I can?"

The boy nodded so many times Argent lost count.

"All right, lad, I'll return with her straightaway." McTavish ruffled the boy's light locks and seemed to miss Jakub's flinch as he addressed Argent.

"Looks a bit like ye did as a wee boy. Is he yer git?"

The short and burly officer had been hired barely out of boyhood, himself, to work at Newgate. Due to a sick mother and an absentee father, he'd been more than willing to take bribes from Blackwell, Argent, and their band of criminals back in those days. Though he'd risen through the ranks to inspector at Scotland Yard, his loyalties had never faltered so long as his pockets were full of coin.

He was their man on the inside, and they did favors for each other when they could.

"He's *not* mine." The idea was preposterous.

McTavish leaned in, lifting a conspiratorial hand to hide his mouth. "Are ye certain? I've likely a few bastards peppering the streets from the randy days of my prime. Ye never can be sure, can ye?"

Argent glanced over at the inspector from beneath a sardonic brow. "I've never sired a bastard." He let his low voice make his unmistakable point. "I promised I never would."

McTavish hadn't been there the night his mother had died, but he'd seen the aftermath. He'd been the only one to clean his mother's blood from Argent's catatonic body the night after and deliver him into Wu Ping's protection.

He'd been the one to look the other way as Argent took his bloody revenge.

He didn't know why, but Argent found the former guard's presence unsettling even after two decades. To look into the inspector's soft, understanding Scottish eyes was to glimpse a past best left alone.

"Aye, well, I'll be after his mother then." He put on his hat and straightened his coat as though going outside instead of down a hall and into the wings of the theater. Winking down at Jakub, he left.

Silence yawned in a room where chaos had only just reigned. It didn't belong here in a place of such riotous color and cheerful disarray.

Argent and the child stared at each other warily, and he tried not to think about how the room smelled like Millie. At least the boy's tears had ceased. Somehow that . . . improved things.

Exponentially.

"Thank you." Jakub's soft, somber voice echoed as loudly as a gun blast between them.

Argent blinked, but was saved from the expectation of a reply as the child uncurled his fingers from the implements he'd been protecting, and bent to retrieve his short easel and set it to rights. He restored the canvas to its place and took an inordinate amount of time centering the piece.

Argent didn't know what to do with gratitude. He'd never before been faced with it. Should he clarify just exactly what he'd done to deserve it? Which, in essence, was nothing now that he thought about it, because he didn't save the boy from capture, or his mother from a deadly ambush, out of any altruistic spirit. He'd done it because Millie LeCour was going to pay him for the deed.

With her body.

A foreign sensation coiled in his chest as he watched Jakub's small hands deftly and compulsively arrange the supplies around the canvas. His tongue tasted wrong and his skin felt—smudged somehow. What unsettled him the most was that the distasteful feeling seemed to be directed at himself.

Millie LeCour stared out of the canvas posed in a dress of emerald green, standing in a disarray of roses. The colors were heavily applied, and the nose completely skewered, but her smile, high cheekbones, and heavy dark hair were unmistakable.

Drawn to the painting, as he was to its subject, Argent took a step forward, then another. "You're . . . painting your mother." He stated the obvious, painfully aware that he could think of very little to say to a child. As he constantly had to remind people, he refused to harm or assassinate them, and therefore very rarely found himself in their company. The only child he came into contact with on any semblance of a regular basis was Faye Marie, Blackwell's infant girl, and she did little more than squawk, drool, and put things in her mouth that had no business being there.

He'd never before considered that they actually might have to . . . interact with her in the years to come.

"I'm going to give it to her on her birthday," Jakub ventured, studying his work and pushing his spectacles up the bridge of his small nose.

"It's a remarkable likeness of her."

Swiveling his head on his thin neck to study him, the boy's exaggerated eyes narrowed. "You're saying that to be kind," he accused.

"I say nothing to be kind," Argent informed him stiffly. "If it was a dreadful painting, I'd advise you not to give it to your mother, as it would make a terrible gift."

A tiny lip quirked upward and the boy motioned him forward. "The nose is off," he challenged.

Another step brought him closer, and the floor didn't fall out from beneath him. "I'm sure that can be fixed."

Nodding, the boy bit his lip and turned back to the canvas. "Do you know what is the most difficult about painting her?"

"No," Argent answered honestly, and reached for a strip of linen that looked clean enough, thrusting his suit coat up his arm and wrapping it around the knife gash to stem the bleeding while the boy's notice was absorbed elsewhere. It wasn't bad enough to need immediate attention. He'd have to stitch it later.

"Mama has dark eyes, like these I painted, but there's a light . . . behind them. *Inside* them. I can't—I can't get it just right. I don't know how. I have a feeling the trick isn't in the eyes, themselves, but in the shape around them. In the brow, and the cheek, and . . ." His little shoulders drooped and he speared him with another solemn glance. "You probably think I'm talking nonsense."

Argent shook his head and finished the one-handed knot on his makeshift bandage. "No. I know exactly to which light you are referring. I've noted it on more than one occasion."

With a tentative caution, the child peered over his shoulder. "Is that why you kissed her?"

"Partly." Argent might not know much about children, but he knew better than to describe all of the other reasons he'd kissed the boy's mother. And why he'd been in her vicinity to begin with.

Shyness gave way to sly temerity. "Are you going to kiss her again?"

"Yes."

Straightening, Jakub lifted his chin and stuck out a rather concave chest. "Are you going to marry her first?"

Something heavy dropped from the top of Argent's stomach into its depths. "What in God's name would make you think that?" Women didn't marry men like him. Ever.

Jakub wrinkled his button nose. "At school, Rodney Beaton said if a man kisses a woman on the mouth then he has to marry her or the woman is ruined." Anxiety stole back into his expression as his spectacles made their unruly way back down his nose. "You're not going to ruin Mama, are you?"

Argent couldn't bring himself to answer that, couldn't examine the question too closely, not while his blood still sang with violence and the picture of bespectacled innocence blinked up at him with unsettlingly familiar eyes.

Ruin had many different meanings, all depending upon the perspective of the deciding body. In some circles, standing in the same room with him would be enough to ruin a woman. Imagine if they were privy to what he planned to do to her once he got her alone. Among the whores he'd used, they didn't seem to be particularly ruined by him. In fact, one or two had been in a snit when he'd opted not to employ them again.

Which made no sense, whatsoever.

But . . . ruin? After Millie had spent her obligatory night with him, would she consider herself ruined? The oily feeling returned and for the first time in decades, Argent wanted to squirm away from even himself.

Why should it matter?

Looking away, he muttered, "Rodney Beaton sounds like a first-class idiot."

"That's mostly what Mama said, but that's because I asked if you were my father. Do you want to see my treasure?" he asked, brightening.

Argent choked on a swallow, and the chatty little being again assumed any sound that wasn't a no was automatically an ascent.

Father? The notion would be hilarious if it wasn't so sobering.

Retrieving the small box he'd been clutching during the tussle with Dorshaw, Jakub motioned for Argent to take a seat in a plush chair and pushed his spectacles back where they belonged.

Argent complied for lack of a better thing to do.

Jakub's voice turned rapturous. "Look," he breathed, unlatching the box and pulling it open.

Argent frowned. "It's—paint." Lord, he hoped it was paint; the alternative would have made even him a bit squeamish.

"Not just *any* paint," the boy insisted, his features taking on the kind of reverence only seen in a religious icon. "This particular shade of crimson is produced from the plucked wings of the cochineal beetle in South America. It's the truest red. The most beautiful and costly. I've only ever used it for the roses in Mama's painting. At first, I felt sad for the beetles because their wings were taken from them, and they could no longer fly. But then, I thought, if

I was a cochineal beetle and someone asked me to give them my wings for such a color, I'd do it. Gladly."

Obviously the boy had never been locked up. Never been trapped behind walls of iron and stone looking at the sky and actively hating the birds that could come and go at will. "Were I granted the ability of flight, I wouldn't give it up for anything in this world."

For some reason, Argent didn't have such a hard time meeting the dark blue gaze of the child in front of him, not even when the boy studied him in that stoic way of his.

"You think that way because you're not an artist."

"Fair enough." But they often painted the walls with the exact same shade of red.

"But, I believe, we can think differently and still be friends, can we not?"

Argent shrugged. "I don't see why not. My mind seems to work a great deal differently than almost all of my allies. Doesn't stop us from attaining our goals."

Jakub latched his treasure and put it away. "I like you, Mr. Argent," he announced. "I like that you don't lie to me because I'm not yet a man. You can go on kissing my mother if you want, so long as you don't ruin her."

Christopher stopped just short of informing the child that he didn't require his permission. All traces of fear and tears had disappeared in their short but diverting conversation. Young Jakub was passionate about his art, and discussing it with someone had distracted him from his ordeal with Dorshaw. Argent didn't want the distraught boy back, wouldn't begin to know how to calm him down until his mother arrived. Tears were decidedly a woman's purview.

Also, a memory two decades gone tugged at the inky darkness of his past, threatening to surface from the cold void where it was locked away. A boy's fierce vigilance over his mother. An instinctual responsibility that fell on thin, young shoulders in the absence of a grown man to protect and shelter this pitiful family of two.

This acceptance. This . . . permission. It was rare, and it came from a place of respect not easily won and trust not freely given.

Argent nodded at the boy. "I—"

"Jakub!" The frantic call accompanied by the sound of running feet set both of them on alert. *"Jakub."*

"Mama?" the boy called, sounding infinitely younger.

Millie exploded into the room in a flash of color and sobs. The boy was wrenched off his feet and pulled against a bosom heaving with panic and strain. "Jakub, my son, my boy, *moja słodka piękna syn.*" She simultaneously dissolved into hysterics and her native language.

Relieved of his need to be brave, the child clung to his mother with both arms and legs and released tears of fear into her neck. They stayed like that for a long moment, weeping. Clinging. Long enough for Inspector McTavish and a man just as heavily made up as Millie to file into the small room.

Argent had to take the entire moment to recover from the shock of seeing her again. Almost like he'd forgotten in the moments they'd spent apart just how dynamically beautiful she was up close. That beauty struck him like a physical blow.

The newcomer's eyebrows, already drawn comically high and darker than his silver hair, crawled dangerously close to his receding hairline as he inspected the scene. His impeccable black evening suit and gloves as white as an angel's hide were strained at every possible seam. "I say!" he boomed in a voice more suited to the stage. "Is the lad cut? There's a spot of blood on the carpets."

Argent hid his wounded arm behind his back.

With a sound of distress, Millie sank to her knees with her son, setting him down and running her hands over his hair and his face. "God, Jakub, are you bleeding? Did he hurt you?" She ripped open his tiny jacket and searched for injury.

Jakub made a grunt of protest and wriggled out of her grasping fingers, the stress of an all-male audience overriding his need for maternal care. "I'm all right, Mama." He sniffed, composing himself. "He didn't touch me . . . He was after you."

"My *heavens,*" the elder man exclaimed.

It took Argent a moment, but he recognized the man as the dramatic master of ceremonies from when he'd seen the play.

"I'm absolutely agog, how did you survive?"

Jakub pointed to where Argent held vigil by a mannequin laden with shawls. "Mr. Argent told the man to get the fuck out."

McTavish covered his snort of laughter behind a fit of coughs.

"Jakub!" Millie gasped.

"What?"

Her multitude of ringlets caught the lantern light and gleamed as dark as the eyes that darted up to stare at Argent as though only just realizing he was in the room.

He expected censure for his profanity in front of her boy but, in truth, he couldn't identify what swam in her gaze along with her tears. She didn't look angry.

Argent said nothing, deciding that was the safest course, and kept his own features firmly neutral, though he abruptly felt anything but.

"What I can't figure is how the villain got backstage." The theater employee pulled a white handkerchief out of his pocket and handed it to Millie, frowning when she used it to wipe Jakub's nose instead of her own eyes.

"Dear Lord." Millie's brow pinched with concern

"Do you remember anything else the intruder spoke of, lad?" McTavish asked, a pencil poised over a notepad he'd produced from the depths of his suit.

Jakub's eyes turned dead serious. "He said he wasn't going to hurt me . . . just you, Mama, and that he was going to deliver me."

"Deliver you where?" Even beneath her layers of paint, Millie's skin visibly paled.

The boy shrugged. "I don't know. Mr. Argent told him not to say your fuckin—"

Millie pressed her fingers over her son's lips. "Let's not repeat anything else that Mr. Argent said until you and I have a talk, all right?"

The boy nodded and his mother sent Argent a look that would have withered a lesser man.

Jakub nodded again and continued once his mouth was released. "He didn't say anything else, Mama. The man threw a knife at Mr. Argent and he smacked it, right out of the air!" The boy became more animated as he mimicked Argent's movements and pointed to the chink in the arabesque wallpaper where the knife had been embedded.

They all turned to examine it.

"Then Mr. Argent *kicked* him against the door." Millie had to lean away in order to dodge the errant foot of her son. "And took the knife from the wall and they *stabbed* at each other, but Mr. Argent made him drop his knife, and then threw him on the ground, and they rolled." The boy spun in a vertical adaptation of the motion. "And Mr. Argent pinned him down with a knife right above his eyes." A stabbing motion with his small hand sent a visible flinch through Millie. "He told me to look away."

"And did you?" the old actor asked, his eyes wide and enraptured by the story.

"I did, but then the police arrived. And Mr. Argent said—" The boy clamped his lips together between his teeth and pushed his glasses up for the umpteenth time. "I think I know which word you don't want me to say, now."

Millie reached out and softly took her son's hand, pulling him back into her arms where he squirmed for a moment, then relented. "You were such a brave boy." Argent could feel her trying to capture his gaze, but he couldn't bring himself to look directly at her.

"Where are these knives now?" McTavish queried.

"The one that was dropped is under Mama's skirts."

Millie made a choked sound and gathered armfuls of her costume until the blade was uncovered.

McTavish bent to retrieve it. "I should collect yers too, Argent, for evidence." He took one look at Argent's expression and blanched. "Or, ye keep it, this should be sufficient."

"Egad, man, did it truly occur the way the lad described?" The foppish man skirted mother and child and approached Argent.

"More or less."

"Well, Mr. Argent, was it? You are a champion if there ever was one. I am Mr. Kelsey Throckmorton, the master of ceremonies and stage manager for the Royal Opera House at Covent Garden, and let me be the first to extend you our sincere and humble gratitude for your heroics tonight on behalf of the belle of our stage."

Argent doubted there was anything sincere or humble about the man, but he nodded to him all the same.

With an overdramatic gesture Mr. Throckmorton asked, "Are you a particular . . . friend of our Miss LeCour's?" The question was so rife with innuendo it should have put off an odor.

Millie intervened. "Due to the danger I'm in, I've employed Mr. Argent for protection."

"Well." Throckmorton gave Argent a very thorough once-over. Twice. "That must cost you quite the pound of flesh."

Argent nodded again. He didn't have the weight quite right, but he'd certainly guessed the currency.

Chapter Thirteen

To Millie his regard was like a tangible caress reaching through the layers of her clothing and consciousness to touch places she'd previously been unaware of.

The year prior, she'd taken Jakub to the fair and a traveling snake charmer had the most extraordinary creature in a glass box. A long-fanged terror, the length and width of her arm, with a dark, unsettling rattle at the end of his tail. The performer had called him a viper of the New World and explained that when the creature coiled into a perfect spiral, it was at its most dangerous. The rattle warned that attack was imminent. And when the beast struck, Millie had never seen speed and lethal force of the kind before or since that day.

When Christopher Argent spoke in his low, silken voice, it evoked the memory of that warning rattle. One note, one inflection that rarely changed. An unmistakable warning that death could strike at any moment.

"Your gladiator is worth every penny, I'd wager," Throckmorton mused.

Something in the actor's voice set McTavish to squirming. He buttoned his coat and inched toward the door. "Miss LeCour, Argent, I'm certainly glad tonight ended as it did. I'll leave ye to yer evening for now, but expect a follow-up in the days to come."

Millie stood and only released Jakub with one hand,

which trembled as she offered it to McTavish, though her grateful smile was abjectly genuine. "Thank you, Inspector. I shall sleep better tonight knowing you have that fiend in your custody."

If Argent allowed her to sleep at all.

"A sentiment I share." McTavish paused. "And might I say I'm a rather fervent admirer of yers. I saw ye in Paris two years ago, if ye'd believe it. I'd just wandered into the theater needing to hear some of the Queen's English, and it was one of the most enjoyable experiences of my entire trip."

"You are too kind." Millie turned and addressed Throckmorton. "Please make certain that the inspector here has tickets to the next production, gratis, of course."

"Of course," Throckmorton agreed genially, though his eyes dimmed when McTavish quit the room.

She couldn't bring herself to look at Argent though his regard still raised chill bumps on her skin. Gratitude overshadowed her fear. He'd done as he promised and protected her boy.

But at a price.

Every time her eyes found the silent, disturbingly still man, his body hurled words at her that she'd rather ignore. His tremendous shoulders bespoke an uncompromising strength that hinted at a way of life far beyond her comprehension. What must a man do to build a frame such as his? What feats must he endure?

His arctic eyes said, *Approach at your peril.*

When in his vicinity, every survival instinct she possessed alerted the primitive woman within the cultured lady. *Run,* it told her. Run as fast and far as you are able, and pray that he doesn't choose to follow.

But part of her acknowledged there would be no escape. Not from him. He wasn't the sort of hunter to cull the weak from the herd. He honed in on his prey and was relentless in the chase, precise in the capture, and absolutely lethal.

Millie understood now, more than she had before, that evil had her and Jakub in its sights. That her destruction would be its persistent goal, turning her charmed reality into a twisted nightmare.

Christopher Argent was a creature born of nightmares, a man who looked evil in the face and challenged it to a duel. Millie acknowledged that in this instance, she didn't need a white knight, but a shadow that could traverse the darkness with the cunning and speed of that lethal viper.

It was the only way she and her son would survive this. He'd proven that tonight, when he'd saved her precious child. Every time she looked up at him, she was reminded that everything in this world had a price. And she'd gladly pay it for the boy clinging to her hand.

Her belly quivered.

It was time for the devil to collect his due.

"Let's get you home, my son." Millie gathered herself and Jakub, but the stage manager blocked the door.

"But darling, you forget, the theater benefactors will be gathering at the Costumes and Cocktails soiree in the grand foyer. How would it look if our star was not in attendance?"

Millie made a sound of disbelief. "But Mr. Throckmorton, after such an ordeal, you couldn't possibly expect—"

"No, no, of course *I* wouldn't, but the benefactors, you see, and the contract you signed . . . what would you say to the lawyers and solicitors?"

"I don't know what I'd say to them." The look she directed at Throckmorton caused him to step back. "But I'd take a word or two from Mr. Argent's vocabulary. Now I am bringing my distraught son *home* this instant and putting him to bed."

"But if you don't go, they might not pay you—"

"They'll pay her." Argent's voice cut through the room like a guillotine. "And you'll step out of her path."

The stage manager blanched.

Millie put a hand to her own throat. Heavens, that voice could probably command the sea if he so desired. Mr. Throckmorton trembled, and the assassin behind her hadn't even issued a legitimate threat.

He hadn't needed to.

Jakub tugged on her hand. "I'm not sleepy. I don't want to go home yet. I'm hungry."

"T-there, you see," Throckmorton stammered. "We'll serve food. Bring dear Jakub and your . . . protector. They're both well behaved enough to charm the contributors."

"Please, Mama?"

Millie looked down at Jakub, and then finally over to Argent, whose face could have been carved of stone for all it gave away. Did he want her to stay, to draw out the anticipation? Did he want to take her home, to collect what she owed him?

She couldn't tell. He gave her no cue.

What was she supposed to do with that?

A part of her wanted the charming Bentley Drummle back. He'd been so expressive, so friendly and interesting. Or was it interested? Either way, when they'd danced he'd swept her off her feet, quite literally, and though he'd made her nervous, she hadn't feared him.

What a fool she'd been.

And what an accomplished actor he was.

"I suppose we should stay long enough to make an appearance," she acquiesced. "And anything Mrs. Brimtree prepared would be cold by now."

Jakub made a face.

"Oh, wonderful! I'll just go check on the preparations whilst you . . . attend your toilette." With that, he rushed out the door with an impressive speed for someone of his size.

Millie glanced at her reflection in one of the vanity's many mirrors and grimaced. She was a sodden mess. Hassan's masterfully lined eyes were ruined by her tears of fear and subsequent relief.

"Lord, I look dreadful." Collapsing onto her vanity bench, she rested her face in her hands for a moment until two small arms encircled her waist.

"Just smudged, Mama, we'll fix it."

Millie patted him, her chest swollen with love and still more abject gratitude that he'd been spared a terrible fate this night. "I'll fix it. Why don't you gather your things and I'll have a stage boy hire a carriage and pack it out?"

"Yes, Mama, but do let's hurry. I am hungry." He scrambled to his corner and meticulously began to pack up his art supplies.

Facing the mirrors, Millie turned the wick up on the lantern, illuminating her red eyes and fraught demeanor. Her hands shook as she reached for her powder; she met a pair of intense blue eyes from behind her. He still said nothing, so she took his lead and kept her own confidence, blending her makeup with movements that had become as familiar as breathing.

It seemed as though her gaze were an unruly lapdog, and he held the leash, jerking her notice back to him with undeniable dominance every couple of seconds.

"I—wish you wouldn't stare like that, it isn't polite."

"Shouldn't you be accustomed to people watching you?" His eyes deftly followed her hand as it swiped new rouge on her cheeks.

"It's true, Mama, people stare at you always," Jacob chimed in from the corner.

Perhaps she should stop encouraging the little darling to speak his mind.

The liquid kohl felt pleasant and chilly next to her warm, puffy eyes as she applied the liner with a brush.

She'd never get it as good as Hassan had, and her trembling hands made it all the more difficult, but she finally swiped an acceptable line and darkened her lashes, as well. Crimson rouge turned her mouth into a rose petal. Finished, she stood and gathered a shawl, pulling it around her sixteenth-century costume.

Argent rose when she did, his shoulders filling the space in which he stood. How had this dressing room ever contained more people than this with a man of his size in here? She couldn't avoid him. She couldn't face him.

He was so tall. So remote. His height removed him from anyone in his vicinity, forcing him to look down upon them like a mountain would the hills beneath it.

And soon enough, she'd *be* beneath him.

Something warm and wet awoke within her. Something dormant until this very moment, or maybe it had never existed until now. Until him . . .

"I'm ready, Mama."

Thank God.

She took Jakub's hand, and he squeezed. "Your hands are cold." He giggled. "Even through your gloves."

"Sorry, *kochanie,*" she mumbled absently as she all but dragged him toward the door. Her hands and feet *felt* cold, as though all the blood had drained from them and now hurried to her pounding heart and rushed in her throbbing ears.

The large assassin shadowed them down the hall, without her bidding him to do so, and though she knew he was working on her behalf, it still made her spine tingle to have such a man behind her.

Actors and stagehands alike stopped to ask after her and Jakub, showing their concern and gladness, but then demanding the entire story. She begged off, promising to regale them later and trying very hard not to resent their curiosity.

Millie paused at the door that led from the stage to the carpeted staircase that would take them to the grand foyer below. She took a bracing breath and affixed a smile to her lips that she forced into her eyes with painful effort.

They wouldn't stay long, she thought as she pressed through the door. The carpets beneath her slippers were plush and silent, though the dark red that she'd once found enchanting threatened to give her a headache.

Peering over the dark banister embellished with gold filigree, Millie noted that some of the cast had already arrived. Rynd, the Othello to her Desdemona, tall and handsome, stood out like a dark and sinewy wolf in a pen full of fluffy, bleating sheep.

He made twice the predator, kissing every lily-white glove and charming every vapid lady with an off-color compliment and a saucy grin. Jane, her dearest friend, deftly avoided the roaming hands of their husbands in the corner by the punch bowl and hors d'oeuvres.

Millie looked down on them with trepidation. Like sparkling butterflies, the noble ladies of the *ton* drifted from one to another in a swirl of silks, chiffons, and pretense. Their escorts clustered in dapper, expensive black suits, their hands gesturing with the fervency of moth wings in pristine white gloves.

What if someone in the crowd below wanted her dead?

Charles Dorshaw was imprisoned now, to be sure, but he was a hired hand. The second one to make an attempt on her life in as many weeks. Was this what her life had become? Every admirer and theater enthusiast would now be a suspected enemy? She would look for malice beneath propriety.

And for what? What did anyone have to gain from her death?

She started at an abrupt outburst of applause, and blinked rapidly as she became aware that the entire assembly had turned their delighted faces up to her. She'd been announced.

This was her cue.

Unwrapping stiff, cold fingers from their death grip on the banister, she lifted her hand in a wave, hoping the warmth and delight she shoved into her smile didn't look as brittle as it felt. Adding a little modesty to the expression, she descended the stairs gripping Jakub's hand like a lifeline.

Argent was only a step behind her, and she speculated at how many people were really concentrating on his cold, brutal, and imposing features. Did anyone recognize him? And if they did, was it because they'd hired him to end her life?

Chapter Fourteen

At the sound of Mr. Throckmorton bellowing her name, Millie swallowed the buttered crab crumpet her son had handed to her and ran her tongue over her teeth to make sure no vestiges of food lingered. Screwing on her smile, she turned to the stage manager, inwardly cursing his name with the gusto of a foulmouthed dock pirate. She'd been in attendance at the soiree for a grueling hour and a half. Indeed she was pretty certain she'd met everyone, smiled at them, complimented them, and done her best not to outright ask if they might have a reason to wish her demise, or Jakub's capture.

Her cheeks felt weathered, and she worried others could see them twitching with strain. She'd only just found a moment to eat, could she not be left in peace?

Christopher Argent, mysterious as always, lingered behind her the entire evening, and said little unless it was to offer a brief answer to the myriad of questions thrown at them from every direction. Everyone from her acting associates to the Marchioness of Woolerton wanted to know just who was this new companion of hers. Nordic nobility, perhaps? An Irishman? Someone from the emerging wealthy industrial merchant class? Or worse, an American?

As she and Argent deftly fielded their queries, Millie found herself struggling to not ask a few intrusive questions of her own, such as, had any of them recently employed an assassin or two? Though perhaps people in this class used an unscrupulous proxy for such dealings, like Mr. Dashforth, so the likelihood of them recognizing Mr. Argent was very slim.

Throckmorton reminded her of a French bulldog as his round, squat body bounded up to her with unabashed enthusiasm. "Millie, darling, I want to introduce you to the most important people you may ever have the pleasure of making acquaintance with." He tugged on her elbow toward a pair of couples retrieving champagne from a footman who balanced several crystal glasses on a silver tray.

An uncommonly tall and especially thin gentleman with hair the color of honey and eyes the color of a summer sky handed champagne to a petite, dark-haired woman with exotic, catlike features.

Mr. Throckmorton motioned to them and whispered behind his bejeweled hand, "Lord and Lady Thurston, the Earl and Countess Thurston. Please make certain to compliment them heartily as Lord Thurston has been a longstanding contributor to the theater."

Millie nodded, used to this sort of thing. Half her job as an actress seemed to be charming potential donors. "What about the other two?" she whispered.

"The Viscount Benchley and his wife. Lord Gordon St. Vincent, the Viscount Benchley, is Lady Thurston's younger brother. He's a notorious letch and ne'er-do-well with not a shilling to speak of until his father, an earl of some wealth and consequence, leaves him the title and estates. Pay him no mind unless Lady Thurston seems to think you should."

"I see." Millie nodded, casting a longing look back toward the table, first at her son, who stood next to the ever-alert Argent, and then at the food. With a preparatory smile, she lifted an invisible curtain and began to play her part.

"Lord and Lady Benchley, Lord and Lady Thurston, may I present Miss Millicent LeCour, the pride of the London stage?" Throckmorton thrust her forward.

Millie beamed at them all and dipped a curtsy. With practiced charm, she said, "What an exquisite pleasure to make your acquaintance. I do hope you enjoyed the performance."

"Now if you'll kindly pardon me, I see the Duke of Renton over there and he's promised me a cask of his famous wine." Throckmorton abandoned her to his guests with practiced ease.

He would pay for this.

Gordon St. Vincent was, indeed, handsome. Lean and elegant in the way of poetic gentlemen, but with robust good looks, curly dark hair, and high color that belonged to an enthusiast of the outdoors.

"*Enjoyment* is a crass word for what we experienced due to your transcendent performance, Miss LeCour. I was so personally enraptured by you that I demanded Throckmorton make an introduction. And now that he has, I have decided we simply *must* become better acquainted." The young man's enamored fervor was a common occurrence in Millie's experience, though gentlemen usually waited until their wives were out of earshot before taking such obvious liberties.

Millie cast a glance at Lady Benchley, a plump woman with pleasant features and the most astounding wealth of auburn hair she'd ever seen, who stood physically apart from the family, both figuratively and literally.

"A pleasure to meet you both, Lord and Lady Benchley."

The viscountess stepped toward Millie and her husband, but he held up a hand as though to warn her off.

In an instant, Argent was at Millie's side, his elbow

grazing hers with a strange, electric sensation that she credited to the wool of his evening coat. She glanced at him, and though his features remained the same as ever, she read a tension in him. A ready wariness that made her uneasy.

Did he know these people?

The ladies certainly gawked at him with wide eyes, and their fans fluttered with more haste.

She paid particular attention to them all, her anxiety thrumming closer to the surface. Nothing struck her as out of the ordinary, though Argent stiffened next to her as Lord Thurston bent over her hand. Which seemed odd, really, because it was Lord Gordon St. Vincent whose kiss had lingered for much too long.

A sharp breath from the sentinel beside her drew everyone's notice, and Millie was able to retrieve her hand from Lord Thurston's clutches.

She gestured to Argent. "I'd like you to meet my escort, Mr. Argent."

Lady Thurston's fan fluttered as she dipped a curtsy. "Mr. Argent, did I not see you enter the offices of our solicitor, Sir Gerald Dashforth, earlier today?"

"I'm sure you didn't," Argent replied lightly.

"It's only that there aren't many men of your size," she remarked blithely. "You're quite unmistakable."

"Except there must be, because you are mistaken." Argent said this with a tight smile, and Millie could feel her brow knit together as she glanced up to him. Dashforth was the name of the solicitor who'd hired Argent to kill her. He had, indeed, gone there this very afternoon. Why lie about it?

"A damn shame about old Dashforth," Gordon St. Vincent chimed in. "Scotland Yard found him garroted this very afternoon."

Millie gasped, her hand covering her mouth. Though

Argent didn't react to her outburst, Millie knew he'd done it, that he had killed the man after leaving her in the baths. Why? Had it been warranted? Had they fought each other, or had Argent committed cold-blooded murder only hours before?

"See here, Gordy," Lord Thurston chastised his brother-in-law. With his dark blue eyes blazing, Millie thought that he must be frowning under his silver-peppered mustache. "The ladies needn't hear about such violent behavior, especially when they so narrowly missed it. We don't want them distraught, do we?"

Gordon waved him off. "They're the ones who insisted we come tonight." His lascivious gaze drifted back to Millie. "And I'm utterly glad we attended."

Argent's fists tightened at his sides.

Adept at dodging unwanted attentions, Millie turned to Viscount Benchley's wife.

Lady Benchley's voluptuous form appeared more statuesque in comparison to the slender St. Vincent's. The unfortunate cut of the lace on her dress didn't seem to be helping matters at all. She was tall for a woman, almost as tall as her husband, which perhaps explained why he preferred not to stand next to her. Millie found herself pitying the viscountess, as the slump of her wide shoulders expressed more about her than any polite words ever could.

Her smile created charming dimples, though, and Millie was struck by the abject beauty of her jade eyes. If she'd only look up more often, and perhaps worn more becoming gowns, she'd be a rather lovely woman. Millie truly envied her thick, voluminous hair.

"You were wonderful tonight, Miss LeCour," Lady Benchly ventured, and your costume is lovely. I adore the fashions of the mid-sixteenth century. All those pearls and luxurious velvet; I find it terribly romantic, don't you?"

"Utterly romantic. And thank you for your kindness."

Millie offered her a genuine smile, though both her mind and pulse were racing. These people . . . why did they put Argent off so? Did one of them want her dead?

"It takes a certain . . . economy of figure such as yours, Miss LeCour, to wear a style like that and not make it look like a Bedouin tent." Lord Benchley stepped forward and addressed his wife with barely leashed disdain. "Some women are lucky that velvet is no longer the fashion, aren't they, my dear?"

Lady Thurston heartily agreed, a malicious enjoyment glittering in her eyes. "Yes, and that color would make you seem a ghastly yellow, Philomena. Only someone with porcelain skin and lovely dark hair like Miss LeCour could bring such a historical garment to life."

To call the expression on Philomena St. Vincent's face crestfallen would have been putting it kindly. Something about the bruised, wretched unhappiness drawn upon her features left no doubt that the woman was ill-treated and entirely lonely. Her eyes returned to the floor, and desolation rippled from her in an almost palpable wave.

Instinctively, Millie rushed to her rescue. "Oh, but Lady Benchley, what any woman wouldn't give for your uncommonly lovely hair, and those breathtaking eyes of yours. Your coloring, milady, is indeed enviable."

"I've always preferred dark hair and pale skin." St. Vincent kicked dirt on his wife's proverbial coffin. "The contrast is rather . . . exotic, wouldn't you agree, Thurston?" The brothers-in-law both examined Millie in a way that caused her to fervently wish she were fat, and golden-haired.

"You are too kind to me, Miss LeCour," the viscountess informed the crimson carpets.

Millie wanted to escape this cruel, miserable family as quickly as possible, and began to think of excuses to do so.

"You really are," Lady Thurston agreed. "Much too kind to her." Her shrewd, dark eyes drifted down to Jakub and sharpened to a razor's point. "And *who* is this charming dear boy?"

"This is my son, Jakub." Millie didn't want to introduce Jakub to these awful people.

Her son clutched her skirts with one hand, but offered a shy bow as his manners dictated.

"A son?" Gordon St. Vincent let out a chuckle that ended on a bitter note. "Would that either of us knew what that was like, eh, Fenwick?" He elbowed his brother-in-law in a gesture of collusion, but the earl merely slid him a look of exasperation. "I'm getting too deucedly old to be the dashing young St. Vincent heir anymore. I've been married five years, and Fenwick twice that long. You'd think an heir would appear after a decade from one of us."

A terrible stillness permeated the undertones of the gathering. Glasses clinked around them, and the chandelier glimmered off noble opulence. The assembly's diamonds sparkled with the effervescence of their expensive champagne as they laughed and drank and by all accounts enjoyed themselves. Every one of them oblivious to the dangerous vibrations building in their corner that Millie couldn't quite understand.

Just who *were* these horrid people, and what the devil was going on here?

"What lovely blue eyes your child has." Lady Thurston bent to inspect Jakub and then straightened to tug at her apathetic husband's sleeve. "It's extraordinary that her son's eyes should be so blue when Miss LeCour's are so dark, don't you think so, darling?"

"What?" The man covered a yawn with the back of one white glove. "Oh, certainly, my dear. What did you say his name was?" he asked disinterestedly.

Millie glanced up at Argent, signaling for him to save

her, but he stared at Lord Thurston with uncharacteristic intensity. "Jakub, my lord, his name is Jakub."

In an instant, Lord Thurston resembled a hound *en pointe*.

Millie wanted to be mistaken when she saw the wonderment with which he considered her son. She wanted to shove Jakub behind her skirts.

"Jakub, you say? You don't come across that name often, do you, boy?" Fenwick gave Jakub an arrested stare.

"No, milord," her son answered solemnly.

"It's more commonplace in our native Poland." Millie had to strain a bit more to moderate her voice. Something had opened a pit of dread deep within her. She had the sense she'd stepped into a den of vipers, and not for the first time, she was relieved to have their king at her side.

"Poland?" Thurston could have been struck in the face for all the astonishment he conveyed. "How old are you, boy?"

"I have nine years, sir."

The look Lord Thurston gave Millie could have incinerated every building in Covent Garden. She read confusion, anger, and disbelief in his wrathful glare.

"You're being ridiculous, David, really." Katherine Fenwick took her husband by the arm. "Can't you see you're distressing the child with your silly questions?"

"I think he's shy," Lady Benchley ventured. "Perhaps we're embarrassing him with all our notice?" She offered Jakub a kind smile.

"Yes," Lord Benchley hissed, his hand snaking out and seizing his wife by the elbow with bruising force. She paled and bit her lip, her large eyes filling with pain and moisture. "Why unsettle the child with our consideration when it is Miss LeCour who should be the focus of our undivided attentions?"

Argent stepped forward, cutting off Millie's caustic

reply. "Miss LeCour's attentions are already promised to *me* this evening." Though his tone was pleasant, his glare could have frozen the flames in the candles, and left no question as to the salaciousness of his insinuations.

For all they knew he was a lover, staking a claim. Most actresses had consorts in the open, why should she be any different?

And still her cheeks burned, because this was no act. She'd promised him that tonight she was his.

He turned to her, the arrangement of his features communicating nothing, but something about the way he pressed toward her and Jakub with his size conveyed to Millie that he'd had enough. "The carriage is waiting. Excuse us." He guided her toward the door without so much as a by-your-leave.

Millie had to admit, she appreciated the expressions of outrage and indignation he'd left in their wake, though she did *not* appreciate being herded like so much sheep.

"My cloak," she protested.

"There's a blanket in the carriage," he said through gritted teeth.

"How would you know?" She paused, searching for Mr. Throckmorton in the crowd and noting all the whispers directed at her from behind lace fans and snifters of expensive liquor. "Not all the hired carriages have blankets, and I can't just take my leave without—"

Argent bent down to press his lips close to her ear. "If I have to listen to those fucking people for one more moment, I'll spill their entrails on the floor in front of everyone. The choice is yours."

Millie could feel her eyes peel wide, and knew those who stared at her assumed her lover had just whispered something salacious and lustful in her ear.

How wrong they were.

It wasn't the violence in his threat that shocked her the

most. It was the ardent manner in which they were delivered. Heat flickered in those words, the first heat she'd heard in that ever-arctic voice of his. And Millie had the feeling that if any warmth trickled to the surface, an inferno billowed beneath it.

"Very well, let's go." She clutched Jakub tighter and followed him out to where a row of lavish carriages lined Bow Street.

Millie pressed a glove to her heated cheek; the chilly air felt good and the darkness enveloped her with a strange sort of release, though the thought of poor Philomena St. Vincent weighed heavily on her conscience.

"I think Lord Benchley hurt Lady Philomena, Mama," Jakub worried aloud.

"I think so too, darling. What a villainous beast. I'm of a mind to tell someone."

The other theatergoers parted for them on the narrow walk as Argent led them in the direction opposite to Flower Street where a police wagon lurked and something dark was being scrubbed from the paved stones.

"Telling anyone wouldn't do you any good," he informed them dryly. "St. Vincent is within his rights as a husband to treat her how he likes."

"And I'm within my rights as a woman to kick him in the—" She looked down at her son, whose eyes drooped with weariness. "The shins," she finished, deciding he'd heard enough vulgarity for one night.

Argent turned and considered her from beneath a heavy brow. "If you like, I could—"

"Don't—finish that sentence." She held her hand up. She'd never even struck someone in her life, she wasn't about to go around flippantly ordering their murders.

No matter how badly they deserved it.

He shrugged and paused next to a luxurious conveyance with a resplendent matching set of dark stallions.

"Surely we're not . . . absconding with someone's carriage," she whispered.

His look could have dried all the lakes in Cumbria. "This carriage is mine, and I've already had someone stow Jakub's art supplies inside. *And* your cloak."

Though the carriage had no footman, the driver leaped down and opened their door.

"Thank you, Mr. Argent," Jakub called as he scrambled inside. "Mama, it's soft in here!"

Millie faltered, peering into the blue silk and velvet interior with an impending sense of finality. She felt like the proverbial sacrificial virgin. This was the point of no return. The threshold from this side of her harrowing day, to the other side. To his domain. Or lair. Argent seemed like the kind of man who would have a lair. Like a troll, or one of the monsters from the penny dreadfuls.

Or the devil.

A glance back at him pressed her to take the driver's hand and allow him to lift her inside.

She'd been a fool to even consider she'd had a choice.

Chapter Fifteen

Now she was alone with a monster.

Or might as well be, for in the quarter hour it took to be free of the carriage traffic on Bow Street, Jakub had slumped into Millie's lap, and the only sound that permeated the thick silence between them was his soft, intermittent snoring.

"We could have walked, you know," she stated. "I reside on the next street over, and we'd be there by now."

"We're not going to your apartments. I'm taking you somewhere more secure."

She'd known that, somehow, but she'd wanted to hear him say it. "But the Brimtrees, they'll worry."

"I sent word."

"Of course you did," she huffed. The highhanded lout. Lord, she would have some explaining to do when she returned home. "Did you warn them? Are they safe?"

"If you're not there, it does mitigate the possibility that anyone else would attempt to collect on the contract, so yes, they're safer."

Millie peered at the man seated across from her in the carriage. There wasn't a lantern illuminating the inside, so only the glow from the streets seeped through a few cracks in the velvet drapes and slashed pale shards of light across his still form. One of those shards drew a jagged line over his eyes, one ear, and the blue silk upon which he rested his head.

She'd been right in her earlier musings, that dark blue behind his head painted his disconcerting eyes an even lighter shade. Something like a glacier floating above water. They looked almost inhuman, in a way she'd not noticed before. It was as though darkness sought him out, as though shadows settled upon him, recognizing one of their own, and he siphoned strength from them. This was where he belonged. Cold, eerie nights full of danger and blood.

"Did you murder Mr. Dashforth?"

"Did you fuck them all, or just him?"

They spoke at once, but his question rang through the carriage, snuffing hers into oblivion.

Millie released a shocked gasp that resembled a cough and didn't speak until the next time she heard her son snore. "I—*heartily* beg your pardon," she spat.

"Thurston, did you only fuck him, or did you have Gordon St. Vincent as well? They're a randy lot, and Gordon St. Vincent and his father, the earl, often have those masqueraded, orgiastic gatherings you described. Is that why they give so much to the theater? Do you pay them in trade . . . like you're paying me?"

Millie could count on one hand the times she'd been struck truly speechless. In fact, most people made the context a somewhat ironic paradox because they spoke in order to point out their speechlessness. But outrage and disgust paralyzed her tongue to the roof of her mouth and she could only stare in dumb amazement.

"I don't ask to condemn you." He correctly read the unmitigated outrage on her face. "Only to clarify the situation. We've both obviously had intercourse—"

"I'll thank you to keep your voice *down*." She put her gloves over Jakub's ear, and though he twitched, the rhythm of his breathing didn't falter.

Argent's lids shuttered his expression. "I'll admit . . . I wanted to kill them, though they'd done me no disservice and issued no insult. I *wanted* to spill their blood. To break every part of them that had touched you, starting with their fingers."

"Don't." Millie held up her hand against him.

"It's why I had to make this bargain, I expect. Why I must have you. Because you make me want to—" He paused, eyes moving in their sockets as though searching for a word. "You make me . . . want."

"Stop," she hissed in a dramatic whisper. This habit he had of chilling and concise honesty. It unsettled her. Disturbed her. She, who lived among people whose livelihood depended on being someone else a great deal of the time. Performers, the lot of them, much of their memorized rhetoric spilled over into their lives, and they borrowed from the minds of great thinkers and emotional writers to express their own needs, to seduce, and to survive. They were students and conveyors of the human condition, and a great part of that condition was deceit.

But not this strange and stoic man. He revealed what others wouldn't dare. His uncommon fearlessness wasn't contained to the physical, but also to the emotional. For someone so impervious to emotion, he certainly wasn't oblivious to it. And Millie was starting to believe that he shared with her the entirety of his limited emotional experience, at least the ones that pertained to her.

A man who didn't lie. Who didn't flatter, or seduce, or elaborate.

Did such a man really exist?

"I've upset you," he observed. "Perhaps because I've insinuated that you're a prostitute?"

Millie glared at him, mostly upset because, in all honestly, she couldn't say she wasn't one. "Not that it's any of your business, but I will tell you with absolute certainty that before tonight, I'd never in my life been introduced to those wretched people."

"You seemed to enjoy their company." His brow lowered, casting a shadow over his gaze. It was apparent that he didn't believe her.

"It's called acting. I was merely being polite. You can't honestly believe I enjoyed a *moment* of that interaction?"

"I know nothing about what you enjoy."

"Obviously." The sharpness in Millie's tone surprised even her. Was it wise to speak to a professional killer in such a manner? Likely not. But wisdom was never really something she'd been credited with an abundance of.

Unfortunately.

She had the habit of speaking before her thoughts told her the better of it, and maybe now was a good time to start working on that.

They were silent for a long moment, listening to the clip of the horse's shoes against the cobbles, or the sound of Jakub sleeping the undisturbed sleep of the innocent.

"My mother was a prostitute." The words were spoken so softly, Millie wondered if she'd imagined them.

"What?"

He leaned forward, releasing his features from the light. "Her name was Christine, and she was a whore."

Millie blinked, her breath faltering as he leaned closer in the darkness. "Why would you say that to me?" she whispered.

He shifted. "I don't know. I've never said it to anyone else. Perhaps I told you because I wanted you to understand that I meant you no offense. I don't share society's opinion of prostitutes. Because of the lustful nature of a man's needs, or maybe because of the intrinsic beauty of the fairer sex, a woman's body is a commodity, one that men barter for with land and titles and sometimes even kingdoms. So why then, when a woman sells her own body for food, or survival, or even pleasure, is it called a sin? Or a crime? What has marriage become but sanctioned prostitution, the buying and selling of female flesh for the begetting of heirs and so forth?"

Millie understood in that moment that Christopher Argent would never cease to astonish her. She couldn't even begin to answer that question. Partly because his point made a great deal of sense, and partly because he'd left out so many variables. What about love? What about two souls, and *yes*, bodies, committing themselves to each other for the entirety of their lives? There was protection of joint properties, and the promise of a man to hold to one woman and care for the children they had together.

But, in all honesty, how many marriages did she know of that had more of a basis along his perception than hers?

Well. Drat.

The carriage rolled to a smooth stop, blessedly cutting off the need for a reply.

But then, a new fear arose. They'd arrived . . . somewhere. The place he'd planned on stashing them until he could guarantee their safety.

Until she'd fulfilled her part of the bargain. Before they embarked, she had to know what had happened this afternoon. "Did you murder Mr. Dashforth?" she repeated.

His jaw worked over the answer before he gave it to her. "Yes."

"Why?" She hoped—no—prayed that he'd give her the answer she needed, the one that could appease her smarting conscience. That would calm her growing panic.

Argent leaned forward, eyes leaving the slash of light and his great body invading her space, her air, until she could feel his warm breath on her chilled skin.

"Because he threatened your life, hired Dorshaw to kill you, and take your child. He told me he wouldn't relent." His hand lifted, and Millie flinched, so it dropped back into the shadows. "I'm going to kill anyone who means you and your son harm." His voice was hard as stone in the darkness. "Can you live with that?"

Millie considered for a few shaky breaths. Her son was draped limply in her arms, secure in the notion that she, his mother, would protect him. She was all he had in this world, and she had to accept that she didn't have the skills or the necessary brutality to keep him safe during this nightmare.

"I—I can." Millie wanted to take the words back, but knew she'd never be able to.

Knew that she'd meant them.

She started when he opened the door and leaped to the ground without the need of the steps. Turning, he held his arms out and gestured for her to hand him Jakub.

Millie hesitated, feeling as if she were about to put a bunny in the jaws of a wolf. But, she realized, she was in for a penny, might as well be a pound. He'd promised not to hurt them, and he'd proven himself by his treatment of Jakub thus far.

Lifting his shoulders, she rolled her son so Argent could lean in and take the boy, one arm beneath his knees, and the other behind his neck. Jakub twitched and snorted loudly, but settled into Argent's heavy arms, and turned his head into his suit coat, where he promptly drooled on the lapel.

If Argent noticed, he paid it no heed.

The driver lowered the steps for her, and she thanked him as he steadied her until she was on solid ground.

Millie straightened the skirts of her costume, looked up, and gaped.

Pillars the color of rich cream provided a contrasting circle to the precise angles of stories and stories of pale stones. Neat hedgerows provided friendly cover to imposing iron gates. Millie reached out and used one of those stones to prop herself up.

"You . . . *live* in Belgravia?"

He nodded as the driver unlocked the gate and pulled it open wide enough for them to enter. "Blackwell thought it best if one of us were stationed at each end of the park whilst in London. He's in Mayfair, and I'm here in Belgravia keeping an eye on things, as it were."

"And this is *your* . . . house?" At his urging, she stumbled through the gate and made her way on unsteady legs to the arched front door. To call it a house seemed like a sacrilege. A Grecian temple was more apropos.

He followed with his usual long strides. "I believe most of us here in Belgravia lease from Lord Grosvenor, the Marquess of Westminster," he mused.

The door swung open on well-oiled hinges and a tall, white-gloved butler stepped out with the march of a soldier.

"Master Argent, welcome home." His voice seemed to propagate mostly in his astoundingly large nose.

Argent nodded and climbed the few marble steps to the door. "Welton,"

The butler did not stand aside to let his employer pass. "It is customary, Master Argent, for the guest to enter the home first. Especially if that guest is a lady." He flicked a meaningful, birdlike glance from dark glass-bead eyes, down to where Millie stood at the bottom of the stairs, her breath puffing from her open mouth.

"Oh." Argent stepped to the side and waited.

Lifting her skirts, Millie hurried up the stairs and paused at the threshold before crossing it at the butler's behest.

She didn't know what she expected to find inside the stately mansion, but this most certainly wasn't it. In the grand marble foyer, beneath the indecently expensive Irish crystal chandelier and lovely blue French wallpaper was . . .

Nothing.

Other than the faded rectangles and ovals on the paper, stained skeletons of a previous tenant's art, Millie could find no signs of occupancy.

Her slippers echoed off the bare walls and floors with an eerie and empty sound. Where had he brought them? She turned to Argent with anxious questions in her eyes and he was looking about the place as though he'd never seen it before.

"Welton . . . I didn't think about this, but I need you to find a place for the boy to sleep. I don't think we have any—"

"Already done, sir. When you mentioned you might have guests I ordered a room for the little master here on the second floor overlooking the park. Follow me, if you please." Hands clasped stiffly behind him, Welton took the left side of two grand staircases and Argent silently followed. He carried her sleeping son as if he were no heavier than an afterthought, and more precious than gold.

As she trailed them in the dim house, she couldn't miss the way Argent's muscles shifted beneath his coat, absorbing his movements and keeping the boy as comfortable and immobile as possible.

The gesture seemed so easy, so simple, and yet so incredibly out of character that Millie caught herself on a soft sigh.

Christopher Argent was truly an enigma. Empty house, empty eyes, empty heart . . . or so she'd thought.

But what if she was wrong about him? What if his heart was not so vacant as she'd initially assumed?

Intricate lanterns lit the hallways of his home, made ever wider by their lack of objets d'art, and only interrupted by thick, dark wood doors.

Welton paused at one on the left and opened it, sweeping a hand for them to step through. It became instantly obvious that he knew the visiting child would be male. Done in shades of green, the chamber couldn't have been more of a contradiction to the rest of the house. Toys, models, books, and all manner of furniture surrounded the modestly sized bed like a besieging army.

"This was kind of you, Mr. Welton, but I don't think we'll by staying long enough to make all this worth your trouble." Millie turned to the aging butler.

Welton sniffed, and looked down over his considerable nose. "Not at all, madam, it is my job to see to the needs of any guests under my master's care." Though his features were neither soft, nor friendly, Millie could swear that he winked at her.

"Well, that is appreciated." Trailing Argent to the bed, she feared he'd trip on something or other, but her worry proved needless. She bent to pull the blankets back and looked on as he took care while settling Jakub beneath the counterpane.

The bed was more plush than she'd expected as she sat and began to undo the laces on her son's shoes. Argent stood by and watched, his constant regard making her usually nimble fingers clumsy and slow.

"Why not leave the shoes?" he queried.

She looked at him askance. "I'm making him comfortable, and I don't want his shoes to dirty the sheets."

He nodded and waited until both boots were resting by the bed.

Standing, she began to divest Jakub's tiny limp form from his jacket.

"Why make him comfortable, he's already asleep?"

Exasperated, she stood, putting her fists on both hips. "Are you going to stand sentinel all night, or could you possibly allow me a moment with my son?"

His jaw clenched, and for a brief second, she worried he'd refuse.

"I could have lost him today," she said more gently. "I just need a few minutes."

As he glanced down at Jakub, his jaw worked to the side, then he nodded, shifting to one foot to move around her.

Millie's sigh of relief was cut short by his giant hand gripping her upper arm with all the strength of an iron shackle. His eyes burned down at her, a molten flame melting the ice she'd begun to expect from his gaze.

She didn't know now which she found more terrifying.

"Ten minutes." His hand tightened, but then something flickered in his eyes and she caught what she could have called a wince before he released her. "Ten minutes and then you're mine." He swept to the doorway that Welton had vacated.

"I'm done waiting."

Millie didn't breathe until the door closed behind him.

Ten minutes. She almost couldn't consider it.

Her hand shook as she pulled the blanket up over her son, brushed a lock of his hair off his forehead, and watched those angelic eyes flutter behind closed lids. Good dreams, she hoped. Something that didn't include this new world of theirs full of danger and assassins and the consequences of the past.

Ten minutes.

Or nine, now. As she looked down into the face of her precious boy, she knew it would take all the time he'd allotted her to prepare, but she'd do what she promised. The curve of his round cheek glowed in the soft light of the lantern, and as she pondered it, Millie found herself wondering about the man to whom she belonged for the night.

He'd mentioned a mother. A whore. But in the darkness of the carriage, she thought that she'd heard something like nostalgia lurking in his otherwise monotone voice. A man like Argent . . . It was easier to think he'd been birthed from a shadowy hell-mouth in some dark, forbidden place. Already a lethal, brutal man with no conscience. It was as if he'd been put together by something darker and infinitely more cruel than God. Like pieces were missing.

But that couldn't be, could it?

Once he'd been small like the child in front of her. Helpless. Maybe even innocent.

Had he been born, as some were, with the desire to kill? With the urge to take a life? Or had he been created by some dastardly villain who shaped him into the man he was? What if his missing peices had been ripped away from him? What if his brutality, his proclivity for violence and bloodletting, reached into the bedchamber as well?

Tears pricked Millie's eyes and she rapidly blinked them away, she couldn't tell if they were tears of fear or of compassion, but she did know one thing. She hated to cry for no reason. Besides, these questions were useless, because in a matter of minutes, she'd know the answers.

I'm done waiting, he'd said.

Well, she supposed they both were.

CHAPTER SIXTEEN

The consistent sting and burn of his stitching needle did not produce the effect Argent desired. Of course, the thread he kept on hand in the washroom pulled the sliced flesh of his forearm back together, but the pain did little to alleviate the erection abrading against his trousers. He couldn't tell which discomfort irritated him more, the cut or his cock.

Since the slice was a defensive wound on the underside of his dominant forearm, he had to seek out the only mirror in his entire cavernous place and use his less dexterous hand to do the stitching, while trying to work backwards from the reflection in the glass.

His efforts at a clean stitch had been thwarted more than once, and he'd had to start over. In fact, he might be doing more damage to the skin than good. He hadn't initially realized how long the gash was, though it wasn't incredibly deep. The bandage had kept it from bleeding too much, but carrying the child had caused it to ooze.

Ten minutes. Maybe he should have given her more time.

He'd divested himself of his bloodstained shirt and bade Welton bring him a clean bandage.

Welton set the supplies on the long bench built into the wall beneath the only washroom window. "If you'd allow me, Master Argent, I could stitch your wound in a jiffy," he offered.

"I'm not in the habit of letting other people near me with sharp objects, even if it is only a needle." Welton knew that, of course, but the man always offered.

"Very good, sir, but might I suggest you put on your clean shirt lest you frighten the lady."

Brows drawing together, Argent considered it. Perhaps he should have been better prepared for this. For the first time in a score of years, he took a moment to truly study his reflection.

He really was an unsightly bastard. Though he knew his strong features could compel others at times, he was fairly certain his body would disgust them. His torso stood as a large chronicle of a life of abject, unceasing violence.

Argent flexed his shoulder and arm, smooth muscle rippling beneath a web of badly healed burns stretched over a body that had grown exponentially in height and girth since the wound had been inflicted.

While Welton unfolded the starched white shirt, this one loose and casual, Argent counted two bullet wounds, seven knife gashes, and he couldn't even imagine what his back looked like. He'd once been wounded by a cattle prod a sadistic guard had brought to make the prisoners work harder.

That had been a terrible day. A terrible, blood-soaked day. He was pretty certain those scars still remained, though he'd never much cared to look.

What would Millie see when she encountered him like this? A killer? A protector? A coercer?

A lover?

A monster was more likely.

"I think you're correct, Welton, I think I should like that shirt."

It took some doing for the two of them to dress him and keep the shirt clean, but once he was buttoned into the garment, the right sleeve rolled up past his elbow, he resumed the tedious chore of stitching the flesh closed.

"I will be nearby if you or Miss LeCour have need of me," Welton informed him, more inflection or meaning in his voice than Argent had ever before noted.

Brows drawn together in concentration, Argent nodded and was left alone.

Christ, but it was difficult to do anything requiring so much dexterity with the most insistent cockstand he'd ever had telling him the wound could wait.

The woman could not.

However, fucking a woman like Millie LeCour with a seeping gash in his arm seemed barbaric, even for him.

He somehow wanted to be certain that blood never once touched her perfect, porcelain skin. He had no qualms about bathing in it, but it should never touch a woman like her.

A mother. One who worried about things like shoes in the sheets and the comfort of a sleeping child. When he thought of the way she'd swept Jakub's hair from his closed eyes with all the tenderness and love a woman could possess, a flutter of something soft and foreign pressed against his breastbone. Like a hummingbird was trapped there, looking for a way out.

And it was that little flutter beneath his ribs that made him catch his breath.

The washroom door creaked a little as it opened and Argent gritted his teeth. "Welton, hand me the vodka from the cupboard over there. I think this wound has been open too long. I don't want it to turn septic."

The cupboard door opened and closed while Argent cursed the unsteadiness of his hand as he made one of the stitches wider than it needed to be.

"It was *your* blood on the carpet in my dressing room, wasn't it?"

Argent could count on one hand the number of times he'd been truly startled. Every time had resulted in pain, and this time was no exception, as he pulled too hard on the string stuck in his skin at the sound of Millie LeCour's voice.

She held the bottle of vodka like sacrificial wine against her antiquated bead and velvet costume, and approached him like one would a wounded bear. "You've been hurt this whole time."

Argent didn't know how to respond, as the statement had sounded more like an accusation. Also, her hair had fallen from its net into a wreath of messy curls spilling over her breasts like an onyx waterfall. How the devil was he supposed to put words together when she looked like that?

He wanted her. *God*, how he wanted her.

A frown pulled at the corners of her red, red lips and she slipped by him to set the bottle on the window seat next to the clean bandages, which she pushed to the side.

Argent had paused to observe her, his arm only half stitched, wondering just what she planned to do next.

She sat. Looking up at him, she gestured to the space next to her. "You're making a mess of your arm. Let me finish."

He glanced at his handiwork in the mirror. Her observation was correct, the few stitches he'd been able to accomplish might as well have been done by a blind and simple child. He'd always doctored his own wounds. It was safer for a man like him not to show others his weaknesses.

"I'm nearly finished," he hedged.

"You've only started," she argued. "Now sit down, I know what I'm doing."

It had been a lifetime, it seemed, since someone had

dared argue with him, let alone issue an order. He stood for a moment, deciding what to do, and then, only because no alternative instantly presented itself, he stepped over to the window seat and lowered himself next to her. "How do you know what you're doing?" he queried.

Millie turned to the bottle and retrieved one of the bandages, an air of efficiency that he hadn't yet noted about her settled on her features. "I've two elder brothers and a younger one. Someone always needed stitching in my home."

"Where are they now?" he asked. More startled than she was, he expected, by his curiosity about her.

A frown touched her eyes that made him sorry he'd asked.

"Two of them immigrated to America, and my eldest brother and I . . . we're not close."

"Why not?" he asked alertly.

Tipping the bottle to moisten the cloth, she set it down and reached for his arm.

A shock of sensation bloomed over his entire body when her fingers found his skin and cupped his arm in her small, gentle hand.

Argent was a man used to holding still. Used to waiting silently for his prey to step into his trap. But this time, he froze for an altogether different reason.

Like a seasoned hunter, he could feel the hesitant anxiety within her, and knew that though she ventured close, any sudden movement or harsh word would send her skittering for safety. He couldn't remember the last time anyone had reached for him with something other than the intent to harm.

And, though she was about to inflict pain on him, the pleasure of the gentle press of her fingers as she steadied his arm surpassed any anticipation he'd had thus far.

"This is going to burn," she warned, avoiding the question.

"I know." He'd irrigated deeper wounds than this with alcohol. He was quite familiar with the teeth-clenching pain of it.

Stretching the wet cloth over her fingers, she was the one to wince when she dabbed it on the cut. But to him, the searing sting did something it had never done before, singed its way down to his already turgid erection. Tightening it. Flexing it.

Argent bit down against a wave of lust so strong he had to swallow a groan.

Setting the cloth aside, she took the needle from him, her fingers grazing his, almost intertwining, and he had to stop himself from grabbing her hand. Holding it. Threading her fingers through his until—

"I'm going to do my best to be gentle. I know you men tend to fear stitching needles more than bullets." With a slight smile, she exerted a negligible amount of pressure in order to make the two edges of the flesh come together before she quickly but elegantly pressed the needle through them both.

"I don't fear stitching needles. I'm rather used to them." He'd meant the words to encourage her, but he could tell by the way her frown deepened, they'd had the opposite effect.

"No doubt," she murmured, not looking up from the row of tiny, precise stitches she was building. "I realize, Mr. Argent, that I haven't properly thanked you for saving Jakub tonight. This injury was sustained on his behalf, and for that, I don't believe I can ever repay you."

Argent didn't know what she meant. She *was* going to repay him, as soon as his wound was bandaged. Indeed, as he sat there in her thrall, his arm captured in her gentle grip, he was beginning to believe that, though he'd saved her life, he was still getting the better end of the bargain.

Her body. Her pale, perfect body would bend over for him. Expose herself to him. Providing him a warm, soft sheath in which to lose himself for a while.

"Is there anything that frightens *you,* Mr. Argent?" she asked.

He gave the question due process. What did most people fear? What had he to fear that he hadn't already experienced and survived? Starvation, torture, rape, pain, beast or man? "I can't think of anything," he answered honestly.

Skepticism glimmered up at him for a scant moment before she returned to her work. "Not even death?"

Only if he died before tasting her again. Only if he was denied the ecstasy he would find between her thighs before he kicked open the gates of hell to claim its throne.

"Death is inevitable. To fear it is to waste energy."

She let out a soft sound of disbelief. "So you're a suicidal assassin, then?"

"Not particularly. I take precautions. I don't stay in one place for an inordinate amount of time. I don't eat at the same establishment twice, or visit the same whore, or establish a routine whereby I could become complacent. Or ambushed."

He could see that she fought an emotion from declaring itself through her expressive features; he wondered what it was. "That's certainly no way to live," she whispered.

Argent shrugged. "It's an excellent way to not die."

"But . . . but what about loss, don't you fear that?"

"What have I to lose?"

She jerked a little harder on the current stitch than the previous ones, but he didn't let on that he'd noticed as he watched her discomfiture grow with every passing moment of silence. "Don't you have family?"

He shook his head. "Dead."

"Loved ones?"

"I love no one."

"What about this grand and beautiful house? You must have a great deal of money."

Again, he responded in the negative. "I have more money than I could spend in three lifetimes. This is the first house I've ever lived in and, though I have use for some of it, I'm not essentially attached to it in any way. I've lived in many other places."

When she looked up again, he saw a strange desolation in her eyes that baffled him to no end. "Where have you lived?"

He was glad they were talking . . . it made him less likely to slice the thread, press her against the wall, and heave into her for the two thrusts it would take for his full arousal to release its seed. He was so hard. So fucking ready.

Distraction was an excellent way to endure physical torture. Wu Ping had taught him that at a very young age, and Argent had found exceptional use for it. Besides, he enjoyed her voice.

He searched his memory for the answers to her questions. "I'd a room in Wapping for a while after I traveled with a band of pit fighters, and slept where I could. Then before that, Newgate."

"Newgate Prison?" She gasped. "What did you do?"

"Railroad work, mostly, and fight training with a kung fu master who'd been nabbed for embezzlement."

"No, no. I mean, what crime did you commit to get incarcerated? It couldn't have been . . . you know . . . what you do, because they would have hanged you otherwise."

Argent could sense her distress brimming to the surface, and wondered how much more information he should impart to her. He couldn't comprehend the soft, bruised look in her eyes, nor the change in her voice's pitch. She didn't particularly like him or hold him in high esteem. He'd tried to kill her, not once, but three times. In scant moments from now, he was going to fuck her for payment.

And when he'd disposed of all who posed a danger to her and her boy, he was going to walk away from them. To return to the shadows and leave them to the light in which they lived. It had occurred to him, while sitting in Dorian Blackwell's study and watching the man he'd often thought was almost as ruthless and unfeeling as himself adore the woman he'd claimed, that he might want a similar situation. Someone he could see every day. Someone he could fuck when he wanted. Someone else to stitch his wounds and fill the silence with something more pleasant.

But he'd been a fool to consider it, and this conversation proved it. If he had nothing to lose, he had nothing to give. And what woman would want that? He wasn't charming unless trying to lure someone into the darkness where he could kill them. He wasn't educated, though Dorian had taught him to read, and he did make use of the books in his library upon occasion. He wasn't principled, scrupulous, kind, romantic, or interesting.

He didn't feel things like others felt them, if at all. He didn't waste his time on guilt, worry, or empathy. Up until a few days ago, he'd considered himself nothing more than a machine, a hydraulic contraption with cogs and wheels that required fuel to work, sleep to function, and whores for the release of pressure and the maintenance of equilibrium.

This woman caring for him had taught him differently, but he wasn't convinced of an improvement. All she'd done was to uncover some kind of void he'd been hiding. Some deep, cavernous—no, *bottomless* pit of desire and unfulfillment which he had no bloody idea how to contain.

Her sex was what it called for at the moment. What it demanded.

But Argent had a feeling it wouldn't stop until it claimed her soul. He couldn't let that happen. This demon of insatiable emptiness was his own, and he had to do his best not to show it to her.

Best to warn her away.

"I was born in Newgate while my mother served a fifteen-year sentence for prostitution, burglary, and assaulting a nobleman. She'd been seventeen when she was arrested, and twenty-eight when she died."

"She . . . died in prison?"

"Yes."

"How?"

The void within him opened, screamed, began to swirl with awesome force and insatiable demands. It warned him. It calmed him. It gave him something to focus on.

"In a pool of her own blood."

"No!" The back of her hand covered her mouth, and a small bit of his blood stained the soft tips of her fingers. She reached for him, but stopped herself in time, noting the blood for herself, and examining her fingers with a somewhat horrified expression.

Bloody fuck and writhing hell. It had begun already. Blood on her hands.

His blood. On. *Her.* Hands.

No one could spend any good amount of time in his presence before they were covered in it.

No good could come of this.

"They released me when I came of age." He attempted the comfort angle again. "I've done all right for myself in the fifteen or so years since."

She stared up at him for a long while, her dark, dark

eyes swimming in pools of unshed tears. Argent found himself wondering if anyone but his mother had ever conjured tears on his behalf.

Not fucking likely.

When she blinked, they spilled over, leaving mesmerizing tracks in her makeup.

He had the ridiculous notion to lean over and kiss those tears. To lick the salt from her body and digest it, make it part of himself. To swallow her sadness so he could feel some of his own.

It was long overdue, he imagined.

The urge hardened inside of him, reminding him that if he licked that warm tear, it would only turn to shards of ice in his mouth.

"Don't pity me," he snapped. "No one wants to fuck a woman while she cries."

He watched the sorrow dim and the well of emotion dry up with a sense of conflict, that he'd done something wrong, but for the right reasons.

"I suppose that's not true, there are many men out there who enjoy your tears, who would delight in turning them to screams," he corrected himself, the hummingbird flutter behind his breastbone freezing and plummeting to its death within the void. "You should count yourself fortunate that I am not one of them." His gaze flicked to his wound. She'd done an excellent job. "I think you're finished."

With a narrow-eyed sniff she looked down. "So I have." He thought she'd be cruel then, that she'd yank and pull and tear, if only to punish him. But she quietly and calmly snipped at the thread, tied it, and secured the bandage over her handiwork.

It was time, and she knew it as well as he did. He could see that knowledge written all over her face.

Argent stood. "There's a basin and soap for you to wash." He pointed.

Wash off the blood. For there was no place for it where he was taking her next.

This was one contract Argent was certain he must see through to the end.

Chapter Seventeen

"If you think for *one* moment that I'm setting foot in *there,* you've taken leave of your senses."

Argent glanced from the room where he slept, to Millie's obstinate jaw and crossed arms, then back. If he wasn't inside of her soon, he was fair certain he'd lose consciousness for lack of blood to his head. "Our agreement is such that you're mine tonight," he reminded her through clenched teeth. "That means however, whenever, and *wherever* I want you." He motioned to his bed.

Argent had been watching people for a long time, and he knew with a surety he'd never before encountered the look on her face. It landed somewhere between dumbfounded outrage, and dawning horror. "I should have known." She took a few steps back. "You *are* criminally insane. Touched. Out of your *mind*."

"What the devil do you mean?"

Her finger jammed toward the door he held open for her. "That! That . . . dark closet. I wouldn't keep an animal I liked cooped up in there. It's barbaric. I won't do it, I tell you."

Scratching his head, he took a second glance. It was roughly the size of his cell at Newgate, and they'd slept two to a room. "It's more than large enough to fit the two of us," he pointed out. Well, horizontally anyhow. If they were to lie vertically, their feet would stick out of the door.

"I didn't agree to *this*." Her hand pressed against her chest as though to keep her heart inside of it. She glanced over her shoulder, three times, taking further steps backward. "You are *not* locking me in there."

"But . . . it doesn't even lock from the outside." He closed the door and jiggled the handle, opening it again, as though demonstrating to a simple child how such a contraption operated. "See?" What was wrong with her? She stared into his chamber as though it contained medieval torture devices. Squinting into the dark room, he frowned. His bed might be nothing more than a thin mattress on the floor and a few blankets, but it certainly wasn't the rack. Once he'd initially removed the shelves contained within, he thought it had opened up the place exponentially, though not enough for an iron maiden or anything.

He realized, a little belatedly, that he'd chosen this pantry because the rooms in his home were simply too spacious. Once your entire life had been contained in a prison cell, open spaces often seemed too exposed to sleep in.

Of course, Millie wouldn't have such a view, would she?

"I don't know what kind of perverted madman would bring me to a palace, and have his way with me in a pantry, but I do *not* consent. I'll take my chances on the streets." She took a few more steps back, and shuddered.

Argent took a step toward her. "Like hell you will—"

"Master Argent." Welton materialized from the shadows, his face placid and droll, as always.

"*Not now,* Welton," Argent snapped.

"But sir," the butler insisted. "I've come to show your *guest* to the chambers I had made up for her."

Millie's wide eyes leaped from Argent to his butler and back with unmasked skepticism. "Are you both toying with me?"

Welton sniffed. "Certainly not, madam."

"I didn't instruct you to do that." Argent studied Welton

from narrowed eyes. The man had come with the house, and had proved handy to have nearby, once Argent had made it clear that if he ever said a thing about his comings and goings to the police, Argent would snap his neck.

Slowly.

Five years, and Argent had gotten used to having the old codger around. He never questioned his place, and was a font of information regarding the world of the *ton* and the circles in which Dorian and Argent now maneuvered.

"I am an English butler, Master Argent. It is my job to provide you and your household with whatever may be required *before* its lack is noted." He, too, glanced into the space behind the door to which Argent clung and sniffed through one side of his prominent nose with an air of disdain. "It is not customary for a female, spouse or guest, to share the . . . chambers of the master, and so she is afforded her own for him to visit at his leisure."

Millie's other hand joined the first over her chest. "That is your . . . where you sleep?"

Argent remained silent, curiously loath to claim it. The way she was looking at him now, her eyes swimming again, thrummed an unpleasant chord deep in his gut. If she would pick one emotion and decide to land upon it for longer than a blink, he'd greatly appreciate it. The speed with which she swung from horror, to disdain, to sympathy had him feeling as unsteady as a toy ship in a typhoon.

He just wanted her. Now. His mouth needed to be on her again. But not like before, not frozen with fear as she'd been in her apartments. Or angry then resigned as he'd had her in the baths. He wanted her as she'd been that first time at the Sapphire Room. Hungry, willing, and bold.

If you don't kiss me, I'll die.

He hadn't truly understood what she'd meant at the moment she'd said it. Though the longer he was denied her mouth, the more the words made sense.

"Right this way, madam, if you please." Welton gestured down the long hallway with a stiff bow and marched toward a large, arched door at the end.

Blinking away a rather dazed expression, she cast a very different sort of look at the neat pallet on the floor before sweeping past it to follow in his butler's wake.

Once they'd entered the chamber, Argent made the first personal conclusion about his butler in five years. Welton's favorite color was green.

Argent didn't focus on the domed ceiling depicting seraphim and mortals alike engaged in some form of romping. The excess of potted trees, flickering lanterns, and delicate wood furniture that lent the room a forested feel all blurred behind the woman gliding into the midst of all the frippery.

"Welton," she breathed. "It's like . . . like an enchanted forest."

"Thank you, madam." With brusque movements Welton turned down the dark coverlet on the bed, uncovering butter-beige linens stitched with tiny leaves that matched the drapes tumbling from the canopy. Next he poured water into the basin from the ceramic pitcher and fluffed the few towels on the stand.

"Welton," Argent growled.

"Yes, sir?" His butler turned to him.

"Get out."

"Of course, sir." Never breaking form, the butler bowed again to them both, and left.

Argent turned to Millie, who stood in the center of the room regarding him from under disapproving brows. "You could have thanked him," she reproached. "He's really very good."

"Take it off." The words left his mouth the moment he thought them.

Her breasts lifted in an audible breath and stayed there. "You . . . mean . . . my dress?"

Striding to the washbasin, he retrieved a cream towel and plunged it into the warm water. "I mean your makeup. I want to see you."

She approached him in an arc instead of a straight line, her hands clutching her skirts and her teeth chewing at her bottom lip. She held her hand out for the towel and he gave it to her, stepping back so she could use the mirror.

Her reflection added magic to the experience that Argent could never have guessed. He could see the tumble of her hair and the curve of her ass from behind, as well as her face in the mirror. A face so beautiful that his chest ached if he looked upon it for too long.

After a tense moment, she picked up the soap, dipped the linen, and ran it across a portion of the fabric before lifting it to her face. She washed the kohl from her eyes first, their shape morphing from long to round.

"Most men prefer me with this on," she remarked nervously. "It—covers all the imperfections and accentuates the beauty."

"You have no imperfections," he said honestly.

Her movements stalled, and she stared at him with a queer sort of surprise on her face.

Argent didn't give a dusty fuck how other men preferred her to look when they took her. She was his now. Tonight. That was all that mattered.

Except, he had the troubling desire to murder every man who'd ever seen her like this. Who'd ever drunk the ambrosia that was her lips. He knew the impulse was illogical, understood that he was a bleeding hypocrite. Hell, he even knew she was a liar. She'd denied any acquaintance with Lord Thurston, but she'd fucked him. Had had a child by him.

He didn't care about the lie. Everyone lied to save their own skin, he didn't expect any different from her.

But to think of that middle-aged twat with his soft, aristocratic hands on her . . .

A fire ignited beneath his lungs, and suddenly danger shimmered between them. It fed the violence of his need.

It took thirty years of trained self-control to stand an arm's length away from her and watch clean, pale skin emerge from beneath the powder, and soft, pink lips glow from beneath the slick rouge.

Once she'd scrubbed everywhere with the soap, she bent down and cupped her hands in the basin, splashing her face and drying it.

When she straightened, he was behind her, and her lips parted with a soft gasp as he *finally* put his hands on her. Her shoulders were warm through the fabric of her gown, and Argent realized his hands were cold and clammy.

"You shouldn't open your mouth like that," he warned. "It makes me want to fill it with something of mine." His hands slid around to the front of her, the chilly pads of his fingers brushing at the exposed skin of her chest, inducing a shudder down the entire frame of her body. "My fingers, my tongue, my cock, I don't care. I just know that it's warm and wet inside of you."

She snapped her mouth closed and stood stock-still beneath his touch. Her breasts rose and fell beneath the low bodice of her dress in rapid bursts. She was tense and wide-eyed in the mirror, small nostrils flaring.

He'd thought he'd just wanted that mouth, those full, soft lips pillowing his. But he'd been wrong.

He wanted to consume her with so much muscle-clenching need that he couldn't possibly decide where to begin. He felt strong and dominant, like a true hunter. If she'd retreated, if she'd run, he'd have given chase. He'd have pounced on her and bit down on her neck, submitting her to the indignity of his lust.

But she stood. Still and panting. Waiting. Trembling.

"Are you going to fight me?" he asked, and didn't breathe until she answered.

"No."

God, but her features were perfection, her skin so flawless, so tantalizingly fine. Her face a perfect oval, her cheekbones high and proud. To look at her was intoxicating . . .

To touch her was divine.

He remembered how he'd sat in the shadows of the opera box and salivated over the white flesh glowing incandescent in the light of so many lanterns. He'd dreamt, no, fantasized, of all that soft skin beneath his fingertips. And now he had it.

He could barely believe it.

His hands felt large and clumsy as he drew them from her chest, over the thin flesh of her clavicles, and swept at the curve of her dainty neck.

"Just please," she said, panting. "Don't—don't be cruel."

"I won't," he growled, a promise he made to himself as much as to her. His hand reached around to the satin of her cheek, and pulled it until her chin aligned with her shoulder. From behind her his breath teased at the tendrils of hair by the dainty shell of her ear. "But neither will I be kind."

He took her mouth with his, plunging his tongue inside in a slick parody of what his body was about to do to hers. But first he had to taste her. If he only had one night, one time, then he'd spend it with his mouth on her. Tasting the salt of her skin, the syrup of her lips, the sweetness of her tongue. He didn't just want to kiss her, he wanted to *devour* her. To taste everywhere she was white and tender. Everywhere she was pink and lush.

As long as she didn't tell him no. As long as he never climbed on top of her. Because he couldn't. He couldn't split her legs apart and hold her down with the weight of his body. He didn't do that.

He *never* did that.

Small, tentative fingers rested over his hand on her cheek as she slightly turned into him. Her pliable mouth opened beneath his, and she began to return his kiss in soft, uncertain strokes. Every one of her movements ignited tiny fires of bliss in his loins.

Her scent filled his nostrils and held him prisoner. Soap, sweat, and something that reminded him of late summer berries. Everything about her enticed him, and the clenching of the muscles beneath his stomach pulled a sound from his throat so desperate, it could have been a plea.

In that moment, he could feel that she lost her fear.

And he lost his mind.

Suddenly, his lust had teeth, and it chewed through him with the hunger of a pack of winter wolves. It ripped through his veins with the violence of the wild, and he plunged his hand into her hair, pulling it back and exposing her neck to the firelight.

The sound she made startled him, because it was one he'd never heard before. An answering hunger. A sibilant whisper of submission.

Fuck. He'd planned to rip her dress to shreds. To fill his hands with the pale breasts that had tormented his memory since he'd seen them in the bath. He wanted to see, touch, and taste all of her. To draw the experience out so that the memory would last him a lifetime.

But with one groan, she'd undone him. Stripped him of whatever humanity he'd possessed and turned him into nothing but a creature of inflamed, violent need.

His hand still twisted in her hair, they stumbled to the bed. Once in front of it, he bent her over and tossed layer after layer of heavy skirts up her waist.

"What are you doing?" she gasped, her voice laced with

a new hesitancy. It was too late now, he was too far gone. Blood pounded in his loins so powerfully the pleasant ache had turned into raw pain.

"Fucking you," he gritted out. Finally his hands found her undergarments and they became a casualty of his frenzy.

"Like . . . this?" She rose up on her elbows to look back at him and he seized her hair, pressing her cheek into the covers.

"I only fuck like this." As he pulled his cock from his trousers, even the pressure of his hand threatened to overwhelm him. It had never been like this, though. Not ever. If he had a thought that was his own, a moment to stop and consider, he might fear this power she had over him. The way she siphoned his control until there was none left.

"Don't look back at me," he ordered. He couldn't look her in the eyes. She'd see too much, or he would; either way it would be his undoing.

She took in a deep breath and closed her eyes, as though preparing herself. "I won't."

He looked down and nearly came. Her ass was pale and perfect, curving into long, slim legs that disappeared into black stockings.

Christ Almighty. He wasn't going to last long enough to get inside of her.

He closed his eyes and ran his fingers through the soft hair at the apex of her thighs, relieved to find it moist. She was ready.

Her breath hitched when the throbbing head found her opening, but she didn't move or struggle. In fact, her hips curled, lifting back and pressing toward him. Coating his already weeping tip with her wetness.

With a groan born half of pleasure and half of exquisite pain, he bucked his hips forward and plowed into her.

He was ripped in separate directions as two phenomena he'd never before experienced tore his consciousness to shreds.

Something like a pop, or a tear, as he drove into her body.

He registered resistance. Even as he thrust again, and yet again.

Her flesh clenched him like a fist as he moved within her. Tight. Too. Fucking. Tight. Her body pulled and strained at him, forcing a release. Even though the darkness behind his eyelids exploded with the pulses of pure rapture pouring from his cock. His teeth ground together as he withdrew, his seed bathing her pale thighs.

The pleasure, it felt like it would never stop. That *he* would never stop. The burning began at his spine and shot from his body in long, wet throbbing waves. He hadn't known that for all the depths of pain a man could endure, the spectrum of pleasure was equally excruciating.

But then he saw her eyes squeezed in pain. Noted the trembling of her chin until she pulled her lower lip into her mouth and bit down.

And his pleasure was strangled by a terrible knowledge. Millie LeCour had told him the truth today. And for years, she'd been lying.

When she said Lord Thurston and Lord Benchley had never had her, she'd been honest.

But her lie, her lie was much larger than her truth.

Because when Argent looked down and saw the blood, he knew beyond a shadow of a doubt that Jakub LeCour was not her son.

Because up until only a moment ago, Millie had been a virgin.

Chapter Eighteen

Well, Millie thought as she felt a wet cloth roughly swipe at her bare thighs before her dress was tossed back over her flanks. All in all that wasn't . . . so bad. A bit of a pinch, is all, maybe a tearing sensation, but she'd experienced more pain removing a fake mustache and beard a while back when they'd accidentally used too much adhesive. That had brought tears spilling and her skin had been raw for an entire day. This didn't even register on that scale.

The painful part, at least, was over rather quickly. Somehow, Millie had been under the impression that the actual act, itself, lasted quite a while. In fact, she was experiencing a troubling sense of unfulfillment.

Kissing Argent had caused an ache to bloom between her legs, a moist, throbbing, sweet sort of insistence that hadn't yet subsided. His hunger, his need, even his foul language had created an answering call from inside her that she hadn't at all expected.

From what she'd gleaned from the whispers of the other actresses and the bawdy scenes in performances, this business of intercourse was supposed to culminate in some sort of . . . climax. A rhythmic sort of affair with a very vocal *to do* at the end. She'd also heard that a certain pride came from bringing a man to his completion quickly, because it meant your skills as a lover were that much more advanced.

Millie decided to be proud. Her end of the bargain was complete, and she'd sealed the contract with her body. Nothing to it, really. She couldn't even remember why she'd been so worried about it. Yawning, she remained prostrate on the fluffy counterpane for another moment, wondering what the silent assassin was about.

"Do you mind if I . . . can I sit up now?"

He said nothing. Had he left? The man moved about silent as a ghost, and could very well have slithered away without a word.

He'd better *not* have done.

Pushing herself upright, Millie turned to perch on the edge of the bed and came face-to-face with brilliant blue flame in the form of the wrath burning in Argent's eyes.

He towered over her, wide as a Titan and just as dangerous, fists clenching and unclenching at his sides.

Drat. He knew.

"I could kill you," he murmured through a tight jaw.

Millie blinked, offering him a charming smile, doing her best to diffuse a potentially explosive situation. "A man in your line of work really shouldn't be joking about that sort of thing."

He stepped forward, his leg pressing into the folds of her skirt, but he didn't touch her, not yet. "You think I'm joking?"

"I don't see what you're so—"

"That boy is *not* your son," he growled. "You lied to me!"

Millie narrowed her eyes, forgetting any thoughts about charm. "Jakub *is* my son."

"You must think me an ignorant fool; you didn't expect me to notice your virginity? You didn't think I'd see the blood?"

"I didn't think you'd *care*."

The blue flames in his eyes sputtered and died, and his entire body turned to stone.

Millie stood and thrust her jaw forward, proving that it could be just as obstinate as his. That her eyes could contain as much fire as his could ice.

To her surprise, he retreated, stalking to the washbasin and bracing both hands on it, looking down into the sullied water there. She didn't think he realized that she could see his face in the mirror. That the indecision and doubt broke through his marble façade, and behind it, something altogether bleaker shone through.

Millie stepped forward. "For the last five years I've provided a home for Jakub. I've loved him, I've cleaned up after him, I've stayed awake all night cooling his fever and washing his little body with my tears of worry. I assuage his fears, and I applaud his accomplishments. When there was little to eat, I went hungry so he would grow strong. I gave you my . . ." She paused, emotion clogging her throat and brimming in her eyes. "That. Boy. Is. My. *Son*." She jammed a finger toward the door in the direction of the room where Jakub slept. "And I am his mother. And God can damn the bastard to hell who says any different."

Lord, but what they'd just done had left her raw. Not her body so much as her heart. This was something she'd not expected. Something she'd failed to prepare for. She felt fragile in a way she'd never experienced, and for no logical reason. How dare he barter for sex and then punish her for giving him what he wanted? Just what did he think she owed him now?

"You should have told me." He lifted his head as though it weighed a thousand stone, his accusatory gaze finding her through the mirror.

"I'm sorry I wasn't a hundred percent honest with you from the beginning, *Mr. Bentley Drummle*," she spat. "But up until you came into my life, this secret has kept us safe.

And I've done what I had to to keep *him* safe." Her voice broke. "To spare him the awful truth."

Because the truth was too horrible. Too violent. She didn't want Jakub to grow up afraid.

"That awful truth could be the key to this entire situation, have you ever thought of that?" He turned to lean against the heavy basin, crossing his arms over his massive chest, his shirtsleeve still rolled up above his bandage.

"I've thought of little else." Millie focused on that bandage, not realizing she sat back down until the bed caught her. She studied the skin of his arm, freckled beneath light, copper-colored hair that didn't quite match the dark auburn locks he'd swept out of his eyes. "But who have I to trust in this world? To confide in . . . ? You?"

This time it was she who couldn't bring herself to look him in the eyes, and so she stared at that arm, wondering if the freckles were caused by his time in the sun as he worked on the railway. An innocent boy doing a convict's work.

"Tell me," he ordered in a lower voice. "I'll listen."

It was more than she'd been offered from anyone else. "I hardly know where to start." She sighed.

"Start with who gave birth to the boy down the hall."

Millie nodded, her heart feeling very close to the surface of her chest, as though calling to anything sharp that would pierce it. It would take very little to break her at the moment, and she hoped that he couldn't tell. The ruthless man leaning against the basin could do it without a thought. Without remorse.

"My name is Millicent Karolina Lapinski," she told his arm with an unblinking stare. "Agnes, Jakub's birth mother, was my best friend in the world. She was born Agnes Mertenskya and she lived on the Polish side of Ripen Street in Whitechapel with me. We had strangely similar upbringings. My father died when I was young, hers abandoned them. My mother drank herself to death, hers took opium. We both had a handful of brothers, but she had two sisters, as well."

Agnes's face surfaced from the murky depths of the past, a ghost unavenged but not forgotten.

"We both left Whitechapel as soon as we could, and I forced her to join an acting company with me, even though she was painfully shy. We changed our names. I picked something I thought sounded Parisian and sophisticated. Agnes changed her last name to Miller, after the first man she fell in love with, who was the first of many to break her heart."

Millie finally looked up into Argent's enigmatic features. She'd never wished more fervently than she did now that she could see into someone's heart. Read their thoughts. He gave her nothing, as usual. "You see, Mr. Argent, that is where Agnes and I differed. All she wanted was the love of a good man. And all I wanted was the love of the entire British empire, and I knew that I could not have both. I couldn't allow myself liberties, or pregnancies, or marriages. So I never did. I remained unattainable, and I knew that would make me a star."

A mirthless sound escaped her throat. "Compared to the struggle of fighting for my son's life, I realize how trite all of that seems now. But . . . Jakub has changed everything.

"Agnes never told me who Jakub's father was. Only that she loved him, and was convinced that he loved her. She said there were circumstances, ones she would never share with me, that kept them apart. I knew when she would go and meet with him because she would leave Jakub with me for the evening, and then she was melancholy for days after.

"One afternoon, when Jakub was four years old, she gave me a letter and asked me not to read it, but to keep it safe. She told me the letter was from Jakub's father, that he finally was leaving his childless wife and legitimizing Jakub as his heir. I'd never seen her so happy, so delirious with hope. She kissed Jakub and me, and left him with me for the evening. She told me that she and his father were meeting to plan their future, that she would tell me everything when she returned but . . ." A catch of emotion broke her voice.

"She never came back." Argent said what she could not.

Millie could feel her face crumple and hid it in her hands. "I was so angry with her that day because she'd taken my favorite pair of gloves. But I got them back when Chief Inspector Morley brought them to me, covered in . . . in her . . . blood. The gloves had my initials in them. They never found her body, only parts. Only . . . one part. Her womb. The place she'd carried dear Jakub for all those precious months. Cut out of her, like an animal. That's when . . . when I knew he was in danger. I switched acting companies and made Jakub mine." Her chest hitched on a few sobs, and her fingers caught a wave of tears. She thought she'd finished mourning for Agnes, but the pain and fear of losing her friend, the subsequent stress of five years of bringing up a child when she had no idea how to do so, broke upon her with the force of a building caving in. The weight was compounded by the near attack on Jakub this evening, her exhaustion, and the fact that she'd just given her virginity to a man and not three seconds later she was sobbing in front of him. Like a ninny.

"What if he'd been hurt tonight?" she wailed. "What if I'd been killed and he'd been taken God knows where? Who would have kept him safe? Who would have loved him if I was gone?"

Big hands cupped her elbows and lifted her to stand. "Stop this." A cold but gentle command. "I—I don't like to see your pain."

She knew that about him, and her humiliation seemed to make her cry harder. "I can't," she said between hiccupping bursts of grief and fear.

"You and your son survived the night. I will ensure the safety of you both, as I vowed to do. Every threat to you will be decimated, I swear it."

Giving in to a reckless impulse, Millie surged against him, throwing her arms around his torso and burying her tears in his chest. For every few that fell, one or two were tears of relief, of gratitude, of wonderment that a man would come into their lives to destroy it, and become their savior instead.

She'd expected him to be cold. To be still and frozen, or worse, rebuke her. But Millie didn't care, she'd do enough holding for them both. She just needed to lean on something, on *someone* heavier and stronger than she was. If only for a moment, she needed to put the weight pressing her into the earth on someone else's shoulders. And his were so large, so impossibly wide. Couldn't they support her for just a moment?

At first he stiffened, his arms flaring up from his sides in surprise, and still she clung to him, her sobs already beginning to lose the strength of a tempest. Against her damp cheek and ear, a stirring began that turned into a thrum. The thrum became a beat, an ever-increasing rhythm, and listening to it soothed her, somehow.

Maybe because she'd truly believed him a man without a heart. And here was evidence of it, right beneath her ear.

Then he did something extraordinary. His fingers twined in her hair once again, but he didn't draw her away. Instead he pressed her close, closer, cupping her head against his now racing heart. His other hand inched across the expanse of velvet covering her back. Were he anyone else, she'd call his movements tentative, hesitant. But

Christopher Argent never hesitated. He was afraid of nothing, not even death. He'd said as much. So it bemused Millie when he couldn't seem to decide on the correct place to rest his hand on her back.

His breaths were heavy, but measured, as though he controlled them. She could hear his lungs fill in the cavern of his ribs. Her breath began to coordinate with his. Short, deep inhales, hers interrupted by hiccups. Long, smooth exhales, each one releasing more and more tension from her shoulders.

Lord, but he was firm. Hard. A monolith of strength and power. She knew she could strike him, scream at him, push him and rail at him and he would weather it, unfazed. Unaltered. Unmoved. So she didn't. She sank into him instead. And he stood there, silent and still, letting her fingers cling to the muscle of his back and her tears soak his shirtfront. He gave no meaningless words of comfort. No platitudes or humor to distract her from her feelings. Just silence, and breath, and an infinite patience she hadn't known any man alive could cultivate.

He was so different from the beast who'd pressed her bent body into the bed a dozen or so minutes ago. Something had softened within him, as well. She could feel it. A tension was missing from his muscles, a fervency from his manner.

He seemed . . . relaxed. Like a bear in his den, drinking in the silence, reveling in the darkness.

He'd forgiven her lie.

Millie didn't know how long they stood there like that, but her crying had ceased eventually and she was reduced to a few sniffles. It surprised her how much better she felt, and though she was embarrassed, she still didn't want to let him go.

"Forgive my hysterics," she ventured. "I think the events of this night have left me rather overwhelmed. Every time

I think of poor Jakub alone with that man . . . he must have been so frightened." Tears clogged her throat again, and she forced them aside. She was done with that.

"For such a young lad, your son was very brave." Millie could hear Argent's words in two ways, released into the room, and rumbling in his chest. She liked his voice like this, the way it sounded from the inside.

"Was he?" She let out a rueful breath. "I never thought of him as brave."

"Why not?"

"Well, he's not like other boys, rambunctious and rough. He's so . . . so stoic and quiet."

The sound of amused disbelief Argent made bounced her head off his chest a little. "I'm sorry, are we discussing the same boy?"

An answering smile coerced her lips to curl. "He's rather taken to you." She pressed her head against the hand in her hair and he allowed her to look up at him. "You don't know how rare that is. He's generally such a shy child, much like Agnes was, actually." She let out a great sigh and brought her hand up to fix a button on his shirtfront. Enjoying the intimacy of their closeness more than she should, enough that she was loath to let go of him.

He didn't release her, either. So they conversed like this, standing in each other's arms.

"I worry about Jakub sometimes," she confessed. "He's so softhearted. So gentle and clever. At his tender age, he knows so much more about everything than I do. He reads more books, and remembers it all, I vow. I encourage him to go out and play, but he'd much rather be inside, painting or working his figures, practicing the piano or watching us rehearse." She finished with the button, smoothed her tear stains, and had begun to fidget with his collar. Nothing was wrong with it, of course, not with Welton on the job, but Millie did two things when emotional or anxious. She talked and she fidgeted.

Argent had yet to move, and she didn't let herself stop to wonder if he thought her ridiculous. She spent all her time being charming and listening to others. No one had ever been interested in her thoughts and fears about being a mother.

"It's really rather wonderful," she continued. "Having him around all the time. But I'm beginning to fear that I'm coddling him too much. Or that I'm failing him, somehow. I suppose I should make him stronger, or tougher. The world out there is so difficult and cruel. What if I'm making him weak, how will he protect himself?"

Argent still had locks of her hair in his hands, and he rolled her curls over his fingers like one would a fine sand. "He has a mother like you to protect him. That is enough for now."

His words lit a small glow of warmth in her heart, and she hoped that he could feel it radiating from her. "How could I not? Do you know what always made me glad that he didn't have a father?"

"Hmmm?" Argent brushed the hair from her neck and arranged it down her back, exposing her throat and shoulder. She didn't tremble in fear this time. She barely gave it a thought.

"A father, especially a nobleman, would want him to be a hunter, or a soldier, or something equally manly. He wouldn't understand his artist's heart; maybe even hate him for it."

"Not every man would see things that way." Something in Argent's voice made it impossible for her to look up.

"I suppose it doesn't matter. I never did find out who his father was. I don't even know if he's the one who's after us."

"That's the reason you should have told me the truth from the beginning." Argent said this as less of a rebuke this time, and more of a statement. "Because I think I know who Jakub's father is, and I'm almost certain he's the one who wants you dead."

Millie's lungs emptied of breath. As dramatic reveals went, his was unparalleled. She was afraid to ask. Unwilling to know. And yet, her ignorance had to be the worst form of torture.

As she opened her mouth to demand he tell her, Argent asked. "Do you still have that letter? The one your friend Agnes gave you from Jakub's father?"

"I do." With a sick sense of dread building in her belly, she reached down the left side of her corset, where'd she'd sewn pockets in each of her underthings to carry the two documents that were most important to her for years and years. The papers proving she was an English citizen, and the letter Agnes had given her all those years ago. She couldn't remember the last time she'd needed to produce either document, but having them next to her skin always made her feel more secure, somehow.

After five years, the fine paper had faded and dark creases marred the masculine script, but as Millie pressed the two sides of the broken wax seal together revealing a phoenix at rest, something sparked in her memory.

Unfolding it to study as she had done countless times before, she turned her shoulder to Argent so he could read it along with her.

Dearest Agnes,

Too long have I allowed us to be kept apart by convention and society. What seemed so dire in the past years together now has become a trifle in the months I've spent without you. I've come to understand that life is fleeting, and we only have the one to live. How can I finish the rest of my days without you and my son next to me? That's right, my love, more than anything I want to claim Jakub as my son, the legitimate and legal heir to my titles, lands, and legacy. I've already secured the proper papers from the crown.

I'm divorcing my wife and leaving her all of our assets in town. I am so miserable with her, so utterly unsuited. For once, I am glad that she's never given me a child, as it makes leaving her excusable. I'll take you to the country estate in Yorkshire where we will marry. And you will live there with me as my lady, and my wife, everyone be damned.

She's become increasingly suspicious and, dare I say, unhinged, so we must do this quietly until we're out of the city. Please meet me at the little tea room by St. Augustine's at half past two and I'll give you a train ticket and some money for you to make our plans. It's safest that you tell no one until what's done is done.

This is the beginning of the rest of our lives together, my darling.

All my love,
D

"So she never told you who this man was," Argent stated.

Millie looked over her shoulder. "She promised she'd tell me when she returned that night, but . . ." She swallowed some fresh grief. "Are you saying that you know this man?"

"I'm saying *you* met this man and his family tonight. I believe this letter was written by Lord David Albert Fenwick, Earl Thurston."

"Oh my God." The letter shook in Millie's hand. "*D* for David. It makes sense, doesn't it?"

Argent nodded. "Sir Dashforth, the man who hired Dorshaw and . . . myself . . . to murder you and take Jakub, is the Fenwick family's solicitor. And, though he also worked for the St. Vincents, his wife's family, this bird here on the seal, the resting phoenix, is eminently displayed on the Fenwick family crest."

"How did you know that?" Millie asked, wide-eyed.

"It is my business to know."

"Your business . . ." she echoed. As if she were his business now, because payment had been rendered. Glancing at the bed, Millie took her time folding the letter and placing it back into her corset, unable to look back at him. "What—what do we do next? I can't take this to the police, can I? I have no proof that it was he who hired Dorshaw, or even that he hired Dashforth to contract out to you. And . . . if they find out Jakub isn't mine, they could take him from me."

"That's what you hired me to fix," he clipped. "Speak nothing of this to the police."

"You're going to . . . kill him, Lord Thurston?"

"He murdered your friend, ordered your death, and wants who-knows-what with his son. He'll be tied up in Essex tomorrow. I'll kill him the day after."

Scheduling a murder, as one would a hair appointment or high tea. "What about Chief Inspector Morley?" Millie suggested. "He said there were more women dead by the same killer. More children missing . . . You don't think they were all connected with Lord Thurston, do you?"

"I think they were casualties of Dorshaw. I think he was the man they hired all those years ago to murder Agnes."

Millie's eyes widened. "Why do you think that?"

"Because Dorshaw likes to cut on people and leave organs behind. Especially women."

She shuddered. "Then perhaps we *should* tell Chief Inspector Morley; he's investigating what happened to all those other women. He'd want to know who'd ordered those deaths, at least to let the families know that Dorshaw has been captured."

"You would have me give Thurston to the police? Their record is not exactly stellar when it comes to prosecuting a peer of the realm for the death of prostitutes. If you want to keep Jakub, keep him safe, what other recourse is there than the one I offer you?"

"Agnes was not a prostitute, she was an *actress*," Millie huffed.

"That's not what they'll say at court, if it even makes it that far. You know as well as anyone that society makes only a minute distinction between the two vocations."

Millie retreated from him, making her way to the window on unsteady legs. She was beginning to feel the aftermath of what they'd done. A dull ache in her loins and a stinging in her heart. "Must you be so cold all the time?" He was right, of course, and she resented him for it.

"I must be what I am," he answered cryptically.

What this ugly world made of him, Millie thought, staring out into the night. The bright, late-winter moon sparkled off the frost that settled on the cobblestones and clung to the garden. This was a perfect time and place for him, this part of the city, this time of night. Still and so bitter cold, it drove everyone away. Inside.

For fear of catching their death.

Millie had never considered murder before, let alone ordered one. That made two things in one night she'd never done. Two sins she'd never committed, carried out in this very room.

She, too, must be what she was. And before everything, she was a mother, and a mother protected her child, even at the peril of her very soul.

"Then do what you must," she murmured, a pang of insecurity slicing through her. "Is the price I paid . . . enough?"

"It was sufficient."

She whirled to face him, her ego smarting. "Sufficient?" Damn his face carved of stone and his heart of ice. *Sufficient!* Honestly. If she'd received a review like that from a paper, she'd have torn it up and thrown it in the fire.

"It's what we agreed upon, was it not?" he said carefully, studying her face with an arrested expression. As if he didn't understand what she was thinking.

"Well . . . yes—" Technically, she supposed so. Then why did she feel so unsatisfied? What was she looking for from him? She knew he'd liked it. *Sufficiently* . . .

She should know better than to seek validation from a man like him, but something in her thrived on it. Had she done it right? Was that all there was to do? Just lie there until he finished . . . Was he disappointed at all? Did he *feel* anything? Because she was little more than one pulsating, raw emotion wrapped in a pretty package. She'd thought she'd seen a crack in the glacier, a bit of frenzy followed by a few moments of intimacy. Not passion, per se. Nor tenderness, but a whisper of . . . something. Some warmth behind the bleak void of his eyes.

Had she imagined it? Was she creating it for the sole reason that her own feelings for this strange and lethal man were becoming more opaque?

"Sufficient." She sighed, then nodded. It was enough. Either way he was still going to do what he'd promised.

"I'd slaughter every soul in this city if it meant you'd let me fuck you again." That blue fire had returned to his eyes, the flames licking at her from across the room. "If you would just—" His mouth clamped shut, and he shook his head, whether at her or to himself, she couldn't be certain. "It was sufficient, it was what we agreed upon. But it *wasn't* enough, damn you." Turning on the heel of his boot, he stalked to the door, slamming it behind him and leaving her alone in a shaft of cold moonlight.

Chapter Nineteen

Christopher rose at dawn, as was his habit, and dressed in the loose-fitting silk trousers he wore for martial art training. Stepping out of his room, he paused to study the closed door at the end of the hall. Did the woman behind it sleep well, or was she plagued with fitful dreams? Did she sincerely trust him to keep her alive? How did she fare, he wondered, after last night's encounter?

Turning, he strode toward the stairs, feeling the need to punish himself physically with some brutal drills. A drop of awareness trickled down his spine, and he paused to glance back at Millie's room, expecting to see her standing there.

She wasn't, but his feet remained rooted to the floor as he, again, contemplated the door and the woman who slept on the other side.

Millie.

He'd taken her virginity. Coerced it from her. Mounted her like a randy stallion and pushed inside of her like a brute.

Christopher pressed his lips together, as the contrasting memory of her unparalleled warmth combined with the cold discovery of her blood on him. He'd washed the evidence from his body that night when he'd bathed after leaving her room. His fingers had lingered over the wet patches her tears had left on his shirt and, in a moment of unguarded sentimentality, he'd lifted the garment to his cheek in the chance he might catch some of her warmth left from where she'd clung to him.

He'd sent a bath to her, as well, hoping to assuage the tight and uncomfortably oily sensation he'd been unable to escape from. No matter how vigorously he scrubbed, his skin felt tainted by his own impulsive, undignified need.

Was this what shame felt like?

If so, he didn't at all like it, or its bedfellows, whom he'd hesitantly identified as doubt, regret, and concern. He'd lain up half the night picturing Millie in her canopied bed, vigorously hating him, or worse, hurting because of him.

Where there was blood, there was a wound. One he'd created, one that nature had made necessary, to be sure, but even so . . .

It troubled him in a way it never had that he'd caused her pain. Which bemused him further because pain was his business, was an intrinsic part of his life. He'd been born to it. Pain had honed him to a razor's edge, a weapon as sharp and lethal as any blade. So why would it bother him so much that he'd caused her even the slightest pinch?

Because she'd met his sharp edges and rough ways with softness and amiability. Because beneath all that smooth, creamy skin and sweetness, was a woman with untold courage and strength. Because she'd fallen apart in his arms, and he'd somehow helped to stitch her back together.

Because the thought of her hurting set his muscles to twitching and an uncomfortable fury simmering through his veins. There in his cavernous hallway, surrounded by emptiness, something cold and sharp found him. Something he thought he'd left in the iron darkness of Newgate. It washed over him with the breathtaking shock of the Thames in winter, bringing with it a myriad of rapid-fire questions ricocheting through the quietude.

Fear?

What about when this was all over and he was no longer at her side? Who would protect Millie and her son from the dangers that lurked in the shadows? From men like him? What if someone else hurt her?

The thought had barely formed before he found himself at her door, pushing it open and plunging into the dark room. With the heavy drapes drawn closed, he could only make out little silvery motes of dust sparkling in the sliver of daylight that filtered through the slit in the curtains. Making his way to the window, he bashed the meat of his thigh on an unfamiliar piece of furniture and swallowed a grunt before he reached it and threw open the drapes.

Turning, he caught his breath as the silver rays of dawn illuminated her dark hair with angelic beams of light. Millie slept curled on her side, her knees drawn up and her elegant fingers cupped ever so slightly in repose. Her skin, nearly as pale as the linens upon which she lay, created the most stunning contrast to the inky curls draped behind her on the pillow.

Christopher had seen her from every perspective imaginable. On stage, glittering like the empire's crown jewel. In the shadows, lids heavy with desire. At the bathhouse, naked, wet, and slippery. Bent over this very bed, exposed, lush, and warm.

But not like this. Not quiet and unguarded, the electric life in her eyes dormant and the smile she shared with the world hidden behind slack, slightly parted lips.

The ridiculous notion to kiss her soft mouth awake caused Christopher to swallow profusely.

Twice.

He didn't dare move, couldn't trust himself not to do something idiotic, like curl himself around her body and cradle her against him. To use his own mangled flesh as a shield for her perfection.

She looked so young like this, her black lashes fluttering

against cheeks flushed pink with warmth and slumber. It struck him just how small and helpless she really was. Granted, the bed could have comfortably been rowed down the Thames by a dozen burly sailors, but her slight form and delicate bones barely seemed to interrupt the mountain of covers Welton had piled over it.

Soundlessly gliding to the bedside, Christopher lurked over her, his hands clenched, and arms tensed. Never in his life had he possessed anything so beautiful. Even the mansion in which he resided wasn't technically his. He knew he could afford things, anything really, but it had never made much sense to him to accumulate objects he might lose. If the philosophies of Sifu Wu Ping had taught him anything, it was that desire leads to disappointment, and attachment only brings suffering.

Christopher was well acquainted with suffering in all its forms.

In the middle of this room, draped in soothing colors and lovely, filmy things, a dangerous desire flared inside of him with such ferocity he shuddered with it. Not the kind of sexual desire he'd experienced with her last night, though he'd be fooling himself if he didn't admit a strong component of that, but a stark pang of yearning that pulsed inside his chest.

For her, for *this,* for all of it.

This strange and unfamiliar fantasy in the middle of his own bleak house. Decorations that warmed the chilly rooms and dazzled the eye. Beds of soft down with a softer woman inside of it beckoning him to join her, to be a part of this fantasy. A fantasy she lived every day. Not just any woman, *this* woman. The most coveted female in the empire and several countries on the Continent.

His woman.

Christopher shook his head to clear it of the errant thought. Millie wasn't an object to acquire, she was another human being. One with desires and attachments of her own. One who'd never tempered herself with training, hardened her body with punishment, or inflicted violence upon another. And yet, an instinct, primitive and possessive, surged through him with the intensity of a tidal wave. Only one word carried through the quiet, still morning and braved the tumultuous storm swirling and screaming inside of him, barely contained by his sinew and skin.

Mine.

No. *No,* he berated himself more firmly. Millie wasn't his. He could *not* possess her and refused to become attached. She was a possession of the stage, she was beholden to her son, and she belonged to her adoring public.

He belonged to no one.

Breathing around the strange dull ache in his chest, Christopher whispered her name. He'd not come here to lay claim to her, no matter how intensely his body urged him to do so. He'd promised to protect her. And to keep that promise, he knew he must teach her to protect herself.

Because he could not always be with her. She'd made him vow to leave her alone when their arrangement was through.

But a woman like her was never alone. Never lonely. Constantly surrounded by friends, fans, and a loving son, her life would be full of others.

Yes, he'd leave her. But it was Christopher who would be alone.

Again.

Always.

The dull ache became a cold stab, and Christopher said her name, louder this time, hoping to pull her out of her world of dreams. She slept the sleep of the innocent. No weapons within reach, no weight pressing her down in the night, threatening to consume her the moment her eyes closed. No bitter knowledge that the only way to protect oneself from the danger in the shadows was to become one with the darkness, a creature from the depths of the abyss.

The very thing that goes bump in the night.

Harsh, cold reality awaited her here in the daylight, and he needed to prepare her for it, or he'd never sleep again.

"Millie." He said her name with force, reaching down to touch her shoulder. Even through the overlarge night-gown, her bones felt fragile beneath his hand. It would take nothing at all to break her. But he knew if his large, brutal hands ever did her harm, he would be the one who shattered.

He could think of this no longer without losing his sanity . . . his control.

Tightening his grip on her shoulder, he shook her gently. When she did not stir, his brows drew together, and a small chill formed in his gut.

Was she well? Had she done herself some harm during the night?

Was she breathing?

Seizing the covers, Christopher flung them from her, bellowing her name in a low, desperate tone he didn't even recognize as his own.

She sprang to life with a strangled sound, limbs flailing, and were Christopher a man with lesser reflexes, he would not have caught her wrist in time before her fist connected with his face.

Glassy, frightened eyes stared at him for a moment from a tangle of unruly hair until they darkened with anger.

"Get dressed," Christopher ordered. "I have a few things to teach you."

Each time Millie blinked, a different emotion peered out from her bleary eyes, none of them particularly flattering. Confusion, annoyance, indignation, and then accusation. "What—what time is it?" she asked, her voice husky with sleep as she pressed her palm to one twitching eyelid.

Her voice. He'd only heard that register once before.

If you don't kiss me, I'll die.

The loose bodice of her nightgown slid down her arm, baring her creamy shoulder and skimming the curve of one breast.

Instantly his body reacted, his cock swelling with such momentum, he felt a pang of discomfort low in his belly. He hadn't been aware his hand was tightening on her wrist until she winced.

Instantly, he released her. "It's just after dawn," he clipped. "Now put some clothes on."

Millie narrowed mulish eyes at his bare chest, her jaw thrusting forward in a gesture that was becoming somewhat familiar. "*You* put some clothes on," she snapped. "And wake me at a more decent hour." Scowling, she grasped at the covers and heaped them on top of herself, before rolling away from him and sinking back into the bed.

Christopher stared at the bundle she made with a sense of pure, frustrated astonishment. "It was my impression that the later the hour, the less decent it becomes."

"Your impression is wrong," her sharp voice informed him, somewhat muffled by the coverlet. "And if you wake me before nine in the morning again, I'll pâté your liver and have it with my breakfast. Now get out."

It was a rare person, indeed, who dared to question him, let alone threaten him. Frozen in place, Christopher found himself at a loss for what to do next. How did one make a recalcitrant woman do what she was told?

He'd have to ask Dorian.

But for now, he was faced with eerily unfamiliar territory. He knew, of course, that the *ton* rarely rose before noon. Millie, he supposed, was a similar creature of the night, beholden to delight and entertain the paying crowds until dawn.

His eyes shifting uncomfortably, he tried another approach. Enticement. "If I sent Welton up with some tea, would that help to rouse you?"

"Not if you value your butler," she said around a shuddering yawn.

"Pardon?"

She punched the pillow and fluffed it before settling back down. "If you send Welton in here before nine in the morning, I'll send him to the devil."

"What's at nine in the morning?" he asked before thinking.

She didn't answer, her breath slow and deep.

He stepped closer; she couldn't have fallen asleep again in that short of a time.

"What's at nine in the morning?" he repeated, louder this time.

She jerked and made a very unladylike sound, halfway between a growl and a snort. "I have an appointment," she muttered.

"Appointment? What sort of appointment?"

She mumbled something that sounded like "forgetting to get washed and beaten."

"What?" Christopher asked sharply.

"Kindly leave," she huffed into the pillow. "It's the middle of the cursed night."

Glancing at the window, Christopher developed a scowl of his own. He opened his mouth to inform her that it was not, in fact, the middle of the night if the sun was up.

She beat him to the chase. "And close the bloody curtains on your way out."

Speechless with complete amazement, he complied, thinking to himself that a lash from her sharp tongue ought to open the vein of anyone who'd dare accost her in the morning.

He shut her door behind him, wondering to himself just what hour of the day she became less dangerous than him. He'd probably wake her then.

It turned out that "forgetting to get washed and beaten" was Millie's incoherent sleep language for "Mrs. Loretta Teague-Washington." Even Argent, a social nonentity, had heard of the brassy, scandalous American whom the *ton* had fondly nicknamed the Sorceress. An hour with her was supposed to erase ten years from your skin and guarantee your desirability on the marriage market.

Christopher's eyebrows met over a frown as his carriage swayed across the cobblestones of London, back toward Millie's apartments on Drury Lane. Millie sat opposite him, arm to arm with her son, her hair plaited in a simple chignon and dressed in the same costume he'd fucked her in the night before.

He'd not thought to send for clothing.

Trying to ignore the memory of the wine-red skirt tossed above her creamy ass, Christopher shifted in his seat as his trousers became decidedly smaller. The heated recollection gave way to the unpleasant question of Millie's reasons for seeking out Loretta Teague-Washington's services.

Marriage?

His frown deepened to a scowl and he glared out at the bustling city with uncharacteristic temper. She'd informed him that she wasn't in love with anyone. However, she owed him no fealty or friendship, and therefore wasn't beholden to share her innermost confidences with him.

Also, the institution of marriage infamously kept very little company with love. Perhaps she wanted what many women desired. A rich husband. A secure future. Someone contracted to take care of her when her youth and beauty faded. An eventuality he couldn't even fathom.

A legitimate name for her son, perhaps?

Whatever her reasons, if she married, she'd belong to another. Christopher's jaw locked with such force, he felt a slight headache prick at his temples.

"You're rather quiet this morning," Millie observed gently. "Is anything amiss?"

His eyes swung back to her, and he let out a few cyclical breaths, hoping to use his control over his energy to calm the thumps his heart seemed to insist upon whenever his gaze rested on her genuine smile.

The mild concern in her gentle gaze was the direct reverse of the woman she'd been at dawn. In fact, she'd been the picture of bright-eyed courtesy ever since she'd wandered out of her bedroom at ten, teacup in hand. The contrast somehow disturbed Christopher's very sense of equilibrium.

"I'm delaying any conversation until noon," he informed her. "Until I can be certain that the hour is safe."

Millie tilted her head in a questioning way as, next to her, Jakub's eyes widened with warning. "Safe?" she echoed. "Why wouldn't it be safe?"

"The last time we spoke, you threatened to pâté my liver," Christopher reminded her.

"That's ridiculous, I don't even like liver pâté."

"You also promised to murder my elderly butler."

Her eyes widened. "Welton? Why ever would I do such a thing? I adore Welton, and *I'm* not a murderer." Her features conveyed the unmistakable message in her words.

She was not the assassin here.

"You are decidedly more prone to violence, it seems, at dawn."

She shook her head, regarding him as though he were

the one who'd lost his mind. "Did you have some strange dream? A nightmare perhaps?"

Christopher was beginning to wonder . . .

Jakub, who'd been glancing back and forth during their exchange, chimed in, his falsetto a calculated study in circumspection. "You woke her before nine o'clock, didn't you?"

"I'm afraid so," Christopher confirmed.

The boy shook his head with a very mature compassion. "You should not have done so," he reproached gently, though he remained the picture of solemn masculine commiseration. "Mama is not to be woken before nine in the morning, and if you wait until ten, then you're the better for it."

"I'll keep that in mind." Christopher nodded his appreciation, which drew a gap-toothed smile from the boy.

Millie's astonishment bordered on indignation as she made a tight sound. "I haven't the slightest idea what you two are on about," she huffed, then turned to peek at them hesitantly. "Am I such a monster in the morning?"

"Yes," both Jakub and Christopher answered at once.

"Well." Her lips tightened.

"It's all right, Mama." Jakub rushed to soothe her, placing his small hand over hers and giving her a few consoling pats. "I'm a monster if I take naps, remember?"

Millie smiled and leaned down to kiss the top of his head. "You're always an angel."

"I'm a monster at night . . . in the dark," Christopher confessed with an amused sort of smirk. An ironic revelation amidst a supposedly innocent conversation.

"Are you, Mr. Argent?" Jakub asked.

"The worst kind of monster, I'm afraid."

The child turned back to Millie. "There, Mama, you see? We are all monsters sometimes."

This time, Millie didn't so much as glance down at her

son, her brilliant dark eyes holding Christopher in some kind of thrall as they stared across the enclosed carriage. "So we are," she murmured.

Finding it a marvel that even in the wan light of the carriage, her skin seemed to shine with a luminescence he'd never before encountered, Christopher ventured forward. "I may have been a monster last night. I may have done—rather monstrous things." He'd never apologized in his life, but merely admitting the fact that what he'd done to her last night might have been wrong released some of that oily sensation from his soul.

Jakub returned to glancing between them as the intensity grew, his incomprehension obvious as he pushed his glasses up his nose. "Was he a monster, Mama?"

Millie's eyes shone with something Christopher couldn't even begin to name. Something cautious and yet . . . soft. "No, *kochanie,*" she said, her voice barely above a whisper. "No, he wasn't."

Chapter Twenty

"Just *where* the blazes have *you* been sleeping?" Loretta Teague-Washington flipped a long, peroxide-blond ringlet away from her face before planting her hands on her ample hips.

Guilty color tickled Millie's neck as it crawled toward her hairline from the collar of the peach day dress she'd only just changed into.

"In bed," she evaded, stepping to the side as Mr. Émile-Baptiste Teague-Washington hefted Loretta's many bags and cases, disappearing down the hall that led to Millie's dressing room.

"Whose bed?" the woman demanded. "His?" She gestured to Argent, who hovered over her like a storm cloud, heavy and threatening.

Millie pressed her hands to her burning cheeks, grateful Jakub was in the kitchen with Mrs. Brimtree having a snack.

Ignoring her mortification, Loretta stepped closer to inspect Millie's skin. "I have to admit, you've never looked so dewy before. Never glowed with such . . . vigor. What have you been doing to your skin? Who have you been seeing behind my back? Are you stepping out on me, woman?"

Millie shook her head, having forgotten how Loretta's smoky voice could fill a room nigh to bursting. "I—I don't know what you mean."

"Nonsense." The buxom woman flapped a hand at her as she bustled over to one of her cases, flinging open the latch, and then turning back as though forgetting why she'd done so. Her perfect style and smooth, porcelain skin made it impossible to guess her age. She was either a mature thirty or an age-defying fifty. "Your eyebrows get all pinched when you lie to me. You're either using something different or you're getting that radiance from sharing a bed with this brawny Viking, here." She winked up at Christopher, who remained unhelpfully stoic.

As adept an actress as she prided herself on being, Millie couldn't hide her guilty look in time. Loretta's smile slid over her cheeks with a sly languor. "You hussy." She laughed.

"How did you—I mean—who else knows?" Millie pressed a hand to her heated cheeks. News in London traveled with the speed of a steam engine, but she hadn't thought anyone had known she'd slept at Argent's Belgravia mansion the night before.

"I wasn't even certain you had a lover, until you just confirmed it." Loretta gave Argent an appreciative once-over, her eyes touching on his broad shoulders straining the stitching of his expensive gray waistcoat. "And who could blame you?"

Mr. Teague-Washington gently nudged Millie with his elbow as he passed, which elicited a sharp breath from the assassin behind her.

" 'Bout time you had a man to call your own, chère," the coffee-skinned Cajun boomed in his luscious baritone, flashing her white teeth and charming dimples. "My lady and I hear of your troubles, and we say 'ain't right she got no man to protect her.' But now we see she do." Mr. Teague-Washington's lips appeared extra dark on his Irish-American wife's cheek as he wrapped a long, lanky arm around her plump shoulders and tucked her into his side. It was that disparity of skin color that had caused the couple to flee their home in America. That country might call itself the United States, but some divisions still ran so deep, it would likely take them centuries to progress past the rifts. Europe tended to be more accepting of interracial marriages, especially among the demimonde, and at the very least it was legal.

Loretta squeezed her husband fondly before advancing on Millie. "I only knew you hadn't been sleeping in your own bed, or you would have been using the lavender and white lily tincture I gave you for the eye compress and you wouldn't look so damn puffy." Gripping Millie's chin in her strong fingers, she lifted her face to the light and narrowed Irish moss-green eyes in observant disapproval. "Unless you've been crying."

Millie grimaced, worried that the strain of recent events was beginning to show. "It's been a trying couple of days." Glancing into the mirror at her right, she gave herself a quick appraisal. Her hair did seem rather dull, perhaps missing its usual luster and bounce. The skin around her eyes and brow was pinched with tension and a little swollen from last night's bout of tears. She did note the glow Loretta had spoken of. She could see the iridescence in her skin, the unholy knowledge in her eyes, as though the secrets of the darkness had been revealed to her.

And not all of them had been dreadful. They'd been wicked, though. So very wicked.

Behind her, Christopher's reflection regarded her with that ever-present alertness. He stood too close, loomed too tall and wide.

Looked too fine.

When she'd first met him, she'd thought his eyes dead and cold and utterly indecipherable. But now, when he looked at her as he was doing, she read volumes in their depths. Beautiful things. Terrible things. Words and desires she dare not indentify, because they would set her entire world aflame.

Lord, but this man was dangerous.

Loretta made a noise of appreciation and fanned herself. "*Mon Dieu,* but you two must set those bedclothes on fire."

"Loretta!" Millie exclaimed.

"Well, hey now, if we were all planning on being polite, you'd have introduced me to your Viking ages ago." Loretta winked again, showing that she meant no malice.

"Oh dear!" Millie turned to the Viking in question. "Mr. and Mrs. Teague-Washington, meet my—um—meet Christopher Argent."

"A pleasure, Mr. Argent." Loretta gave Christopher a handshake every bit as firm as her husband's. "You've caught the woman every man would give an eye for."

"So I have," Christopher remarked without a crack in his enigmatic façade.

"I can see why; you've strength enough to handle her."

"Loretta, *please,*" Millie begged.

"I know, I know, you stolid, persnickety Brits can't stand a bit of bawd if it has any truth to it. Are these rumors I've heard circulating about true? That you survived not just one, but two attacks by a killer?"

Millie paused to consider her answer carefully. Of course, the madness the night before at the Royal Theater would have circulated through the late-night crowd of the demimonde rather quickly. And most people already knew about the time Argent had broken into her house and kissed her senseless. Though they now likely assumed Dorshaw had perpetrated both crimes.

Argent had been meaning to kill her at the time. She'd do well to remember that.

He *was* a monster. He had no qualms about it. So why couldn't she see it when she looked at him? What was wrong with her, that his brutal features and dangerous skills somehow compelled instead of deterred her?

Perhaps because he was currently using those skills on her behalf, not against her.

"I have been the target of such a man, yes," Millie answered carefully.

"You poor thing." Loretta reached for her, and pulled her against a generous bosom, squeezing the breath from her lungs before releasing her just as abruptly.

"Sounds like some dark hoodoo to me." Émile-Baptiste made a strange sign with his hands and then spat.

"Surely does," Loretta agreed. "You know that gypsy actress, calls herself 'Contessa' and puts on a bunch of airs that don't belong to her . . . I heard she put the evil eye on you that time you got the part of Carmen over her."

"She need be looking to a holy man to remove the curse, and then she be safe from the evil," Mr. Teague-Washington remarked soberly.

"Curses and superstitions don't hire killers, people do," Christopher remarked.

Loretta's eyebrow, a dark confession to the pretense of her hair color, climbed her forehead. "Where'd you find this ray of sunshine, a morgue? Doesn't have the doughy hands of an idle lord, he *works* for his fine suits. What do you do, Mr. Argent, are you an undertaker perhaps?"

Christopher's shoulder lifted, though he remained unperturbed. "Close enough."

The stylist smirked. "Can't say there isn't much to appreciate about a plainspoken man. Well, come on back here, Millie darling, and let me work my magic." Loretta gestured toward the hall that led to the dressing room. "Not you." She thrust a perfectly manicured finger at Argent, who'd made to follow them. "The time between a woman and her stylist is a sacred and mystical rite. You menfolk have no business interfering."

Argent glanced at Millie. He looked very large and very out of place in this richly appointed, warm, and overstuffed home. Her handful of rooms seemed to contain enough furniture, knickknacks, antiques, and various oddities to fill his entire vacant mansion. Framed playbills hung next to Moroccan lanterns over Grecian table statues, which posed next to faux Egyptian papyri and a vase full of arranged peacock feathers rather than flowers.

Surrounded by such feminine bohemian chaos, Argent's marble skin and monochromatic suit contrasted with the brilliance of his short auburn hair. He looked so hard. So brutal. A mysterious shadow caught within an explosion of color. The image was dynamic, and both women stopped to appreciate it for a moment longer than necessary.

"I think I'm going down for a nip and a smoke at the pub," Mr. Teague-Washington cut in, obviously not amused. "Care to join me, Mr. Argent?"

"Thank you, but I'll stay." Argent claimed a corner of the olive-green couch.

"So long as you stay out of our way," Loretta reminded, all but dragging Millie down the hall. *"Je t'aime, mon cœur,"* she called to her husband, as she had every week she'd visited Millie over the last two years.

"Et vous, mon âme," he sang back to her, closing the door behind him.

I love you, my heart.

And you, my soul.

The ritual usually caused Millie to smile. Today it made her feel bleak, somehow, or guilty, as though she'd spied upon a private sacrament of which she'd never be a part.

Oddly depressed, she sank into the high-backed arabesque velvet chair Loretta pulled out for her, feeling like a wilted flower.

"I'll start with your hair and work my way down."

Loretta said this at the beginning of every appointment. Taking the few pins out of Millie's hair, she began her treatments with a concoction of rare oils and herbs native to the American continent like "jojoba" mixed with a tincture of yucca root and wild rose. Once she oiled the tips and the scalp, she wet the rest of it with her fingers and trimmed the uneven ends with a sharp razor.

Scents of musk and wild, unfamiliar earth infused the room with an exotic fragrance, and for the first time in days, Millie began to relax.

"Where did you find this Viking of yours?" Loretta asked, her voice transforming into something more melodious as her ritual took hold of them both.

"He found me, actually."

"I see. Is this an affair of the heart, or of a more . . . conjugal nature?" Only Loretta could get away with asking such a blunt question, and for some reason, the relationship between the stylist and her clients was more circumspect than that of a confessor to his priest.

And still, Millie couldn't conjure the words to describe what Christopher was to her, exactly. Assassin turned protector. Villain turned lover.

"We have an . . . arrangement," Millie evaded.

"That arrangement have anything to do with the fact that you've been in danger and that brute out there looks like he could break a man in half with his big bare hands?" Loretta might be brash and brassy, and a bit uneducated, but she was anything but stupid.

"I'd be lying if I said it wasn't." Millie sighed.

"Well." Loretta twisted her hair and pinned it to the top of her head and wrapped it, letting the oils sink in and do their job before she washed it out. "You wouldn't be the first woman to invite a dangerous man into her bed in exchange for his protection . . . done it a few times, myself, before I found Mr. Teague-Washington."

"Really?" Swamped with a strange sense of relief, Millie inwardly blessed the woman for not calling her a prostitute.

"Oh sure." Next came a mask of honey, beeswax, white lily, and lemon juice applied to Millie's face with a wooden applicator, to tighten the skin and shrink any pores or imperfections. "Protection comes in many forms. Money, food, shelter, strength, and sometimes just a dangerous know-how and a willingness to kill. Looks like your Mr. Argent out there could provide it all."

"Indeed he can." Leaning back, Millie closed her eyes and enjoyed the sensation of the warm, thick syrup spreading on her beleaguered skin. Many women in her profession took a "protector." In most cases, the term only meant that she had a man who paid her as his mistress. The protection was from poverty, from starvation, and often from the fate of the cruel streets filled with foul men and, even worse, disease.

Now, when Millie confessed to having a protector, she'd mean it in a more literal sense of the word. Though the services rendered had been the same.

"You have to tell me," Loretta whispered conspiratorially. "How are his skills in bed? Is your Viking any good? How many times did he give you *la petite mort*?"

The little death, that mysterious climax so many women went on and on about. The cause of the panting mewls and bellows she'd heard in her days of sharing thin walls with fallen women.

Millie fumbled to cover her inexperience with a shallow explanation. "I really couldn't say. We've only—I've only lain with him once."

The smooth movements paused before resuming more gently. "Don't fear, darling, it often takes lovers a couple tries to learn each other's needs. To become familiar with their pleasures and their desires."

"Does it?"Millie queried before she thought the better of it.

"If I can give you one word of advice, never use your acting skills in bed. Do not portray pleasure you do not feel. You're doing neither of you any favors."

"Acting during—why would you do such a thing?" Millie wondered aloud.

Loretta's voice was softer now, more motherly than it had ever been. "You're not as worldly as you would have us all think, are you, darling?"

"I've not had many lovers," Millie confessed.

A soothing noise of understanding purred from the older woman. "You're one of the smart ones. I feel I must say, a man such as that, so large and so . . . well, I don't imagine he's gentle."

Millie shook her head slightly, so as not to interrupt Loretta's work.

"A man like that spends his life giving orders and having them obeyed. Women submit to him and other men follow him, he's only ever learned by doing because no one dares issue him a command." Millie heard Loretta's voice warm with a wicked smile. "Know what a man like that needs in bed? I can give you the secret to his pleasure, and yours."

"What?" Millie asked, forgetting that she need never share his bed again. It surprised her how much she desired this information. Wanted to employ it.

"A woman to tell him just what she wants."

"You're joking." Millie gasped.

"Not at all. Think on it a spell."

She did. She thought about it the entire time Loretta let the honey mask dry on her face while she rubbed an oil mixed with sugar on her arms and hands to exfoliate and remove any rough skin.

It wasn't enough, damn you.

Those words he'd gritted out at her the night before sent a secret thrill straight to her core. It hadn't been enough. Though she knew he'd found his pleasure, she also understood that she somehow hadn't . . . finished. That the twinge of pain she'd experienced as he'd entered her had been followed by little pulses of pleasure. She'd wanted him to move deeper. She'd wanted him to touch . . . somewhere else. That little bud of pulsing flesh that resided above where he'd entered her. It had bothered her late into the night, aching, tightening and clenching around nothing but emptiness. She'd wanted to touch it, herself, but didn't dare. What if she told him to do it? Would he? Argent wasn't a compliant man, to say the least, but Loretta seemed to know what she was talking about.

"Those hot-blooded men love it when you tell them where to touch you and how. When to use their tongues, how long and how hard to take you, and in the most explicit language you can muster."

Millie's mind snagged on only one thing. "Their . . . mouths?"

"Oh darling." Loretta patted her hand with sympathy and went on about her business. "Tell me, do you think Mr. Argent is going to stay at your skirts for a while? That he'll speak for you?" Loretta asked in a carefully neutral voice.

"No." Her reaction to the answer surprised Millie, a sense of desolation coiled within her. "No, our arrangement is . . . finite."

"Probably for the best," the woman said gently. "Men with eyes that cold often come with a hot temper. You'd be wise to take care with him. Give and take some pleasure, and then say your good-byes before the first clash or snit makes everything awkward . . . or dangerous."

Millie nodded, her mind racing too swiftly to form a coherent sentence.

Would a few failed assassination attempts count as a *clash* or a *snit*? It was impossible to tell, and inconceivable to ask such a question. Goodness, how had this become her life?

"Were you not engaged in a flirtation with that chief inspector over at Scotland Yard?" Loretta asked. "What was his name, Morrison, Morton?"

"Morley, Carlton Morley."

"Yes, that's the bloke. Whatever happened with him?"

Millie shrugged, conjuring the handsome, angular features of Sir Morley. "I only mentioned him to you because I thought he was charming, intelligent, and kind. We've known each other for a handful of years and I've always found him attractive and his presence . . . calming. I highly doubt the interest was mutual. He's very focused on his work."

"Attractive and kind is not a bad place to start." The woman wrinkled her nose. "But charming and calming have nothing on that big, strong brute out there. Women like us, we need a little danger in our lives in order to keep it interesting. Sometimes what a woman needs is a man who can pick her feet off the floor and have her against the wall, if you understand my meaning."

It took Millie a moment to capture Loretta's meaning, and her eyes widened as the conjured image awakened that ache in her nether regions. Would Argent do something like that? Against a wall or maybe—Lord, why was she even entertaining such salacious fantasies about such a broken man? He was a killer. A *murderer* by trade. He was naught but a necessary evil in her life. The serpent king she employed to consume the vipers who would do her and her son harm. She'd do well to not mistake the way her nerves sang when he was close to be anything but a primal warning to her that danger was near. She shouldn't let it entice and thrill her.

Oh, but it did.

"What my Émile said was the truth," Loretta continued conversationally. "We do worry about you some nights. It might do you some good to find a man to settle down with. I can only work my magic for so long, you know, and no matter how much money you give me, time does get us all in the end." She peeled the mask off Millie's face as she said this, dabbing on a toner of rose water, brandy, and witch hazel once the skin was revealed.

Millie made a noise of affirmation in her throat, still locked inside her churning mind until she could finally voice her worries. "The difficulty is, there are plenty of men offering to warm my bed and line my pockets, but I've never received a legitimate proposal of marriage. I'm a woman men want to possess, to bed. They want me to tempt them, to seduce them, to fulfill *their* fantasies. Though, when they hear that I plan to remain on the stage for as long as I am able, none of them want such a woman for his bride. A wife is supposed to follow her husband and support him in his endeavors, not the other way around."

"Speak for yourself, darling." Loretta snorted. "Émile does little but carry my heavy things, pleasure me senseless, and make me laugh. And that suits me just fine. The man would rather be fishing than working, but that means he brings home supper, at least, while I pay the banknotes. His people live off the land, and that's hard to do when I drag him from city to city. I wouldn't think of putting him to work in a factory so I could sit on my duff at home and get thicker."

"But you and Émile are a rare and lovely couple."

Loretta gave a fond half smile. "That's as true as it is kind of you to say, darling." She bustled over to her cases and extracted clippers, a block of beeswax, and a rough bit of leather she'd use to trim, shape, and buff Millie's nails and cuticles with. "I brought up the idea of settling down because I was at an appointment a few days past with Lady Harriett Crenshaw, Viscountess Russell. And, as you may know, she is sister to *His Grace* Collin Talmage, the Duke of Trenwyth, who is recently returned from the Indies. Rumor has it that he's looking for a wife, and Lady Russell informed me he is a *great* admirer of yours and is angling for a chance to make your acquaintance."

"A duke?" Millie's fingers twitched beneath Loretta's masterful ministrations. Women like her, ones from the tenements of Whitechapel, never allowed themselves even the private fantasy of capturing a title as lofty as duchess.

"Rich as Midas, big as your Viking, and beautiful as a bronze statue of Adonis, so long as you don't mind that he has only one hand."

"Oh?" An article flashed across her memory. "I think I read about him in the paper. No one knows exactly how he lost his hand, do they? Didn't he recently return from the Indies with that marquess they call the 'Demon Highlander'?"

Loretta nodded. "Laird Ravencroft, the very same. Two more decorated officers than Trenwyth and Ravencroft never existed, though the Highlander returned with all his bits intact."

It astonished Millie how little she actually wanted to meet this Lord Trenwyth. A national hero, a wounded soldier, and a duke, besides. "You're forgetting, dear Loretta, that dukes do not marry actresses, it just isn't done."

"This one would. He famously, or perhaps infamously, does whatever it is that he likes. And, as something like fifth in line to the throne, he can afford to disregard convention." Loretta let that thought linger in the sunlight and settle as she held up Millie's finger to the light to check the evenness of a nail before buffing it. "If you're of a mind, once you're finished with your arrangement with the Viking, Lady Russell and I could set up an introduction, though I wouldn't keep a man like him waiting."

"Indeed," Millie murmured. A duke. Could she give up her life, her career, to become a duchess? For Jakub, she could. Of course, he'd never be the heir to the title, but the life and advancement that kind of familial connection could afford him would be worth the price she'd willingly pay. Not that the price was lofty. There were worse things than becoming a duchess to a handsome duke, she supposed. Much, much worse.

"I do need to start thinking of the future, don't I?" she mused. For the past week, she'd been so busy worrying about her own survival, she'd let everything else fall to the wayside. Argent had become a very large part of her life in such a very short time. Since the moment she'd seen him on that balcony, he'd dominated her thoughts. Since the time he'd pressed that hard, full mouth to hers, he'd overwhelmed her senses.

And now that he'd been inside of her, she could scarce think of anyone else. Here she was, presented with an opportunity to seduce a duke. The highest available peer in the empire. And all she could think about was the bleakness in Christopher Argent's pale eyes that contained a void too deep for even her to fathom. The contrasting primitive ferocity of his desire.

Now that she'd shared a night with him, submitted to his strength and need, a treacherous curiosity pervaded her every waking moment. It was as though something that had lain dormant her entire life had been awakened.

She couldn't bring herself to fantasize about a duke who was the equivalent of a Greek god. It was Christopher Argent who invaded her very evocative imagination. Hard, lethal, and brutal.

Except for the moment he'd held her, when he'd surrounded her with his strength and rested those lethal hands on her back with such tentative care.

She'd never forget that moment. She'd never be rid of the mysterious assassin, even when he walked out of her life and disappeared back into the shadows.

CHAPTER TWENTY-ONE

Millie had been right when she'd assumed Argent had a lair. Dark, cold, and frightening, it was everything she'd imagined it to have been but for one detail. It happened to be located in one of the grandest ballrooms she'd ever ventured into. Even the windows stood two stories high, heavy drapes drawn, and the ivory ceiling with gold embellishments and handpainted icons vaulted higher still. The two grand chandeliers required to light the immense length of the space dripped with expensive crystal and, tragically, more than a few cobwebs.

Her slippers made a forlorn sound as she glided to one of the flickering gas lamps and turned the intricate knob. The flame gleamed off the strange and terrible tools of his trade. Blades of every conceivable length hung from mounts on the wall. Pistols rested on a misshapen stand covered with black velvet that Millie suspected had once been a pianoforte. Other things, for which she couldn't even begin to imagine their uses, hung from hooks or rested on stands, just waiting to inflict themselves on someone's flesh.

Which of these, she wondered, would he have used to end her life? The weapons, already macabre, took on a menacing gleam, and Millie's first instinct was to cringe away. To flee this place.

Turning from the wall of artillery, she gasped as hulking shadows rose from the glossy, dark wood floor, the effigies of violent practice, human-sized statuary upon which to enact the art of execution.

Why had he wanted her to come here, to meet him in this terrible place?

Upon returning from her apartments, his carriage weighted down with a few days' worth of clothing and sundries, he'd ordered her to convene with him in the grand ballroom alone within ten minutes.

Apparently, he was fond of that distinction of time. Ten minutes.

Perhaps he felt the most at ease in this room, surrounded by his arsenal. Maybe he didn't want her to forget who he was, *what* he was, whilst they formulated a plan on how to rid her of those who would see her dead.

She supposed there were many who would be revolted by this room and its contents, and maybe she ought to be. But somehow, during all of this, Millie had begun to leave her trepidation of Christopher Argent by the wayside. Strange, opaque emotions began to take the place of her apprehension. Some she dare not name, and others she shouldn't allow herself to explore.

Curiosity chief among them.

Stepping forward, she reached trembling fingers toward the rack of knives, selecting one with a large handle and a wicked-looking blade. It was heavier than she'd expected. The handle cool and unyielding beneath her grip. It felt dangerous to hold it, as though it made her a more treacherous person. And, she supposed, it did.

Lifting the blade up to the light, she caught her reflection within it. Just one wide eye and a pale cheekbone. What must it be like, she wondered, to take a life? To thrust such an innocuous device into someone's flesh, severing their veins and spilling their life's blood on the ground.

Her reflection tightened, as the thought made her want

to weep. It must be just dreadful. To gaze upon the fear in someone's eyes, to see their pain, to witness the moment they knew their life was over. To witness their regrets. No wonder Argent was so cold, so passionless. How could he perform his hateful employment otherwise?

He'd been unable to execute his duty the night he'd come for her. What had truly stayed his hand? He'd admitted that his physical desire for her was the impetus for her survival. Deep down, Millie knew she had to believe it was more than that. That somewhere in his broken heart, Christopher Argent didn't want to be an assassin. That he found no pleasure in the taking of a life, but was merely a victim of circumstance and the product of a society that had failed him, utterly.

Was she being a fool? Was she excusing an evil man because he was going to do an evil thing on her behalf?

What did that say about her own culpability?

Millie's sad sigh echoed back at her as she pushed the thought from her mind. This room was the most well used in the entire spare mansion, she observed as she turned to inspect it. He *lived* here. His very essence permeated the warm shades of the walls and turned them into something eerie. If Millie had to conjure a manifestation of his mind, of Argent's very existence, this grand ballroom would be it. Bones and structure of rare beauty, indeed, of flawless design and composition. A dark and phantasmal interior, unable to fulfill its intended glory because instruments of death, of cold violence and merciless destruction, dominated the entire vast room until it was filled with emptiness and the expectation of pain and blood.

Even the shadows.

It was from one of those shadows that Argent melted like a silent apparition. His cold blue eyes glinted like the steel in her hand from an expression equally as hard.

Startled, Millie gasped when she saw him, the knife

slipping from her fingers and clattering to the floor with an ominous echo. Her mouth opened, though no sound escaped, as she took in the pure awe-inspiring vision before her. Though she'd given her body to the man, she'd never truly had the opportunity to *see* him.

Not like this.

Naked to the waist, he wore only a pair of exotic-looking blue silk trousers that flowed about his long, thick legs as though to hide their movement. Bare arms bulged at his sides from the golden slopes of his massive shoulders. Millie's mouth went dry as moisture collected somewhere lower. So many, many scars marked him. His thick torso, ribbed with strength and muscle, was a lesson in violence. Gashes interrupted his ribs and the hard, straining ridges of his stomach. And, dear God, his shoulder and the swell of the bicep below it was a webbed mess of gnarled skin. Like a burn, but perhaps worse.

This was a man who evoked fear in the hearts of all who would see him thus. So why not her? Why did the thrill that washed her spine in shivers have nothing to do with apprehension?

Because she hadn't known. Hadn't had a clue that he was this—this *beautiful*.

"Did I alarm you?" he asked, correctly interpreting the cause of her astonishment.

"A-a little," she confessed. It was a very different thing, Millie realized, to *feel* the strength of a body and to *gaze* upon it. Many times over the handful of days she'd known Christopher Argent, his unequaled size and might had been manifest to her touch. In the way his hands gripped her. In the swells of his arms beneath his coat, or the hard planes of unyielding muscle she pressed her cheek against in order to hear his heart beating.

But to appreciate his raw, brutal masculinity with only the sense of sight was a truly unparalleled experience. He was, in a word, *magnificent.* Again he evoked the image of a fallen angel, for it seemed to Millie that such obvious physical power could belong to no mortal man. That here in the realm of coarse and inelegant humanity, such precise and chiseled limbs could not exist unless shaped of some other earth than flesh. Marble, perhaps. Or iron.

Hadn't he mentioned that he'd worked forced labor on the railway? He had been forged in the quarries and iron yards of prison.

"Do I frighten you?" He stalked closer, taking a circular approach instead of a straight line.

Did he have to ask? Couldn't a man such as him, a predator, sense the fear in his prey? Was she afraid? *Yes.* She was terrified. Not just of him, but of herself, of the frightening heat spilling through her. Of the urges compelling her toward him. Of the dark and carnal things she wanted to elicit from him. Today, right now, he was the stoic assassin, violent and cynical and ready to be about the business of killing.

This man wouldn't hurt her, she was *almost* certain.

He was most dangerous as the man from the night before. Wild and aroused, hungry for a satisfaction only she could bring him, and willing to take it if need be. And what Millie feared the most, was that she wanted him to. She wanted to give it to him again, and this time, take the pleasure that was her due. She wanted to tell him what to do . . . Which shocked her as she'd never before experienced such an impulse.

For a fee, she could now wield his lethality like that knife in her hand. Thrust him at her enemies until their blood painted the ground and her child was safe. There was a dangerous sort of hypnotic power in that knowledge. That a man like this would attack at her slightest command.

But what if she could take it further? What if he allowed her the same command over his body in a more carnal fashion? What would it be like, to order his hands upon her, and to have him comply? To direct his strength and command his pleasure? To withhold his climax until she'd had her own. To make him beg for her mercy, as others had pleaded for his?

Lord, something was wrong with her. She had to stop this. She had to get control over herself before she did something utterly idiotic. Something they both regretted.

"You startled me, is all," she lied. "I've never seen you . . . like this."

"Yes, well." He glanced down at his own torso. "Welton said you might be appalled by my scars. Would you like me to find a shirt?"

"No!" Millie protested. Then, realizing she'd spoken too fervently, she cleared her throat and tried again, diverting her eyes from the feast of fascination that was his bare chest. "That won't be necessary, Mr. Argent. If you would just, um, tell me what it is you . . . needed to discuss with me here, I'll leave you to your . . ." She gestured to the room at large, uncertain what exactly it was he did in this room. "Your exercise."

He prowled toward her, the flow of his pants causing him to look as though he floated over the polished floor rather than walked across it.

It struck Millie, not for the first time, how silently he moved for such a large, *large* man. He slithered close, too close, this king of vipers, and the warmth from his bare skin washed Millie in stomach-clenching awareness.

"You mean to tell me, my body does not disgust you?" he asked, something glimmering from the depths of his eyes that she'd not yet seen.

Millie was loath to call a man like this self-conscious or bashful. And yet, that strange attentiveness he conveyed nudged her for an answer.

"No," she said again, slower this time. "Indeed, I find it rather more diverting than disgusting."

She'd the sense she pleased him, though he didn't smile.

He did have scars, but to her they represented a very intriguing combination of mystery and masculinity. They were a testament to his fortitude and vitality. The only reason she'd erase them, would be to make it as though they'd never been. To spare him the agony of their wounds. She wanted to press her lips against each one and somehow clear the memory of the pain from his mind.

That impulse became so intense, Millie literally found herself blinking away tears. And again, she was thrust into dangerous territory. There needed to be less between them and more *in between* them. More darkness. More space. More clothing.

He leaned closer, and Millie wondered if he realized what he was doing, bringing that hard mouth toward hers. She put her hand out to stop him. To demand that he tell her what he wanted and let her go.

But the moment her hand touched the fine webbing of scars on his shoulder what escaped was, "How did this happen?" She snatched her hand back and held it to her heart. Not because the burned skin had felt uneven and yet unnaturally smooth beneath her fingertips, but because touching him had felt better than she'd remembered.

His eyes narrowed on the hand she held against her as though she'd bemused him, or perhaps rejected him. He didn't turn from her, though his gaze dulled and he looked away.

"Years ago, on the railway line, an enemy attempted to drown me in hot tar. I was able to fight him off, but not before some of the tar spilled down my shoulder and part of my arm. I couldn't get to it before it hardened on my skin."

Millie couldn't think of one thing to say, so instead she

reached out again, pressing her hand to his taut shoulder as an aching fury threatened to smother her. "D-did you . . . kill him?" she finally gathered the courage to ask.

He nodded, both of their eyes trained on the smooth, pale hand she held against his scarred flesh. "Caved in his skull with a rock, but the damage to my body had been done."

A dark pleasure speared through her, that the man who'd caused him such an injury had met such an ignoble end.

"How did you remove the tar?" she asked around a thickening voice, already knowing the terrible answer but feeling that she owed it to him to listen. "Did you have to—tear it away yourself?"

His shoulder flexed beneath her hand, power rolling under remembered pain. "No, actually. In Newgate, two ruthless boys, the Blackheart Brothers, Dorian Blackwell and Dougan Mackenzie, spent all night ripping away bits of my flesh along with the tar. We'd formed an alliance some years before when Dougan had saved my life by pulling us out of the deadly prison ship lines and into the railway gang. Though we worked well together, we were all violent youths, and so avoided each other when possible. But that night of my pain and their patient work solidified loyalties between us all."

Millie's eyes misted. She couldn't even begin to comprehend the torture he'd endured. "Are you—still loyal to them?" she queried.

He remained staring at her hand as though it puzzled him. "Dougan is dead now, for all intents and purposes, but Dorian Blackwell and I have spent a lifetime trading terrible favors. And thus it will ever be, I expect."

Terrible favors. Millie drew her hand away slowly. How easy it was to forget, to ignore the monster born of nights such as the one that left this terrible brand on his flesh. These scars should serve as a reminder, a reminder of the stains on his soul. They should repel her instead of attract her. They should evoke fear instead of compassion.

But when it came to Christopher Argent, things never seemed to be as they *should* be.

"Have you ever hurt anyone, Millie?" he murmured.

It took her a moment for the question to register, so distracted was she by the electric tingle in her hand. "I—I'm certain I've said things I'm ashamed of, that I've done underhanded—"

"No," he interrupted. "I mean, have you ever physically hurt anyone? Cut them, struck them. Broken them."

Millie took an involuntary step back. "Never," she whispered. "Why would you ask me such a thing?"

His eyes turned a liquid blue in the lantern light before he turned from her. "It is the reason I brought you here," he explained as he moved to the wall and selected a knife with a deeply grooved handle. "I want to teach you how."

She couldn't marry the duke, Christopher Argent decided as he, yet again, fended off a surprisingly strong attack to his throat. A man would need both hands to be able to handle a woman like this. It had taken her some time to overcome her fear of hurting him, but once she had, Millie seemed to find a previously unexplored enthusiasm for violence.

He knew he should feel ashamed again, for listening to the lady's conversation back at her apartments, but the feminine murmurs had drawn him down the hall, and on the list of his sins, eavesdropping was relatively low.

He'd caught Chief Inspector Carlton Morley's name, but missed most of what they'd said about the man. He'd most definitely heard about Lord Trenwyth, however. And the crux of that conversation was like a knife to the belly every time he remembered what they'd said.

Millie wanted a hero.

And Argent was anything but that. He was, in effect, the very definition of a villain. A hero-maker, as so-called good men would brag about his demise.

Chief Inspector Morley certainly would.

Argent had encountered Trenwyth only once, at a session in the House of Lords he'd attended with Dorian Blackwell years ago. The duke was one of the only men tall enough to look Argent straight in the eye, and in doing so, they'd recognized each other. Not from a previous introduction, but as one killer distinguishes another. For a moment, Trenwyth, Blackwell, and Argent stood in the midst of maybe the most civilized building in the known world and circled each other like wild predators. It was as though a wolf, a jaguar, and a viper converged upon the edges of their respective territories and had to decide whether to fight or to parlay.

It was Dorian's wife, Farah, who'd saved them from such a decision by stepping into the circle and dazzling them all with her smile, thus creating neutral ground.

Christopher had forgotten that day until this one. Had thrust the unnaturally handsome duke from his mind, as the man had gone off to India to amass a higher body count, and Christopher had remained in London.

To do the very same.

But Millie couldn't be a duchess. The impediments of that court would become shackles after so long. She would despise marriage to a military man, barking orders and regimenting her day. Crawling on top of her night after night, pressing her into the bed as he used her perfect body to forget the atrocities he'd committed in the name of the crown.

At that image, a low rumble clawed its way out of his burning chest and escaped between his clenched teeth. Millie's eyes widened upon his face, and she took a step away from him.

"Don't get frustrated with me," she reproved with fire sparking in her dark eyes. "I don't do this for a living, and I'm trying very hard to learn." Planting her balled fists on her hips, she studied him for a moment longer, and then blinked as a softer, more apprehensive expression overtook her lovely features. "Did I—hurt you?"

"No," he said, rubbing again at that sharp ache in the cavern of his chest, not missing the way her gaze followed the movement with an arrested expression. Christopher looked down, and then dropped his hand. Was he . . . lying to her? Had she caused this pang in his chest? Was she the reason he lately felt like one large open wound?

"Swipe at my feet again," he ordered, needing to divert himself from these destructive thoughts. "Then throw enough force behind your body to bring me down. Should you ever need to use this maneuver, you *run* before your assailant hits the ground. You get to safety."

"Right." With a look of determination, her foot shot from beneath her skirts and swept at his legs.

"Other foot," he corrected her.

"Why? This one's closest and it's the one my brain seems to want to use." She attempted again, truly throwing him off balance. Argent could have merely recovered if he'd wanted to, but instead decided to teach her a lesson.

He went down backward, but not before he seized her and pulled her down with him.

They landed in a heap of her skirts, Christopher on his back, his knees and elbow bent to control his own fall, one arm shackled around her. Her hands were trapped against his chest, her body sprawled on top of his, legs skewed to either side of him.

"That's why," he muttered.

She writhed and struggled against him, yanking and pulling with all her strength to escape his grip, but Christopher barely had to exert any pressure to keep her his captive. Her struggles created the most delicious friction against his prone body, and the rasp of silk against his cock, pressed closer by her proximity, exacerbated an ever-present problem. He'd been half hard ever since he'd thought he'd caught a flash of appreciation in her gaze as she'd scrutinized his bare chest. Now, with her body writhing, lithe and wild above his, lust screamed through him with excruciating ferocity.

He knew the moment she realized, as she immediately stilled, her body going slack against his, the only movement between them created by their quickening breath.

Christopher closed his eyes, employing every technique he could conjure to help him ignore the inviting warmth centered where her legs parted over him.

Nothing worked. His flesh had become one large, pulsing conduit of sensation. Her weight a delicious pressure everywhere they touched.

"What do I do now?" she asked, her voice a breathy whisper against his skin.

Were he to do what he wanted, what his body screamed at him to do, she'd be beneath him in a moment, helpless and spread wide. All he'd have to do is rip her undergarments away and . . .

"You try not to find yourself in this position by listening to my instruction," he gritted from between clenched teeth.

She paused for a moment, before slowly pulling back to look down at him.

Christopher allowed it, his arm sliding from her back down to her waist and over where the curve of her hip would be were it not covered by so many layers of heavy fabric.

"I wonder . . ." Her husky voice vibrated through him, sending shivers of yearning down his spine that arced to his turgid sex with agonizing need. "I wonder, Mr. Argent, if you take instruction as deftly as you give it."

Christopher froze beneath her, his entire being focused on the growing heat between her parted legs, creeping closer to his aching arousal with the graceful arch of her body as she continued to sit back.

"Never," he breathed. He obeyed no one.

"Not even if I ordered you to claim my lips with yours?"

All the moisture abandoned his mouth and Christopher stared at her in stunned silence, certain that he'd misheard her. "What?" he asked.

Her eyes flashed unnaturally bright in the dimness, pools of pathos and a disquieting reflection of his own desire. Christopher knew it had to be a reflection, for a woman like this could never feel the raw, primal hunger that clawed at him now.

"Kiss me," she commanded, rolling her hips back until she was pressed intimately against him, her voice containing a growing desperation that might not entirely pertain to the carnal heat building between them. "Kiss me like you did the night we met. Like a man who captured my gaze across a glowing room and seduced me with a waltz. Touch me as though we are back in that dark corner beneath the stairs of the Sapphire Room and you are Bentley Drummle, nothing more than a harmless, charming businessman."

"Millie," Christopher warned, confused by the almost frantic need in her eyes. By the fear and strain that seemed to underscore her passion.

"Kiss me like you never meant to kill me."

Unable to take any more, Christopher reared up and stopped her lips with his own. His bare arms gathered her close, and held her trembling body against his solid one as the searing heat of their mouths fused them together.

She was shaking. Was she still frightened of him? He'd meant to teach her some techniques to make her feel safer, to empower her, but all he'd succeeded in doing was reminding her that she was in danger. That not too long ago, the biggest threat in her life was Christopher, himself.

Didn't she know that she'd never been in real danger from him? He wasn't a man of many words, and so conjuring the comforting phrases she needed was as foreign to him as Punjabi. But how could she not know? How could the care with which he held her now, the way in which he tempered his strength, not prove that he'd never truly posed a threat? Could she not feel his reverent deference, in the yielding of his mouth to her tongue?

Her arms clenched around him, fingers digging into his back as she dragged her lips over his again and again. Her body melted against and around him.

"Touch me," she demanded once more, her breath hot and sweet against his mouth as her fingers twined into his hair. "This time, do not leave me wanting." Her nails scored against his scalp until she curled her fingers and pulled.

The pain drew a pleasured groan from him as it seared all the way to his cock. His vision blurred until her skin, her face, was the only thing he could see. His sensitive hearing only caught the rasp of the fabric of her dress against his skin, or the wet sounds of their frantic kisses. Heart pounding, he feared how powerless he felt as his hands trailed down to her knees. He could do little but obey her, desired nothing but her pleasure.

Gathering fistfuls of her skirts, he burrowed beneath them with desperate fingers. They both gasped when his hands found her thighs and began their journey upward. He paused at the tops of her stockings, held in place by the most intriguing contraptions, but a rhythmic clenching that had begun in her lean muscles spurred him onward.

A small ribbon lay against the smoothness of her inner thigh, and he somehow knew to pull it. The blessed thing bared her to his touch.

The curse he uttered was more a vibration than a word when he at last grazed the soft nest of heat between her legs. Her desire coated his fingers in liquid fire as he found the slick flesh he blindly sought.

"*Yes.*" The word flew out of her on a hitched breath and he inhaled it, a masculine triumph swelling up from the abyss.

His fingers caressed soft, turgid flesh and slid amongst folds of hot, slippery skin until a delicate sound from her throat gave him pause.

"There." She sighed, her fingers tightening in his hair.

It had been the most erotic word Christopher had ever heard in his life. He dragged his mouth away from hers long enough to explore the curve of her jaw, as he used her little gasps and soft moans as a guide.

This must be what religious men felt as they fell to their knees at an altar. This unworthy rapture. This unholy desire. This need for redemption.

Christopher became a pilgrim of her pleasure. Watching her expressions as carefully as one would a map of the stars. His thumb circled the soft nub above the entrance to her body and her head fell back, exposing her throat to him. He fell upon the pulse at her throat like a vampire, laving and sucking at it to help appease his own roaring hunger.

Every time she ground against his arousal was pure agony . . . but he couldn't stop. Not yet. He could feel her climax building inside of her, and if it was the last thing he did before he died, it would be to watch her come for him.

A searching finger found her opening, and his thumb continued its gentle assault on her flesh as he sank inside of her.

Christopher could sense the moment the stars beckoned her to join them.

Her release drenched his fingers in a warm rush and

with it came a surge of wild, primal satisfaction he'd never before known. Her knees clenched around his hips and a strangled sound escaped her. Her hands clawed at him, and she curled forward, her teeth bearing down on the sinew of his shoulder as waves of shudders gripped her.

He stayed with her as she rocked over him, lost within the pulsing of her flesh. She was ready for him, soft and wet and yielding. His cock reached upward toward her, offering to replace his hand, hoping she would allow him inside her goddess's body.

Somewhere in the house, a high voice rose in an unmistakable call.

"Mama?"

Millie tensed under his touch as Christopher bit out a string of harsh curses she'd likely never heard used in the same sentence. Heaving them both up, he set her on her feet and pulled away when she reached out to steady herself.

"Mama? Where are you?" Jakub called, closer now.

She stood on unstable legs, blinking as though trying to orient herself, placing a trembling hand low against her belly.

"Go," he barked.

Her brows drew together, as mystified by his sudden burst of temper as he. "I . . . I—"

"Go to your son."

"Mama?" An element of anxiety injected itself into the boy's call, and that seemed to pull Millie back into herself.

She cleared the pleasured huskiness from her throat to reply."I'm coming, *kochanie,* stay where you are." Sending him one last voluminous look, full of meaning he couldn't begin to identify, she brushed at her skirts and hurried out. The click of her shoes made a sharp, lonely sound as they carried her away.

Once the door closed behind her, Christopher allowed his legs to give out, using one of the pillars to support his weight. The warmth of her release chilled on his hand as a memory gripped him.

Mum? He'd called his mother that, rather than *Mama.* But he'd found her in the dark, much like Jakub would have found his mother here had he not warned them. Christine had been grunting beneath a man, spurring him on with foul words he could tell she did not mean.

It was the first time Christopher had ever felt the urge to kill. Hatred had filled his young body with a force he'd not been old enough to understand.

That night they'd filled their bellies with warm food that had tasted like ashes on his tongue.

Because his mother fucked for survival . . . just as he'd forced Millie to do.

The pillar abraded his back as he slid down to the floor. Fate was indeed full of cruel and heartless irony. He'd murdered every man he could remember touching his mother. It had taken him years, but he'd done it as a sort of tribute to her. As a promise that he'd never take a woman beneath him and trap her there for his pleasure. That, whatever atrocities he committed, he would never be like those men.

And now . . .

Burying his head in his hands, he emitted a low sound that echoed accusingly back at him in his empty room of terrors. Of all the men he'd learned to hate, he never felt such loathing as he did for himself.

Chapter Twenty-Two

Whenever Millie couldn't sleep, she tiptoed to Jakub's bed and snuggled with him for a moment. She reveled in the little-boy smell of soap and sweat with the slight chemical tinge of the paint permanently stained to his hands.

Perching her candle on the bedside table, Millie lifted the long, thin wrapper she'd brought from home, and rested her hip on the bed before leaning over him. He slept on his back with his mouth agape, and she pressed a finger to the bottom of his jaw to shut it before kissing his downy cheek and taking a moment to stroke his hair a few times.

A bath had soothed her aches and cleaned away any remnants of the day, and brushing her hair out and braiding it by a crackling fire had made her pleasantly drowsy.

However, the moment she'd crawled into bed, she'd come alive. Her body was tired. Exhausted, really. But her thoughts tumbled over themselves like a litter of unruly puppies. The events of the past few days revisited her. Some intriguing, some troubling. Some repulsive and some titillating.

Lord Thurston, Jakub's father, and his dour-faced wife, Katherine. Poor Mena St. Vincent and her awful husband. The encompassing fear she'd faced when a white-faced stagehand had told her someone had attacked her son.

The sweet relief of holding him in her arms.

Losing her virginity. The idea of a noble marriage. Her illicit encounter with Argent only hours before . . .

Argent. Her silent sentinel. Cold and large as a Roman marble statue, and just as ponderously well crafted. Would that he were chiseled out of something more forgiving. Something less forbidding. If only he were earth and ash, flesh and blood like all the rest of God's creatures. Instead of shadow and ice.

He had to be, didn't he? Because there was heat when he kissed her, and fire when he touched her.

Agitated by the memory of his caress, she'd risen from the foreign bed and sought her son, hoping to find clarity in the presence of his innocence.

But tonight it did little to calm her turbulent spirit and, not wanting to disturb his slumber, she pressed one last kiss to her hand and brushed it onto his cheek. Standing, she retrieved his candle and padded to the door, reassuring herself with one more glance before slipping into the dark, empty hallway.

A sound echoed off the walls and chilled her blood. A cry of distress. One so full of helpless torment and piteous rage, it tore at her heart.

Millie would have thought a tortured spirit haunted these bleak corridors if she'd not recognized the exact source of the deep, awful sound.

Argent. If that stoic, stone-faced man was making such a noise, then the devil himself must be flaying the assassin alive.

Her breaths may as well have been cannon blasts in the silences between the disquieting noise. Millie's candle trembled in her hand as she inched along the wall of the corridor toward the closet that separated most of the sleeping quarters from the stairs.

She pressed her ear to the cool wood door, but a knock and a powerful scream drove her back. It sounded as if a desperate scuffle raged in the insufficient space on the other side. Why would a man like him banish himself to such a tiny, uncomfortable place? He was master of one of the largest manses in London, and she doubted his long, large frame could even stretch end to end in there.

Could it be that because of his birth in prison, larger rooms made him uncomfortable? Perhaps he felt more at home in a room the size of a small cell. Lord, that was pitiable. But he chose to sleep in there, for all the noise he was making, and . . . should he have nightmares, they were perhaps the renderings of a buried conscience. Perhaps when one spilled so much blood, it stained not only their hands, but also their dreams.

Caught in a moment of indecision, Millie wondered if she should leave him to do battle with the darkness alone. An instinct as primal as life, itself, told her it wasn't safe in there. That to open that door was tantamount to sealing her own fate.

A low, tight cry rent her heart in two. It was the sob of a helpless child mingling with the snarl of a wounded beast. If he'd been crying for help, her hand might not have reached for the latch. But that awful sound, it had no place in this world. It was the cry of a soul that knew it had been abandoned to the devil, one of agony layered over hopelessness.

Millie couldn't comprehend the depths of suffering that could produce such a sound. That could produce such a man.

Her candle flickered as she pulled the door open, casting shadows and dancing light on his prone, writhing body. Hand flying to smother her own horrified gasp, she inched closer to the thrashing giant, for in such a small closet, she only had inches in which to move.

Sweat slicked the temples of his hair as he fought invisible enemies from his back. As far as she could tell, he wore nothing but a white sheet that was now tangled over and around his heavy, muscled limbs. Even in the dim light Millie could see his scars.

She didn't take time to ponder again how dazzlingly large he was, or how the strain of his muscles rippled so close beneath his skin that veins pressed against the swells of his arms.

His breath hissed through teeth gritted and grinding together, his features taut with torment and rage as his chest bucked against the floor as though someone had thrust a knife through his heart.

A tremor of sympathy overtook her, and Millie leaned down to touch his scarred shoulder, to wake him from whatever hellish dream held him in its thrall.

His warm arm twitched beneath her fingertips.

And then she was beneath him, steel biting into her throat. Her candle and its holder made a muffled sound as it hit the carpet, plunging them into complete darkness. His crushing weight pressed her into the thin mattress, impeding her breath, but she dare not make a move, dare not struggle upward lest he cut her throat.

His breath rasped through the dark, hitting her cheek in hot bursts. He was both death and sex straining above her, a knife against her throat, his erection hard as steel cradled between her legs.

"Christopher?" His name escaped her as a strangled gasp. "Christopher . . . p-please . . . don't."

A moment passed that may have been the most frightening of her entire life thus far, before a string of blistering words fell from his mouth to her ear.

"Do you have a weapon?" he demanded in a voice made harsh by sleep and anger.

"A weapon?" She wanted to shake her head, but it was impossible . . . and useless. "Why on earth would I?"

To say he relaxed would be likening a tempest to a

storm, but somehow his relief was palpable. "You're not here to kill me?"

"Heavens, *no*."

"Then . . . have you come to fuck me?"

Stunned into silence by his vulgarity, Millie blinked up into the darkness. Her heart beat like the wings of a trapped butterfly, rushing blood lower and lower until she could no longer feel the knife, only the hard length wedged between her slightly splayed legs.

"Millie?"

Her name was a groan of supplication on his lips. He was breathing so fast, as if he'd run the span of the city.

"Yes? I mean, no! I mean—you said my name . . . so I answered. Not . . . yes to the . . ."

"You said *my* name," he whispered, grinding against her with a long, sleepy movement of his hips. "I want you to say it again. I want you to answer the question."

"Q-question?" An uncomfortable ache stirred to life between *her* legs, feeding her fear and, at the same time, distracting her from it. What question? Oh, he'd asked if she wanted to fu—er, to make love to him.

Might they have earlier, if they were not interrupted? She'd been asking herself that very question all evening.

He dropped his mouth to her ear, his cheek pressing against hers, the beginnings of a beard abrading her skin. She'd been wrong about the moisture at his temples and hairline. It wasn't sweat, but the fragrant dampness of a recent bath. He smelled clean, but his words were anything but. "I asked you if you came in here looking for another fuck? A better fuck. A longer fuck."

She should say no. And yet, after she'd nearly seduced him this afternoon, how could there have been a question left in either of their minds?

"You were . . . dreaming," she stated lamely.

"I *am* dreaming," he said against her hair, his lips

rooting until they found the shell of her ear, the curve of her neck.

"I . . . I came to wake you." Dear God, what was happening? She bloomed like a tea rose beneath him. Pink and vibrant. Her breasts felt swollen where they were crushed against his chest, and she had to rock her hips away from where his sex dug against hers because it was just too much. Too big. Too . . . enticing.

"If you wake me, I'll kill you." The threat poured from his lips like honey over jagged shards of ice. The knife made a heavy *thunk* as he embedded it somewhere in the wall and she could breathe again. That was until he replaced it with his lips at the soft, sensitive hollow at her throat.

"You had a nightmare," she explained, bringing her hands up to press ineffectually at his heavy chest.

"I've lived every possible nightmare." His tongue was hot velvet against the hollow between her ear and her jaw. "But I know this is a dream."

"How—" Her breath hitched as his teeth nipped at the place where her neck met her shoulder, sending warm chills that turned her bones to liquid. "How do you know?"

"Because I've had this dream every night since I met you." His lips trailed over her jaw, her chin, her clavicle. His anger had turned to hunger, and Millie could feel it building. "And sometimes it becomes its own nightmare."

"What . . . h-happens?" Millie ventured, understanding that he truly believed himself still asleep. And he truly might kill her if she woke him.

"I have you beneath me." His voice was dark, darker than the absolute night within this room. "Which would never happen while I was awake."

"Why?"

"Doesn't matter. Not here." His hands came alive, falling to the curve of her waist. "I tell you to stop me, to push me away. I tell you to run from me. I tell you I am nothing for you but death and blood."

"And . . . what do I do?" What should she do? She should run, while she still could. If he would still let her. But somehow his weight had turned from crushing to delicious. And his mouth left little trails of pleasure in their wake.

"If it's a nightmare you scream and you run in fear. You lock me in here alone for an eternity. If it's a dream, you kiss me, and we fuck."

Every time he said that word, her sex clenched on an aching emptiness that she didn't understand. She wished he'd stop.

She wished he'd say it again.

He laved the lobe of her other ear and a warm, wet rush between her legs had her biting her lip to keep from groaning.

"You feel so real, because I've been inside you. Because I know the warmth of your skin, and the scent of you." He pulled back, his body tightening into that signature stillness of his, coiled to strike. "Which is it to be tonight, Millie? A dream, or a nightmare?"

Not allowing herself another thought, Millie seized his shoulders and pulled him down to her lips. She couldn't be the cause of a nightmare. Not for him, who had lived so many.

His groan was lost in her mouth, and Millie somehow wrapped herself around him like he was her anchor in the darkness. Her fingers barely met around the width of him, but her legs . . . oh, her legs could wrap around his lean hips and lock him against her, against that place that throbbed in such a way she thought she might go mad.

Despite his words, his dreamlike exploration didn't last. She may have initiated this kiss, but she was a fool if she thought she'd control it. Not only that, but she hadn't been prepared for it, for the pure blistering intensity of it. His lips were hard, yet full. His movements raw and unapologetically carnal. He kissed her with a wicked mouth, one that issued threats and vulgarities and brutal, albeit sometimes endearing, honesty. He kissed like a man unused to kissing. No artfully applied maneuvers or sensual variations. He kissed like a man about to—to fuck. Like he wanted to pour himself into her, or perhaps crawl inside of her. *This* was a dominant kiss. A shameless kiss. The kiss of a man who knew his sins and granted himself absolution.

This was the kiss of a killer.

So many anxieties and alarms clamored about in her restless mind, and with every sweep of his velvet tongue, with every grind of his pressing hips, they became quieter and farther away until only their two panting, clinging bodies were left in the close and intimate darkness.

Millie thought they may have lost themselves at this moment. Perhaps she'd ceased being who she was and he left himself somewhere else. They were no longer actress and assassin. Mother and hunter. They were man and woman. They existed for this moment. In this kiss. And if either of them breached, they would both cease to be.

Or perhaps find themselves and remember why this was wrong.

If this was his dream, Millie also never wanted to wake. She felt safe here, in the hold of a dangerous man. How could that be? Why did she trust him so?

Over her gown, his big hands found her breasts and engulfed them. She could feel the roughness of his palms through the thin fabric. The calluses brushed her hardened nipples and drew a soft sound of surprise and appreciation from her throat.

Her palms smoothed down the muscled ridges of his shoulders, testing their width. The webbing of his scars softened her heart, enough that she lifted her lips and pressed a kiss to his shoulder.

He tensed and made a sound she couldn't identify. Encouragement or censure, she couldn't tell until he spoke. "Don't be kind to me," he ordered roughly, and tore her nightgown down the front. "I don't know what to do when you're kind."

He bent to claim her breasts with his mouth. His hands lifted and molded them as his tongue circled the buds until her entire body felt like it was burning. His licks turned to nips, and then tugs, drawing small whimpers from her throat. She writhed against his touch. The darkness fueled her boldness, hid her blushes, and intensified every sensation.

She'd never considered how lovely it would feel to lie beneath a man. To cradle something so warm and large was shockingly tantalizing. A pose as eternal as time, itself, but in that moment Millie felt as though she were experiencing something unique.

His rough chin scratched at the soft valley between her breasts, and she stiffened when she realized his mouth was drifting lower, leaving her upper half completely exposed.

"What are you doing?" she whispered.

"Your scent on my body, on my hands, drove me mad with hunger," he said against the plane of her quivering belly. "Once I bathed I wanted it back. I want to taste you until you say my name."

Dear sweet Lord, she couldn't let him do that. It was too wicked. God, who was this man? Where was her terse assassin? Where was the man who bent her over and took her with her clothes left on? The one who'd pleasured her in the ballroom earlier and then pushed her away and disappeared? Who knew that in his dreams he was so utterly sexual? That he could set her blood to burning and mortify her at the same time?

Those rough palms pushed her legs apart, making room for his broad shoulders.

"Wait," she breathed, overwhelmed, overstimulated, and suddenly very self-conscious.

"No." His teeth nipped at the thin, sensitive skin inside her thigh as his finger split through the wet folds, coating him with her slick desire.

She bucked at the sensation as it branded its way through her blood. His other hand reached around her thigh and pressed her abdomen down, holding her hostage for his pleasure.

"I love you like this. Spread open and wet for me," he confessed roughly. "I wanted you like this . . . I just can't—" He broke off, silent for a tense moment.

Can't what?

His finger slipped inside her and her entire body heaved beneath the sweetness of it. All breath left her lungs in a pleasured rush.

"Just like I remember," he murmured against her thigh. "Soft . . . tight . . . drenched."

Untried muscles clenched involuntarily around his finger and he let out a soft curse.

"Sorry," she gasped.

"Don't ever apologize to me . . ." he said tightly, eliciting a breathy sound when he withdrew his finger, and joined it with another. They didn't slide inside her easily, but pushed, their way somewhat eased by the slick moisture there.

"So tight," he growled. "You were so fucking tight . . . Christ."

She couldn't speak, only gasp and whimper as his fingers worked their way out of her before plunging back in again. She *felt* tight, and aching.

To her ultimate disappointment, he pulled his fingers from her and she whimpered her displeasure.

"I could taste you every night," he moaned.

Sweet Jesus, had he just licked the fingers that—

"I need to taste more of you, Millie." He pressed her thighs wider with his shoulders. "I need it all."

His mouth descended, latched onto the exact place she'd felt raw and aching. The contact seared her so abruptly she cried out and contracted. His tongue was a warm weight splitting up the center of her sex, his fingers sank to the knuckle and stroked her from inside.

The darkness exploded into lightning, becoming a white flash that surged through her body on a raw cry. She felt shattered by bliss, beaten with pleasure. It surged through her in brief, intense surges that had her hips lifting against his restraining hand, shoving at it, and then retracting from it.

Even when the storm passed he didn't pull away. His tongue replaced his fingers, a wet and shallow thrust inside of her, drawing out every drop of her release in audible swallows.

Collapsing to the mattress, Millie stared up into the darkness, too amazed, too pleasured to be astonished by his wickedness. She closed her eyes, feeling the soft glide of his tongue on her hot flesh, feeling pressure building again, enjoying the vibration of his moan against her newly sensitized skin. Then he captured the soft protuberance with his mouth. Sucking, then flicking, then tugging.

And again she went flying. Riding his mouth like she would a wild beast, her shoulders peeling off the floor, her cries echoing off the ceiling. This time she flew too high, the pleasure turned into a burn, and she made a wild grab for his hair, yanking until he detached on a snarl.

"I'm not finished with you." He strained against her grip.

"I can take no more," she said, panting. "Please."

Her limbs felt like pudding, soft and weak. Her lids heavy.

"Is it always like that?" she asked softly. "In your dreams."

"You've never tasted so good."

"Is it like that with every lover?" she wondered aloud.

"I'll kill any other man who gives you pleasure," he said savagely, then paused for a handful of audible breaths.

"What is it?" she crooned, reaching down to thread her fingers in the silky thickness of his hair, his face turned to press against her, his lashes closing against her wrist.

"I don't want this to be over," he told the darkness. "I don't want to wake."

His lips brushed against her thigh. His kiss was more of a nuzzle that melted what was left of her heart. "No man has ever fucked you." Possessiveness underscored his gentle tone. "I wonder if anyone has touched you, if they've tasted you. If you're truly, only mine."

"I am," she whispered, and the veracity of those words struck her with an astounding force, and she stilled.

He crawled up her body in a slow prowl. Slowly, tentatively he lowered himself over her, pressing her breasts back into his chest, and shuddering as his erection slid against her open thighs. She opened trembling legs wider, accommodating for his bulk settling atop her. He was warmer than before, and she sensed a hesitation beneath the hunger.

"In my dreams I am a beast." He sounded hollow and she wondered how he could in such a lovely moment. "I hold you beneath me. So you can't escape."

A bit of cold air hit the heat between her thighs, producing a shiver. "I won't stop you," she said, stifling a yawn of pleasured drowsiness. He felt heavy and warm, like a blanket of desire and sex. He could stay there all night if he wished and she wouldn't complain one bit.

Captured in a bittersweet battle between consuming desire and profound regret, Christopher plunged his arms beneath his dream-lover and buried his face against her hair, knowing it was as inky as the night surrounding him.

He knew how this dream ended. A seductive fantasy

that brought him to the brink, and then he woke on a tortured groan with his cock in his hand. Spilling his seed in a hollow parody of the bliss that everything building up to it had promised.

He hated that moment. Hated everything about it. About himself.

The dream had never been this good.

And it never would be again.

"I'm sorry I hurt you last night, when I took you." He gave the words to dream Millie that he could never say to her in the daylight. She knew, didn't she? She knew that he'd not meant to hurt her. That he didn't know she'd been a virgin. That for all the lives he'd taken and the carnage he'd wrought, the sight of her blood made him feel sick and panicky.

The fingers threaded through his hair stroked softly, came to the edge of his scalp and circled back to his hairline to run through the same path.

He'd loved when she'd yanked it earlier. It nearly made him come. But this . . . this was different. Better, almost. It turned his lust from a bite to an ache. As insistent and demanding but less . . . savage somehow. For a man who was born in hell, that singular touch was sweeter than the idea of heaven.

"I want you," he confessed. "I want you like this . . . beneath me."

"Then I'm yours." She lifted her hips, pressing the wetness of her sex against him in a gesture so infinitely sweet, it nearly unstitched him.

Rolling his hips, he found her opening and gently slipped the head of his shaft inside of her heat, sheathing himself inch by aching inch. She was as tight as he remembered, but nothing tore this time, nothing barricaded his way.

She gasped and the sound did something delicious to his chest. It swelled somehow, expanded.

"Ohhh." Her elegant hands feathered over his back. "That's so . . . much."

"Too much?" Had he hurt her? Even here, even in his dream, he didn't think he could go through that again.

"Don't . . . stop," she cried between heavy breaths.

He didn't think he could. Blood poured the fires of lust through every nerve, and if he pulled away now, it would surely kill him. It was her fault. She was too sweet, too soft. She was everything a fantasy should be, and somehow more.

He glided back and drove forward again, reveling in her small sounds of pleasure. Only in a dream could something feel this right. Could the icy void become a warm, velvety sheath. A cradle of silken flesh and soft murmurs. Only in a dream could he rediscover what wonder felt like.

He gave himself to her in deep, slow thrusts. Lost part of himself with each stroke. Something came alive inside him, grew, glowed, and pulsed. He wanted to shrink from it, from the pressure, from the pleasure, but he was a man of pure primal lust now. Made of nothing but carnal instinct. Her little, high mewls drove him forward until it was not enough. It was never enough. It would never *be* enough. Desperate to get deeper, he slipped one of her legs over his shoulder, angling himself so deep that he thought he felt her womb.

Her sob touched him as deeply as he penetrated her. Soft hips spread beneath him in sweet feminine submission.

"Come for me," he demanded on long, almost punishing thrusts. "Say my name . . . One . . . more . . . time."

"Christopher." His name was ripped from deep in her throat. "*Please.*" A plea or a prayer, he couldn't tell. It didn't matter. She whimpered, then screamed. Her body clenched around his cock, bore down on him with a throbbing pressure so intense, he couldn't fight it.

He closed his eyes, battling the ecstasy building in his abdomen and preparing to burst from him. He clung to the moment, held as long as he could.

Now he would wake. Now he would lose her—

Hot release spilled through him and he gasped his disbelief as his breath expelled along with his seed. He couldn't draw air back into his lungs. Could do nothing but jerk and strain as every muscle clenched, held prisoner by pleasure. Consumed by sheer unadulterated bliss. It pulsed from him, poured from him, bathing her womb with warmth and further easing his last desperate thrusts.

The tempest passed as abruptly as it had hit him, and in its wake left a crushing destruction. Horror turned his blood to ice, even as the heat of lust still sang through him.

"You're . . . still here." He stood, the wetness of his manhood against his thigh an awful cold burst of reality.

"Where else would I be?" He could hear the confusion mingling with something else in her voice that made it husky and thick. It sickened him. Regret? Fear? Pain?

Christ. The things he'd said to her. The things they'd just done . . .

She'd been—she *was*—beneath him. She'd shivered when he settled above her.

He'd held her down . . .

Fuck.

"Christopher?"

He stumbled blindly toward the door, kicking it open and making his way on weak legs down the dim hall. He was running. Running from the darkness. From the lily-white woman of his dreams.

From the fantasy that had quickly become a nightmare.

CHAPTER TWENTY-THREE

Christopher's knuckle split as it glanced off the rough wood stump he'd weighted down with stones in his training room. Rain pelted the windows and cast the room in late-morning gray, turning his implements into shadows.

Cursing his lack of concentration, he welcomed the sharp, stinging burn like an old friend. The pain would bring focus, the blood would foster clarity.

I want you.

Then I'm yours.

A harsh sound ripped through the emptiness of the room, a growl he could barely identify as his own as he clenched his wounded fist and drove it into the wood again. And again. And again.

He'd trained like this his whole life. Wu Ping had started with sand, building calluses on his knuckles and the outsides of his palms. Then they'd moved to buckets full of pebbles, and wood after that. Finally he'd been punching the walls of the prison, painting the stones with his weakness until his skin was so rough, it no longer broke.

The blood meant he was growing too soft. That he was getting weak. That he could be broken.

Come for me. Say my name.

Christopher . . . please.

He was no stranger to entreaties, to pulling people beneath him and silencing their pleas. But hers cut through him like a jagged stone. Had she been begging for release, or had she been pleading with him to release her?

He couldn't tell. He couldn't remember. Part of him was glad he didn't see her last night, that the memory of fear or pain on her face wasn't branded onto his mind's eye.

Goddammit, it was supposed to have been a dream. With her, it had always been a dream. Words like that didn't come to him when he was awake. Needs as primal as those didn't belong in daylight. Men like him didn't leave a woman wet and writhing.

They didn't care to.

He. Didn't. *Care.*

This time, it was the wood that splintered beneath his fists.

He'd been at this for what felt like an eternity, trading his obsessive mental mortification with the physical kind. Sweat ran down his naked torso in chilly rivulets, blood pulsed, pushing his veins close to the skin. Muscles swelled and burned.

And still he couldn't forget the softness between her thighs, the bliss of holding her beneath him, of grinding his hips down against hers.

He'd coerced her. Treated a virgin like a common whore, took her from behind like one. Ripped into her like a barbarian, but at least *then* she'd consented.

And still he'd cringed from what he'd done.

Don't . . . stop.

He rummaged through the haze of lust and frenzy, desperately trying to unravel the meaning behind those words. In his dream, she'd been goading him on, encouraging him to take her.

In his nightmare, he'd taken her against her will.

In reality, he'd spilled his seed inside a woman for the first time in his life. What if she was—What if they'd made a—

"Fuck. Fuck. *Fuck.*" He punctuated each new blow with a bellow of frustration.

"I wouldn't let Mama hear you say that." A small voice permeated the echoes of his vulgarity with a gentle reproach. "She doesn't like that word."

Wonderful. He'd said it fucking plenty last night, hadn't he?

Jakub stepped from the doorway and ventured into the room, pausing to study the weapons in the rack beneath the second-story walk from which a climbing rope dangled. His pale fingers closed over the little wooden handle of his garrote with fascination.

Christopher opened his mouth to tell the boy to leave, but what came out was, "Have you seen her?"

"She's getting dressed." Jakub caressed a set of throwing daggers next.

"Is she . . . all right?" Cursing the tinge of anxiety in his voice, Christopher clenched his wounded fist.

"Why wouldn't she be?"

There was no safe place to go with that question.

"Don't touch that," he barked.

Jakub's hand jerked away from a shiny pistol and seemed to bury itself in the pocket of his little trousers in shame. "Sorry," the boy mumbled, then brightened. "Did you break that?" He jogged over to the log, settling his hand on the fresh split with reverence before he craned his neck to look up. "Welton said to come down and look for breakfast after I dressed, but then I heard a crash. You did that with your fists?"

From this angle, those blasted spectacles made the child mostly a set of gigantic eyes with a few skinny limbs dangling from them. Christopher had difficulty looking down at him.

"You must have to be terribly strong to hit something that hard."

The wistful note in the boy's voice tugged at him, and Christopher looked down to see Jakub run a finger over the split in the trunk with his brows drawn into a frown.

"I am terribly strong, but you don't have to be to do damage like that. It takes knowledge, discipline, and agility more than strength." He walked to a shelf in the corner, reaching for a cloth with which to wrap his knuckles. Eyes snagging on his bandaged forearm, Christopher flinched at the memory of Millie's gentle care.

"Mama could never do that," Jakub argued. "Nor could I."

"Nonsense." Christopher turned back to the boy, rolling the bandage over his hand. "The martial art I practice was taught by a female monk in the East decades ago. It was said she could shatter stone with a flick of her finger."

"That's just a story," Jakub scoffed.

"A story told to me by the master who taught me to fight. He was a very small man, smaller than your mother, and I saw him shatter bricks in his palm."

The boy snorted. "Stop teasing me."

"I've never teased anyone in my life."

"Then you're lying."

Christopher frowned, crossing his arms over his chest. "What makes you think that?"

"You won't look at me."

Their eyes collided and they glared at each other for a few narrow-eyed seconds before the boy's mouth twitched, tightened, then broke into a smile.

Grunting, Christopher broke away from that smile, from the answering amusement it produced, and went to the basin in the corner and began to wash the sweat from his skin.

"Your trousers are funny." Jakub trailed after him. "They look like a dress."

"Aren't you supposed to be at breakfast?"

"Do you use those weapons on people?"

Christopher froze with the cloth half dipped into the water. Jakub's innocence did not belong in this house. Nor did his mother's. And, bastard that he was, Christopher had taken hers last night. But the boy's was worth saving. His lack of guile, his big-eyed curiosity, his exuberance.

Hadn't he been that way once? Before . . .

"I do." Shit, he should have lied.

"Couldn't you teach me?"

"No."

"But . . ." The boy's voice dropped back to the solemn note Christopher had heard before. "There are people after my mother. Bad men. I could protect her if I knew how."

Dropping the cloth back into the water, Christopher closed his eyes against a wave of something so intense, it locked his limbs. He recognized that note in the boy's voice. A mixture of worship and fear, of a little boy's fierce, protective love for his mother, and the anger big enough for a grown man that ignited when that love was threatened.

It didn't matter that Millie's body had never carried the boy. She was his mother. Love glowed between them, a love he'd seen before. A love ripped to shreds and lost in a pool of . . .

"You don't have to worry about that," he vowed. "*I* will protect her; I'm here to protect you both."

"But will you always be?"

The question tore the breath from his chest and Christopher had to struggle to inflate his lungs. "Get that knife over there," he ordered. "I'll show you a few things."

"Welton." Millie ran across the butler marching through the empty dining hall. "Have you seen my son—What on earth is that?"

Welton foisted the prickly-looking oddity forward with both white-gloved hands, his chin rising several notches.

"This, madam, is called a 'pineapple.' A gift to the master, from the Countess Northwalk."

Reaching out, she tested the sharpness of the tufted stalks and the rough scales of the oblong fruit. "I've heard of these, someone told me the Duke of Milford had a hothouse that grew them—Wait . . . The Countess Northwalk? She sends Mr. Argent exotic fruits?" A twinge of displeasure stole through her. Lady Farah Blackwell, Countess Northwalk, an heiress in her own right and wife to arguably the most infamous and wealthy man in the realm, sent gifts of a morning to a reclusive assassin. Why? What sort of arrangement did they have? And, more importantly, why did Millie care where Christopher Argent procured his produce?

"Lord and Lady Northwalk are friends of the household," Welton announced proudly.

"Indeed," Millie murmured, wondering if it had been terribly unkind of her to assume that Christopher had no such thing as friends. In fact, hadn't Argent said something the night before about a long-standing loyalty to Dorian Blackwell?

"Well, acquaintances, at any rate," Welton amended.

Acquaintances, and yet here was a gift from a married woman . . . Was there something going on between her protector and the countess? If someone were to be brave enough to cross the king of the underworld, it would certainly be the master of this house.

"I was just going to add the fruit to the breakfast menu, but I'm not sure when Master Argent and the young master will be finished in the ballroom." Welton looked down his spectacular nose at Millie, one brow cocked with insinuation.

"What are they doing in the ballroom?"

"I'm sure I don't know." It seemed this morning that Welton's nasal haughtiness was tinged with something else. Not warmth, exactly, but a purposeful optimism, perhaps, that made Millie feel accepted.

"Thank you, Welton."

"Very good, madam." Turning on his heel, he resumed his soldierlike march through the empty dining hall, presumably to the small solarium in which they were to take their breakfast.

Millie wandered in the opposite direction, through the grand, desolate entry and toward the French doors, where the right-hand one stood ajar. The echoes of serious conversation filtered from the opening, and Millie paused to smooth the teal silk gown down her front and check her hair for any escaped tendrils.

Nerves fluttered in her stomach at the thought of seeing him again. Her might-have-been assassin. Her protector.

Her lover.

The manner in which he'd fled from her last night left her confused and uncertain. Two emotions particularly foreign to her, especially when it came to men.

In general, she found men easy to understand, charm, and read, thereby making them uncomplicated company. They were creatures of ego and artifice. They smiled with their wolfish teeth whilst scheming with their eyes. Their weaknesses included flattery, their virility, and challenge or conquest, power, wealth, and sexuality, respective and interchangeable throughout. Anything that made them feel like a predator was enjoyable, as long as they could master it without too much effort.

Some prized intellect. Others physical strength and prowess. And still more chased possessions or influence. Some were cruel, others were kind. Some jolly, others solemn. They loved to compete, and shamelessly display their wealth, power, or consequence over each other. They were fascinating creations of alternating primitive instinct and societal constraints.

Not Christopher, though. He was such a unique and complicated animal. An enigma, really. What was it that drove him? Money, it seemed, was important, as he made a great deal of it, but he didn't seem to spend it on much of anything. Certainly not on creature comforts. He possessed a grand house, at the behest of someone else, but he slept in more distasteful conditions than the servants would. His clothing was well made, but far from ostentatious.

As for ego and artifice . . . he didn't seem to understand either concept. He lied to kill. Or to survive. But not to protect himself from judgment or awkwardness. He accepted his strengths and skills at their value and correct measure, owned them without a speck of modesty, but also without ego. He never exaggerated, nor did he undermine. Seduction was an art he didn't practice. Flattery was as foreign a language to him as Greek or Arabic. He kept his relationships, such as they were, confined to arrangements. Contracts, whether on paper or understood, ones with very set parameters of which he refused to step out of bounds.

So when he said he wanted her, when he told her she was beautiful, that he dreamed of her. He'd meant it. He meant it more than any of her admirers had ever meant a single one of their poetic words.

And yet he was tethered by nothing. A boy born in a cage, taught little but cruelty and survival. Then he was thrust into this world and had to make his own way, falling upon the only skills he'd ever mastered.

Violence and death.

But there had to be more to it, to *him,* didn't there? Despite what he claimed, he was not without emotion. The tortured dreams he suffered. The things he'd said to her. Unapologetic illicit things at first, but then he'd given her needful words, and the most selfless pleasure.

All because he'd thought the only way she'd come to

him was in a dream. The reason being, he believed nothing good ever happened to him while he was awake.

What if she changed his mind? What if she brought good into his world? Was there hope for a man with so much blood on his hands? Millie hadn't thought so before, but after last night . . .

Lord, but she was thinking nonsense, wasn't she? A romantic fool, that's what her brother Merek had always called her. And he was probably right.

"They take my spectacles and then push me down." Jakub's voice carried through the door, distracting Millie from her thoughts. "I can't see to take them back."

What was this? Millie hadn't known anyone had done her son violence. That he hadn't confided in her stung, that he confided in Christopher now intrigued and concerned her.

He'd never had a father, nor had she provided him much in the way of male companionship. Certainly, he knew her fellow actors, and there was Mr. Brimtree, of course, but due to Jakub's reclusive nature, he'd never connected much with any of them. Was it testament to her failure as a mother that the first man her son seemed to bond with murdered people for money?

Quite likely. She winced. But he had saved Jakub's life . . . there was that . . .

"You don't have to see them clearly." Christopher's voice rumbled off the ballroom walls with all the resonance of thunder. "You focus on the space between you and your opponent, no matter how blurry your vision may be. By not looking directly at them, you notice all of them. You can tell where the next strike is coming from almost the moment the thought is formed in their minds."

"I want to try," Jakub demanded.

"Like water," Christopher reminded. "Take the path of least resistance, but don't let anyone stop you."

Shifting her weight, she leaned against the half-open door, remaining quiet and in the shadows.

What she saw stole her breath.

Sweat glistened on his body, trailing into valleys and grooves made by mountains of strength. And still, for all his sheer size, she detected an almost preternatural grace in his movements, though whether innate or practiced, she couldn't begin to speculate. She couldn't believe that she'd traced that muscle with her fingers, followed the tight columns down his back as they rippled with rhythmic movement. She'd been pressed against the twin mounded cords of his abdomen, felt their distinct shapes lunging against her flesh.

Her fingers twitched with the memory of him, and the memories only served to awaken new curiosities. He stood in his domain of strange and indecorous tools, a *man*. Hard and dominant and overwhelmingly potent. Sinful and solid and scarred.

And gently patient with the almost ridiculously small boy lunging at him with artless, wild blows.

She should say something, do something, other than play voyeur to this moment. But, how could she when the ground beneath her was no longer stable? It rocked under her feet like a ship on the waves of an approaching storm.

What must it be like to possess the heart of a man like that? To even think it had to be some sort of blasphemy.

But his blasphemies were delicious, weren't they? His wickedness brought her pleasures in the dark and—

"Mama?" Two pairs of blue eyes swung to where she stood with unsettling synchronicity.

"Jakub, darling, Welton has set out breakfast, it isn't polite to keep him waiting." Millie hated the breathless note in her voice.

"But we were in the middle of a lesson." Jakub reared

back, settling into some kind of fighting stance. "I have a center line, and no one can push me off it. Well, Mr. Argent can, but no one else. I can punch anyone who tries to touch me in the throat, or thrust the heel of my hand into his nose. Also, I can pry off a kneecap with a knife, even a jam knife, Mama. And—"

"Jakub," she said more firmly, realizing Argent had taught her son the same things he'd shown her only yesterday.

He hid his mulish frown by looking at the floor. "Yes, Mama." He slunk past her, his shoulders so dramatically slumped that she wondered if she'd also let him spend too much time in the company of actors.

"I'll be along, *kochanie,*" she said more gently. "I need to discuss something with Mr. Argent."

As he plodded down the hall she heard him mutter to himself, "I *knew* I shouldn't have mentioned the kneecaps."

Watching her son, her heart squeezed. Was he being bullied? How did she not know?

Christopher had moved to the basin and was wiping his flushed face, neck, and chest with a damp towel. Millie found herself transfixed again by the muscles rolling in great waves down his back, tapering into narrow hips and disappearing into those strange trousers with the most enticing curve at the backside.

The last time they'd been in this room together . . .

Blinking, Millie tore her gaze from that particular part of his anatomy, clearing her throat and her thoughts. Her embroidered slippers were soft-heeled and she could hear the swish of her heavy skirts on the floor as she approached him.

He tensed, but didn't look at her. Aside from the bandage she'd placed on his forearm, his knuckles were wrapped as well, pinpoints of new blood seeping through.

"You're going to resemble an Egyptian mummy before the week is out." She tossed a smile into her voice, and mixed it with a pinch of genuine concern. "Are you all right?"

"Don't do that," he snarled, turning to pin her with a belligerent glare before his eyes darted away. Gone was the gentle teacher who'd only just shared the space with her son, and in his place stood a glistening god of wrath. "My mother used to do that."

"Do what?" Millie stepped back, utterly confused. "Worry about you?"

"Pretend you're all right." He paced the floor in front of her, three steps to the right, and three back, glaring daggers at the space between them. "She'd fuck the guards for an extra piece of bread, then hide the bruises behind a split-lipped smile when she handed it to me. It sickened me then, and now it's worse because I . . . I'm the one that . . ." Plunging his hands into his lush auburn hair, he gripped it tightly before planting his restless feet and towering over her. "I won't have it, not from *you*."

"I don't have any bruises," she told him softly. Of course, she'd felt a few twinges of use on and in her body, but they'd merely served as a reminder of their affair. She hadn't minded them in the least. "You've done me no violence." Millie reached out her hand, but he flinched away. Pressing her lips together, she knew she needed to tread carefully here. This was not the cold, calculating, ruthless assassin she'd come to know. The man in front of her was a different creature altogether, one with his armor and ice chipped away. Exposed, raw, and just as dangerous.

Perhaps more so.

"I'm no better than *them*."

"Than who?"

"I held you down. I made you bleed. I—I *forced* you to fuck me."

"*Forced* is a rather strong—"

"I *forced* you to fuck me so I wouldn't *murder* you." He swiped at the basin, sending it crashing into the far wall with a terrible cacophony of splintering wood and shattering porcelain.

"Well, if you put it in those words, it does sound a little—"

"I slaughtered them for it. They were my first kills." He resumed pacing. "And now I've become one of them."

Millie was certain no one had ever seen him like this. Wild and distraught. Working himself into a frenzy. She wanted desperately to understand his meaning, but most of the information remained locked within the vaults of nightmarish memories. He must have fought them in his dreams, those mysterious "them." How many, she wondered, had mistreated and abused him? It had to have been a collaborative effort, to create such a man as this. A committee of evil deeds and violent men. She knew she should be afraid, could feel the adrenaline coursing through her body, again warning her to run.

But she stood her ground, because an intrinsic knowledge told her they were both standing on the precipice of a wall. A wall of ice. And the audible cracks in that wall were beginning to perhaps make him feel unstable. But at any moment they could break away, and she had to be there for it. For him.

"Who are *they*?" She stepped forward and he retreated, balling his fists, though she somehow knew he wouldn't strike her. "What happened to your mother?"

"They held her down . . . on her back." His breath sawed in and out of his lungs, the ice in his eyes had melted into an inferno. The flames blue, burning with a rage hotter than any she'd ever before encountered. "They held her beneath them and she didn't fight. She only begged for *my* life, told me to look away, but I didn't. I memorized their faces. *I* fought back, and because of me, they gutted her."

Millie's hand flew to her mouth, her belly clenched in sympathetic response, both for his mother and for her son. Hot tears welled with painful force and spilled down her cheeks.

"I screamed and screamed and no one came." His voice broke, but it was the only indication he felt anything other than anger. "I spent the night in a lake of her cold blood, and then next day *I* gutted four men. It took me years to kill the guard who'd facilitated her death, who wanted to teach her a lesson, and not before he killed another boy." His features told her he was reliving a memory that would sicken her, and he enjoyed it. "Blackwell and I took turns with him. To this day I'm not certain who dealt the killing blow."

"Oh, Christopher . . ."

"Don't be kind to me!" He roared. "I am *not* a wounded child to be pitied. Your tears are wasted. I am *Argent*. I am the most famous villain that no one has ever truly met and lived to tell about it. I've killed more men in the Underworld War than could fit in your precious theater. I've beaten men to death in cesspits for money. And what do you think I felt? Victorious? Avenged? Guilt? Pleasure?"

"I—I don't know." Millie's hand moved from her mouth to cover her throbbing, bleeding heart.

"Nothing," he said darkly. "I felt nothing. I *feel* nothing."

"That isn't true," Millie insisted, her voice trembling with tears. "I don't believe it."

"No? I've fucked whores and the randy widows of powerful men I was hired to kill. You think I cared about them? About their pleasure? I didn't. I don't. I only fucked them because they let me. I took them like dogs, like animals, but at least I never held them beneath me. They could always escape . . . but you . . . *you*." A large wooden beam with pegs like a coatrack splintered beneath his blow, flying into a column and crashing to the floor.

Millie flinched and locked her knees, forcing herself not to take a retreating step from his gathering rage. It had been brewing inside him for years, for more than a decade. He needed to let it out. He needed to break things. "You're not going to shock me," she informed him gently.

"I'm not trying to shock you, I'm telling you the truth. I watched you die on that stage and there was a part of me that knew I could never see it again. That I should have walked away and left you to the mercies of someone else. I could sense myself turning into this . . . this fiend. And still I tried. Then you begged me not to hurt your son. You said the same words she did that fucking awful night." He scrubbed his face with rough, brutal hands. "God, I *am* a monster."

"But you *didn't* hurt my son," she argued.

"Oh, but I have done, don't you see? I hurt him because I hurt his mother. I took your innocence. I made you pay for your life with your body."

"He doesn't know that!" Millie's cheeks flamed, not because of his terrible confessions, but because of the scandalous one she was about to make. "Also . . . truth be told . . . I've never enjoyed making a payment so much."

He froze. "Don't, Millie. Don't grant me absolution or forgiveness. I. Held. You. Down."

"I wanted it," she insisted. "I knew when I opened that door, when I woke you . . . a part of me *knew* what was going to happen. And I wanted it to."

Some of the flame in his eyes flickered and danced and he made a strangled sound.

The urge to hold him overtook her with such ferocity, her arms ached. Lord, what he'd been through, what he'd survived. Most men would have broken, would have fallen to the earth and lost their minds, or taken their own lives. He'd hidden the shame, the horror, the desperation in a placid lake of darkness. Of blood. And then froze it solid to lock it away.

Unfortunately, it seemed, she was just the storm to dredge the wreckage up from the bottom.

He gaped at her, speechless and stunned, his mouth slightly parted, giving her time to close the gap between them. Reaching out, she spread her fingers over the thick muscle covering his heaving chest. He was still damp, but she didn't care. He smelled of clean sweat and male, a musk that she'd never thought could be pleasant. Arousing, even. But it was. Whatever this man was made of, the essence of him called to her. Appealed to every sense.

He regarded her as if, for once, she were the hunter, and he the ensnared prey. Beneath her hand, his flesh, hot from exertion and emotion, twitched and flexed. And beneath even that, his heart pounded against her palm.

"I feel that there is something here between us." Her fingers spread and she stepped closer, pressing her other hand against his chest. "Something more than just a business arrangement. I think you feel it too, growing from the most impossible circumstances."

He remained silent but for his heaving breaths and pounding heart, and Millie went on, taking his lack of rejection as encouragement.

"I know you've done unspeakable things. That you've suffered immeasurably. And I ache for you, Christopher."

"No one calls me 'Christopher.' I told you, I am Argent." But slowly, so slowly, his hands reached up to cover hers. Hard and rough as brick, but tentative as a moth's wings.

Millie smiled up at him, enjoying the way his eyes snagged on her lips. "After all we've done together, I think I've earned the right to call you by your name. You asked me to last night, remember? And to me, you are *Christopher,* a man I—I'm fond of and intimate with. A man who used to be a boy, a boy like my son, whom I love more than I can bear sometimes."

The prowling beast in his eyes retreated, the fire banking into something more warm than scorching. His chin was directed at the column off to the right, his gaze darting about the familiar room. But it always landed on her, glancing off different parts of her, off the places where they touched.

"That boy, the one you used to be, he's beneath all this, I know it. And he feels it all." She pressed at the smooth chest beneath her, and felt some of the cold iron of his muscle melt beneath her hands. "His innocent hands are somewhere inside these scarred ones stained with blood."

"I have killed *so many,*" he murmured. "Don't you know that it's too late for me? Don't you realize that if there is anything but oblivion after this life, I am well and truly damned?"

"But wasn't it Dickens who said 'I hope that real love and truth are stronger in the end than any evil or misfortune in this world.' Look at this, Christopher." She turned her gaze to encompass the shattered, splintered casualties of his rage strewn about the marble floor like fallen soldiers. "This is proof that, despite what you think, you have the ability to feel, and to do so is not always pleasant, I know, but it is necessary for human life. And we're *alive,* you and I. And because of it, there is hope. Hope and truth and the possibility of love. I believe they can pull you out of the mire, if you let them."

He studied the carnage with the same dark look that Millie imagined the devil, himself, used to survey all the realms he lorded over. "You think—you think I live in a mire? One you can pull me out of?" His voice had calmed, his breathing slowed.

"I think you live in a shell," she answered. "A grand,

large, rather expensive shell of a house. But it's no home, Christopher, it's a place to live, but not what a person needs to *feel* alive."

His hands tightened over hers and she rushed on with the desperation of a general charging uphill and still gaining the high ground.

"You thought last night was a dream, and I believe there is some truth to that. I don't think either of us dreamed that pleasure could be so intense, that our bodies would fit together so perfectly. That we would *feel* so much. I enjoyed being beneath you, and I would do it again."

"No. You won't." His face hardened and Millie could hear the crackle of the ice as it climbed and clawed its way back over his soul, engulfing the man beneath it. She was losing him.

"Christopher . . . wait," she begged, as though they were racing, and he'd pulled too far ahead for her to see him anymore.

"You become my woman, what then? Who profits from the bargain?"

"I'm not asking for promises," she amended. "It's not a question of profit, it—"

He flung her hands off him and retreated to the door. "What do I have to offer you but corpses and shells?" His voice . . . his cold, cold voice, it had returned. It leached the warmth from the room, froze the heat of last night's memories with the hard actuality of his violent life. Of the existence he'd carved for himself out of stone and ice. "I will give you the corpses of your enemies, of the ones who wish you and your son harm. But make no mistake, woman, I am not a man who can give you a life. For like this house, I am nothing but a shell. A walking corpse. And just because I didn't kill you, doesn't mean I won't destroy you." He turned to leave.

"Christopher."

He paused, his hand on the door frame, but he didn't turn to her.

"*Please,* look at me." He couldn't go. They couldn't leave it like this.

His knuckles tightened on the door frame until they whitened, and still he never so much as glanced back. "Go have breakfast with your son, Millie," he ordered tonelessly. "I have an appointment to kill his father."

This time, she made no move to stop him.

Chapter Twenty-Four

It was certainly surreal to enjoy delicious tea in such an elegant parlor when one's lover was off killing your child's father somewhere.

Millie found it impossible to focus on the lovely Lady Northwalk's conversation, though she did try to smile into the woman's disarming gray eyes and notice how well they matched the silver of her finely crafted chair.

People died every day, didn't they? Someone was murdered in the city all the time. Innocent people, young people, the elderly, the helpless, they were all occasional victims. And people like her knew about it, felt sorry for it, and went about their own lives. Not because they were heartless, but because they didn't know what else to do.

So why was she obsessing about the death of a man who'd ordered her own murder? Who posed a threat to her son? To his *own* son. It made no sense, and yet she couldn't escape this impending dread. This feeling that something very wrong was about to occur. She knew a crime was even now being committed, that someone who woke this morning and dressed and maybe enjoyed jam with his toast wouldn't wake tomorrow to do so again.

Was this vengeance, murder, or justice? Were they *certain* it was Lord Thurston who'd lured Agnes to her death? Of course it was, who else could it be? Who else would have profited from Jakub's mother's disappearance? His father. The man who stood to lose everything, including his barren wife's entire fortune, were anyone to find out. He had to be disposed of, didn't he? It was the only way she could ensure Jakub's safety. She'd sell her soul to the devil for that boy.

And maybe, by sitting in this lovely room the color of Christopher's eyes, she was signing the contract in blood.

So be it, she thought, listening to the peals of laughter filtering from down the hall where Jakub entertained the Blackwells' delighted toddler with their nanny, a bawdy woman named Gemma.

This whole thing had begun in blood. The moment Chief Inspector Morley had returned her glove, stained with Agnes's blood, and recited the horror of her dearest friend's death, Millie must have known the bloodshed was not over. For years she'd been waiting, wondering if the man who'd left Agnes's womb on the cobbles of London would return for her.

Or for her son.

She'd taken steps to make certain he wouldn't, done what she'd had to do. Every step culminating in this arrangement with Christopher Argent. That cold, tortured, beautiful, lethal . . .

. . . Blind, irritating, *stupid* man.

He'd been silent to the point of infuriating when he'd scooped her and Jakub into his carriage after their late breakfast and deposited them at the Blackwells' Mayfair mansion with terse instructions not to leave Dorian Blackwell's sight. Of course, the Earl and Countess Northwalk had been delightfully accommodating, but the intensity of the morning, and the life-altering events of the previous night, had left Millie feeling drained and irritable. Helpless, and maybe a little bit rejected. This was all so new to her, this ledge upon which she balanced. One wrong move, one bad decision, and her heart could be broken or lost . . . and so could her life.

"Miss LeCour . . . Millie, are you all right?" Farah held the teapot poised in the air, her delicate features a picture of patience and concern.

"I'm sorry." Millie summoned a brilliant smile. "What were you saying?"

"I was asking if I could refresh your tea."

"Please." Holding out her cup, she added a dash of genuine apology to her voice. "I didn't mean to be rude. I suppose I'm still having a hard time believing my luck. I never imagined I'd be a guest of the illustrious Lord and Lady Northwalk."

Farah, dressed in lavender and lace, her hair and eyes as stunningly light as Millie's were dark, sent her a perceptive glace from beneath pale lashes. "Don't you mean the *infamous* Lord and Lady Northwalk?"

"I prefer *notorious*." A shadow stirred from the giant leather chair that had been pulled next to the fire, whereby Dorian Blackwell, the *notorious* Blackheart of Ben More, effectively hid his features behind a book.

Millie wondered if he held the book that close to spare her his startling visage, or because he could only read out of his one good eye. Millie had heard he lost the use of his other one in the Underworld War, and that it had lost all pigment, but the earl was now wearing an eye patch, and she had a hard time telling if she was disappointed or relieved. Even with the patch, Blackwell's features were frightening enough. His one good eye seemed to ritualistically and ruthlessly assess and calculate. She felt as though only after a few moments in his company, he knew all her secrets, understood her weaknesses, and could dismantle her body and mind if he had the notion. He was large and dark as the devil and just as handsome, or would be if not for the permanently sardonic expression.

That all changed when he looked at his astonishingly angelic wife. Millie had liked Lady Northwalk immediately, and after watching her interact with her adoring, almost obsessive husband, all suspicion about Farah's involvement with Christopher dissipated like the smoke of a snuffed candle.

"Yes, my love, you've succeeded in making yourself notorious, haven't you?" she teased. Farah set the teapot down and offered Millie the sugar. "It's so amusing that you should express your sweet sentiment, because I was only just examining my good fortune at hosting the one and only Millie LeCour, London's darling of the stage." She took a dainty sip. "Won't all of society be green with envy when I tell them I had your exclusive company to tea?"

Millie beamed at her, then let her smile die in slow increments. "I only wish . . . that we'd become acquainted under different . . . better circumstances."

"As do I." Farah's small, compassionate smile was artlessly genuine. She'd have made a terrible actress, and that endeared her to Millie quite a bit. "But I hope you feel safe and comfortable here, until Argent comes to tell us you and your lovely son are out of danger and takes you back with him."

Millie stared down into her tea, her other gloved hand squeezing into a fist, mirroring the action of her heart. "I don't think he'll take me back with him. Once he . . . once everything is all said and done I think our . . . arrangement will be over. Our contract settled."

The heart that felt strangled by a squeezing fist now dropped like a lead weight.

Gently, Farah set her teacup down and regarded her with the same excessive curiosity she had when she'd seen Millie and Jakub for the first time. "How long have you had an . . . arrangement with Argent?" Her arrested expression belied the casualness of her tone.

"Farah," Dorian rumbled.

"Oh, I don't mean to pry," Farah rushed. "It's only that I've known Argent for a few years now and I must admit this is unprecedented. He must be very fond of you and your son."

Lord Northwalk turned his page with a forceful gesture and cleared his throat.

"I don't mind the question," Millie murmured. "I've only known Chr—Mr. Argent several days." Though it did seem like a lifetime. Or perhaps the last time she felt as though she knew herself was a lifetime ago.

"He is handsome, isn't he?" Farah asked conspiratorially. "And, despite being a bit phlegmatic, he really is charming at times."

"As charming as a typhus epidemic," Millie quipped into her teacup.

Blackwell's book seemed to give a strangled snort.

"Oh dear." Farah's golden brows, a touch more golden than her pale hair, drew together. "Are you cross with him?"

"Of course she's cross with him," said the book. "He's an idiot."

"Are you reading, or having this conversation with us?" Farah asked her husband.

"I'm reading."

"Then I'll thank you not to slander your friend in front of his . . . his . . ." Farah stalled, and Millie wished she could help the woman. She didn't know what she was to Argent, either. Didn't know if there was a word for it, exactly. And all the ones that sprang to mind were distasteful at best and descended into criminal.

"Argent doesn't have friends," Dorian muttered. "He has people he'd find it a little more distasteful to kill."

"He's saved your life more than once," Lady Northwalk pointed out. And, Millie remembered, Dorian had been there that terrible night to help remove the tar from Christopher's arm.

"Only because I returned the favor and/or I paid him a great deal of money."

"Oh tosh." Farah turned back to Millie. "Ignore him, he's an incurable grump today. Those two would die for each other and neither of them have the emotional capacity to admit it."

The man behind the book fell silent and Millie found that more telling than a confession. Though she had the impression that if Dorian Blackwell were to truly wake up grumpy, they'd find a few more bodies floating in the Thames than usual.

"Christopher *is* an idiot," Millie agreed with a little more vehemence than she'd intended.

Farah scooted to the edge of her chair, managing to make even that movement seem dainty and graceful. "Millie, dear, has he been cruel to you?"

"If you don't count the three assassination attempts, then no."

"Three?" The book snapped shut. Millie found herself the sole focus of Dorian Blackwell's dark, unsettling attention. He studied her for a long moment, disassembling her and examining her for spare parts. Firelight glinted off hair as black as her own, the rest of him bathed in the waning light of the fading afternoon still spilling in from the open drapes.

Millie met his stare with an unflinching one of her own. She was an actress, and if she knew a thing about her craft, it was to hide the nerves she battled. It was not wise to show weakness to a man like the Blackheart of Ben More.

"Did you know, Miss LeCour, that Christopher Argent has never *attempted* an assassination in his life?" He delivered his words with the carelessness of a nobleman, but they landed with a mountain of meaning. "Once he marks a victim, their every breath is borrowed from a miracle. He's gone into a building full of the deadliest men, and been the only one to emerge. Christopher Argent does not *attempt* assassination. He's mastered it." Unfolding his tall, powerful frame from his chair, he prowled to the dainty jewel-blue couch across from her, identical to the one upon which she sat, and claimed it. "And yet, here you are."

Millie squirmed beneath his stare. Up close, Dorian Blackwell was more than unsettling, he was a force of nature. A force to be reckoned with.

"I think Argent is a secret romantic," Farah said, looking inordinately pleased with herself.

Millie and Dorian both turned to stare at Farah as though she'd lost her mind.

"Or have you forgotten, dear husband." Lady Northwalk smiled at Dorian as though she'd made a joke. "That Argent once held my own contract in his hands, and instead of collecting on it, he turned it over to you."

Blackwell's eye narrowed. "That wasn't romanticism, that was self-preservation. He knew that if he didn't prevent your death I'd have waged a battle that would have made Waterloo look like a mere squabble between spoiled children."

Farah reached for Dorian, putting an ungloved hand over his. He looked down at it for a moment and what Millie saw in that look caused her to blink back emotion. There was more deferential veneration in Dorian Blackwell's world for the slim woman's pale hand than a zealot had for his god. How would it be, to be loved like that?

"He could have killed me and been rid of me and you'd have been none the wiser," Farah pointed out.

"*I* would have known," Dorian insisted.

"My point is, I believe Argent wanted us to find each other." She tightened her hold on Blackwell. "And the point my husband is trying to make is that if he left you alive, if he took it upon himself to protect you, then you must be very special to him, indeed."

Millie could never have admitted this to polite society, but there was something that told her these two would understand the nature of their arrangement. "I paid him for his protection," she admitted. "He wanted me, and I . . . gave myself to him."

Dorian shook his head. "He's wanted things in the past. Women, included. And he's paid for them or gone without. *You*. You are something else. And he is an idiot."

"Why do you keep saying that?" Farah queried.

"Because, from the way you and Argent were acting when he brought you here, I surmised that she likely offered him her heart, and he quickly and thoroughly broke it."

Millie studied the floor, again impressed by how perfectly it would have matched Christopher's eyes. "Not broken, Lord Northwalk, but bruised," she confessed.

"Do you know about the circumstances of his birth?" Farah asked.

"Yes."

Dorian's brows lifted. "Are you aware of how his mother died?"

"I am."

"And you obviously know about his . . . vocation." Lady Northwalk tapped a tiny divot in her chin with the finger of her free hand.

"I've seen his scars," Millie told them. "I realize what he's done and what he's capable of doing. He thinks he is damned, but . . . I still believe he's worth redeeming. I'm willing to try, but he . . . he . . ." Millie swiped at a stray tear of hurt and frustration and wondered miserably if it wasn't for the best. She could only give him her heart if he'd hold out his hand to take it. She wasn't the kind of woman to toss it to someone who didn't want it.

"Like I said . . ." Dorian kissed his wife's hand and flipped open his book. "An idiot."

Farah nodded, but leaned across to Millie and touched her knee. "Men like Argent . . . like . . ." She motioned to her distracted husband with darting eyes. "They need—"

"Miss Farah, Miss LeCour?" The nanny, a skinny pale woman with frizzy, ash-colored hair, rushed into the parlor, bony hands wringing her white apron. " 'Ave you seen yer boy?"

Millie shot to her feet, followed by the earl and countess, a burning coal of dread ripping through her chest as though she'd taken it from the fire and swallowed it whole. "I thought he was with you," she croaked.

" 'E was, miss, 'e was, but I was changing Faye's nappy and 'e begged off to the loo." The woman, Gemma was her name, went impossibly paler, her big dirty brown eyes completely ringed with white. "I thought 'e's gone too long, so I went about lookin' for 'im, when 'e didn't answer, I thought 'e came lookin' for you."

Icy fingers of dread squeezed all the air from Millie's lungs. She turned to Blackwell. "Could anyone have gotten in? Could he have been taken?"

Blackwell strode to the door. "Does he have a penchant for hiding?"

Millie shook her head, the room spinning with the movement. "Not at all."

"I'll check the second floor, but the likelihood of anyone breaking into *my* home is slim to none. I have a man on each story and multiple guards."

The door chimed down the entry hall of the house and Millie launched herself past Blackwell, her hope flaring. It was just a mistake; he'd been playing in the yard. She'd be so stern with him, so angry, but she'd kiss his precious face first.

Yanking the door open, she found a rough-looking man in a nice suit standing wringing his hat much in the same way as Gemma had. " 'Ello," he said in an accent that belonged nowhere close to the fine streets of Mayfair. He addressed his greeting above her head, so Millie knew Blackwell stood directly behind her.

"I don't know if this is important or not, but Chappy seen a boy head down the street and head into the park. 'E thought the boy was carrying a knife 'alf his size, and up to no good. Did 'e come from this house?"

Millie seized the man. "Did he have on a blue jacket?"

"I fink so."

Dorian said a few things Millie had never heard before and pulled her back into the house, thrusting her toward Farah. "I'm going to the park to look for him. I'll take Harker here and Murdoch. You stay and lock the door. I'm leaving Mathias and Worden with you."

"Sod off," Millie hissed. "That's my son and I'm going with you. Thurston is likely already taken care of, and with him gone I'm out of danger. But if Jakub is in Hyde Park by himself, anything could happen." What on earth could Jakub have been thinking? He was such an obedient boy. It was so unlike him to go anywhere without telling her first.

Dorian shook his head. "Argent said—"

"We just agreed Argent is an idiot." Millie threw his words back at him. "And so are you if you think you'll stop me."

Dorian glanced back at his wife, who was bouncing a fussy toddler on her hip and nodding to him. "Fine, but stay close."

To assassinate someone during the day took more finesse than under cover of night. Christopher Argent stood in his casual suit coat next to Lord Thruston's hedgerow at

St. James's and stifled a yawn. To maintain optimal conditioning, he generally kept strict sleep and training schedules. Last night had changed everything.

In every possible way.

Patience was a virtue to most, and a necessity to him. Today, patience was something he would have murdered for.

Literally.

Something was wrong. He wasn't himself. In fact, he could feel his sense of self slipping through his fingers like a mooring rope in a tempest. His shoulders gathered into a tense bunch, threatening to engulf his neck. His stomach twisted and roiled, refusing sustenance. His hands were twitchy, his lungs tight, and his legs restless. He wanted to sprint far enough to outrun the desire and desperation banked in his loins. He wanted to climb into a dark hole and hide from the memories that stalked him through the streets of London like a pack of starving beasts. A part of him wanted to wallow like a dog in the bed they'd shared, engulfing himself in her scent. The other half kept scrubbing his clammy palms on his trousers, as though he could rid them of the recollection of the texture of her creamy skin.

But they wouldn't forget. *He* would never be rid of her. Millie LeCour would forever be a part of him whether he saw her again or not. She owned some sort of distinction that he couldn't identify. She was his first, she was his only, and his every. However, those sentiments remained incomplete, didn't they? He needed to fill in the missing bits, but he didn't dare. Couldn't possibly.

He'd been her first, her only lover. And he was going to walk away.

Because he was afraid. Afraid of her. Afraid of himself. Afraid to hope, to want, and . . .

To feel.

He was a fucking coward. He knew it, and now she knew it as well. He could see it in her eyes when he'd left her.

That's why it was better not to look.

Spotting the slim, elegant form of Lady Thurston stepping from the manor gate, he noted which pocket she slipped the key into before Argent gave the woman his back and leaned casually against a stone post on the corner of the property. He used the time it took for her to brush behind him to check the windows of Thurston Place to make certain no one was looking. He counted her steps without glancing over his shoulder, taking into account her size, stride, and adjusting for any momentary pauses. With his honed senses, he could make out the moment she passed behind him, and he turned to trail her for less than a half minute, the time it took to get the precise angle within the foot traffic of St. James's to pick her key from her pocket without her knowledge. That accomplished, he took three more steps, and then smoothly changed direction, back toward the mansion.

According to the man Argent had watching Lord Thurston since the night Argent had fought in the pit, he had learned that the earl was a creature of habit, which made his job easier. At half past five Thurston retired to his library to enjoy a cigar and a port or Scotch to relax until the evening meal. Now, at three quarters past the hour, he'd been given enough time to pour his drink and begin to enjoy his cigar.

The cigar he would never finish.

Glibly, as though he belonged there, Argent unlocked the gate and strode inside, immediately ducking into the long, late-afternoon shadow cast by the western wall and its hedgerow. Staying to the shade, he circled the gardens, using them for cover until he aligned with a clear path to the back trellis covered with thick ivy. The latticework threaded through to cover a large pipe and gutter that served to hold the wood structure in place. If he distributed his weight as evenly as he could, it should hold . . . If not, he knew how to minimize the damage of a fall and would have to enter on the main or lower floors, which was not optimal due to the amount of staff having their tea and meal below stairs before they had to bustle to feed the household.

The top floors would be deserted of staff, thus providing him with ample time and privacy in which to conduct his business.

A sprint and one-legged leap off the brick wall brought the trellis into reach, and Argent hung from one arm for a breathless moment. On a strong swing, his other arm caught the trellis and he climbed with a hand-over-hand ascent that became exponentially easier once his feet could do some of the work. At this angle, even so far up, he was effectively invisible from the street, but anyone who dared peek out the second- or third-story windows would catch him immediately.

With one last grunt of effort, he used his upper body strength to swing from the trellis to the third-floor balcony, the door of which, to his delight, stood ajar, gauzy fabric billowing in the gentle breeze.

Argent had hoped to use his garrote, to watch Jakub's villainous father struggle against the cord as it cut into the skin of his throat, slowly filling his airway with blood and then horribly undoing the curl of wire within the man's neck, pulling tight and snapping the spinal column in the process.

Argent filled his lungs with calming breath as his hands began to tremble. What was this? Rage? Anticipation? Perhaps an infuriating combination of the two? This was too dangerous, he shouldn't want it this much.

"Your death will be slow and painful. I was paid extra for slow and painful."

Argent froze. That melodic, conversational voice could only belong to one man. A man he *knew* he'd have to tangle with again, but not so soon.

Not today.

Drawing his long knife out of its sheath, Argent tucked it against his arm and slithered into the library.

The splash of entrails spilling onto the floor assaulted his senses. The sound, like the buckets of steaming water the shop owners splashed over the dirty cobbles every morning on the Strand, only a little muffled by the fine carpet. The sight, like the unraveling of a gruesome rope, or something a Scotsman wouldn't mind eating. Then there was the smell.

Argent was no stranger to blood, and had no scruples about opening a vein, but the human body was home to all kinds of gore and offal, and he generally liked to keep those bits encased in their respective cavities.

Charles Dorshaw, though, had no such compunctions. He gleefully turned his victims inside out. Often whilst still alive, as David, Lord Thurston, currently was.

Blue eyes identical to Jakub's magnified bespectacled ones peeled open as wide as their sockets allowed as Lord Thurston's scream was muffled by his gag. He struggled uselessly against the bonds tying his naked body to his chair. When he spied Argent, he slumped back, his eyelids fluttering. They both knew he was already a dead man.

"The ironic thing is . . ." Dorshaw continued his one-sided conversation with his victim, as relaxed and unperturbed as a man at his club. "I *prefer* slow and painful, so it's unnecessary to pay me extra as you would most—purveyors of my services." Wiping the blood on the carpets, Dorshaw brought the clean blade's flat, reflective surface to his face and brushed a lock of dark hair behind his ear with a bloody finger. Like a lady primping in a mirror. "But when a client wants their victim to suffer as badly as mine does, when they offer such a vulgar amount of money, it's just bad business sense to turn it down, wouldn't you agree, Argent?"

Argent said nothing, but closed the doors behind him, securing the exit. Dorshaw likely had caught his reflection in the blade. If Dorshaw took care of Fenwick, Argent's own intended victim, he could rid the world of Dorshaw and call it a day's work well done.

"You're going to have to stop interrupting my kills like this, Argent, I'm beginning to think it's personal." Rising from his crouched position on the floor, Dorshaw faced him, tossing his knife back and forth from one elegant hand to the next.

"Did you escape or were you released?" Argent asked coldly.

Dorshaw scoffed, dropping a hand and leaning on Fenwick's shoulder as if it were the back of a chair. "We both know I've never met a prison cell that could hold me for long. Whereas you, however, never seem to escape yours . . ."

"How the devil would you know—"

"Do you want to know what I find curious about you turning up here?" Dorshaw queried, tapping the tip of his knife against his pursed lips.

"All I want to know is how long you'll take to die."

Dorshaw chuckled, his dark eyes dancing with the almost sensual thrill he felt at spilling blood combined with the heady mix of having an edge on the competition. "Oh come now, Argent, you're known for your efficiency, not your cruelty. That's my domain. Don't leave me in suspense. I was given this contract against Lord Thurston exclusively. So that leaves me to wonder what you're doing here and what your business is with Lord Thurston. We don't have to be at odds, you know. I could make him tell you anything you wanted before he dies. We'll call it . . . a professional courtesy."

Argent paused, considering the consequences of stalling. "I want to know what he's doing with the missing boys, if they're still alive . . . and why he contracted against the lives of all those women."

"Women like Millicent LeCour?" Dorshaw's eyes flared, and Argent fought the urge to pluck them out. "Should we ask him? He's bleeding faster than I'd expected, he doesn't have much time." With a cruel yank, Fenwick's gag fell to his throat, and Dorshaw held the knife beneath the man's jugular. "Tell my friend Argent just why those women are dying, and how they're connected to you." Bending his lean, graceful frame down toward his victim, Dorshaw stage-whispered in Fenwick's ear, his lips almost touching the man's honey-colored hair tipped with his own blood. "Tell him just *who* is responsible for all that killing, and *who,* upon occasion, has actually wielded the knife."

"You?" Argent accused, pointing his own knife at Dorshaw.

Thurston's pallor had begun to match the marble in his fireplace. Ivory-white rimmed with blue. Dry, bloodless lips parted, and panting breaths formed his last words. "Those boys . . . they're . . . mine." Tears streamed down his once robust face, the wrinkles becoming more prominent as the veins beneath the skin emptied. "Jakub . . . my son."

"You don't deserve to say his name, you disgusting swine." Argent snarled at the dying man. "Now where are the rest? Are they alive?"

"I . . . don't . . . know . . ." The man's breath dissolved into painful, sobbing coughs.

"Oh dear." Dorshaw tsked. "I feel as though we've run out of time." He petted the earl's hair like one would an ailing dog, then his eyes brightened as though he had an idea. "I suppose I could tell you, as I know where they are, and if they are dead or alive, as I collected on half the contracts, myself."

"Where?" Argent demanded. Thinking of Millie, of Jakub, of all the boys lost and never found, or locked away and not released until it was too late. "Where are they?"

"I said I *could* tell you, but I don't think I will. You were unforgivably rude last time we met, and that doesn't foster feelings of good will, does it?"

Argent brandished his own weapon. "You're going to tell me."

Dorshaw giggled, a high, gleeful sound, waving his own knife. "Mine's bigger and longer, which means I don't have to."

"I'll make you." Stepping forward, he tracked Dorshaw as the wiry man ducked behind Fenwick's chair.

"It's not your way, torturing information out of people."

"It is now." Advancing, Argent tested the knife in his hand, feeling the familiar ridges, knowing how it conformed to his grip. He was going to have his pound of flesh before he put this sick bastard down.

This time, he wouldn't be interrupted.

"Not one more step or I'll shoot you both!" Chief Inspector Carlton Morley bellowed from the library doorway.

Goddammit. Argent froze, knowing his back was the broadest target for Morley's pistol, and Dorshaw was partially shielded by Thurston's fine chair and also, if the angle was correct, Argent's body.

He'd never had much in the way of run-ins with Inspector Morley, but he did know that the Scotland Yard leader hated Blackwell.

This could end badly for him. The only advantage he had was his proximity to the French doors and thereby the closest means of escape. However, it was deucedly difficult to outrun a bullet.

"You're here for Dorshaw," Argent said calmly. "I have nothing to do with this."

"I did, indeed, follow Dorshaw's trail here," Morley stated, his deep voice just as calm and smooth as Argent's, touched with the air of one who wasn't used to having his authority questioned. "But there's a disemboweled nobleman in front of you, and you're holding a knife."

"He's killed half of those women. He cuts on them. Leaves only clothing and some entrails to find. Sound familiar?" Argent dared to look over his shoulder to pinpoint Morley's exact location. "He knows what happened to those boys."

"Did you kill the other half of them, Christopher Argent?"

Christ. Argent gritted his teeth.

"That's right, I know who you are and who you work for, so you'll stay where you stand until my men show, or I'll paint that rare book collection with your brain matter. I'm that good of a shot, so don't even think—"

Morley didn't see the knife Dorshaw threw until it was almost upon him. The inspector was able to turn his torso just in time to absorb the blade into the right shoulder, instead of the heart.

The gun went off. Glass shattered. Morley went down.

Argent whipped his own knife at Dorshaw, who ducked in time to miss a blade through the eye. Another blade was in Argent's hand before the first weapon embedded in the far wall with an ominous sound.

Grinning, Dorshaw also produced a weapon from his boot, remaining where he'd crouched behind Lord Thurston's chair. Sometime between the man's last words and now, the earl had died, and taken his secrets with him.

Fuck.

"Give it up, Dorshaw, I'm blocking your only means of

escape," Argent taunted. "Tell me what I want to know, and I'll make it painless."

"Let me go before the copper's minions arrive, and I'll tell you everything."

"Tell me everything now and I'll consider—"

Fenwick's chair toppled, revealing Dorshaw's sinewy body mid-leap, his knife arcing toward Argent.

Crouching, Argent caught Dorshaw by the hips and used the man's own momentum to throw him over his shoulder and into the wall. Hopefully head-first.

It was too much to hope. The man caught himself, rolling out of the fall, absorbing minimal damage and unfolding to stand with his back to the window. His lip was bleeding, and broken glass had done a number on his skin, but all wounds seemed superficial.

They circled each other, low and ready, testing the reach of their blade, looking for a place to strike.

"What's happening to you?" Dorshaw's handsome face grimaced with disgust. "Protecting a mark, all for a piece of quim?"

"Shut up." Christopher sliced, but the blow was parried.

"Why not just fuck her first, then kill her and collect the money?" Dorshaw smirked. "It's simple enough, even for someone like you."

"I don't enjoy that," Christopher hissed. He lunged again, but caught the edge of Dorshaw's jacket before his blade glanced off Dorshaw's knife. "I'm not like you."

"I know you're not." Dorshaw's smile revealed sharp, uneven teeth. "I'd kill her first, and then fuck her."

Losing the battle for his control, Christopher saw the opening, just the slightest gap in Dorshaw's guard, whether a trap or a mistake, he was going to fucking take it, and there would be two men's entrails staining the Fenwick library carpets.

The click of a revolver action pulled him up short. "Don't. Fucking. Move."

Morley had gained his feet, his right arm curled uselessly around the large knife almost embedded to the hilt in his shoulder. Though his stern features were devoid of color, his left hand, the hand holding the gun, was absolutely steady.

Argent sent him a silent tirade. This was supposed to have been easy. A quick climb, the snap of a neck, and then Millie and Jakub would be out of danger. Men like him, ones that shifted through shadows, they had no purpose for loud and messy guns, not on a job like this. Argent made a silent promise that his pistol would be his new permanent accessory. If rogue coppers were carrying them now, it might be a necessity from here on out.

"Shoot him," Argent commanded.

Dorshaw dropped his knife and put his hands up, backing toward the broken window in the guise of making himself more visible to Morley.

"You heard what I said, shoot him. *Now*."

"I'm unarmed," Dorshaw cried, throwing a bit of fear into his voice for flair. "And you only have this man's unholy word that I'm guilty of anything that transpired here today."

"You . . . threw a knife at me," Morley slurred, a bit incredulous. Argent wondered if it was blood loss or shock making the inspector unsteady; either way, it didn't bode well.

"I was aiming for him," Dorshaw lied, gesturing to Argent. "Upon my word." He took several steps back, inching closer to the window, hands still in the air.

"Shoot, goddammit," Argent snarled. "He's going to escape."

"No I won't. I'm not leaving this city." Dorshaw smirked, glee twinkling in his wild eyes. "I think I know where I'm going next. To catch up with an old friend, the Blackheart of Ben More . . . I hear he has a houseguest who's going to just *die* when she sees me."

Twisting his torso, Dorshaw leaped for the window.

Argent dove after him.

Morley's first shot went wild. He cocked the hammer and tried again, this time hitting the window molding just as Dorshaw slipped beneath it. His third bullet landed so close to Argent's face as he moved to follow, that he couldn't be sure whether it was the bullet or splinters from the windowpane that grazed his cheek.

"I won't miss this time," Morley warned.

"He's getting away, you bloody fuck wit!" Argent eyed the pistol. Two bullets left. Five paces away. If he charged, what were the odds of Morley missing? He considered the inspector's condition, losing blood, his hard lips pinched with the indescribable pain of the blade embedded in his shoulder. His pale hair now slick with cold sweat that trickled down his neck. *Maybe,* Argent thought, maybe he had a chance.

"Didn't you hear him?" Argent demanded. "He's going after Millie. I have to stop him. Lower your weapon."

Morley snorted and swayed. "He said she's with bloody Blackwell." Morley's eyes shuttered, then snapped open. "He'll keep her safe . . . though you were a fool to leave her alone with him." His expression twisted into something bitter, and he thrust the weapon forward.

Argent didn't find it at all unmanly to flinch.

"He's probably squirreled her away to his fucking castle in Scotland . . . and married her," Morley slurred bitterly.

Jesus Christ, Argent didn't have time for a history lesson. Millie, *his* Millie, was in danger. Despite his many contacts, Blackwell may not have any idea that Dorshaw had escaped, that he was descending on his home. And, though there was no place more secure save Buckingham

Palace, itself, Argent couldn't breathe. And didn't think he'd breathe again until Millie was in his arms and Dorshaw was in the ground. Not specifically in that order.

"Hold still!" Morley barked.

Argent hadn't moved a muscle. He was wasting precious time. He had to go. Now.

"I said stop where you are!" The chief inspector made an animal noise of pain, doubling over his injured arm but valiantly keeping his pistol trained. Obviously, his vision swam from shock or blood loss.

"Let. Me. Go," Argent warned quietly, remaining absolutely motionless.

"Never," the man croaked, before falling to the ground in a dead faint, a pool of blood collecting around his shoulder.

Argent would never be able to tell why he did what he did next, but in a split decision, he pulled the rope next to Thurston's desk on the way out, which would bring the staff from the basement. It was the best chance Morley had at survival.

And as Argent slid back into the shadows, jumped the fence, and ran for the Blackwell estate with desperation filling his lungs upon every breath, he knew *he* was Millie's best chance.

An icy dread stole through his entire body; a sense of impending catastrophe gathering in the very air that whistled past his ears told him that he might already be too late.

Chapter Twenty-Five

Chaos reigned at the Blackwell household. A dozen men gathered in the yard drawing the notice of curious neighbors. One of them opened the gate as Argent shoved his way through the gathering onlookers, and pounded up the drive at a dead run. A heavy weight burned within him, that sense of impending doom flaring into a frantic knowledge.

Bursting through the front entry, he bounced two men off the walls in his haste to get to the parlor. "Millie?" His heart beat her name, though even as he dashed into the room and searched every face, a part of him knew he wouldn't find her.

Farah held a sobbing Jakub to her breast, stroking his hair as silent tears rolled down cheeks pale with worry. A harried Gemma bounced Blackwell's fussy daughter, her own tears spilling onto the child's dress. Murdoch, Blackwell's grizzled Scottish steward, sat in the corner holding a bottle of Ravencroft's finest whilst his lover, Gregory Tallow, held pressure to a bleeding torso wound.

"Where is she?" Argent bellowed.

"Argent." Blackwell's cool, dark voice behind him preceded the man's gentle hand on his shoulder.

Strengthened by desperation, Argent turned on Blackwell and shoved him against the far wall, blocking out the varied sounds of shock and dismay. "Where. Is. Millie?" Argent slammed him again for emphasis.

Blackwell put up a hand, staying the approaching men drawing their weapons. "It's only been a matter of minutes. I'm gathering men to search for her, Dorshaw took her from Hyde Park. He can't have gone far."

Argent stepped away with a desperate sound, took two paces, pulled at his hair, and then turned back, landing a hook to the jaw that not even Blackwell could have seen coming. "How could you let her out of your sight?" He swung again, but someone grabbed his wrist. He threw the bastard off, lunging for Dorian, only to be grappled by two men, one on each arm. A third, the one he'd tossed aside, snaked a thick elbow around his neck from behind, putting pressure on his throat.

The monstrous arm could only belong to Frank Walters, one of the biggest men alive, and famously a gentle giant, his wits having been stolen by one too many bashes to the head in prison.

Another of Blackwell's men seized his middle. And still it took all their strength to keep Argent from tearing the Blackheart of Ben More to shreds.

Argent had helped to train these men, this underworld army, and he'd never regretted anything more in his life. "You had one job," he yelled. "To keep her *alive*. How the bloody hell did she get into the park?"

" 'Twas my fault, Argent," Murdoch confessed through his gray beard. "I didna see him coming at me until he nigh well skewered me. I lost yer woman. I'm damned sorry for it."

"H-he needs a doctor," Tallow stuttered. "He's losing too much blood."

"One's been sent for," Farah said.

Dorian swiped at the back of his split and bleeding lip, his disfigured face contorted into an ugly sneer. "You'll answer for that," he vowed, but then he glanced past Argent toward his wife, and a grim sort of understanding settled upon his cruel features. "But it'll wait until after we get your woman back."

"If anything happens to her I swear to Christ, I'll—"

"Stop it, all of you," Farah ordered from behind him. "You're upsetting the children."

"It was me!" A tiny voice cut through the masculine growls with high-pitched clarity. Little feet pounded on the wood floors until Jakub stood in front of him, his spectacles fogged with emotion and his skin patched red with grief and fear. The child collapsed against him, thin arms surrounding his thighs and wails of grief wetting the side of his shirt. "It was me, Mr. Argent, it was *my* fault." The boy lost his breath to sobs before he could continue. "I—I wanted to help you. I wanted to use what you taught me to keep her safe. I—I took a knife and snuck away to find you."

Something crumpled inside of Argent, and again he struggled against the men holding him back.

In front of him, Blackwell nodded at Argent's subduers, and he was released. Sinking to his knees, Argent allowed Jakub's arms to encircle his neck and bury his little face in his throat, unleashing a tempest of tears against his skin. "He's going to hurt her and it's my fault," the child cried. "I *can't* lose her. She's my mama. I want her. I want her *back*. I'm sorry, I'm sorry, I'm so sorry."

Argent wanted to believe the pressure in his throat was due to the clinging boy. More than anyone, he understood exactly the helplessness causing the violent spasms of grief and horror ripping through the tiny body heaving against his. Suddenly he found his arms around the boy and, as he held the distraught child against him, the decades-gone memory of his own fear and helplessness shuddered through every muscle and left him one raw, open wound.

He'd wanted her back, his mother. Begged her not to leave him. Cried and cried for help. Sobbed his apologies against her cold body. It had been *his* fault. If he'd not fought back, she might have lived. The guilt and rage had drowned the child he once was in a shallow pool of her blood.

"I want Mama," the boy whimpered. "I want her back."

"I do, too," Argent said hoarsely, meaning it with every fiber of his being. Dragging Jakub away from him, he looked the boy right in the eyes, somewhat hidden behind the smeared glass. "I'm going after your mother, but I have to leave now. Do you promise to remain here, upon your honor?"

Jakub wiped his runny nose on his sleeve and nodded, fat tears still streaming down his miserable face. Argent took him by the shoulders and shook him gently. "Listen to me, Jakub. No matter what happens, this *isn't* your fault. The blame lies solely on the shoulders of the man who took her. Do you understand me?"

Jakub swallowed, biting hard on his lower lip.

"You were being brave. You wanted to protect your mother. There's nothing in the world more honorable than that. But until you're a man, you have to leave that to me."

"I promise, I'll do anything." Jakub surged against him. "I'll do anything if you bring her home."

Argent stood, the boy locked in his arms, and met Blackwell's suspiciously bright eye. The Blackheart of Ben More's jaw was clenched, his chin may have been unsteady, and the man whom he'd met only the year after the tragedy of his mother's death nodded to him. A silent vow. He'd also lost his mother violently, and Argent knew the memory still haunted the man.

Turning to the room of wide-eyed and moist-eyed spectators, he deposited Jakub into Farah's reaching arms.

"We'll look after him, Argent," she reassured him. "No matter what."

Argent nodded and turned to leave. He was going to tear this city apart, stone by fucking stone, if he had to. He was going to bring Millie home.

"He'll take his time with her," Blackwell said in a low voice, falling into step behind him as he left the parlor. "We have a good chance of tracking them."

"We?" Argent clipped through clenched teeth, every heartbeat that passed a moment Millie could be hurting, or worse. Wrenching open the door to Blackwell's study and pulling the statue lever that uncovered the panel of weapons behind the wall, Argent claimed an arsenal.

"You didn't mean to find her alone, did you?" Blackwell handed him a pistol, which he stowed beneath his jacket before selecting a few scabbards and throwing knives. "I wouldn't have found Farah without your help."

"I wouldn't have lost Millie without yours," Argent bandied back, shouldering past Dorian to stalk toward the entrance.

"I didn't know Dorshaw had escaped police custody." Blackwell trailed him with long, powerful strides. "And I was fair certain you'd taken care of Thurston by then."

Argent jogged down the front stairs of the Blackwell mansion, his mind on one thing.

Millie.

"I couldn't very well keep her from searching for her son," Dorian continued.

"You could have tied her to something."

"Fair enough," Dorian ceded, reaching out to block him from flinging the gate open. "Regardless of that, I'm coming with you, and bringing my men along. We'll find her faster if we're all looking."

Argent whirled on Dorian, but was stunned to see all

who surrounded him. Blackwell, Tallow, and even Walters, along with a few others he knew from Newgate. Wei Ping, Wu's nephew, held a nasty-looking curved metal pipe with blades thrust through the edges. Murdoch, of course, had his pale face pressed to the parlor glass.

He knew these men. Knew their weaknesses, knew their strengths. Had worked, fought, killed, and bled beside them. Dorian and he had done the impossible, organized these cutthroats and criminals into a well-oiled machine.

Argent had always thought he'd been alone, that he was on one side, and the entire world on another. There were faces of men whom he still wouldn't turn his back to in a dark alley, but they were here, ready to do his bidding.

Free of charge.

Whether out of loyalty, fear, advancement, or true sentiment, it didn't matter. To Argent, it still meant something.

"I think he's taken her to the tunnels." He addressed them all, referring to the ever-growing intricate network of underground waterways, trade routes, and smuggling networks that had wound beneath the city since the time of the Romans. "Rumor's always had it that Dorshaw lurks down there like a sewer rat. It's why they never find the bodies, not even the police will venture in certain places beneath ground."

"That's our domain," someone said. "We'll find 'im down there, and we'll fetch Miss LeCour. She'll be back on that stage in no time, you'll see."

"Do whatever you can to save her." Argent pushed open the gate and strode through the milling crowd of gaping gentry that parted in the wake of his wrath. "But Charles Dorshaw is *mine*."

Millie had been afraid before in her lifetime, for many reasons. She'd portrayed fear and terror on stage a myriad of times. She'd run from imaginary villains, and a few real ones in her day. But until this moment, Millie realized she'd never truly experienced fear in its raw, terrible, uncomplicated entirety. She'd heard all the analogies: weak with fear. Paralyzed by it. While they provided apt description of the condition, she didn't think the Bard, himself, could have found words for what she currently experienced. Because she very much doubted any existed. Her entire *body* was afraid. Her heart and head throbbed with it. Her limbs trembled with such force, she was almost grateful for the iron chains holding her arms above her head, as her legs threatened to give out at any moment. Her stomach churned with bile. Her mouth felt dry, and she couldn't seem to swallow around her heavy tongue.

Where was she?

An ancient-looking iron gate interrupted bleak stone walls and a close, moldy ceiling. She could hear the trickle of water somewhere in the distance, but it sounded more like rain hitting cobblestones than the rush of a river. Two lanterns sputtered on short wicks and Millie stared at them, willing them to stay lit, her immediate fear being the dark. The thick, heavy chains from which she was suspended were bolted to the stone and mortar maybe three feet above her head on each side.

She was alone for now, but for a rickety wooden chair and a long, sturdy table. Strange, grimy stains settled into the wood of that table and dripped from its legs, fueling her certainty that people had died in this room. Many people.

And there was no doubt in her mind that she was next.

This was a place for demons, maybe underground. A place that never saw the sun and was hidden from heaven. All those lost to this place were abandoned to their cruel fate.

Millie thought of Andromeda offered to the monster to appease jealous gods. Where was her Perseus? Did Christopher know she was missing?

Would he even look for her?

Her chains scraped against the stone as she struggled against them, trying to wrench her wrists this way and that, hoping to make them small enough to slip from the manacles. It didn't work, of course, but she couldn't help herself. The air seemed too thin, and she gasped for it, hating the desperate little noises escaping her throat. It smelled like death in here, like rot and age, and fear. Stone dust peppered the dirt floor with more of the same.

How had this happened? One moment she was searching for Jakub with the jolly and capable Murdoch, and then a familiar tall man with dark hair thrust a knife in Murdoch's belly and promised her in the loveliest voice that if she didn't come with him, he'd dismember her child.

She'd agreed, of course, but he'd hit her anyway, so hard that she'd seen stars dance behind her eyelids, and the time it had taken him to drag her underground was lost in a haze of dizziness and pain.

"Jakub?" she croaked around a growing lump in her throat. "Jakub, are you here?" She couldn't see through the darkness past the iron gate, and her greatest fear was that Jakub was out there in the shadows somewhere. Afraid. Alone. Or worse, *not* alone.

What if the monster was with him?

Renewing her fruitless struggle, she cried his name. "Answer me. Anyone? I'm here, come and find me!"

She called to whoever lurked out there in the darkness. To another hostage, to a would-be rescuer, to Charles Dorshaw, she didn't care. If he was in here with her, then he wasn't with Jakub. He wasn't harming her son.

The darkness answered her with terrifying, soul-crushing silence. She couldn't stand still and listen to it. While she still had breath left in her body, she had fire in her soul, and she would do whatever she could to escape. Which, at the moment . . . was nothing. The manacles held her fast, the stones revealed no weaknesses, and the door was on the other side of the cell.

Drat and blast and bloody hell.

Her growl of frustration echoed back at her as she jerked and yanked on her chains, pulling with all her strength. Which, admittedly, was far less than impressive, but she had to try. Dust spilled on the ground beside her. Especially the right side. What if that bolt were loose? The chamber seemed old enough, and if enough people had been held here, as desperate as her, struggling just as hard . . .

She tried not to think of that.

Leaning to the left, she levered her weight against the wall as much as she possibly could, and pulled on the chain with a grunt of effort. More dust fell. Encouraged, she leaned to the right, trying to get a different angle, and tried again. Shards of mortar joined the dust on the ground.

Her heart lifted. Trying different angles, she pulled and strained, training her eyes on the loosening bolt. Her wrists ached, the skin threatening to break. In tiny increments, the plate held by the two bolts separated from where it had been driven deep into the wall. If she could just keep going, she might get a hand free.

And then what?

She paused to gasp in a few breaths, shortened from exertion and fear. The flat iron plate the bolts secured for the chain could make a good weapon, there was that. And if she got one hand free, there was hope for the other.

Then she could worry about the gate. Studying the chains there, she knew a padlock of some kind held them in place. Millie had a few lock-picking skills gleaned from her brother Anzelm, before he left for America. Maybe she could find something—

The shadows shifted beyond the gate. Someone was out there. Was it her Perseus? Or the monster?

She knew the answer before the key turned in the ancient

iron lock. It reached to her through the darkness on a wave of malevolent, maniacal evil.

Charles Dorshaw, he had come for her.

The chains clinked ominously as he pulled them from around the bars, one by one, as though each link represented the last of the minutes in which she had to live. The gate swung open, and Dorshaw oozed into the small room.

He studied her with the most terrifying gaze. He looked at her in the way she imagined a proud father would regard his grown progeny, a strange mixture of accomplishment and anticipation for the future.

"For a moment there, I thought you'd slipped through my fingers, Miss LeCour," he said pleasantly. "But with Argent at Lord Thurston's, I knew you'd be vulnerable." Turning, he secured the chain again, wrapping it twice around the bars, and clipped a lock the size of her hand through the links. Then, he set about turning the wicks up on the lanterns that were set in both of the far corners of the small room, flicking his gaze back and forth from her to them and then adjusting. She'd seen Mr. Howard, the stage manager, do something quite similar before each performance.

Millie wondered what sort of horrific production Mr. Dorshaw had planned for the evening and a succession of tremors overtook her.

"Where is my son?" she demanded in a surprisingly steady voice. "What have you done with Jakub?"

Plucking his white gloves from thin, graceful fingers, he regarded her from beneath his lashes with a cryptic smile. Small lacerations interrupted his handsome visage, none of them deep enough to scar, but they added to his menace. "I assure you, I don't know where your son is at this precise moment."

"If you've so much as touched him, I'll see your heart

separated from your chest," she threatened, surging against her chains.

More of the mortar gave way, but if Dorshaw noticed, he didn't mention it.

Lust flared in his eyes. Lust, possession, and unholy anticipation. She'd seen it before, on the face of a different assassin, but she'd welcomed it then.

He sidled closer, that terrible little smile lifting the corner of his split lip. "My, my, Millie, does Argent know how fierce you are? How merciless? Is that why he wanted you so badly, I wonder?"

Wanted . . . past tense. Millie couldn't fathom why that should matter at a time like this, why she would even mark it, but she did, and it pierced her like a hunter's arrow.

"Where is my son?" she screamed at him, kicking out, but falling short as he stood just out of reach.

"I didn't lie to you." He shrugged, his expression never changing. "I don't know where your son is, I never had him to begin with. I imagine he's back at the Blackwell residence by now."

It was relief that did her legs in. She sagged against her chains until her shoulders protested. "Oh thank you, God," she whispered.

"Don't thank Him just yet, perhaps save that for when you meet Him." Dorshaw strolled to the left wall and removed a gray stone, uncovering a generous nook. From within it, he pulled a satchel and replaced the stone. The satchel he set on the long table, and each instrument he withdrew from it was more horrifying than the last.

Millie's eyes widened and her heart leaped another increment with the appearance of every new item. A bone saw, a hand drill, a scalpel, some sort of forceps, and a few things she'd never seen before and couldn't comprehend. Dorshaw was a madman with a doctor's implements.

In that moment *she knew*. She knew he was the man

who'd killed Agnes all those years ago. Knew that he'd left her friend's womb and her own bloodied gloves for the police to find.

"Why do you do this?" she asked. "How can you be so evil?"

"It's my vocation," he explained patiently as he organized his tools with the precision of a physician. "We all have to eat, don't we?" He let the disgusting implication of that statement hang in the air, and Millie felt the blood drain from her face.

"If this is nothing but a bargain for you, might we strike another?" It had worked for her before. If money was his motivation, she'd give him everything she had.

He tossed her an apologetic look. "It's too late for that sort of thing."

"Why?"

"Because, my darling, what we have here is a triangle of Olympian proportions."

Millie shook her head. "I don't understand."

"We all have our singular talents, don't we?" He picked up the scalpel and turned to her. "And yours, dear lady, is capturing the heart. I've seen you do it on stage, delivering your lines in such a way that by intermission, everyone is already besotted with you, including myself, I'm not ashamed to admit. I've watched you on many occasions." On any other face, his sly smile would have been charming. But as he moved closer, Millie's blood turned to ice.

"But your talents reach beyond that, don't they?" he continued. "You beguile men. You understand them. You've made a boy that is not of your body love you as fiercely as he would any mother. You've stolen the heart of the man even *I* was convinced was the most coldhearted, unfeeling killer in the empire. To be loved by the frigid, disciplined Christopher Argent . . . what must that be like?"

"I'm sure I don't know," Millie spat. "He doesn't love me. We had a . . . physical arrangement, that is all."

He laughed then, a musical, happy sound, ruptured by the stones. The echoes of his mirth turned demonic and brought unhallowed tears to Millie's eyes. "Don't be a willfully blind fool," he said tenderly, approaching her from the side this time to avoid the lash of her foot. "You have, indeed, beguiled the poor man, so much so that he doesn't even know which end is up anymore."

Reaching out, he caressed her cheek with the back of his fingers, and she flinched away from him, though her chains held her fast. "So lovely," he whispered.

Millie wrenched her neck as far away as she could. "You disgust me."

"I know." Dorshaw chuckled again. "There are many things that Argent and I have in common, other than our taste in women, of course. One of which is that our work keeps us so busy, we don't have the time to properly woo a woman. And, when there's competition for the affections of the lady we desire, things become so much more complicated, and so we must take matters into our own hands."

Millie gathered her courage, looked him in the eyes, and asked the question she knew she didn't want the answer to. "What do you mean?"

The cold bite of steel pressed against the base of her throat, and dragged lower, slicing through the gauzy fabric at her neck and chest, to dip in between her cleavage.

Millie stopped breathing.

"You've stolen the heart right out of my chest, Millicent LeCour." Dorshaw's eyes burned with earnest intensity. "My only recourse is to return the favor."

Chapter Twenty-Six

Millie let anger drown her panic. She must stay angry if she was going to remain alive. Fear made her weak and reckless and muddled her thoughts.

"Argent is coming for me," she lied. "He'll find you."

"I have no doubt he's looking for you." Dorshaw's scalpel pressed against her breast, not hard enough to break the skin, but with just the right amount of pressure to let her know that he was a master of this blade.

Some of Millie's anger gave way to the panic she desperately tried to smother.

"No one will find you down here. No one ever does." Dorshaw traced the outline of the tops of her breasts with the scalpel, the lace giving way beneath the blade. Millie would never forget the sound of fabric cut by a surgery knife. "You belong to me. Don't you see? I've *won* you. Body, heart, and soul. You'll become a part of me." He pressed an ear to her breast, listening to her heart, and Millie had to stop herself from tossing the contents of her stomach all over him.

"It doesn't matter what you do to my body, you'll *never* have my heart," she vowed. "It belongs to my son." The other bits were tattered by a man more lethal than this one but not even half as mad. "And my soul is my own."

"But is it, though?" Seizing her sliced décolletage, Dorshaw ripped it away, baring her corset. "I've learned that a mother's love is an extraordinary thing. Almost superhuman in nature. Mothers are stronger, more desperate to live, more accustomed to pain and fear and worry." He leaned in, pressing his mouth to her ear. "They're so much harder to break than other women. Take your friend, for instance, dear Agnes. She fought like an animal. She called Jakub's name up until the end, you know."

"You beast!" Millie screamed. A ball of something dark and heavy expanded behind her ribs. It gripped her in its clutches, brushing all fear and reason aside. "You bloody wretch!" She spat at him. Hoping he'd hit her. Wishing he'd do something to break her out of this near-hysterical rage. "You'll pay for what you've done to her. I vow it. If I have to come back and haunt you, if I have to trade my soul to the devil, so be it! I will have vengeance for her life. And mine."

He was hard; she could see it through his trousers. His breaths were labored and his eyes bright, and his hands trembled. He wiped her spittle from his cheek with his free hand and then licked his palm.

Millie gagged.

"Look what you do to me." He held up his tremulous scalpel and made a sound of disbelief. "You are certainly not like the others. You're special, Millie LeCour. How bored you'd have been with Argent. He's such a cold fish. Such a wounded bird. But you and I, we're alike. We're creatures of life, of passion, of expression and experience. I've never wanted a woman while she was still alive. Not like—" Swallowing hard, he turned from her then, and Millie immediately began a succession of desperate movements as he rummaged through his satchel, this time producing some sort of clamp that could only be used to pry something delicate open and hold it there.

Millie's movements became more frenzied as she struggled and swayed. No matter what happened down here, he was *not* coming near her with that thing. If she wasn't surviving this, she wasn't lingering, either. She wouldn't be fodder for his sick amusement. She'd fight him to the last. She'd *rather* be dead while he carried out whatever indignities he had planned for her.

He picked certain instruments, inspected them, and set them on the edge of the table. "I wonder, my love, how much pain do you think you can take before you offer your heart to me? How much fear and horror can you behold until you're bartering your soul? As much as a mother who's borne her child in her own body? Is there a difference with a surrogate?"

The first bolt gave, and Millie rattled her chains to cover the sound, in the guise of a fruitless feminine struggle. "You'll never know, you evil monster."

He paused, and for a breathless moment, Millie thought he would turn around and put a stop to her struggles. But he resumed his work, organizing unneeded tools in his satchel. "Evil monster? Am I, though? Is there such a thing as evil?"

She actually paused to gape at him. "You *murder* people. For money, for pleasure. You take their lives from them, from the people they love."

"Yes, but doesn't your lover also do that?"

He had her there.

"He doesn't delight in their pain. He doesn't do these . . . these sick experiments."

"Argent has never delighted in anything. God, he's such a yawn." Dorshaw snapped his satchel shut and strolled to the corner to stow it in its hiding place. "I would say that making love to him must have been like swiving a corpse, but the simile would be inappropriate considering my specific proclivities."

He glanced back at her after putting the satchel where

it belonged, and Millie froze as she captured his gaze with her own.

"If you think of it in these terms, I'm really not so bad." He smiled encouragingly. "I've killed a few dozen people in my lifetime. Maybe a hundred. More than some, less than Argent. But do you know who can claim more casualties than even us?"

Millie shook her head, desperately trying not to glance upward, and praying he wouldn't, either.

"The queen, for one," he said smugly. "Pretty much any regimental soldier. An executioner for the crown. I met men in America who almost single-handedly slaughtered entire villages of native women and children. Beat and raped and burned them all, and other men bought them drinks in the taverns. But *I'm* evil?" Shaking his head, he gave a sigh of disbelief. "I think of myself as more akin to a predator in the wild. In order for me to survive, there must be casualties. But I don't take more than is needed. I'm not at all greedy." Turning, he crouched down and lifted the stone that would seal his satchel back away.

This was her chance, it was act or die.

Clenching her teeth against the strain, Millie gave one last powerful yank on her chain, directing all the movement at his turned back. Slack appeared when the other bolt gave.

The plate fell to the floor, and she retrieved it before Dorshaw turned. Aiming it at his head, she threw it with all her strength.

She fell short of her mark. The square plate hit him in the shoulder, drawing a snarl of pain and ripping through his coat, but not debilitating him.

Thinking quickly, Millie rolled the chain toward her, end over end, until she, again, held the plate in her hand.

"You vicious *bitch*." Dorshaw lunged for the table, but

she moved at the same time, aiming the plate as carefully as she could. She'd always been excellent at this. Once, she'd had to throw a flaming baton at a trapeze artist every night for six nights a week plus matinees.

A scream of rage ripped through her as she let the plate fly. This second throw landed on the side of his head, felling him with a very unmanly sound of alarm. The force of it wrenched Millie's shoulder painfully, but she didn't care. Though blood had begun to well from the wound at his temple, Dorshaw's eyes were still open, and his chest lifting with breath.

"That was for Agnes." Millie could feel her strength fading, her free arm beginning to tremble under the weight of the heavy chain and plate. He was wounded. Bleeding from his shoulder and head. She was too gone to care, too angry, too afraid, too close to getting herself free. All she had to do was kill him with her next throw, because she knew she only had one left before her energy gave out.

"This is for all those poor mothers and their missing boys." Summoning a strength she hadn't known she possessed, she flung the plate again, aiming right between the eyes.

Dorshaw rolled away and the plate landed harmlessly next to him. He seized her chain before she had a chance to pull it back. "I'm going to send your defiled corpse back to your lover," he threatened, keeping the plate in his hand as he crawled toward her. Blood and dirt muddied the left side of his face, creating a demonic mask. "Your death will not be quick. You will twitch and struggle."

She was still chained to the wall with one hand. Had no other weapons at her disposal. Once he was in range of her boot, she kicked at him, but his hand snaked out and captured her ankle, which he used to pull himself even closer.

"You will see your blood mingle with the dirt. You'll watch the demons come for you, and you'll welcome them if only to escape the horror of my face. If only to flee from the knowledge that it was *I*, a monster, who ended you, and that I will systematically assassinate every person who would miss you, until even your *memory* is dead."

Millie jerked and struggled, kicked and twisted as furiously as she could. He might be wounded, but he was still so terribly strong. Fueled by pain, and fury, and insanity, he pulled himself up her leg, grasping at her skirts until they tore. His added weight put painful pressure on the shoulder still secured above her head.

Then she saw it. Her last chance. Perhaps no one would ever find her here and she'd die somewhere beneath the ground, but at least she could keep him from her son. From Christopher. At least he wouldn't have to see her in a puddle of her own blood.

Because she somehow knew that would break what was left of him.

Maybe they would comfort each other, Jakub and Christopher, and remember her fondly. But they'd be alive. She'd make certain of it.

A clamor rang in her ear, the sound of footsteps. An incessant ringing. Suddenly she felt as though she were submerged in water. In a lake of fire and fury. She could only see her enemy. Could only hear his every breath that was a personal offense to her. She could already hear a demon calling her name, and the voice was painfully familiar.

Seizing the chain Dorshaw held in his hand, she used the slack to quickly wrap around his neck and then with a battle cry that would make a banshee proud, she pressed her knee against his throat and pulled the chain tight.

Christopher hated the catacombs. The smell reminded him of prison. Moisture and decay mixed with the echoes of the misery and treachery of the past etched into aging stone.

But he would die down here before he left without Millie.

Fear and helplessness was something he'd thought he'd left in the past. But since he'd realized Millie was in the clutches of his enemy, a man arguably as dangerous as himself, he hadn't been able to expand his ribs enough to take in a real breath.

He'd lost his training. He was no longer just like water. He was a flood. Crashing through the gate of the Hyde Park tunnel, he used a lantern to light his way. The dust and frost had been disturbed by more than a few footprints. It was impossible to tell which ones were fresh.

Forging deeper underground, he sprinted down the tunnel. He could hear the footfalls of Blackwell and his men, but didn't wait for them. The passageway divided into three, and Argent searched the ground for clues. Fewer footprints here, but none of them belonged to those inconceivably senseless high-heeled boots Millie favored. Thrusting his lantern forward, he paced back and forth, studying every inch.

There. Two thin drag marks leading to the tunnel off to the left. Too small and close together to be made by a cart.

He didn't let himself think of why she was being dragged. Of what harm might have already befallen her. He couldn't, or this awful, dark despair would rear up from the void in his soul and choke the life from him.

Steep, crumbling stairs led him down to an underground waterway, from which numerous arched stone tunnels branched. A dozen at least.

"Fuck!" Argent hurled the lantern at a wall. The explosion caused by glass and lantern oil against the stones stopped everyone else in their tracks.

"I sent for Crenshaw to bring his hounds," Dorian said, coming up behind him and handing him a torch. "But he may be several minutes."

"We may not *have* minutes," Argent barked, staring into the oil-fueled flames and feeling his own blood run colder and colder.

"We can split up in the meantime," Blackwell suggested.

Yes, Argent thought. He had to do *something*. He addressed the dangerous men behind him. "Each man takes a tunnel, go three hundred paces, mark your place and double back. Look for drag marks, scraps of clothing, flickering lights, holding cells, *anything* you can find. We'll meet here and then venture farther if nothing turns up."

"I'm coming with you," said the Blackheart of Ben More.

"Every tunnel needs—"

"I counted. They're covered. I'm not leaving your side."

With a grunt, Argent turned and they silently jogged three hundred paces through a labyrinth with absolute vigilance. It was maddening. Every footfall could be bringing him closer to her, or taking him farther away. There was no way of knowing. The earth was either packed dirt or stone. Sometimes disturbed, other times not. But he found no sign of her.

They beat half the men back to the hub, and none of them could meet his eyes. "Sorry, sir," the one called Chappy muttered. "I couldn't find no'fing."

Argent contemplated separating the man's head from his shoulders out of anguish and violent frustration before a frantic echo sounded from their left.

He felt sick. Whether with hope or dread, he couldn't tell. Surging down the tunnel from which the clamor ricocheted, he almost trampled Gregory Tallow, the slim, wily invert with a dreadful stutter.

"I—I didn't hear them u-u-u-until I was almost b-back here." Tallow panted, pointing down the tunnel. "S-s-s-screams,"

Screams.

"Millie!" Argent shot into the darkness, his long legs eating up the earth, faster than he'd ever run before.

"Argent?" Blackwell's voice sounded far away. "Argent, wait for—"

The tunnel wound in sharp, perpendicular turns rather than snakelike curves. A few other doors and iron gates shot off into dark directions. It smelled like death down here. Like terror and pain and blood.

Then he heard it. Distant and chilling, like the sound of a reaper whispering in his ear.

Screams. *Her* screams.

"Millie!" He ran faster, sliding around turns and pushing off walls. His legs felt alternately strong and weak. She was *alive*. She was in pain. She was screaming. Desperate sounds of strain and fear punctuated by moments of terrible silence.

God, what was happening to her? What sort of unspeakable terrors had Dorshaw already enacted? He hadn't had her in his clutches for long . . . but every moment was a drop of blood, the slice of flesh, the space of a breath.

Every breath she took was precious. Every inch of skin was beyond priceless.

Though he'd never heard anything so horrifying in his life as the sound of her cries, Argent prayed for them to continue. They were his beacon in the dark. They were his torment. His hell. But he needed them to find her. So he could rescue her.

So he could pull every scream of hers from Dorshaw's own throat a hundredfold.

Dorshaw's malevolent voice repeated through the catacombs. His awful threats invoking a dark, evil rage within Argent's chest.

He turned the corner and caught the dim flicker of lanterns on stone. His vision narrowed. Chains rattled against walls. A struggle ensued behind those bars.

"Christ, no . . . *no*." With a burst of speed, he leaped for the narrow ancient iron gate.

And nearly choked on his astonishment.

Millie, *alive*. Her dark hair in wild disarray, her shimmering teal bodice torn away and milky breasts heaving above her black silk corset. Her dark eyes snapped with an unholy fire. Her teeth were bared in the savage imitation of a lioness, the chain manacled to her delicate wrists wrapped around Dorshaw's neck as she used her knee for leverage. Her slim elegant muscles strained against the skin of her bare arms.

In that lightning flash of a moment, Argent knew two things:

That her fierce strength was waning and she might not be able to hold the struggling, bleeding Dorshaw in check long enough to choke him unconscious. And—

That he was in love with her.

"No," he whispered. Not certain which fact terrified him the most.

Drawing his pistol, he trained it on Dorshaw, but the angle made a shot too dangerous. At this caliber, the bullet could go through Dorshaw and puncture Millie.

Besides, he wanted to get his hands on the man with a relish he'd not thought possible.

Standing back at an angle to avoid ricochet, Argent shot through the thick iron lock.

The sound reverberated against the stone with deafening force, but Argent had been prepared for it, and he wrenched the chains off the gate and kicked it open.

The blast of the pistol broke the haze of bloodthirsty rage holding Millie in its thrall. She knew who'd come for her before she looked up. She trusted that she was safe, that this nightmare was over. Because a man who somehow continued to perform incredible, nigh *impossible* feats had kicked down the gates to her prison, liberating her body and soul.

The lanterns set his hair ablaze and glittered off eyes the color of the frozen north. His strength and prowess magnified the depth of his wrath as he entered, the pistol still smoking in his hand.

Millie realized that she'd been so, so wrong about him. All this time, she thought she'd made a deal with a demon. With the devil himself perhaps. That she'd signed her sinful contract in blood. That he was a man forged in the depths of hell and, as such, irrevocably doomed to a life of darkness and despair.

But that was just not so.

Christopher Argent was her fallen, avenging angel.

Not a seraphim. Nor a cherubic innocent garbed in white. But a guardian. A warrior. A boy who had traded his halo and wings, and perhaps even his soul, for a knife and a garrote and ultimate vengeance. He'd been baptized in blood and now he rose from the ashes, something hard and sinister and unholy, but ultimately redeemable.

He had a heart. She could see it in his eyes as he drank her in.

His arrival revitalized Dorshaw, whose struggles increased as her strength waned. She could feel the trembling now, the burning in her lungs and the aching of her muscles. She wanted to think that she could have done it. That she could have saved herself, that she could have taken a life. But it became clear that she would never know.

Christopher said nothing as he reached her and gently pried the chain from her aching fingers. His nostrils flared and taut muscles tested the seams of his shirt as he took a moment to thoroughly examine her, unspoken questions twitching on his hard lips.

"I—I'm all right."

Nodding, he turned his attention to Dorshaw, and

Millie couldn't help but feel a slight touch of compassion for the villain.

Without seeming to put forth any effort, Christopher pulled the chain tight. Dorshaw's eyes bulged, but an awful squeal of breath still struggled into his constricted throat. Exerting just the right amount of pressure, Christopher leaned down and put his cold, brutal, *beautiful* face the space of a breath from Dorshaw's.

"Your death will *not* be quick." Christopher repeated Dorshaw's words to him, as a vein popped out on the dark assassin's straining forehead. "You will twitch and struggle."

And, indeed, he did. His boots made terrible sounds as they scraped across the dirt in frantic, panicked reflexes. Hands pawed at the chains, then at Christopher, but he ignored them as he pulled the chains incrementally tighter, knowing *just* how much pressure to exert.

"You'll watch the demons come for you, and you'll welcome them if only to escape the horror of my face. If only to flee from the knowledge that it was *I*, the *superior* monster, who ended you."

Millie had never seen the throes of death this close before. No matter how evil the man had been, it was hard to watch him die, but she forced herself to. She wanted this. Wanted to experience this, knowing it would change her forever. It was the only way she'd not look for Dorshaw in the shadows. That she'd not see him down every alley, waiting for him to pounce. If she watched him die, she could let him go.

And so she did. Attached to the chain that killed him, she watched him struggle his last, and finally understood how one could take pleasure in the taking of a life.

When it was done, Christopher let the body drop to the dirt.

He wouldn't look at her. Didn't touch her.

"Christopher?"

While he searched for a key, other men spilled into the room like a foulmouthed river of peril, filling up the small chamber until she could no longer see the gate.

Their exclamations of pleasure and surprise at finding her alive were at once endearing and overwhelming. When she felt the first manacle fall away, she made a small noise of relief, and Christopher crowded her against the stone wall to unlock her other wrist.

His closeness was like a balm. He was a pillar of hard, warm muscle that directly contrasted with the cold stone at her back. Once free, she melted into him. His arms enfolded her and they stood like that in silence. In absolute stillness. Words escaped them both, but every sentiment passed between them with such intensity, to try and vocalize them would have cheapened the depth of their consolation.

The room fell quiet, as one by one, each of the men stood witness to something they'd never thought would transpire, and that they wouldn't soon forget.

Christopher Argent, the largest, coldest, deadliest assassin any of them had ever heard of, swept a half-naked Millie LeCour off her feet, and held her to him and said not a word as he carried her out of the London underground and out into the night.

Chapter Twenty-Seven

Farah held Millie's hand through the entire police interview. Had Chief Inspector Morley not been stabbed, they might have been able to keep the police out of the entire ordeal, but too much had transpired in one day to keep hidden.

Morley had indeed survived his wound. A doctor was seeing to him in his bachelor terrace mere blocks from the Blackwell manse.

Lady Northwalk's soft blue receiving room, with its jewel couches and crystal lanterns, felt like a palace next to the pit Millie had been carried out of. She'd been allowed a tearful reunion with Jakub, and she'd tucked him in so sweetly, allaying his fears and his awful guilt. She hadn't wanted him to overhear as she recounted the events of the night to the police.

The villains of this nightmare, it seemed, had both been defeated. Lord Thurston had obviously been ordering the deaths of previous lovers, of women who'd borne him sons, in the most despicable way imaginable.

Only a few troubling questions remained: what had happened to those boys, the illegitimate sons of a madman? What had Dorshaw done with them? And who had paid Dorshaw to kill Thurston? Lady Thurston? The dreadful St. Vincents? The murdered Mr. Dashforth?

The police were going to keep looking for the missing

boys, but at this point, everyone knew they were searching for corpses.

Millie and Jakub, however, had escaped such a fate, thanks to Mr. Argent, and were safe to return to their lives as they wished.

Sometime after a very terse and awkward conversation with the police, Christopher had slipped away from the chaos. Millie felt his absence like a palpable irritant. An itch beneath her skin and a pang in her heart. One moment he'd been hovering behind her, big and silent and pulling curious glances from the myriad of coppers and criminals milling through the halls of the Blackwell estate. Though he didn't excuse himself, and no one remarked at his absence, she *felt* the second he'd slithered away. The shadows were colder. The air less full of masculine potency.

She was alone in a room full of people.

Signing a few autographs and playbills after all was said and done, she thanked the police who had absolutely *nothing* to do with her rescue. She'd relied upon her practiced charm until they left, and sagged inside the coat Argent had given her as Dorian rudely ushered them out.

Was it truly over? Did things just . . . return to normal? How could they? Millie couldn't even fathom what normal had been only days ago. She couldn't remember what it felt like to be carefree. She couldn't seem to consider the days *before* . . .

Before she'd been kissed by a killer.

"Millie dear." Farah squeezed her hand, soft gray eyes full of understanding. "I'm going to insist you and your son stay here for the night. I've already had the staff draw a bath, as I'm certain you wish to wash that horrid place off you."

As always, the countess looked as fresh as a spring orchard blossom in a high-necked lily-white gown bedecked with sage-green ribbons and stitched paisley skirts.

Millie could only nod, a melancholy exhaustion weighing her shoulders down. "You've been so kind," she said. "I don't know how I can ever repay you."

"Nonsense." Farah helped her to stand and looped an arm through Millie's in a show of support. "Friends don't think in terms of compensation."

"Speak for yourself." Blackwell sauntered into the room appearing much too relaxed for a crime lord covered in dust who'd only just been host to half the police force of the city. "I always think in terms of compensation."

Farah rolled her eyes heavenward, as though praying for strength.

"The exception being this case, of course," the Blackheart of Ben More amended, casting a chastised look at his wife. "You are most welcome to call upon us for anything you need, Miss LeCour. My wife has quite taken to you, and any means at our disposal are yours for the asking."

Millie couldn't think of a thing to say, and Dorian Blackwell seemed to understand as she stared at him, dumbfounded. He nodded, moved to kiss his wife on the temple, and merged with the shadows of the hallway, doubtless in search of his own bath.

"I wish to look in on Jakub one more time," Millie murmured.

"Of course you do." Farah guided her up the main flight of stairs, their steps muffled by lush ivory carpets, and down toward the nursery where Jakub slept in a small but well-appointed guest chamber. "He was so afraid for you, but he was brave. And *so* sorry. I hope you're not terribly cross with him. Your son loves you dearly."

"I'm not angry with him in the least," Millie said. "It makes me sick to think of what could have befallen him, but I feel as though he's chastised himself enough for slipping away. And he's not the kind of boy to forget such a hard-learned lesson."

"No, I don't suppose he is." Farah smiled fondly. "In fact I—"

Jakub's agitated voice drifted into the hall, and Millie quickened her step, though she and Farah both paused at the contrasting baritone of Argent's reply.

"I don't think I'll ever be able to sleep again," Jakub confessed, his voice anxious and waterlogged.

"I brought your mother back as I promised, and you're both safe here. There's no reason to be afraid."

"Then why can't I stop weeping?" Jakub hiccupped.

Heart clenching, Millie made to rush to her son's bedside and sweep him into her arms.

"Do you want me to fetch your mo—"

"No!" Jakub cried. "No, don't get her!"

Millie paused, hurt trickling down her ribs.

"I don't want her to see me. I can't face her! Not like this."

"Why not?" In the face of the storm of youthful distress, Christopher's cool, temperate voice was a strange and effective balm to her son.

"I don't have a f-father." Jakub sniffed. "Which means . . . I'm the m-man of our family. She has no one else. I'm supposed to protect her from distress, aren't I? I've not done a very good job. I'm not acting like a m-m-man."

Millie's hands flew to her mouth; the shame in her son's voice was too much for someone so young. Had she made him feel this way? Had she put the responsibility of her happiness, of her *loneliness,* on his tiny shoulders?

She ached for him, for he would not know that his sire died only this afternoon. That of anyone in this house, save Lady Northwalk, his blood was the most noble. He was the bastard son of an earl and an immigrant. Raised by a woman who knew nothing about children, who knew nothing but how to love him.

What if that wasn't enough? What if *she* wasn't enough? Again she wanted to dash in there, to scoop him up as she did when he was so small and would wrap his arms and legs around her and cling and cry until she cooed and kissed all his woes better.

Farah put a staying arm around her shoulders, giving the doorway a meaningful glance.

"I told you before, I don't have a father," Christopher said softly. "Never have done."

"Did you even know who he was?"

The bed squeaked a bit under the stress of a heavy weight, as though Christopher had sat.

"No. My mother named me after herself. Told me that my father wasn't the sort of man who deserved a namesake, and I believe she was right."

"Your mother's name was Christopher?"

"Christine." The name sounded dusty on his voice, as though he hadn't said it in a lifetime.

"Did you protect her?"

Millie closed her eyes, her trembling hands still covering her mouth as tears burned behind her lids.

"No." Christopher's voice was tighter, darker, but retained its infallible composure. "But you must understand something I didn't at your age. Mothers like mine, like yours, they don't gather strength from *your* protection, but from protecting you. Your mother needs you to be a child when you're a child. And then a man when you become a man."

It was true. He was so unbelievably correct. If it weren't for her son, for her fear for him, her love of him, she'd never have had the ferocity and strength she did in the catacombs.

Jakub stopped crying, and was so incredibly silent for a moment while Farah and Millie clung to each other, each of them filled with an understanding of what this conversation might be costing the assassin. And what Jakub might be gaining from it.

"Really?" was her son's watery question.

"Really. When I was your age, my mother thought of all kinds of clever ways to keep us occupied. To keep me happy, and—brave. She did it for me, but I think—I think it helped her as well."

"My mother makes me teach her things that I learned at school, or from a book." Jakub's voice lifted, and Millie found it so bittersweet that he understood why. Sweet that he knew she cared, bitter that he'd found her out so young. "She pretends to misunderstand everything and repeats it back to me all wrong and we laugh and laugh."

"There, you see? You mother . . . she's . . ." Millie held her breath, her heart balanced on his next word.

"Mr. Argent?" Jakub asked.

Millie winced, wishing her son had waited one more moment, so that she could have heard the words Christopher hadn't articulated.

"Hmm?"

"What did your mother do when you couldn't sleep?"

A heartbeat went by.

"What does *your* mother do?" Christopher asked shortly.

"I don't know. I always sleep."

An eternity went by.

"She . . . she sang." Christopher's voice thickened. "We sang."

"Sang what?"

"Songs, of course."

"*What* songs?" Jakub asked with affectionate exasperation.

"I—hardly remember."

"Not even one?"

The mattress creaked with a shift of movement. "Perhaps one."

"Sing it for me?"

"No."

"Please?"

"Absolutely not."

"I refuse to sleep until you do," Jakub cajoled.

"So be it. You'll be quite exhausted for a very long time."

"Will you at least tell me the name? Maybe I know of it?" Jakub was starting to sound like himself, and Millie couldn't be more grateful.

"Very well," Christopher consented. "It's an old Celtic tune. She called it 'Hush.' "

"I know just the one!" Jakub crowed. "Old Mrs. McMasters used to sing it to me when Mama was on stage. Are you Scottish, Mr. Argent?"

"Couldn't say. It's a possibility, I suppose."

Jakub's high, small voice broke through the night with heartbreaking sweetness.

Hush Hush in the evening,
Good dreams will come stealing.
Of freedom and laughter
and peace ever after . . .

"I . . . don't remember the next bit." Jakub sighed.

The hand that Farah didn't have around Millie flew to her heart as Christopher astounded them both when he softly sang.

Ye'll smile while you're sleeping.
And watch I'll be keeping.
Hush hush now my darling
No tears til the morning . . .

If her eyes had been dry, if her heart had been free, at that moment everything would have changed. But Millie learned something about her would-be assassin turned mercenary lover that it never would have occurred to her to know, *regardless* of the length of time he allowed himself to stay in her life.

Christopher Argent had the voice of an angel.

Dorian bade Chief Inspector Carlton Morley to sit before the man fell over. He looked as pale as the late-winter moon filtering in through the windows. Regardless, here he was, *again,* in Farah's sitting room in the middle of the night with an emotionally unstable assassin whom the inspector had shot at only hours before.

Morley must have more between his legs than Dorian had given the inspector credit for, he mused.

Farah was busy seeing to Miss LeCour and, without her to mediate, Dorian wondered if he was, indeed, going to get blood on the carpets.

Either way, this ought to be interesting.

"To what do we owe the pleasure of your visit?" Dorian asked in a perfect mockery of his wife's earlier civility.

The left sleeve of Morley's gray wool suit coat had been neatly folded and tucked under, as his arm was held immobilized beneath it by a sling around his neck. He sat heavily, then winced. "I came as fast as I could."

"Yes," Blackwell acknowledged, lowering himself to the sofa. "But you've missed the party."

Argent remained standing, regarding the chief inspector with his usual aloofness.

"I was pleased to hear that Miss LeCour had been recovered." Morley glanced up at Argent. "And that Dorshaw was defeated."

"No thanks to you," Argent said stonily.

Agitation brought some color back to Morley's cheeks. "If I'd have been apprised of the situation *before*hand, I would have—" The inspector began to tilt over, and caught himself with his good hand, upon which he leaned heavily.

"You would have what? Fainted?" Argent snorted. "Don't make me laugh."

Dorian found himself searching his flawless memory for a time when Christopher Argent had ever laughed. He came up with nothing.

"I've seen a lot of blood," Morley admitted. "But not my own, not like that. I've never fain—that's never happened to me before."

"An explanation you've likely kept to the bedroom up until now." Blackwell chuckled.

Golden features darkening, a vein in Morley's neck pulsed, but he remained as cool and composed as Argent, himself. Blackwell had to give the man credit, he was difficult to rile.

"I would have come to finish you off if anything had happened to her," Argent threatened. "Everything that transpired today is on *your* head. Your useless men had Dorshaw in their custody and managed to lose him. I would have ended him then if you'd not interrupted."

Dorian could feel the heat building inside of Argent, and it stunned him. For a man he thought was made of ice, the assassin certainly had a fire smoldering beneath it all.

And the intrepid Miss LeCour was the fuel.

"I. *Know,*" Morley said through clenched teeth.

"Let us speak plainly, Inspector." Dorian leaned back in his chair, catching his chin in his hand and regarding Morley with abject curiosity. "Why have you come? Surely you didn't drag yourself from your recovery bed to be castigated by us for the ineptitude of your institution?"

Jaw set, aristocratic features waxy and sweating from pain, Morley closed his eyes for a moment, as though gathering courage. "I'm drowning, Blackwell. Drowning in blood, the streets are awash with it."

"As they ever have been."

"Yes, but it is changing. There are machines, and guns, and men like us living on fine streets like this. Self-made men, with no noble blood to speak of. Men who've made their money from foreign wars, oppressive mercantilism, and American markets."

Dorian chuckled. "Men like you perhaps. I'm an earl, or haven't you heard?"

"A courtesy title afforded by your wife," Morley argued.

"I'm the bastard son of a marquess, with more noble blood in my small finger than you've got in your *entire* body."

Both Morley and Argent stared at him as though he'd sprouted horns.

Argent had known this, of course, but no one had dared speak of it out loud for over a decade.

Since he'd become Dorian Blackwell.

"A marquess?" Morley grimaced. "Who in the devil—"

"An old Scottish title." Dorian studied the inspector, noting the moment the puzzle piece fit together in Morley's mind. "One held by a Mackenzie, I believe."

"Ravencroft," Morley breathed. "I should have guessed. You look *just* like him. But—that's impossible; he's all of forty or so."

"His father raped my mother."

Morley shook his head, disbelief glimmering in his bloodshot eyes. "You're *brother* to the Demon Highlander?"

"*Half* brother." Dorian shrugged, uncomfortable with the word. "You're acquainted, I believe, fought in his regiment in the Second Opium War."

Morley nodded, his eyes dazed with reminiscence. "Never saw anything like Ravencroft. Charged Chinese cannons like they didn't exist. Bullets, cannonballs, knives, bayonets, they seemed to change their courses midair and curve around him. We all did things—killed people—

but . . . Liam Mackenzie, he was . . . barbaric. Savage. *Startlingly* effective."

The inspector blinked, as though shuttering doors to the past. Dorian found himself wondering what was back there that Morley didn't want to see.

"Yes, well. Runs in the family, I suppose." Blackwell didn't want to talk about his brother. It led to their infamous father, and that was a conversation he wasn't ready to have.

With anyone.

"We were talking about why you are here," Dorian reminded him.

Morley nodded, agreeing to leave the past firmly where it belonged. "I'm here for Argent."

The assassin uncrossed his arms and Dorian leaned forward, wondering if Morley knew how close he was to death. "And you didn't bring an army?"

"Not to arrest him," Morley amended. "To employ him."

Dorian began to wonder if all his speechless moments were going to pertain to Christopher Argent.

Turning to the assassin in question, the chief inspector adjusted his sling. "You didn't have to pull the servant's bell. You could have left me to bleed out. You likely saved my life."

Dorian turned in his seat to stare at Argent out of his good eye.

Argent, the bastard, wouldn't lift his eyes above the fireplace. "The gunfire would have brought them regardless," he mumbled. Whether explaining himself to Blackwell, or to Morley, it was unclear.

"That isn't the point," Morley stated.

"What is the point?" Argent asked with his usual bluntness.

Morley took in a deep breath and stood, swaying a bit before finding his bearings. "I'm putting together an elite contingent of men. Men with very . . . *singular* talents to help rid the city of criminals like Charles Dorshaw. To hunt for missing children and serial murderers, for anarchists and terrorists, for people beyond the arm of the law. To do . . . things the police simply cannot."

"You?" Dorian gave a mirthless laugh. "A leader of vigilantes and mercenaries? Like the Pinkertons in America?"

Morley shook his head vehemently. "Not at all." He addressed Argent. "They'd never serve private interests. Instead, you'd be a servant of justice. An agent of the crown. Think of how you protected Miss LeCour. How you saved her from the clutches of a madman, a villain. You could do that for countless others."

Features arranged with incredulity, Argent finally looked at Morley. "I'd be the first villain on your list."

"You'd be granted immunity from the crimes of your past, of course."

Argent scoffed. "I already *have* immunity. You can prove me guilty of no crime. Hell, I even pay my taxes to the crown."

"I could nab you for Lord Thurston's murder." Morley lifted an arrogant brow. "You *were* there. You had a knife in your hand."

Dorian contained his wince, knowing Morley had just lost any chance he'd had with the man.

"You could *try*." Argent's voice should have frozen what little blood Morley had left in his veins. "I've spent enough time as a prisoner of the crown to *ever* do it any favors."

"This wouldn't be a favor, you'd be compensated."

"You couldn't afford me."

Morley made a one-handed gesture of desperation. "I'm offering you emancipation from your current . . . circumstances. A different life. A better path. The chance to be a force for good. To be a better man."

Argent made a low noise and stalked to the inspector, putting his face right into his. To Morley's credit, he didn't back down, even though the large assassin loomed over him a few important inches.

Dorian shot to his feet, ready to intervene.

"It was men in your position who put me on *this* path in the first place. I was innocent once. *We* were innocent." He gestured to Dorian, who agreed wholeheartedly. "And *good*. But inside the walls of your cage, we lost the meaning of the word." Argent shouldered past Morley, who paled further at the jarring impact.

The assassin paused at the threshold, but didn't look back. "If there's blood on the streets, you have no one to blame but yourselves." With that, he disappeared down the dark hallway.

Morley turned to Dorian. "Blackwell, if you could talk to him. Make him understand that I'm trying to change all that. To ensure the future is not like the past."

"Don't look to me." Dorian shrugged. "I'm not in control of his decisions."

"Who is?" Morley asked.

Dorian squinted into the shadows of his own home; noting that Argent hadn't left as he was wont to do, but gone upstairs toward the guest rooms. "That's an excellent question, Inspector. One that remains to be seen."

Chapter Twenty-Eight

Millie was exhausted. Though, it seemed, she couldn't bring herself to snuff the lantern and lie back. Full of alternate scenarios and unanswered questions, her mind seemed to eschew the darkness. Too many monsters lurked there.

Too many memories.

Perched on the edge of a lovely and comfortable guest bed, she stared at the budding bruises on her wrists left by iron manacles, and let the peaches-and-cream bedroom blur into her periphery. Swathed in a borrowed white nightgown, bathed, brushed, and braided, she remained motionless for countless minutes.

Jakub was safe. She was *alive*. The danger was vanquished. So, why did she feel more insecure than ever? What was this strange lump of fear stuck at the back of her throat?

Why did the thought of going back to her charmed and happy life make her so melancholy?

She knew he was there before he made a noise. Perhaps she'd been waiting for him. Because the moment Christopher Argent stepped into the bedroom, all questions were answered. All the anxiety dissipated. And the darkness seemed like a safer place. Because he was part of it, and it was an eternal part of him.

He looked hard and savage. Angry. His face was stone,

but not the cold, grim set she'd come to know. Even though he wasn't looking right at her, she read everything she needed to in his features. This wasn't the man who only a half hour past had sung a gentle lullaby to her son. This was a different beast. Perhaps one she hadn't met before.

Millie wasn't used to heat from this man, let alone the conflagration she sensed from him. Heat and possession and something deeper, more permanent, radiated from his large body.

An answering warmth flared beneath her own skin, and she yearned to meld it with his, lest she be scalded by need.

"You're . . . *alive*." His chest heaved and he had the strangest look in his eyes, as if he'd come upstairs expecting her to be gone, or worse. "I mean—" He cleared his throat. "You're beautiful. That is . . . you look . . . better."

He was acting strange. Well, more strange than usual. And he had been since the catacombs. Though he'd shut her door behind him, he hadn't yet taken his hand off the latch. Millie had a feeling that if she made a move toward him, he'd bolt.

"Come in," she invited, patting the space on the bed beside her. "I haven't had a moment to properly thank you."

"You don't have to."

"Nonsense," she cajoled. "Come here."

He shook his head, stepping backward. "I'm not myself." His eyes were bright, his movements jerky and wild instead of graceful as usual. "But I had to see you." He gave her his broad back, as he turned the latch to leave.

"Don't go." She reached a hand out.

"I should never have come, I'm sorry."

"I'm not afraid of you," Millie challenged.

He glanced over his shoulder. "You should be."

"I know." Standing, she began to unbutton her nightdress, pushing it off her shoulders and letting it glide down the contours of her body. She was unclothed, but it was he who stood naked in front of her.

"I'm alive, thanks to you. I want to *feel* alive." It was all she needed to say.

A palpable shift occurred as he visibly broke whatever chain it was that kept him away from her. Some would call it decency. Others would call it fear. Millie knew it was some complicated mélange of the two.

In the end, need won the night.

He pushed away from the door and his long, powerful legs ate up the paces between them. He'd reclaimed his predatory grace, no longer held in check.

A thrill stole Millie's breath the moment before he reached her, yanked her into his arms, and kissed her harshly.

The lethal potency in him hit her with a palpable wave. Millie could sense it, coiled and deadly, balancing on a dagger's edge. The lust generated by such a dangerous man, unleashed upon her with a fury she'd never before felt from him, was indescribably erotic. His tongue was a smooth invader, claiming her mouth, forcing her teeth apart, and sweeping over hers with sure, rhythmic thrusts. His stubble was rough against her lips, cheeks, and chin.

His hands were rougher.

Roaming everywhere at once, his palms abraded her skin with incomparable sensation. Once they reached the curve of her backside, he ground her against him. The rigid length behind his trousers was hard as stone. She could feel the heat of it pulsing from where it was wedged between their bodies.

She had never wanted anything more, had never been so needy and aching. She craved his weight above her. His body inside hers.

Feeling brazen, she reached between them and cupped his erection. He gasped and tore his mouth from her. His lips gleamed with moisture, and his eyes glinted down at her with an erotic warning. Her name ripped from his throat on a low groan.

"I want to be beneath you." She released him, reaching up to undo the buttons of his shirt, exposing shoulders as tight as cables.

"I shouldn't—"

"Don't deny me," she commanded gently, pressing a kiss to the glossy web of scars at his shoulder as she pushed his shirt down. "Don't tell me not to be kind. I *must* be kind to you, and you must allow it."

He twitched and stiffened when she kissed his shoulder, the skin of his throat, but his arms remained locked around her. After a few indecisive moments, his head dropped to where the column of her neck met her own shoulder and he pressed a kiss there, too.

Millie's heart melted, and so did her loins, becoming soft and wet and ready for him.

His second kiss was more tender, velvety, but just as possessive and urgent as before. It entranced Millie so completely, she hardly marked the sounds of his shirt hitting the floor, or his trousers. He kicked them and his shoes away before pushing her back onto the bed, his strong arms anchored at her back to cushion her fall.

Slowly, rigidly, he settled on top of her, breathing out something harsh and profane against her ear. She could feel his cock as he stretched atop her, hard and insistent against her thigh.

His mouth found hers, questing for consolation. She gave it to him, smoothing her hands down the cords of his back, threading her fingers through his silken hair. She'd expected this moment between them to be explosive and lusty. A frantic, thrusting culmination of a horrific night.

What she hadn't anticipated, was this need to explore the nuances of their desires. She'd never been able to truly look at him when they'd come together in the past. Hadn't thrilled to the way his eyes turned from ice to indigo when he was aroused.

His rough thumbs grazed her nipples, teasing them into hard peaks, causing her to grind against him.

"Soft," he groaned, as though having lost the ability to create full sentences. As he sucked her lower lip into his mouth, his hands drifted down, spanning the indent of her waist, flaring over the curve of her hip.

Millie moaned her encouragement, reveling in the feel of his sleek muscles beneath her palms, in the weight of his incredible body pressing her into the mattress.

His teeth caught at her captured lip as his fingers cleaved the moist cleft between her thighs. A hoarse cry exploded from her as he grazed the small nub of flesh from which raw pleasure seemed to spiral to the farthest reaches of her limbs.

She gasped his name, a climax rolling up from deep within her after only a few soft strokes of his hand. Clutching at him, clenching her thighs together, she rode it, spun out with it. Only vaguely was she aware of the wild sound he made as he explored the tender parts of her throat with his lips and teeth.

She writhed beneath him until her limbs locked with a few last jaw-clenching pulses and then she went limp, resting her forehead on his scarred shoulder as she struggled to regain her breath. Christopher pressed kisses into her hairline and dragged his lips along her jaw. He wound his hand in her hair, anchoring her head back as he studied her lips, then captured them, marking her tender skin with his stubble before pulling away to inspect his handiwork.

She could feel the urgency rising within him. His knee wedged between her legs and spread her wide beneath him.

Millie put a staying hand on his chest and he froze. His eyes closing, as though he knew it was over.

"Look at me," she ordered, reaching up to cup his face.

He flinched, turning his head and clenching his jaw, staring into the dark fireplace past the foot of the bed. His muscles instantly went from molten to cold steel, and his hand tightened in her hair.

Millie was afraid to lose him, but in this moment she knew she had to forge ahead. "I see you, Christopher Argent. I know who you are," she soothed, running her hands over his powerful naked back and up the swells of his biceps. "I want you to see me. I want you to know me."

Exerting gentle pressure, she pulled his obstinate features around to face her, and his gaze hovered right below hers.

"I want you to feel this, not just with your flesh. But here." She touched his chest and felt the kick of his racing heart. She kissed him gently and then settled her head back against his palm. "*Look* at *me,*" she commanded again.

Millie thought she was prepared for what would be in his eyes when he obeyed. How wrong she'd been. In her defense, she didn't believe anyone would be capable of holding the intensity of his gaze for very long.

But she didn't dare look away, lest he read it as a rejection.

Words didn't exist to describe what she saw in the depths of his eyes. *Possession* wasn't strong enough. *Desire* didn't cover the half of it. *Vulnerability* couldn't touch the silent, searing profundity of it.

Millie almost regretted what she'd done, for in that moment she realized she might have unleashed something from a place wilder and more wounded than she'd originally thought. Perhaps Christopher Argent didn't need redemption. It was deeper than that, infinitely more complicated. Millie had a suspicion that what he needed was deliverance. Release. For though he'd been out of prison for some time, a part of him was still locked away there, in the past.

More than she'd desired anything in her life, Millie wanted to be the one to set him free. And this was the perfect place to start. "This isn't fucking," she whispered, running her thumb tenderly along his cheekbone. "Not this time."

His nostrils flared, but he nodded, his unflinching gaze holding on to hers as though it were a lifeline. "Not this time," he agreed tightly.

His possession was unbelievably slow as he sank inside of her, filling her with a heat she'd not known existed. For a moment they stayed like that as his cock stretched her slick channel and throbbed inside her welcoming body. They both stared, stunned by the incomprehensible intensity of the moment. It was like a thousand bolts of lightning converged within them, between them, and they somehow had joined more than just their bodies.

But fused their souls, as well.

"What have you done to me?" he lamented as he took her again, this thrust stronger, gaining a rhythm that set them both to gasping.

Millie met his every stroke with an encouraging lift of her hips as he surged deeper inside of her with each thrust.

He caressed her tenderly, her breasts, her shoulders, her throat, his fingers curling around the soft, delicate column in a gentle imitation of strangulation.

Millie lifted her chin to receive his descending lips, demonstrating her trust, daring him to trust her back.

It didn't take long for her pleasure to build. She fought it, wanting to stay here in this moment. Wanting to watch him as he watched her. But, it seemed, the more she strained against it, the stronger it became, until it broke upon her like the waves against sea cliffs in a tempest. The violence of it was shocking, so much so that his pleased growl was lost in her blissful cries.

Christopher gave her no quarter, the tempo of his hips changed from tender to urgent, then fierce, full of unrestrained power, grinding into her and ripping another climax from her before the first one was quite finished.

She held on to him as he rode her, as the last pulses of delight turned into drugging satiation. He was a wild, primitive beast, his muscles bunching and cording beneath his skin. His head buried in her hair as he made guttural noises with each of his merciless thrusts.

The lantern cast erotic shadows on the ceiling, and Millie watched them with a soft glow filtering through her entire body.

As he flung his head back and buried himself deep inside of her, shouting and straining with the force of his release, Millie wanted to weep. In fact, tears pricked behind her eyes and she blinked them away.

She'd found that word for what had burned down at her from his eyes. She *knew* what was happening between them. Understood why they weren't just fucking.

They both knew it.

This time, they were making love.

Untold minutes passed in blissful silence as they lay next to each other in the golden lantern light. Millie listened to Christopher's breathing regulate, almost as though he commanded it to do so. She wished she were inside his head. That she were privy to the thoughts of a man such as him. He was an enigma, really. A hard man to understand and an even harder one to read. Those small moments of insight she had into his broken psyche only made her want to dig deeper, to burrow in like a mite until there was no way he could be rid of her.

Nuzzling the muscled length of his arm, Millie lifted

its heavy weight and wriggled beneath it, settling her head on his chest. Listening to his heart beat was fast becoming one of her favorite things to do. As she nestled into his warm, solid body, it tensed for an uncertain moment, and then reacted in exactly the way she'd hoped. Arms closed around her, leg bent to make room for hers to entwine with it, even his cheek settled atop her crown.

She might not be his first lover, but Millie was sure she was the first woman to ever snuggle with the mercenary Christopher Argent. That fact gave her a sense of possession, of proprietary status that was among the most exclusive in the world. In the ever-expanding British empire, there were a disparate amount of duchesses, a manifold of marchionesses, and a considerable number of countesses. But in the arms of this man, Millie felt like a queen. Unparalleled and protected. There was nothing in the world that compared. And she'd know. Millie had ridden the euphoria of a standing ovation. Had cashed a banknote with more zeroes on it than she'd expected to see in a lifetime. Had enjoyed the success of acclaim and renown.

Somehow, this quiet moment surpassed all that.

Perhaps because she was in the arms of the man with whom she was falling in love.

Closing her eyes she breathed in the heady truth of it. She loved the warm smell of his skin, clean and sharp and altogether masculine. Loved every scar on his hard body, and every shard of ice in his eyes. She loved how every moment of pleasure and amusement they shared he treated like a rare gift he didn't quite know what to do with, and she desperately wanted to fill his bleak and empty life with joy. To teach him how to be happy. How to laugh. She'd give her entire fortune to hear him laugh.

She knew he was unsure of his heart, not only of what it contained, but if he even had one to begin with. But he did. She'd seen it in his eyes, and her next move was to coax it into her hand. It would be a large undertaking, but she'd done it before. She'd won the love of the whole of Britain, and not a small amount of the Continent, truth be told. If she set her mind to something, she attained it. And her mind, her heart, was now set on the man whose big, naked body she was currently draped across.

Now . . . where to start?

A proclamation of her intentions seemed a bit premature, and if she knew anything about men, she knew that they needed the illusion that everything was their idea so as not to feel trapped or coerced. Christopher Argent might be a strange and singular man, but he was a man nonetheless, and she felt it wise to leave the pace of their relationship up to him. He would need more time to process his feelings, as he'd not done so in quite some time.

And, she supposed, she was getting ahead of herself. What if her feelings for him surpassed his own? What were his intentions, his expectations? Perhaps she should find out. However, one did not just demand such things, did they? Not even of a man prone to sometimes offensive brutal honesty.

She decided to start small. Now that contracts, threats, and coercion no longer precipitated their interaction, she'd need to find something else.

A wide smile stole over her mouth as the perfect idea sweetened the moment.

She craned her neck to look up at him and found him frowning up at the canopy.

Resting her chin on the meat of his chest, she said, "You're a wonderful dancer."

He glanced down at her, the grooves between his eyes deepening. "What?"

"I was just remembering when we first met. I thought you were so handsome, and intriguing, but when you asked me to dance, I was afraid you'd be too big and clumsy to make an effective partner."

His eyes darted away.

So, they were back to that, were they?

Refusing to be deterred, Millie smoothed her hand over his pectoral, then angled south, exploring the taut ridges of his ribs and stomach. "And then you quite literally swept me into that waltz, beneath the blue candelabras, and you were shockingly graceful." Pressing a kiss to his skin, she licked the salt of it from her lips and sighed her contentment. "I've never been so seduced."

His nostrils flared and his lips twitched. A smile, perhaps? Or was it her hopeful imagination?

"I heard you singing to Jakub," she confessed. "You have a lovely voice."

He didn't thank her, but she watched the spread of his reaction coloring his golden skin ruddy. An assassin who blushed? How could she resist him?

"We both know you weren't raised as a gentleman," she ventured, hoping to show him that she was willing to discuss his past, to share it with him. "Was it your mother who taught you to sing and dance?"

His throat worked over a swallow and his eyes found hers again in the lantern light. "It was my mother who taught me to sing, but I learned to waltz elsewhere."

"Oh, really? And just who taught you that particular skill?" Some saucy tart, probably. Millie narrowed her eyes, picturing a pretty blond woman with bigger breasts than hers waltzing with him before bending over and offering up her—

"Welton."

Millie gasped. Then snorted before dissolving into an unladylike fit of giggles that shook the entire bed. "You're . . . joking," she accused over spasms of mirth.

"Why would I be?" he asked in that endearing way of

his, true confusion transforming his features into something younger, almost boyish. "It became apparent to me that in order to take contracts among the *ton,* I needed to be able to blend into their social environs." The more she laughed, the more he explained. "I have trained myself to memorize quite a lot of fighting stances and such that flow from one to the other. Dancing is rather like that, I suppose, just set to music instead of breath."

Her giggles ended on a sigh and she squeezed him fondly. "Do you like to dance?"

His shrug lifted her head where she rested it. "I don't know."

"You seemed to enjoy yourself that night," she reminded him.

"That wasn't me."

Ah yes, that night he'd been Bentley Drummle. Charming, amiable, wicked Bentley Drummle. And yet . . . she hadn't detected artifice during the time they'd spent together that night. He hadn't hurt her, because he'd wanted her. Because . . . perhaps he'd been enjoying himself?

"I would do it again, sometime . . ." She chanced a look at him to gauge his reaction. The darkness gathering in his aspect worried her, but she forged ahead. "Think of it, you could fetch me in your fancy carriage, escort me out, even back to the Sapphire Room if you preferred. We could waltz until we couldn't stand it, and then find that dark corner and finish what we started that nigh—"

"Don't you remember what you said to me?" he asked in a dark voice

"I say a lot of things. Half of them I don't even mean, let alone remember." A chill slid along her skin as she searched her memory.

"I haven't forgotten." He sat up so abruptly she was nearly tossed off him. Throwing his legs over the side of the bed, he gave her his back. "*After this is done with, and we part ways. I never want to see you again.*" His chin touched his shoulder, but he didn't look back at her. "That's what you said, and I gave you my word."

Millie sat up, clutching the covers to her breast. "I—I changed my mind, obviously."

"That's not how this works." He stood, retrieved his trousers and thrust his powerful legs into them.

Millie was so astounded it took her until he was punching his arms into the sleeves of his shirt to reply. "Don't leave." She hated how small her voice sounded, how vulnerable he made her feel. "We just . . ."

"I should have left before all this. I should have gone home." How a man could sound cold and furious at the same time, Millie would never know, but he did. "I should have dropped you here and slipped away. Then none of this would have happened."

Millie didn't understand. Half of her was trying to figure out just where the conversation had turned, and the other half was desperately thinking of a way to make him stop, or at least slow down. "What we did just now, Christopher, it was wonderful. This, between us, it could be the start of something meaningful. Is that what you're afraid of? Is that what you're running from? Because I can help you. Just stay, and we'll—"

He whirled on her. "I run from *no one*!" he thundered. "And I fear nothing. I. *Feel.* Nothing."

"Liar," Millie accused. She knew better, she'd witnessed his emotions, had connected with them and let them feed her own.

"You think *you're* so brave?" He stalked closer to her, his features positively Siberian by the time he reached the edge of her bed. "You think you can help me with *what,* Millie? Clean the gore off my clothes when I return from a kill? Spend my blood money filling my mansion with expensive and meaningless things? Fuck life back into me when I'm dead inside? Don't be ridiculous."

Millie flinched at his cruel vulgarity, but she knew what he was doing. Lashing out, pushing her away. Testing her limits. Thrusting her chin forward, she fought against the hurt and reached for kindness and understanding. "You've been so empty these past years, dead inside, as you say, and you're coming back to the land of the living. I can *see* it. I can feel it." She rose to her knees, still clutching the sheet to her chest and reaching for him with her other hand. "I want to love you, Christopher Argent, and I want you to let me. You don't have to kill people anymore."

"You're wrong." He pulled away from her, just out of reach. "I am a killer. I'm already bound for hell, I don't need baggage for the journey."

"Now who's being ridiculous?" she snapped, her temper perilously close to doing that very thing. "Don't you see? Everyone who ever mistreated you, hurt you, oppressed you, their villainy is perpetuated by *your* hands. You're letting those men who killed your mother shape who you are, or at the very least, what you do."

"Careful, Millie," he warned.

"It's the *truth*. No one has a charted course. Winds shift, tides change, and even if he's fighting against all of that, a man can choose where his journey ends—"

"Unless a man like me ends it for him."

Millie inched forward on her knees. "You could be a different man. A better man."

"Why would you all unmake me?" he fumed, his eyes flashing with silver and blue lightning for the briefest moment as he seized her arm in a punishing grip.

She shook her head. What did he mean by "you all"? No one was trying to unmake him, just the opposite. She was trying to set him free.

He didn't pause to allow her a reply. "I'm a hunter. I'm a *killer.* It's all I am, it's all I've ever been. If you love me, you're in love with a murderer. Could you do that? Could you watch me leave the house knowing that every time I return there's one less person in this world? One more widow, one more orphan, one more soul to condemn me to hell?"

"I—I . . ."

He actually looked disgusted as he released her. "I think you have your answer."

"No." She recovered her senses, reaching out and grasping the fabric of his shirt. "I was thinking about Jakub, I—"

She'd been thinking that they might have made a child. She opened her mouth to remind him that he'd vowed never to leave a bastard.

"Think of what kind of father I'd make."

Her mouth snapped shut.

His features actually softened as he pried her fingers from his sleeve and held her hand in his. "You're a good mother." He kissed her hand and released it, backing away. "Men like me, we don't survive long enough to grow old. We don't have wives and children, we have enemies and allies. The people we care about are liabilities, do you want that for Jakub?"

He had a point, a point that was beginning to make terrible sense. Tears threatened again, and Millie began to hate how many times he'd made her cry. Millie blinked, tears searing hot paths down her cheeks. Why did she always do this? See the impossible and reach for it? Ignore the obstacles in her way? Just assume that she could make something better, greater, just by wishing it so?

Christopher didn't look at her again, but his nostrils flared and his muscles were clenched and turgid as he gathered the rest of his things. "I'm a creature of the darkness,

Millie, and you belong in the spotlight." He reached for the door and opened it, pausing before he left. "But you were right, for what it's worth . . . I did enjoy dancing with you that night."

Millie made a strangled sound as the door closed softly behind him. She'd been accurate when she'd told Farah earlier that her heart was only bruised.

Because now, it was well and truly broken.

CHAPTER TWENTY-NINE

Pain was something Christopher had learned to deal with at an early age. Where so-called normal folk sought comfort and warmth, he'd spent much of his youth just trying to make things a little less intolerable. Comfort made you weak. Hunger made you strong. No matter how horrific, nothing was unbearable, because as long as one was alive, then obviously, it could be borne. Every moment was naught but a moment. Every day was naught but a day. The sun would rise in the morning, night would fall, and the earth would turn around.

These were things that Christopher knew beyond a shadow of a doubt.

People would die. Sometimes because of him, other times in spite of him. The species would propagate. The innocent would suffer. The powerful would build monuments. The world's religions would spill each other's blood, ironically in the name of a God of love. The rich would amass more money. The poor would crawl on top of each other to reach for a piece of bread. Women and boys would sell themselves in the streets.

The sun would rise in the morning, and he would feel pain. Night would fall, and his chest would be a cavern of empty loneliness. The earth would turn around, and his blood would threaten to cease flowing, for it hurt too much to pump it through his veins.

These were the things that Christopher Argent knew.

He'd gone to see Millie again at the theater today, watched her hungrily from the shadows during the early-afternoon dress rehearsal of the play she was debuting this very night. A dramatic comedy about a courtesan and a married lawyer. It seemed she and the director/playwright were very affectionate with each other.

Thomas Bancroft. It gave Christopher dark pleasure to imagine the top five ways in which he'd love to execute the man. Unbeknownst to the playwright, each fantasy became more bloody every time Millie laughed at one of his quips.

Seven times. She laughed seven times at the man. She touched him twice. *He'd* touched her five times whilst adjusting her stage position, putting his hand on her back when they looked over a script together, plucking an errant feather out of her bodice that had drifted there from her headdress. That time, he'd grazed the skin of Millie's bare shoulder and Christopher could tell by the way Bancroft bit down on his lip that he'd done it on purpose.

Was this the kind of man Millie was generally attracted to? Dark curls, soulful brown eyes, lean and elegant with aristocratic features. An easy smile. A gentle touch.

It would be hard for Bancroft to touch her without a hand, Christopher mused, thinking of sawing it off the bastard's thin wrist and tossing it in the Thames.

Christopher had made it almost a fortnight this time without having to see her. Well, half of a fortnight. Almost half. Five days. He'd made it five excruciating days without gazing upon the light inexplicably shimmering from her dark eyes. Without hearing the lilt of her mesmerizing contralto. Five days without taking a full breath into his lungs.

Before that the longest he'd gone was three, so . . . progress, he supposed.

Everything hurt. Everything hurt so much he'd begun

to do what he'd watched countless others do in an attempt to alleviate pain. He'd sought comfort for what things he could control. He'd even taken to sleeping in a bed. It had been overwhelming at first, but once he'd had Welton procure some bed curtains that blocked out the spacious room, he drew them against the light and found that an enclosed bed was, indeed, better than the hard floor of his closet.

He hadn't worked in a handful of weeks, not since his last night with her. He'd go to the theater instead, buy a ticket, sit in the shadows and drink in the sight of her, whisper her lines that he'd memorized. His hands would twitch when someone touched her. His jaw would clench when she was kissed.

Sometimes he'd wish he'd never met her, that he didn't have the memory of her creamy skin singed into his fingertips. That she'd never reached into his soul and confirmed its existence. There'd been a reason he'd buried it in the first place. And now that she'd found it, it belonged to her.

And she'd offered to keep it. *God*, why would she do such a thing?

Now, as he stalked through the gray of the London evening, Christopher was careful not to blink. For whenever his eyes closed, he would see her naked in front of him, lily-white skin smeared with the blood he couldn't wash off his hands. He would see her drowning in it. Tears of crimson pouring from her eyes as she begged him, *pleaded* with him to wash it away. The more he touched her, the more filth and gore covered her.

He dreamed about it at night. Held her dying heart in his hands while she looked on, horrified, knowing that her heart was just another one of his countless casualties.

For the first time in his life, he'd done the decent thing, hadn't he? He'd pushed her away.

The truth of what he'd said to her in his training room hadn't diminished. Just because he hadn't killed her, didn't mean he wouldn't someday destroy her. What did he know about being a man? About being a husband or a father? She and her son were the first people he'd cared about in almost twenty years. The force of his newfound emotion for her would have damaged her eventually, he was certain of it. No one should carry the weight of his past. No one should have to share his empty life. Especially not Millie or Jakub. They were *alive*. And he couldn't say that he ever truly had been. For surely he'd never had much of a life, and the one he'd lived was tainted with evil deeds.

So he'd let her go.

The reality of it stole his strength, and he leaned against a gate with his shoulder, willing his lungs to expand.

What a bloody lie. He'd not let her go in the least. He'd allowed *her* to let *him* go, because apparently, he couldn't seem to stop himself from seeing her.

She'd hated him at first. He'd perched on the ledge outside her window on Drury Lane like a gargoyle and listened when young Jakub asked to see him, ached when she made up ridiculous reasons for them not to.

Her tears when she'd been alone had almost been his undoing. She'd cried. Over *him*. He'd never been a suicidal man, but listening to her soft sobs had nearly driven him to jump. That she or Jakub would have been the one to find his broken body was what had stopped him from acting on the impulse.

Saving her, protecting her wasn't enough to redeem his soul. Deep down she had to know that, even if she didn't accept it at the time.

That wasn't to say he didn't stop trying to guard her and her son. Couldn't seem to help himself. He would fear for her if he didn't see her for too long. He'd conceive dark and terrible things that might have happened to them both, unable to function until he found them, safe and sound, going about their day. Some instinct born of experience told him they were still in danger. That this wasn't over. Though he knew he was being ridiculous, that he was creating an excuse for his obsessive behavior.

Lord, he wanted to be with her now. Wanted the impossible. Wanted to go back to the theater and wallow in the exquisite torture of her presence. But he knew that if he saw Thomas Bancroft put his disgusting fingers on her one more *fucking* time, he'd—

"Argent?"

Blinking away dark thoughts, he looked up, shocked to find himself in front of the Blackwell manse.

Dorian Blackwell descended his stairs with all the regal bearing of a royal. His head slightly turned to regard Argent out of his good eye, he approached the gate and pulled it open. "Has something happened?"

"No." Left without much choice, Christopher followed Dorian up the drive, nodding to the four "footmen" along the path and in the yard.

"Then what, pray, is the reason for your loitering at my gate? You'd been standing there for minutes."

Christopher shadowed Blackwell across his entry and down the hall toward his study, unable to produce an answer to Dorian's question. His feet, rather than his intention, had brought him to Blackwell's door. Yet, he now felt a sliver of ease in the dark presence of his oldest associate. Aside from the death of his beloved mother, Argent and Blackwell had shared the hardest and worst moments of their lives with each other. Perhaps habit had driven him to seek out the Blackheart of Ben More in a time of perceived crisis.

"Do you have something to drink?" Christopher asked.

Blackwell slid him a perceptive glance. "I thought you

didn't drink spirits." He glided to the decanter and filled two crystal glasses without waiting for a reply.

"I didn't." Accepting the generous pour, Christopher tossed it back, taking three swallows to finish the burning fluid. It crawled down his throat and spread from his stomach to his limbs with a warm, pleasant liquidity.

Blackwell was there with the decanter, pouring him another before they each claimed the high-backed chairs by the fire. They sat in silence for a moment, each sipping their drinks, contemplating dark things in the flames. Argent wanted to say something. Wanted to unburden himself, to pour his pain and hatred and his love into the fire and be done with it. He wanted to be cold again, unfeeling. Because then he didn't have to look at himself. Didn't have this horrible yearning for a life that could never be. Wouldn't have the words nagging at his thoughts, lighting tiny fires of their own within him.

Love and truth are stronger in the end than any evil or misfortune in this world.

Millie had believed in those words. Had offered him redemption, in her eyes at least.

Why couldn't he bring himself to take it?

Because I'm a coward, he thought.

"You're an idiot," Dorian stated softly.

"It would be unwise to push me," Christopher replied, just as softly.

"You're also like a brother to me," Dorian confessed in a startling, uncharacteristic moment of unguarded warmth. "So, I can push you if I like."

Christopher couldn't look at him. "Men like us don't have brothers."

"I do, actually. More than one, or so I'm told." Dorian's voice held a note of curious complexity. Not mirth, not acrimony, something in between.

"Do you know them?" Christopher couldn't stop himself from asking.

"Just one. A Scottish marquess. Keeps sending me this damned fine Scotch whisky of his. He's been abroad fighting for the empire and all that, but we've been in somewhat infrequent contact since the death of our father."

"I thought you had your father killed," Christopher mused. He glanced at Dorian in time to see the rest of his drink disappear in one careless toss.

"So I did." Blackwell smirked. "Quid pro quo, I suppose."

Argent nodded, remembering that the late Marquess Ravencroft had paid to have his own bastard killed in Newgate Prison. Maybe not having a father wasn't such a tragedy.

"At any rate, I consider my relationship with you more fraternal than with any of them. We're bound by more blood, I think. Buckets of it. And, over the past decade you and I were the closest thing to family men like us can allow ourselves to have." Dorian seemed to be having as much of a difficult time saying the words as Christopher was hearing them. "We fought and won a war together. We're loyal to each other. We brawl and snarl at each other. And, in the end, we trust—we hope—all is forgiven."

He was talking about losing Millie to Dorshaw that night, Christopher knew. About the fact that nothing had been the same since Christopher had attacked the Blackheart of Ben More in his own house.

And lived to tell about it. That, alone, was a testament to Dorian's admiration for Christopher.

They were both staring hard at the flames again, but Christopher knew Dorian was right. And that he'd just articulated the very reason Christopher had found his gate.

"Brothers, then," he clipped, moving uncomfortably in his chair. "But if you try to hug me, I'm leaving."

Dorian chuckled. "Then allow me to give you some brotherly advice."

"No."

"I'll do it anyway."

Christopher growled. "For the love of—"

"Love," Dorian said firmly, which produced the effect Christopher suspected the Blackheart of Ben More wanted. Christopher's silence.

"Love is exactly to what I'm referring when I tell you that you're an idiot," Dorian stated, finally turning in his chair to gaze at Christopher. "Men like you and me, we don't love like other men do. With patience and poetry and gentle deference. Our sort of love is possessive—obsessive even—and passionate and consuming and . . . well, fucking terrifying sometimes."

Christopher gripped his glass so hard he was afraid it would shatter. "Why are you telling me this?" He wanted to run, but was glued to his chair.

"The walls behind which we endured so much, we carry them with us and I don't think they ever come down. So if we are to love, then that person has to scale those high, solid walls, and once they do, once they go through all of that work . . . they're trapped inside with us."

"Which is precisely why—"

Dorian held up a hand. "The very least we can do is remove a few bricks every so often. Let the daylight in. Make the walls shorter. Do you see what I'm getting at?"

"All I see is that you're beating a poor useless metaphor to death." Christopher didn't want to hear any more. And yet . . .

Undaunted, Dorian continued. "It takes a rare and resilient woman to withstand a life like ours. For most it's just too much. We're too . . . broken. Too brutal. They can't swim upstream through these rivers of blood we've created."

"Farah did," Argent said bitterly.

"I still had to compromise. To make concessions."

"Like what?" Argent asked. "You're still the Blackheart of Ben More."

Dorian cleared his throat. "Would you believe me if I told you . . . half my businesses are actually legitimate?"

"No."

"It's probably best you feel that way, I don't particularly want it getting out."

Argent gaped at Blackwell. He'd known the man was in love with his wife, that he'd searched for her for an eternity, even when she'd been presumed dead. But . . . to go legitimate? He was bloody king of the underworld. Second only to Argent, himself, for the amount of people he'd killed with his own hands. Now he had a daughter. A wife. A courtesy title, not unlike that of the queen's own consort. A life outside of their criminal enterprise that expanded his possibilities.

And he seemed . . . happy. Contented. The sky wasn't falling and the streets weren't burning.

It was beyond conceivable . . . and yet . . .

"I don't know what concessions to make. I can't clean the blood I've already spilled off my hands. And, as I told her, I'm a hunter. I'm a killer. I'm afraid I need to be, that even if I try to stop, I won't be able to."

Dorian regarded him for a long time, that enigmatic eye of his processing his own thoughts. "I think it lives inside both of us. This darkness. This need to be a predator, or worse, play at being God."

Christopher nodded, cursing Blackwell's talent for identifying the crux of a problem.

"You could take Morley's proposition, you know," Dorian suggested.

"Work for the enemy?" Christopher snorted. "Not a chance."

Turning his drink around and around in his hand, Dorian smiled a bit ruefully. "He's not so much my enemy now."

"Since when?"

"We've had mutual interests at times . . ." Dorian answered cryptically. "Prison reform, for one. Getting the same people off the streets, clearing scum from the gutters and the like. You'd be good at that. With your skills you'd probably be his biggest asset. Then, perhaps you and Miss LeCour . . ." He let the insinuation trail away, but the idea took root.

"Millie and I . . ." Christopher's heart clenched. Hope was a dangerous thing. Once it was taken, regaining it was nigh to impossible.

"You might not have to change who you are so much as why you do what you do," Dorian continued. "You don't have to give up your skill set. Even if you don't take this position with Morley, I'll still need you. And as my world . . . changes . . . perhaps yours might do so as well."

"Taking his offer, or yours, doesn't erase what's already been done, Blackwell."

"No," the Blackheart of Ben More agreed. "No, it doesn't. But she fell for you, for the assassin, didn't she?"

"How would you know?" Christopher asked bitterly.

"These walls are well built, but not so thick as to block out everything." Dorian lifted an eyebrow, and a mock salute.

Christopher's frown deepened and heat that had nothing to do with Ravencroft's fine Scotch crept from underneath his collar.

"Also, she told us of her feelings for you." Dorian stood, walking to the window to watch the last of the evening light fade into darkness. "When it comes to women, I know very little," he admitted. "But I've noticed that intention means more than just about anything. If she knows that you're trying . . . If she is secure in how you feel—"

"I don't even know what I feel." Christopher put his glass down hard. Harder than he'd meant to. "I barely know *how* to feel."

"Yes, but you're learning," Dorian pointed out. "We both are, I suppose. Before Miss LeCour, before Farah, you and I would never have attempted this conversation. Perhaps that's precisely why you need her." Dorian's breath fogged the glass with a long exhale. "Ladies tend to be emotional creatures. It's one of the many things they're better at than we are."

Christopher leaned forward in his chair, studying the dancing fire as though it held the answers to the cosmos. A legitimate hunter? An agent of the crown . . . Was this possible? Would Millie even consent to see him again, let alone . . .

Wait, was he actually *considering* this madness?

"What if I can't—"

"What if?" Dorian snarled, slamming his palm against the wall, startling Christopher to his feet. "*Fuck* what ifs. *What if* they're our last chance at humanity, Argent? *What if* they're a gift from the beyond for all of the injustice visited upon us? What if we spend eternity burning for what we've done, for who we've become, but we have the memory of these precious years spent with a goddess?" Black fire flashed in his eye. "I almost let Farah slip through my fingers and you were witness to the misery it caused me. Why repeat that mistake? *What if* you lose her for good because you're too busy being a *fucking idiot* to seize your second chance?"

Christopher's mouth dropped open, but a knock on the study door saved him from having to concoct a reply.

"Mr. Argent, there's someone in the parlor I think you

both need to talk to." Farah's sweet voice drifted through the door.

Argent's heart leaped as he wrenched it open, startling Lady Northwalk. "Millie?" he asked.

She shook her head, silver eyes gleaming with concern. "I'm afraid not. It's Lady Benchley, Philomena St. Vincent."

"What the devil is she doing here?" Dorian wondered from behind Argent.

"She said she has some information about those dead women and their boys."

"But the matter has been closed," Blackwell stated.

"I thought so as well." Farah shrugged. "Mr. Argent, do you know what's going on?"

Christopher stormed past her and into the parlor he was beginning to hate. It had been ages since any good news was delivered in this place.

Hot tea steamed, untouched, on the table in front of where Lady Benchley perched, wringing a damp handkerchief in her hands. The reason for her ridiculous orange hat and veil became immediately apparent when she stood and lifted her head. Tears were not the only cause of the swelling of her eyes. Her nose had been broken fairly recently. Though the resulting mask of bruises had faded to an ugly shade of yellow, the inflammation hadn't completely disappeared.

"Mr. Argent." She stood and gasped as Christopher was followed by Dorian and Farah into the room. "I'm relieved to find you here, actually." Dipping a flawless curtsy with not a small amount of difficulty, she gave a surreptitious sniff and held her handkerchief beneath her nose.

Christopher approached her slowly, and she shrank from him, wincing and holding a hand to her ribs.

"You two are acquainted?" Farah asked, gliding to

Lady Benchley and taking her elbow to help her sink down onto the couch.

Lady Benchley lowered herself carefully, holding her breath until she was settled.

"We were introduced at the theater, *Othello*. You were Miss Millicent LeCour's—companion. Both of you were so kind." Lady Benchley offered a shaky smile.

"You've been injured, Lady Benchley, and you're obviously distressed. Is there aught we can do to help you?" Farah cajoled, taking the woman's hand in her own.

Next to the slim, angelic Lady Northwalk, Philomena St. Vincent appeared more plump and sallow than she had during their previous meetings. The apricot dress and hat didn't help, and neither did the healing wounds. Though, as Christopher studied her, he again noted charming dimples next to her full mouth, and her arresting jade eyes, despite the swelling and redness.

"Call me Mena, please, and I've been seen to, I'm not here about that." Her voice was sweet and young, though the shadows in her countenance were anything but.

Farah's brow wrinkled. "Yes, but—"

"Please," Mena pleaded. "I—I don't have much time. My absence has likely already been noted as I've previously been this afternoon to Scotland Yard." Her chin wobbled, but she visibly composed herself.

"Why is that?" Dorian asked evenly.

"And what does it have to do with Millicent LeCour?" Argent demanded.

Farah cast him a sharp look, but Mena didn't even flinch. The viscountess was no shrinking violet, but a woman used to a harsh tone.

"As you all might know from the papers, my brother-in-law, Lord Thurston, was horrifically murdered," Mena began.

No one said a word, nor did they look at each other.

What Mena St. Vincent knew of the circumstances of Lord Thurston's death was still undetermined.

"I am often the companion to Lady Katherine, his wife, as she is my husband's sister. She's not a kind woman, you see, but we have had a sort of bond with which we can commiserate." Placing a trembling hand over her mouth, Mena swallowed and took a few gulps of air before continuing.

Christopher leaned forward, curling his hands into fists so as not to shake the point from the distraught woman.

"We've both been married for some years now and have been so far unable to produce an heir for our husbands. You see, I've never been able to . . . conceive. And Katherine, she's lost every child she's conceived either in the womb or moments after birth." Mena blinked up at Farah. "I think it's driven her quite mad."

"Why do you say that?" Christopher prodded.

"After Lord Thurston passed, she left for one of their country estates in Essex. I didn't hear a word from her for a month, which worried me because I didn't think that the death of her husband would leave her very troubled. It was no secret that theirs was not a happy match. So, I followed her to Essex to check on her, and there, at Fenwick Hall, I uncovered her secret."

Mena now had both of Farah's hands clenched in her own. "Upon my arrival, I found her out of mourning garb raising five orphan boys. I was surprised at first, of course, but I initially thought that maybe her husband's death had softened her, and that she was trying to do some good in this world. The longer I remained there, it became apparent that the boys were traumatized, that they were being held against their will."

"Christ, Blackwell, do you know what this means?" Christopher turned to Dorian who was already shaking his head in amazement.

"Those boys Morley was looking for, Thurston took them and his wife *knew* about it." Blackwell brought a thoughtful hand to his chin.

Mena nodded, her eyes filling again. "I'm afraid it's *much* worse than you think."

Christopher watched her alertly, puzzle pieces clicking into place. "What do you mean?"

"She was like I'd never *seen* her before. I wouldn't believe it if I hadn't witnessed it with my own eyes, if she hadn't confessed everything to me. As if she were proud. As if she'd done nothing wrong." Tears had begun to roll down her cheeks and drip from her chin, but Mena couldn't seem to let go of Farah's hands long enough to reach for the handkerchief in her lap. "She made those poor boys compete with each other. She kept telling them she'd pick one of them to be the heir to the Thurston title and fortune, and that she'd get rid of the rest."

A mute sense of horror filled the room. Even Christopher felt it.

"Until about five years ago, Lord Thurston was a notorious reprobate. These children, these boys, they were all his . . . illegitimate sons by his numerous mistresses." Mena sent all of them a searching look. "Don't you see, Lord and Lady Northwalk, Mr. Argent, she *killed* their mothers. Not with her own hands, but she hired it done and *took* those poor children into her depraved captivity."

Christopher remembered back to the day he'd lifted the gate key from Lady Thurston's pocket. Fenwick's guts had already been spilled by the time he'd arrived. Had Katherine Fenwick already known what Dorshaw was doing to her husband when she strolled so blithely down the sunny streets of St. James's?

"Did Lady Thurston order the murder of her husband, as well?" he asked bluntly.

Mena paused, her gaze dropping to her lap. "A cruel and unfaithful husband sometimes seems an impossible thing to bear, Mr. Argent," she said quietly, indicating what he'd already suspected. That her wounds were inflicted by her own husband, Gordon St. Vincent. "If Lord Thurston was her only victim, I might not have come here—" Her voice broke. "But those children. They were so frightened. I pretended to be in agreement with her and came straight back to London a week past. I would have gone to the police sooner but I was—detained by my husband." She touched the side of her healing nose gingerly.

"So you've told Chief Inspector Morley this, Lady Benchley?" Dorian asked carefully.

She nodded, more tears sliding from her chin into her lap. "The St. Vincents . . . they're going to find out that it was I who told. There will be—consequences. But I couldn't live with myself if anything happened to those boys. Not if I could stop it."

"You're so very brave, Mena." Farah rubbed her back consolingly. "That was so well done of you. And we will of course help you in any way we can."

"Forgive me, Lady Benchley." Blackwell leaned toward her. "But if Scotland Yard is handling this, it's still unclear as to why you've brought the affair to us."

"The chief inspector sent me here with explicit instructions to tell you everything I confessed to him. He sent men to Essex after the missing boys. Katherine told me that they yet remain unharmed." Mena blinked up at Argent and Blackwell, the uncommon shade of her eyes intensified by her tears. "She told me this *in person,* because she's returned this very morning to London."

A stab of warning brought Christopher to his feet.

"She said she has one more boy to obtain. One she thought had escaped her. The one Thurston had chosen, himself, for his heir." Mena continued on a trembling breath. "I'm afraid that means she has one more of Fenwick's mistresses to kill."

"Millie." Argent almost launched himself over the table at her. Why had she wasted so much time telling the entire infernal story when the most important part was that Millie could be in danger?

"I wasn't certain if it was Miss LeCour and her son or not. Though after Sir Morley told me to come here I began to suspect—"

"Where is Lady Thurston now?" he demanded.

Mena flinched. "S-she was at our home with my husband when I sneaked away. I hired a carriage to Scotland Yard and then here, but that was more than an hour past."

"I have to get to the theater." Though he flew out of the house, Christopher's feet felt like lead weights. He couldn't get there fast enough. Bellowing for a horse, he had to keep reminding himself that he couldn't bloody well run all the way to Bow Street and get there in time.

Once reins appeared in his hand, he leaped astride and kicked the animal into a run.

He didn't know which assassin Lady Thurston would have hired now that Dorshaw was dead, but he would drain every last drop of blood from the man's body. Then he'd go to work on the bitch, herself.

"Hold on, Millie." He breathed into the bitter night wind. "I'm coming for you."

Chapter Thirty

It took an incomprehensible amount of time to prepare for death.

Millie sighed as she opened her costume dress and allowed two stagehands to strap skeins of warm crimson-dyed syrup to her corset, and made a vow that the next role she accepted, her character would *live* to see the end of the play.

It struck her in that moment behind the heavy black curtains off stage left how cohesive life could be sometimes, even if it was in the worst possible way. In her tenure as an actress, she'd portrayed the jilted lover, the temptress, and, of course, the tragic heroine. But this brilliant production had her acting all three parts. A woman who seduced a man, fell in love with him, and then was broken by him. Art imitating life, apparently.

She barely had to act. In fact, all she had to do was open her bleeding heart onstage for all of London whilst delivering Thomas Bancroft's lines. She could already tell the night was a rousing success. She'd never felt this kind of energy from the audience before. Though the play was a bit melodramatic, it had just the right amount of sex, violence, and pathos for everyone to enjoy.

And now, thanks to Christopher Argent, she had a reference for the emotion evoked in each act.

Closing her dress and buttoning it, she tilted her head

down so the makeup artist could check her hair, and pursed her lips so her rouge could be touched up. Lord, it was hotter than usual. She blotted her forehead and hairline with a handkerchief.

"Who are you playing to tonight?" Jane Grenn asked, striking a macabre pose as she fidgeted with the almost comically large knife she'd use to stab Millie to death in the final act.

Millie could only give her friend half of a smile. "Truth be told, I didn't pick anyone tonight." She already had someone to deliver her lines to. A man with ice-blue eyes and a cold heart. She conjured Christopher's face every time she needed the anger to flow, the tears to fall, or the temptation to flare.

If only the man, himself, were so easily summoned.

"That's odd," Jane remarked. "Would this have anything to do with our delicious director?"

Millie smirked. "First I'm cavorting with Rynd and now it's Bancroft? My, how I've moved up in the world."

"Well, if you're not with him, do you mind if I have a go?" Jane and Millie peered over to where the director in question pored over an issue with the prop master, pushing a lock of chocolate hair out of his eye.

"I've no designs on Thomas Bancroft." Millie shrugged. Or any man, for that matter.

One would think after a month and a week's time, the pain of losing Christopher wouldn't be so fresh. That she wouldn't have to fill her days with work and pretense just so she could keep the tears away. Jakub helped to keep her going as well, though she found it harder and harder to hide her sadness from the perceptive boy.

She wondered, not for the first time, if she'd ever see Christopher again. If he'd ever be aught else but a knight in tarnished armor she'd once chanced to love in the middle of a nightmare. She still searched the shadows for a glimpse of his auburn hair. And there were times when she thought she'd caught a glimpse of him.

"Millie, it's your cue." Jane almost pushed her out onto the stage, and Millie composed herself just in time for the lights to hit her with their wave of subsequent warmth. She delivered her lines with practiced artlessness. To those in the breathless audience, she was just a woman thrown to the whims of the world, who refused to accept her lowly place in life. Who captured the heart of a man who was not free, and lost herself to him. They loved her. They forgave her for tempting him into iniquity. She had to capture them completely before they lost her.

That's how the tears were produced. How the tickets were sold. How the heart was won.

"Why did you leave?" she railed in her lonely misery after her fictitious lover had callously abandoned her.

Christopher, why did you leave?

"Was it that you were a man with a heart impossible to tame? Or was I a woman not worthy to do so?"

There, she'd done it. The temptress turned vulnerable. Now for the tragedy. Jane, in the role of the jilted wife—the real victim—would appear with the knife and—

Wait a moment, what is Lady Thurston doing backstage?

And what was that in her hand?

The countess stepped onto the stage, and several of the audience members gasped. Some with delight, but others in the peerage—those who knew Lady Thurston—couldn't contain their shock. A lady of the *ton* as an actress? It just wasn't done.

Backstage had been almost deserted by crew and performers alike.

The brilliant lights glinted off Lady Thurston's pistol, the one she trained on Millie.

The countess looked like the proper society matron

upon first glance, but when one was as close as Millie was to her, the inconsistencies became apparent. Her dress was just slightly askew, as though she'd slept in it. Her hair artfully arranged, but a little too wild, too undone.

The costume artists couldn't have concocted it better themselves.

"Did you enjoy it, whore?" Lady Thurston asked as she advanced, her eyes glittering with malice and touched with madness. "Did my husband woo you? Seduce you? Or did he buy you like the common prostitute you are?"

The audience audibly gasped at her vulgarity, obviously riveted.

"I don't know what you're talking about," Millie stalled, entirely shocked. Why wasn't someone doing something? Couldn't they see she was in danger? That Lady Thurston was utterly mad?

"He was always the type of man who believed in tradition." Lady Thurston sneered. "That a wife was for breeding and a mistress was for loving. Do you think you were special to him? Do you think that he didn't have a *hundred* just like you? That he didn't get bastards on them, too?"

Millie tried her best to compose herself. "It's not what you think," she said, putting out a staying hand. "Your husband was in love with my—"

"Shut up," Lady Thurston hissed. "I don't want to hear excuses from your whore mouth. This is the end of you." She lifted the gun.

Desperation swept over Millie with such strength she could taste it. She felt abandoned. Deserted. As she frantically searched the darkness beyond the curtain for someone, *anyone* to rescue her. Finding no one, she turned to the audience. Unable to see more than the closest members, she dimly realized that they all thought this was part of the production. Fans fluttered like bejeweled leaves in an approaching tempest and hands clasped at heaving bosoms. The crowd sat in their silk and velvet, watching the spectacle unfold with breathless anticipation.

Perhaps tonight they'd get more than they'd paid for.

God, was she truly going to die in front of hundreds of spectators? Would they applaud as she bled out on the stage?

It all seemed too cheap and disingenuous now. Fame. Money. The love of a country who would readily call her a whore. While the murders of mistresses went unsolved and the injustices of men went unnoticed. Suddenly all the suffering and sadness of the world seemed to crash in on her, and Millie wondered if death might be less painful. A soul-deep agony drenched her in pain as she thought of Jakub, of all he'd lost. Of all the things she'd kept from coming to light, to protect him.

He'd have lost two mothers at such a young age.

Would he hate her then? Would he remember her as his mother?

"Don't do this," Millie whispered. "I have a child."

She realized the moment the words left her mouth that it was the worst possible thing she could have said.

Lady Thurston actually snarled, the sound more evocative of a badger than a highborn woman. "You must have felt so smug meeting us in the foyer, introducing my husband to the son he'd thought he'd lost." Lady Thurston drifted closer, insanity baring the whites of her eyes. "I did what every wife should do. I turned a blind eye to his infidelities, which he didn't even have the decency to hide from me. I knew the name of every whore he kept."

Millie shook her head in denial, taking a step back for every advance Lady Thurston made. "You're mistaken. I *never*—"

"I said silence!" Katherine Fenwick screamed, swinging the pistol wildly.

Millie clamped her lips shut. She could see the copper heads of the bullets shining from the barrel of the gun. Fresh fear broke over her, causing her stomach to boil with nausea.

Time. She was running out of it.

"He was going to divorce me all those years ago when your precious son was born." Lady Thurston's voice took on an almost singsong quality. A lilt that only belonged to a toddler or the touched. "To shove me, a countess, into some middle-class London disgrace with the stipend of a pauper while he legitimized his Polack *bastard*. Said he was in love, with an immigrant actress. That she'd borne him a son, and that he was going to marry her and retire to the country!" She turned to the audience, the barrel of the pistol still pointed at Millie's heart. "Can you imagine?"

No one answered, though a buzz had begun in the crowd. Uncomfortable shifting, questions whispered behind white gloves and sparkling fans. *What was going on? Was this really part of the play? A new and gauche Continental performance art, perhaps?*

"Turns out I erred when I ordered the death of the wrong Polack *actress* all those years ago. I thought I was rid of all of my husband's whores by now, that I'd collected all his bastards." She pulled back the hammer of the pistol, the thrill of victory speeding her breath. "After tonight, I will have done. I was going to use one of them, make him say he was mine. But in the end, I think it's best that my husband's line ends. That his title not be held by a bastard."

"You . . . *ordered* Agnes's death?" Rage surged through Millie, thundering through her veins and clearing her throat of fear and tears. The anger felt good, reminded her that she was yet alive. She gained strength from it, and courage. No matter what happened to her, this woman would *not* win. Agnes, her dear sweet friend, would have justice, and the boy they both loved more than life would at least be left his birthright.

"I have evidence your husband wanted Jakub to be his heir," Millie stated coldly. "It's right here." Pulling Lord Thurston's letter out of her bodice, she held it up to a thousand witnesses. "He's officially legitimized Jakub. What's done is already done. The moment your husband died, my son became an *earl*."

Katherine Fenwick screamed, but no one heard it above the gunshot. A puff of white smoke rose from the barrel and several women added their shocked screams to the countess's before all fell eerily silent.

Time. That most precious commodity. It slowed almost to a stop. Everything took an eternity, and yet happened so fast.

Millie expelled a relieved breath as the door to the back of the theater burst open and a man flew down the aisle, hurling himself on long powerful legs. Other men followed him in, ushers and someone in a dark suit with ebony hair. Theatergoers surged to their feet, but Millie could only see *him*. Taller than all the rest and fast, so incredibly fast for someone so broad and thick.

"Christopher?" She whispered his name and the rage faded. She wanted to call it back, to direct it at him, but she couldn't seem to summon it. Instead, her throat clogged with tears and her traitorous heart leaped with joy.

His lips formed words, but she didn't hear them. His eyes, his beautiful blue eyes locked on her, but didn't rise above her torso.

Look at me, she begged. *Look into my eyes.*

He didn't. Instead his lips pulled back in a vicious snarl, and he reached into his jacket as he surged forward, producing a gun of his own. He pointed it toward the stage.

And pulled the trigger.

Millie felt it then, an ache in her side, a twinge in the

muscle and then a burn. Her hand flew to her middle, and came away sticky. She made a startled noise, and then another.

Katherine Fenwick dropped to the ground beside her.

Oh thank God.

"It's not mine," Millie whispered, holding her slick hand drenched with crimson up for him to see. "The blood, it's not real."

"Millie! *No*!" Christopher Argent's cry boomed above all the others.

"It's not mine." Millie lurched forward on feet unsteady with fear. She needed to tell him, but her face had grown cold, her tongue thick and heavy. She could feel the packages against her dress. They'd just been *punctured* was all. The warm sticky liquid was merely honey and coloring.

But how? She paused. Confusion furrowing her brow. Jane had never come out with the knife.

The burn intensified, feeling more like a tear.

Christopher vaulted over the orchestra pit and onto the stage.

Millie cried out, stumbled, and then his arms surrounded her. Those arms were just like she remembered. Hard and strong. He was warm and solid as a brick wall as she slid against him, letting him hold all of her weight that had seemed to become too much for her liquefied bones. He lowered her gently to the ground, bellowing for help, for a doctor.

She'd never seen him like this. His cold, brutal features a mask of terror and pain.

"You're not afraid of anything," Millie reminded him, blinking away black spots from her vision.

"Yes, Millie," he said, panting. "Yes, I am. I'm afraid of losing you."

A cascade of hot tears flowed down Millie's face as she

reached up for him with a cold, pale hand. "But you let me go."

"No, I didn't." He shook his head, grasping her to him; clutching her with a hard desperation of which she hadn't thought him capable. "I thought I could, but I was wrong. You can't leave me, Millie. Because I'll *never* let you go."

Millie's hand went limp and slid to the ground, landing in a puddle of warm, sticky liquid. She could feel it spreading out beneath her, reaching toward his knees. *I don't want to go,* she pleaded to the light above her head. *I don't want to leave him.*

What a tragedy, she thought as the lights above no longer warmed her. That the man she loved had to lose another like this. Kneeling in a pool of her blood.

Chapter Thirty-One

Christopher toppled over the rack of weapons against the wall in his ballroom. Picking up a weight, he hurled it through the window, the glass shattering in a spectacle of moonlit shards. A terror he'd not thought existed weakened his limbs, then the next moment his muscles would surge with strength and fury. His heart threatened to burn out of his chest. He felt feral and trapped and out of control.

Helpless.

He looked down at his hands, still red and sticky with Millie's blood—no, no, not all her blood. A great deal of it was fake. A stage prop. He'd have known that if he'd been in his right mind. He'd had enough blood on his hands to recognize what was real and what wasn't.

Christopher had pressed his palm to her side while the thick liquid overflowed his fingers as he'd tried to stanch the flow. He'd clutched her to him and chanted her name like a madman.

The medics had pried him away from her, and then the fucking surgery had been overflowing with wounded. He hadn't caught the reason before he'd lost it.

A rage the likes of which he'd never before felt had engulfed him. He'd broken things, he'd *almost* broken people.

Then he'd remembered he and Blackwell knew of a surgeon, one of the best in the business, with a proclivity for gambling. Dorian had promised to forgive a fortune of debt if the doctor saved Millie's life, so they'd brought her here, to Christopher's home.

That had been an hour ago and the surgeon wouldn't let anyone into the room. He had insisted that the more people present while he worked, the higher the rate of fatal infections.

It had still taken seven men to tear Christopher from her side.

So now he destroyed everything in his path. Because a helpless rage drove him to it. Picking up a staff, he broke it over a pommel. It wasn't enough. Staggering over to the wrecked stand, he pulled it apart, embedding one of the metal legs into the wall, enjoying the splintering of the wood paneling.

"Argent." Dorian slid into the room, emerging from out of the shadows.

Yanking on the leg, but unable to free it from the wall, Christopher kicked at the broken boards, shattering it beneath his boot, creating huge, fractured holes.

"Christopher," Dorian said more sharply, surveying the carnage with his usual self-containment. "The doctor has finished, he's ready to report."

Christopher met Dorian's eye and knew it was bad. He shook his head and held a hand up against whatever words were about to end his existence. "Not like this, Blackwell. I can't lose her like this. I won't survive this time."

"I know." Dorian rested a hand on Christopher's shoulder. It was the first time the Blackheart of Ben More had ever touched him. "For those of us who've perpetrated so much death, the retaining of life seems even more elusive."

"I don't know what to do." Argent's neck could no longer hold the weight of his head, and he let it drop.

"Someone else has arrived," Blackwell stated evenly. "Someone who needs you."

Jakub.

A boy who could very well lose his mother. The thought drove Christopher forward, and he flew toward the French doors.

He found Jakub in the enormous, empty grand entry, small and clean in a long white nightshirt and a coat. The boy squirmed away from the rotund Mrs. Brimtree and ran to Christopher.

Braced for the child's hysterics, Christopher reminded himself to be strong for the boy.

But young Jakub shocked him by stopping dead in front of his boots and blinking those gigantic eyes up at him, like he'd done that first night after Dorshaw's attack. As always, it disarmed him completely.

"It's going to be all right," the boy said.

Christopher swallowed around a dry throat. "How do you know?" he asked hoarsely.

"Because you're here." The veneration in the child's eyes broke his heart. "Everything always turns out well when you're here."

The doctor, Raymond Cromstock, was a middle-aged fellow with impressive jowls despite his lean frame. He descended the stairs with a carefully composed expression.

It was only after Jakub reached for his hand that Christopher realized it was still stained with blood. Fake and otherwise.

He tucked the boy against his leg, instead.

"The bullet went clean through," Cromstock informed the assemblage. "And there is precious little damage to the organs, as far as I can tell. Her body didn't react well to the shock, but as long as there is no infection or fever, it's my opinion that Miss LeCour is out of danger."

The surge of elation and relief he felt drove Christopher to his knees. He prayed in that moment. Thanked a God he'd never believed in.

"You see?" Jakub said, throwing his little arms around Christopher's neck. "She's going to be fine, as long as you're with us."

But the fever flared in a matter of hours. Christopher and Jakub looked on in helpless horror as she shook with uncontrolled tremors, her teeth chattering though her skin burned.

Despair didn't begin to describe the pit into which he was thrown.

"I just tucked Jakub in," Farah said gently to Christopher as she leaned on the bedpost in the bedroom Welton had furnished all those nights ago. Millie had thought it looked like a forest. "He still believes she's going to wake up any moment. He believes in you that much."

If only Jakub knew that God owed Christopher no favors. But Christopher owed the devil plenty.

"You should sleep and eat something. I'll sit with her and come for you if anything changes." She held out a bowl of soup.

"I slept," Christopher lied as he leaned forward in his chair, the only one in the entire house, the one he hadn't left in almost two days. He hadn't taken his eyes off Millie. Couldn't look away. As long as he stayed with her, watched her chest rise and fall, then he knew she hadn't left him. He'd close his eyes when hers opened. Not before. "And I'm not hungry."

Farah left it alone, handing the soup to Welton, who'd been hovering silently at the basin. "What did the doctor say this morning?" She brushed a dark curl from Millie's pale forehead.

"Her fever broke."

"That's excellent news." The harder Blackwell's wife tried to sound encouraging, the worse Christopher felt. "She'll be back to us in no time." Her face brightened. "I've brought you more good tidings. Chief Inspector Morley closed the matter of Lady Thurston's death. It's not something you'll have to worry about in the future. Also, the police rescued those boys. They were hungry and traumatized, of course, but they're unhurt. We're finding places for them, hopefully together, as they're brothers."

Christopher nodded, because he was supposed to. He wished he cared. Millie would want him to care about something like that. Maybe he would, later. When she awoke. *If* . . . she . . .

"The doctor said that if she was going to wake, she'd likely do it today," he reminded himself aloud.

"Of course." With a soft press of her hand to his shoulder, Farah drifted to the door in a ruffle of skirts. "I'll be downstairs with Dorian if you need me."

He nodded, his head feeling heavy and his neck tight.

In her sleep, Millie gasped, her chest hitching on a labored breath as her fingers twitched.

"Millie?" Christopher rose and searched her face for signs of a change, but found nothing.

Lying flat on her back in the giant bed on the dais, arms to her sides and tucked beneath a mountain of blankets, she looked small and helpless. The warm beige color of the bedding made her white skin even paler. Though her spark was diminished, her magnetic beauty was not.

He'd gone through a lifetime of emotion while she slept.

The last eternity of hours had been spent in this gray sort of daze. As she hovered in between life and death, Christopher also existed in that limbo with her.

But he ached with love. With longing. With profound regret. With a fear that never faded to numbness but lingered so close to the surface his skin hurt with it.

What if she never smiled again? What if those dark eyes never sparkled with mischief, with that light that Jakub had tried so hard to capture in his painting? What if the last memory he had of her truly *alive* was the moment she'd offered to love him and he'd left her in a puddle of tears and cold bedsheets?

He had to tell her. She had to know.

Sinking to her side on the bed, Christopher took her cold, clammy palm and held it in both of his rough, scarred hands, willing some of his warmth into her.

She made another sound, like a cough, but not quite. His heart stopped until she was still again. His eyes stung and burned and he didn't breathe for what felt like a full minute.

Christ, he couldn't take much more of this.

"Millie?" He whispered her name. "Millie, you were right. I *do* feel. It started the night I met you, the moment you blew me a kiss from the stage. It's why I made that damned arrangement in the first place, because I had to touch you—" His voice broke and he had to clear emotion out of his throat. "Every time I said that I wanted you . . . I think I meant—I meant that I needed you. I *need* you, Millie. I need you to wake up. I need to hold you against my heart because it's the only fucking time I feel it beating. If you go, it dies. The last part of what makes me human dies with you. I'll disappear. If you're not on this forsaken planet, it might as well stop spinning until we all fly off into the void. Because that's all there is without you. Emptiness."

He felt something on his face, something hot and itchy. He lifted one of his hands to wipe at it and it came away wet.

Tears? *Fuck.*

It didn't matter. Nothing mattered.

"I would be your blade in the darkness," he bartered. "So you and Jakub could stand in the light. I would never leave you again. I would protect you, support you, and give you the freedom you crave. I would follow you anywhere you wish to go, anywhere the stage takes you. For where you are, that is where my home is.

"I'll take you dancing, Millie," he bargained. "Every night for the rest of our lives. I'll take you anywhere you wish to go. Nothing sounds better than seeing the world with your light shining on it." He cast about for something else, anything that would tempt her back to him. "I'm taking a position with Morley. With Scotland Yard, if you'd believe it. It pays less but I have more money than I know what to do with."

An idea occurred to him on that note. "I'll let you fill my house with things, countless, useless expensive things. Until it's a home, and not a shell. And I'll try. I'll try so *fucking* hard not to be a shell, either. And . . . I'll give Jakub my name. Tainted as it is. No matter what happens, it's his, it's *yours*. Whatever you want is yours. *I'm* yours. And you are *mine* so just *don't* . . ."

He couldn't bring himself to say the word.

"Welton?" The name sounded like a rusty croak on Millie's pale lips.

Shock turned Christopher's limbs cold and he jerked his head toward his butler. He'd forgotten the man even existed, truth be told, let alone lurked in the corner.

Welton? Why the fuck would his name be the first on her lips when—

"Yes, madam?" Welton's eyes were suspiciously bright, the rims red, but his cheeks were dry as though he'd wiped them on the pristine handkerchief he clutched in the hand at his side.

"Did you get all that?" Her voice was barely above a soft rasping whisper, and still it held the glimmer of dauntless spirit and merriment that Christopher recognized as purely her own.

"Of course, madam." The butler's voice was warmer than Christopher had ever heard it.

"Most especially the part about expensive things," she said, sighing.

"Every word."

"Thank you, Welton."

"You're *very* welcome."

It amazed Millie that such a tiny bullet could make her feel like she'd been stampeded by a coach and four. Though any light at all seared her sore eyes and aching head, she knew she had to see Christopher to believe he was really there. That this was truly happening.

He'd professed his love.

She blinked her eyes open slowly. Her head felt muddled, as if she'd been given something that made everything seem like some gilded dream. Including the auburn hair of the man staring down at her as though she'd lost her mind, or he had.

He breathed her name and on that whisper she heard the echo of every beautiful thing that swelled in her heart.

It hurt to lift her hand, but she wanted to touch his face. He caught it halfway up and buried his hard, stubbled jaw against her palm. Pressing his lips to her fingers.

"I was never going to leave you," she assured him. "I love you too much to let a paltry bullet keep us apart."

The strong chin in her palm trembled, the ice in those pale, pale eyes melted into moist oceans of emotion. With a harsh sound ripped from deep in his chest, Christopher dropped his head down, burying it in her shoulder as he visibly fought for control of his lungs.

Millie lolled her head to rest against his, closing her eyes to savor his nearness. He'd come for her. He'd conquered his fear and his pain, and the chamber of ice around his heart. Could this be possible? A happy ending for two souls such as they?

"Did you really mean what you promised?" she asked against his lush hair.

He gave a surreptitious sniff against her shoulder. "About the expensive furniture, you mean?"

"No." She tried to laugh, but it caused the dull pain in her side to turn sharp and burning. "No," she said again, this time much more subdued. "The part about giving Jakub and me your name. Are you going to marry me, Christopher Argent?"

"I should have claimed you the moment we met."

"And I won't have to take another bullet to hear you say you love me?"

He pulled away just far enough to look down at her, to meet her eyes with his own. "I love you, Millicent LeCour," he vowed.

"Good. But don't forget what you said about the furniture." Her breaths became deeper, as sleep tried to claim her again. Her voice was dreamy and light. Everything was golden and lovely. "Oh, and just be warned, my love, our wedding is going to be obscenely expensive, too."

She welcomed the soft embrace of healing slumber, but not before her greatest wish was granted.

It was quiet and low with rusty notes of caustic irony. And yet, it was the most beautiful sound she'd ever heard or could ever hope to hear. One she hoped to provoke many times in the years to come.

Christopher Argent's laugh.

Read on for an excerpt from
Kerrigan Byrne's next book

The Highlander

Coming soon from St. Martin's Paperbacks

A sound like the muffled beating of her accelerating heart pounded on the earth, and Mena leaned against the window in time to see several mounted Highlanders materialize out of the mists like the specters of Jacobite warriors who roamed these very moors a hundred years past.

Her breath caught at the sight of them. Heavy cloaks protected brawny shoulders, though their knees remained bared to the elements by matching blue, green, and gold kilts. They reined their horses to a walk and lurked closer to the carriage, letting the mist unveil them to her wide gaze.

Mena was suddenly aware of how *very* alone and vulnerable she was. Chances were, she told herself, this was the help Kenneth Mackenzie sent for, but she didn't see him among the men. She now counted seven, each one burlier and—dirtier—than the last. On the other hand, they could be brigands. Highwaymen, rapists, murderers . . .

Oh, dear God.

They circled the carriage, all peering inside the rain-streaked windows with not a little curiosity, speaking the lyrical language of the Highlands. She understood it to be Scot's Gaelic, though she comprehended not a word.

Then she saw *him.*

Her mouth became dry as the desert, and a tremor that had nothing to do with the cold ripped through her.

Though he wore a soiled kilt and loose linen shirt beneath his drenched cloak, he sat astride a black Shire steed with the bearing of a king. Dark hair hung long and heavy with moisture down his back, and menace rolled off the mountains of his shoulders in palpable waves.

Whoever he was, he was their leader. She saw it in the way they looked to him, in the deference they used when speaking. If not by birth, then by the physical laws of nature, surely. As the largest, the strongest, and the most fearsome of them all, he towered above the brawny men as he scowled through the window at her.

Even through the mesh of her hat's veil, and the black soot streaked across his features, Mena could see the tension in his strong jaw. The aggression etched into the grooves of his fierce, deep-set eyes. Viewed through the chaotic tracks of rain upon the window, he could have been a savage Pict warrior, bred not only to survive in this beautiful and brutal part of the world but to conquer it.

Mena gasped at the shocking flash of muscled thigh bared to her as he dismounted, and despaired that even on foot his astounding height and breadth diminished not at all. Dear lord, he was coming closer. He meant to reach for the door.

Lunging forward, she threw the lock and extracted the skeleton key just as his big hand turned the latch.

Their eyes met.

And the rain disappeared. As did everything and everyone else.

Mena knew that there were moments in one's life as significant as an epoch. Existence was then split into a before, and an after, and whatever was left as a consequence of that moment illuminated who someone really was. It laid one open, exposing them for honest and brutal inspection and the acceptance that one was inexorably altered forevermore. She'd lived long enough to experience a few of these. Her mother's death when Mena was only nine, her first real taste of tragedy. The first time she'd galloped on a horse on her father's farm and experienced true freedom. Her first kiss. The horror of her wedding night. The moment she was told she'd never be a mother.

So she recognized this as one of those moments, though the Leviathan on the other side of the now-seemingly-inadequate barrier of the window was not the only one conducting the inspection.

What Mena saw in the striations of amber and ebony in the Highlander's eyes alternately terrified and fascinated her. Here was a man capable of inconceivable violence. And yet . . . a weary sorrow lurked behind the incredulity and subsequent exasperation in his glare. He was surprisingly handsome, but in the feral and weathered way the Highlands themselves were appealing.

Mena blinked, berating herself for noticing such a thing of her probable-robber-highwayman-rapist-assassin, and the spell was broken.

"Open the door," he commanded in a deep and booming brogue.

"*No*," Mena answered, before remembering her manners. "No, thank you."

They called Liam Mackenzie "The Demon Highlander."

Over the course of the previous two decades, he'd led a number of Her Majesty's infantry, cavalry, and artillery units. He'd stormed countless mobs during the Indian Mutiny and made his fame when the so-called Indian rebellion had been crushed. He'd facilitated the disbandment of the East India Company with espionage, assassination, and outright warfare, painting the jungles with blood until the crown seized the regime. He led the charge against Chinese cannon in the second Opium War, leaping from his horse over cannon fire and slicing through Asian artillery.

He'd secretly conducted rescue missions to Abyssinia and Ashanti, leaving no trace of himself but a mountain of bodies in his wake. He'd trained killers and killed traitors. He'd toppled dynasties and executed tyrants. He was William Grant Ruaridh Mackenzie, Lt. Colonel of Her Majesty's Royal Secret Highland Watch, Marquess Ravencroft, and Laird and Thayne of Clan Mackenzie 3rd of Wester Ross. A high agent of the crown and a leader of men was he.

So how in the name of all the gods that were ever worshiped on his land could he be struck dumb by a pretty, stranded English governess? It boggled the mind.

He had no time for this. A fire had somehow ignited in the east barley fields that morning and his men were exhausted from tirelessly fighting it. The rain had been a blessing, one that had saved their crops. When Kenneth had ridden up and explained their predicament with the carriage, they'd ridden five miles through the sac-shriveling autumn rain to save her pretty hide.

Had she really just locked him out of his own carriage and then disobeyed his command with a polite *No, thank you*? If he was feeling himself, he'd have ripped the door off its hinges for her insolence. But something about the bruised softness of her vibrant green eyes, the only thing about her he could see with any clarity, had stolen his wits from him.

When their eyes had met, he'd felt the earth shift beneath him in a way he'd never experienced before. Not with the unstable feeling of a peat bog or slick silt beneath his boots, but exactly the opposite. Like the land might alter and align to please the cosmos, clicking into place with prophetic finality.

It was damned unsettling. Infuriating, even.